UNDERCURRENTS

RIDLEY PEARSON

St. Martin's Paperbacks

This is a work of fiction. Any similarity to actual incidents, any resemblance to persons living or dead is purely coincidental. Although based on interviews with law-enforcement agencies and research of actual events, the story herein purposely avoids any likeness to any singular case history. It is, instead, a compilation of fact, technique, and detail a fictionized story born solely out of the author's imagination.

UNDERCURRENTS

Copyright © 1988 by Ridley Pearson.

Library of Congress Catalog Card Number: 88-1014

ISBN: 0-312-92958-7

Printed in the United States of America

St. Martin's Press hardcover edition published 1988
St. Martin's Paperbacks edition/April 1989

15 14 13 12

"SUPERB . . . HARD-EDGED EXCITEMENT
. . . An intricate story, challenging the reader
with misleading clues and perplexing dead ends
. . . Goes beyond the police procedural format."
—*St. Louis Post-Dispatch*

*"GRIPPING AND ENJOYABLE . . . A solid po-
lice procedural with an unusual setting and an
engaging, fully realized protagonist . . . The novel
is filled with interesting, esoteric information."*
—*Times & World News* (Roanoke, VA)

"A COMPELLING saga of madness and mul-
tiple murder told with plenty of suspense . . .
SUPERIOR!"   —Walter Wager, author of
Telefon and *58 Minutes*

"EXCITING, GRIPPING, AND AUTHENTIC
. . . A novel that could well be a psychiatric–
forensic story of an actual case."
—G. Christian Harris, M.D.,
Forensic Psychologist, Seattle, WA

*"Has the makings of a great mystery that sounds
all too real . . . enhanced by a wonderfully descriptive writing style."*
—*Chattanooga News-Free Press*

"A WALLOPING GOOD, HYPNOTICALLY
SUSPENSEFUL STORY that moves along at a
pace so breathtaking it will leave you limp . . .
It is one of the season's more inventive and en-
tertaining crime novels."
—*Greenwich Time* (CT)

St. Martin's Paperbacks Titles by Ridley Pearson

NEVER LOOK BACK
BLOOD OF THE ALBATROSS
HIDDEN CHARGES
UNDERCURRENTS
PROBABLE CAUSE

Dedicated to my editor and
good friend, Brian DeFiore,
for his enthusiasm and
tireless efforts on this book.

ACKNOWLEDGMENTS

Special Thanks To:
Dr. Donald Reay, King County
Medical Examiner
Dr. Alyn Duxbury, University of Washington,
Marine Sciences
Dr. Christian Harris, M.D., P.S.
Mr. Joseph Smith, FBI, Seattle, Washington
Mr. Gary Flynn, Seattle Police Department
Mr. Robert Laznik, Chief of Staff, King County
Prosecutor's Office
Mr. Richard Malm, Seattle's
Pacific Science Center
Dr. Royal McClure, M.D., Sun Valley, Idaho

Editors:
Mr. Brian DeFiore
Mr. Tom McCormack

Research Assistance:
Mr. Bradbury Pearson
Ms. Colleen Daly
Mr. Fletcher Brock
Ms. Aileen Denton

Office Organization and Manuscript Preparation:
Mrs. Mary Peterson

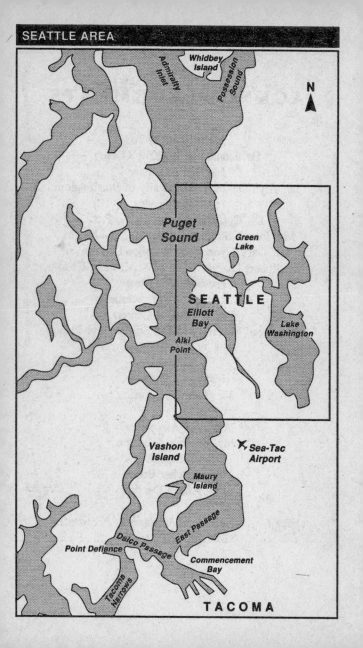

SEATTLE AREA

Admiralty Inlet

Whidbey Island

Possession Sound

N

Puget Sound

Green Lake

SEATTLE

Elliott Bay

Lake Washington

Alki Point

Vashon Island

Sea-Tac Airport

Maury Island

Dalco Passage

East Passage

Point Defiance

Commencement Bay

Tacoma Narrows

TACOMA

SEATTLE

N

Puget
Sound

Haller
Lake

Carkeek
Park

522

5

405

99

Green Lake

513

46th &
Market

University
of
Washington

520

Seattle
Center

Medical
Examiner's
Office

Lake
Washington

Police
Station

99

90

405

Alki
Point

5

Vashon
Island
Ferry Pier

FERRY

Vashon Is.

1

AS HE STEPPED off the jetway, Lou Boldt spotted the child held in the woman's arms, a keen sense of expectation in the young blue eyes as they briefly caught his own. The child attempted to kick loose from her mother, who set the girl down, allowing her to run to greet her father, a rather average-looking executive-type a few people back. It was symbolic to Lou Boldt that the child should pass him by. He felt as if everyone, everything were passing him by, taking no notice. Perhaps it was his own fault. Yes, perhaps he *was* invisible. Perhaps what he wanted was to be unseen and left alone.

He heard the child giggle and found himself tempted to turn around. He loved the musical sound of a child laughing. Was there anything more beautiful? Anything more missing from his life?

But right now the child didn't matter.

The killings had started again; that was all that mattered. He maneuvered his way through the arriving passengers, his mind elsewhere, eyes trained toward the floor as he absentmindedly watched the colorless toes of his scuffed shoes.

He didn't want to believe it was the work of the same man. He had consumed the better part of the short flight from Portland to Seattle struggling with the thought, trying to convince himself it could not be. The killings had *ended* with that horrible scene in the courtroom. He had suffered through that incident—the whole *city* had suffered—and that had been the end of it. But nothing is ever that simple, he now thought, waiting for the line at the escalator to move.

He broke free of the line and, carrying his hanging bag effortlessly, charged down the stairs instead, drawing looks from those to his right who descended silently, their curled fingers gripping the fat black rubber rail for support. There was no rail for Boldt to grasp, nothing automatic about the job before him. Again, he found himself eyeing the dull toes of his shoes in order to avoid a disastrous and embarrassing fall, and he thought he should have them shined.

In the men's room he caught sight of himself in the mirror and realized he looked older than his thirty-nine years. This case was taking its toll. His whole act needed a shine, not just the shoes. The age of his suit reflected a detective's salary; he had spilled coffee onto his new tie—when and where, he had no idea; he had missed a spot shaving, eager to catch the first flight out of Portland; his face was pale and gaunt. And if the sun represented enthusiasm and energy, then he thought his spirit pale as well: he felt tired, nearly exhausted. He splashed some cold water onto his face, then discovered there were no paper towels. He resorted to rubbing his face briskly in the noisy jet of a hot-air dryer, lukewarm air that smelled like urinal deodorizers. The stream of forced air stirred his thin sandy hair into a rooster crown, but Boldt didn't notice.

He wanted to be at the crime scene. Now. Precious hours had been lost. He had no desire to be standing at the curb waiting to be picked up. He, better than most, understood the importance of the crime scene, and the need to get there quickly. Any disturbance at the crime scene could throw him off. He worried that some of the evidence had already been disturbed, its value negated, the site made stale. It gives *you* the advantage, he thought, looking into the dizzying sea of unfamiliar faces of the hundreds of people swarming the sidewalk, wondering: Are you still out there somewhere? Not fully believing it.

Had the wrong man died in that courtroom? Was it possible? He scanned the faces in the crowd, as if someone might provide him with the answers, but of course as a homicide detective, people looked to him for the answers, not the other way around. He was considered the expert. He was the one who had been invited to Portland to speak at a criminology seminar. His topic: *Methodology in the Murder Investigation: The Victim Speaks*.

In any case, he knew he was ultimately responsible. He would have to catch the killer.

If the killer existed.

A two-door Ford double-parked at the curb, its wipers fighting back the drizzle. The driver waved Boldt into the passenger seat. Recognizing the man, Boldt hesitated briefly, bent at the waist, staring from the sidewalk. When things start going against you, he thought, they get going in a big way. When the killings start up again, they send Kramer to pick you up. Wonderful.

Boldt pushed his hanging bag into the front seat, climbed in, slammed the door, and brushed the tiny silver droplets of rainwater from the wrinkled sleeves of his sports jacket, avoiding eye contact with Kramer. No sense in starting this off on the wrong foot. The two men sat in silence. Kramer switched on the wipers and put the car in gear and pulled out into traffic. The radio was tuned to a Muzak station. Boldt leaned over and switched it off. Kramer adjusted his tie and checked the outside mirror. The tires whined against the wet pavement. The wiper on Boldt's side only served to blur the windshield. He looked down and brushed at the stain on his tie.

"You mind?" Kramer complained, elbowing the hanging bag. Boldt tossed it into the backseat. Kramer switched the radio back on. "I'm driving," he explained. "Music helps me relax."

Boldt sighed and laid his head back on the headrest, closing his eyes. The Muzak annoyed him and Kramer knew it. Boldt was a jazz pianist by hobby, formerly by profession—it had helped pay his way through college—and this insipid dribble from the car speaker was as obnoxious to him as a hot dog to a gourmet. Kramer knew it all right. It was lifeless, uninspired, and Boldt realized how perfectly suited it was to Kramer. The two went together like Roy and Trigger.

"How certain are we?" Boldt finally asked. It was the question he had been intentionally avoiding. "About the killings, I mean."

"Certain enough."

"You don't have to sound happy about it."

Kramer toyed with the rearview mirror.

"I didn't make the assignments," Lou Boldt reminded, knowing what was bothering Kramer.

"You want to head out there straight away?"

"Is that the plan?"

"You're the one who makes the plans, right?" Kramer sounded like a five-year-old.

It was a blatant exaggeration. Lieutenant Shoswitz headed the Special Task Force. Kramer and Boldt were sergeants of equal rank assigned to Shoswitz. Each oversaw several pairs of homicide detectives—Kramer from a desk, Boldt from the field. Therein lay the difference, and to Kramer it was obviously an unforgivable slight. He held it against Boldt, despite the fact that neither of them had had anything to do with the command structure within the task force. The captain had issued the assignments in early May, following the second murder and the resulting flood of national press. One article had claimed that Seattle had logged more serial murders in the last decade than any U.S. city—a statement Lou Boldt questioned. As a result of those assignments, the prestigious job—the fieldwork—belonged to Boldt. Now early October, it seemed like years to both men.

"You're as important to this thing as I am. We both know

that.'' Boldt had not made this kind of overture in weeks. But this latest killing meant they could be starting over, so he figured it was worth a try.

Kramer said nothing, softened momentarily by Boldt's attempt. He made a face, changed lanes and accelerated. The Ford sped down the slick highway, frenzied wipers fighting backwash from a semitruck. The Muzak droned from the speaker. Boldt said, ''I would think you'd be happy. I'm the one the press will tear apart. Not you.'' Boldt knew how important the press was to Kramer. The man was always being quoted in the newspapers. It seemed to give him a sense of purpose, a sense of power.

''The press maybe, not the department. Shoswitz is still convinced you're the one who can solve this thing. I won't pretend I didn't try to get our assignments switched—you'll hear about it anyway. You bet I did. But Shoswitz wouldn't have anything to do with it. He said 'the batting order was all set' and there was no use 'changing the infield.' He talks about you like you're some kind of boy wonder.''

''Hardly,'' Boldt groaned.

''You don't have to tell *me* that,'' replied Kramer. ''He said the Jergensen thing was everyone's fault. Mostly the press. I heard him arguing on your behalf with the captain. Said it was you who suggested tighter security at the omnibus hearing. Claimed you'd been making noise about that for a couple years now. That true?''

Boldt felt cornered. ''Yeah,'' he huffed, annoyed that Kramer could make him feel bad about being right.

''Shit,'' Kramer spit out under his breath, and pressed down on the accelerator. The speeding made Boldt nervous. He chewed down a Tums, and strapped on his seat belt. This angered Kramer all the more. He drove faster. ''So Jergensen gets shot and killed for something he didn't do.''

''We can't be sure of that,'' Boldt corrected.

''Certainly looks that way. You and I both know we didn't have much of anything on Jergensen. If Daphne hadn't leaked that report, Jergensen would probably still be alive.

Just plain bad luck that he fit the description of the killer so well.''

"It wasn't Daffy's fault. It was the FBI's BSU profile. A number of us had access to it. Yourself included. Any one of us could have passed it to the press. Whoever did, got a man killed, and I guarantee you it wasn't Daffy.''

"You're always defending her. Why would that be? Why would a happily married man like you always come to her rescue?''

Boldt glared at the man and sat up stiffly. "You're lucky we're doing seventy on a wet highway, Kramer.''

"Always the tough cop, huh, Boldt? I don't buy it. Not from you. I buy the image of the fag jazz musician a lot easier.''

Boldt took hold of the volume knob and turned the radio off. He turned so hard that he accidentally broke off the knob. He stared at it in his hand. Kramer whined, "That's coming off *your* paycheck, not mine.''

Boldt grimaced. Children's games. Kramer always brought out the worst in him. He rubbed his gut. It had given him hell since August. For the last few weeks there had been blood in his stool. And now he had Jergensen's death on his conscience. The man had stolen a television set—for all Boldt knew that was the full extent of his crime. That was why they all had been at the hearing. Any connection beyond that had been speculation by a hungry press.

Kramer pulled the car into the middle lane and slowed down. The drizzle had let up. He switched the wipers to intermittent.

The windshield in front of Boldt grew even more blurry. It made him nauseous. "We're all to blame for Jergensen.''

"And now this,'' Kramer said.

"Yes,'' agreed Boldt, nodding his head slowly. "Now this.''

2

N.W. SEVENTY-FOURTH STREET, three blocks from Green Lake, was quiet, narrow, and steep, lined with tightly packed houses, some of which had been converted into apartments. They passed a tiny island in the center of the intersection that served to slow traffic. Cars were parked on the left side only. Electrical wires tangled overhead in a spider web of black. Boldt wished the wires ran underground. They were an eyesore.

"That it?" Boldt asked. They parked in front of a light green two-story house with a driveway on the left.

"Yeah."

"Take it slow. Give me the first officer report."

Kramer paraphrased, "Victim's name: Cheryl Croy. She didn't show up at work and didn't call in sick. She's a legal assistant—an executive secretary. Two co-workers, a Gail Lumbard, another secretary, and a Richard Rice, a paralegal, came by to have a look around. That was five fifty-five P.M., Monday. They observed the victim's car parked in the carport and approached the back door, which they found locked. The front door was locked as well. They circled the house, whereupon Rice observed an open window in the back. By standing on a trash can he was able to reach the window. He smelled what he regarded as possible decomposition. He did not touch the window or frame.

Lumbard placed the phone call from down by the lake. A patrol arrived shortly thereafter and took statements from both Lumbard and Rice. Because the location was close to Green Lake and because of the previous killings, the first officer had the good sense not to go inside, but to call in Homicide. Our people arrived and established a crime scene that included the entire property. They observed two other open windows, both on the second story." Kramer referred to the photocopies of the reports. "One on the north side of the house, one on the east."

"How far were the windows opened?"

"It doesn't say. I wasn't here."

Boldt made a note to himself. "You said the co-workers came by on Monday?" Kramer nodded. "What was your weather on Monday?"

"Rain."

"Hard?"

"Off and on."

"How about Sunday night? When I left it was nice."

"Yeah. That's what I remember too. Real nice. Started raining about midnight I think."

"So the time of death is estimated between six and midnight on Sunday night," Boldt stated.

Kramer nodded somewhat childlike. "Because?"

"Because of the windows, right? She would have shut them."

He nodded again.

"And because all of the killings are in the evenings." Boldt rolled down his window. "How about the death scene?"

"Don't you want to go inside?" Kramer asked.

"In a minute." He reached out. "You want me to read it?"

"No, that's all right."

Boldt was trying to give Kramer a chance to participate in the fieldwork. He would have preferred to be here alone. At any rate, in a minute, he *would* be alone.

Kramer read from the next report and again paraphrased,

"No ceiling lights on in the entire house. A night-light was operating in the master bath. Nothing from the neighbors, so far."

"Who'd you put on it?"

"Shoswitz assigned it to LaMoia. He entered the premises alone, to reduce the chance of disturbance. This is the cleanest scene we've had yet, Boldt. LaMoia did the initial report. Then Doc Dixon. Then Abrams." Dixon—whom Boldt called Dixie—chief pathologist and King County Medical Examiner, was a close friend of Boldt's, as was Chuck Abrams—Abe—the veteran I.D. technician. "Abrams dusted the place. He was real careful, as usual. LaMoia shot color photos and a videotape. He sketched a floor plan that shows all the angles the photographs were taken from. He filled out a VICAP report and a death-scene checklist while Doc Dixon examined the body." Kramer turned pages.

"Croy was found faceup on the bed, ligature around her neck, multiple stab wounds about the chest. A cross cut into her in the same way. Doc thinks he used a kitchen knife, like he did with the others. A piece of her nightgown is still around her neck, but the nightgown is missing."

"So he kept another souvenir," Boldt said.

"It's identical in every way. He tied her to the bed, strangled her, untied her, turned her over, and left his mark. It's him."

"Have we looked for the nightgown?"

"Thoroughly. Same program. Same guy. He took the nightgown with him. This guy's getting quite a collection. Maybe he'll open a boutique."

"Go on."

"Glass of milk, empty, by her bed. Last mail she had opened arrived Saturday. Monday's mail is still in the box. She had a Sunday paper in the kitchen. Fashion section by her bed. We didn't touch anything we didn't have to. Shoswitz says you can handle it however you want. No evidence of robbery. I.D. lifted traces of that same mud—an oil-gasoline mixture—from the front porch. This is what, the

third time we've found it? Could be from an outboard motor,
chain saw, weed eater. No way to tell. Last contact with
victim not yet known, but believed to be a boyfriend—a
guy named Marquette—on Friday night. We found some
rolling papers in a stash box in the living room along with
about a quarter ounce of smoke. No other paraphernalia.
Japanese vibrator found in her bedside table. Pretty common
unit, sold by mail order. No other evidence of any deviate
sexual practices. That's about it.''

"Fibers?''

"I.D. vacuumed the shit out of that place. Trace evidence
is already at the crime lab. You're interested in the red
fibers, I take it?''

"That's right.'' Several years back, in the name of efficiency, the police lab had been dismantled in favor of a
state-budgeted crime lab. Its services were used jointly by
the FBI, Police, and Fire—charges billed separately to each.
The result was an often overworked, occasionally inefficient
laboratory that analyzed evidence gleaned by SPD's I.D.
technicians or the detectives themselves.

"If there were any we've got 'em. We took six separate
bags, front and back doors inside and out, stairway, and
several in the bedroom.''

"Good.''

"Oh, there's one other thing,'' Kramer said, flipping back
through the pages. Boldt looked over at him. Kramer had
freckles and light green eyes and golden rust hair. He looked
like something out of a Walt Disney movie. "LaMoia noticed a strange smell in the air. Medicinal. It was familiar
to him but he couldn't place it. The bag boys Doc Dixon
used mentioned the same thing. No one could place it.''

"Medicinal?''

"That's what they said.''

Boldt nodded. "I'm going to walk around for a few
minutes. Then I'm going inside. You have the key?'' Kramer handed it to him. "I'll call when I'm through.''

"Back door. We all used the back door. It was dead-bolted. Front door was on a night latch. We assume he used the front door." He added, "I can hang around and wait for you."

"Don't know how long I'll be," Boldt said delicately.

"Doesn't matter. I'll wait. If they need me they'll radio."

"Suit yourself." Boldt watched as Kramer fished the morning newspaper out from under the front seat and turned to the sports pages. Kramer knew everything there was to know about professional sports.

"May I?" Boldt asked.

"Right," Kramer said, as he peered over the pair of glasses he had put on. He handed Boldt the clipboard and a manila envelope thick with photographs.

"Jesus," Boldt said, commenting on the weight of the manila envelope.

"I told you we got a lot of shots."

Boldt shut the car door and turned to face the house.

He searched the clipboard and located the photocopy of the floor plan that LaMoia had sketched. The bedroom was at the back of the house on the second story, down a hall accessed by the front, and only, stairway. Boldt examined the exterior of the house. Two of the curtains were partially opened. He wondered if they gave any kind of interior view from out here. He wouldn't be able to tell for sure until he returned tonight when the lighting would be the same as it had been for the killer. In the months since April twenty-ninth, eight women had been killed in the Green Lake area. Cheryl Croy made it nine. All had been killed in the evening. He'd been over the local patrol reports several times: no nuisance offenders reported in the Green Lake area—no voyeurism, indecent exposure, exhibitionism, kleptomania, or fetishism. He knew well enough that an obsessive-compulsive behavior often led to a more violent crime. Voyeurs made good candidates. None so far.

Boldt walked entirely around the block stopping at each house and looking back toward Croy's. It began to mist heavily again, but he took no notice, except to tug his coat collar up against his thick neck. Not even qualifying as a drizzle, this mist was typical fall weather. The overhead power lines grew shiny. Water collected there and fell to the street in heavy drops. Boldt climbed the hill, his left hip and right knee complaining of high-school football injuries. When he turned around he lost sight of her house completely.

The walk around the block consumed about fifteen minutes. By the time he reached Croy's house again his coat was damp, his hair dark and stringy. He caught himself whistling "Blue Monk." He searched the extreme perimeter of the small lot first, walking alongside a low fence, eyes trained downward. The ground was not yet damp enough to leave foot impressions—something he would avoid at all costs. He found nothing. He reduced his loop by a few feet and began the pattern again. He stopped twice, using his pen to overturn a bottle cap and then a Popsicle stick. Both appeared faded and old. Probably of little use to him, but not useless. Nothing found at a crime scene was useless. He paused by some dog excrement and made note of it on LaMoia's map, which had become wrinkled from the mist. He scribbled a note at the bottom of the page: PET?

These loops took him another fifteen minutes. Not once did he look up to see what Kramer was doing. Boldt uncovered an empty pack of Marlboro cigarettes pressed into the damp earth. It too showed evidence of age and weathering. Nonetheless he made note of it on the wet page and marked its location on the map. His note read: WHO SMOKED? In addition he found a mud-stained broken shoelace, a garden trowel, two cotton swabs with what appeared to be blue nail polish, and five cigarette butts, all Marlboros. None of what he discovered appeared new enough to have a bearing on the killing, but he duly marked each on the map and made several notes. He underlined WHO SMOKED? five times.

He had tucked the manila envelope containing the photographs in the waist of his pants, shielded from the mist by his buttoned jacket. He withdrew it now as he slid the key smoothly into the lock of the kitchen door. He swung the door open on noisy hinges and hesitated before stepping inside. He made note of the sound from the door. He looked into the house: such a normal kitchen, in a normal house, in a normal neighborhood. But something hideous had happened here. *He* had been here.

Lou Boldt could not put himself into the mind of the killer. He wished he could. But he was not a psychologist, he was a cop. The only way he knew something tragic and grotesque had happened here was by the color photographs inside this envelope and the fact that the key fit the door.

He had yet to look at the photographs. He hated the photographs, and what the photographs did to him. He hated this animal who had been here before him. (He couldn't bring himself to think of the killer as anything but, despite Daphne's arguments.) In many ways he hated this job.

At the core of his uneasiness with the job was the uncovering of people's private lives. Murder has a way, he thought, of unwrapping the package and leaving exposed all those private nuances and secrets people spend a lifetime hiding. With no time to bury these secrets, a murder victim is left unmasked, horribly vulnerable, and all too human. Would Cheryl Croy have wanted anyone to know about the vibrator in her end table? Unlikely. Did the grass hidden in her living room make her any less a human being?

Boldt kept a supply of brown-paper evidence bags in the left pocket of his sports coat, disposable surgical gloves in the right. He slipped on a pair of gloves so he wouldn't leave any prints. It was believed the killer wore similar gloves, and it made Boldt think of him as he turned the doorknob.

He stepped into the kitchen. He was invading her privacy now. He had the photographs. He had the reports. He shut the door and looked around.

The kitchen appeared clean and tidy. He made a note at the discovery of several bread crumbs in the stainless-steel sink. The refrigerator handle still retained the shaded mask of black powder used to dust for prints. Boldt opened the refrigerator and studied its few contents. Vegetables, yogurt, real butter, skim milk, cheeses, mayonnaise, mustard, a half bottle of a high-priced California Chardonnay, pickle relish, catsup, fresh pasta, grapefruit in the bottom drawer. No meat. The freezer held Häagen-Dazs bars, a bag of French Roast beans, and several frozen diet dinners. No meat here either. Ice tray half empty and frosted. He wrote down the expiration dates of the dairy products and closed both doors. The dates would give him an idea of when she last shopped. Maybe find a receipt in a shopping bag if she saved them.

The cabinets were neatly ordered and clean. She ate unsweetened breakfast cereals, rice, and Almost Home chocolate chip cookies, and obviously didn't like canned foods. She had an espresso maker, a microwave, a coffee grinder, and a two-slice toaster. He made a note to have the disposal checked; he couldn't fit his hand inside.

He noted that the kitchen window above the sink lacked curtains. He peered outside, into the constantly shifting mist, to see which houses had a view of the window. Several possibilities. He made a note on LaMoia's hand-drawn map.

The downstairs window that had been found open by Croy's co-workers was part of a half bath that was tucked under the stairs and that backed up to the kitchen. Under the sink he found some feminine napkins, an assortment of cleansers, and a toilet brush. Nail clippers, aspirin, and dental floss in the medicine cabinet. Two drops of urine and a pubic hair on the rim of the toilet, indicating use by a man. Boldt made a note and circled it.

He assumed he knew whom he was looking for: the FBI's Behavioral Science Unit in Quantico, Virginia, had created a psychological profile of the killer following the discovery of the second victim, Jan Reddick, back in May. Despite the uncanny success record and accuracy of the BSU profiles, many of Boldt's co-workers placed little faith in what amounted to professional guesswork. Nonetheless, Lou Boldt believed them useful. The murderer was white, between twenty-five and thirty, emaciated, lived alone or with a single parent, was a firstborn or only child, lived within a three-mile radius of Green Lake, was an insomniac, used recreational drugs, and wore blue jeans and basketball sneakers. The difficulty with this profile was the three-mile radius of Green Lake. It created too large an area. In the last six weeks two detectives had thoroughly covered four search sectors. They had twenty-seven to go.

Now, with the discovery of the urine, perhaps Boldt had something. Perhaps not.

He reached the front door and stopped. The report favored the front door as the entrance. Same as the other sites. It bothered Boldt. What was the man's entry? How did he convince her to open the door? Did she know him? Did he pretend to be injured? His car broken down? Was he dressed as a woman? (This last thought resulted from the discovery at other sites of starched red silk fibers that the lab believed to be from a woman's bonnet. The victim had owned no such bonnet. The fibers had been found on the pad of a chair at the death scene, as if the hat had been placed there, or the killer had undressed.) Was that his entry? Was he a transvestite?

From the perspective of a homicide detective there were two key elements to any serial killer's ritual: the selection of victims and the way the killer gained entrance. Beyond these elements the ritual served the interest of investigators only in that it helped to further define the subject's psychological profile. Boldt still had no clue to either.

He stepped onto the first step and tried to put himself inside the head of the killer. It wasn't easy. He had no real idea what it was like to be inside a psychotic mind. He closed his eyes. He wanted to feel wild and driven to kill. Out of control. Frantic. Lou Boldt opened his eyes and began to climb the stairs. Indigestion, maybe. Out of control, frantic? No.

The fifth stair from the bottom creaked beneath his weight. Did the killer sneak in, or did she admit him? Would she have heard this stair creak from up in her bedroom? The stairway seemed to grow more narrow as he approached the top, the illusion brought on by his increased anxiety. With every step now he moved closer to her most private sanctuary; with every step he moved closer to the confrontation; with every step he moved closer to her final moment. He walked slowly but steadily down the now-pulsating hallway, blood drumming ferociously in his ears, eyes stinging. He briefly felt her fear. It began in the center of his chest as something like a tiny bubble and ballooned out of all proportion as he stepped up to her bedroom door. He didn't need LaMoia's map to know which room it was.

He was familiar with the stories of cops who could "become" the perpetrator; who could wander the death scene and interpret the events from the killer's perspective. For Lou Boldt it was quite the opposite: he experienced the overwhelming fright of the victim, the ultimate horror of being someone's victim—and though this rarely helped him to glean any facts, it greatly motivated him. It drove him up to and beyond the points where other cops might stop.

He swung open the door to her room.

As he caught sight of the dried blood he actually heard her shrill cry, only to realize it was a jay outside her window. He mopped his forehead with his handkerchief and stuffed it carelessly back into his rear pocket. He quickly loosened his tie and unbuttoned the collar button. The room was indeed well preserved. A yellow chalk line had been sketched onto the soiled sheets indicating her final position. Without stepping any further into the room, he carefully inspected the mauve walls, the matching curtains. He faced the double bed with its wicker headboard, the oak end table, the white carpet now flecked in that awful shade of brown. To his left, in the corner, was a dresser littered with framed family photographs, and along this near wall a bureau holding a television set and VCR. He dropped to one knee and continued his examination, finally placing his cheek onto the carpet and looking from this angle as well. He spotted a paperback under the bed, spine out. Judith Krantz.

Boldt withdrew the first photograph and turned it over. Croy was naked, bloody, lying on her back staring toward the door. Toward Boldt. Don't look at me, he demanded. But it was he who looked away. As with the other victims, the killer had taped Croy's eyes open using silver duct tape, stretching and distorting her face, leaving her grotesque, oversized eyes swimming in pink empty sockets. Around both ankles and wrists, the telltale lengths of nylon rope were tied securely, although the other ends, wrinkled from having been knotted previously, were untied and hanging off the mattress. A torn piece of her missing nightgown remained around her neck. Except for this odd bloodstained necklace, she was unclothed, her chest riddled with stab wounds, the symbol of the cross severing her breasts and running from throat to navel. *His* trademark. The newspapers had dubbed him "The Cross Killer."

Boldt leafed through the photographs. Close-ups of her face, of the wounds, of the knotted strips of bed sheeting —on and on they went, taken from different angles with different lenses. In color. Frame by frame, they seared an image in Boldt's memory, taking their place alongside those of the others. Cheryl Croy's murder was now a part of him. It would linger inside him, stagnant and fetid.

If I had done my job, he thought, you would still be alive.

In his seven years on Homicide, he had never experienced the all-consuming weight that this case put upon him. Most homicide cases did not involve repetition. It was the repetition that beat him down—his prior knowledge of what he would see before even entering the death scene. He felt as if the killer was intentionally forcing him to relive this same disgusting sight time and again, punishing Boldt for his failure to solve the case. Was this killer conscious enough to want to be stopped—as some serial killers were—or was he dazed and disoriented, wandering aimlessly out there somewhere ready to be trapped by his own psyche and "forced" into another killing?

Nothing about this case was predictable. Even the FBI's Behavioral Science Unit had warned Boldt that the killer did not fit easily into a single profile description. Certain parts of the killing ritual pointed to a psychotic: a spontaneous, dysfunctional individual, often responding to imaginary voices and commands. Other aspects indicated a psychopath: a calculating, asocial, criminal mind. Boldt had been told he had a combination personality on his hands, and for this reason the BSU profile could be well off the mark.

He retrieved the paperback from under the bed. Unlike other items in the room, it showed no signs of fingerprint dust. They had missed it. He opened to the bookmark, which turned out to be a cash-register receipt dated the previous Saturday. Had she intentionally hidden the book under the bed, the receipt some kind of clue? Had Croy recognized her killer from the store where she had purchased the paperback and then had the foresight to slide the book under the bed? He examined the receipt but avoided touching it. He knew a receipt like this had to be torn from a register, leaving open the possibility I.D. could pull a good thumb or index print. He slid it into the manila envelope atop the photographs. As he opened the envelope, Cheryl Croy stared out at him, the thick pieces of silver tape stuck to her face.

Boldt walked to the other side of the room and reconstructed the kill like a film director preparing to shoot a scene. He has something—a handkerchief perhaps—around her neck. She's losing consciousness. He won't let her go off completely. Boldt had been told that would ruin it for him. Instead, he brings her right to the edge of unconsciousness and then releases his tourniquet just in time for her to return. Boldt now watches as the man binds her ankles and wrists, as he ties her to the bed—facedown at first, they now believe—as he excitedly tapes her eyes. But why? What was the point of the tape? What was it she was to watch? They knew his ritual involved a performance, but what performance? There was no evidence of masturbation. Why the eyes? Was he disfigured?

While she is still facedown the killer continues to choke the life from her, and only then does he turn her over and finish the ritual with a kitchen knife, this despite the fact she is most likely already dead. For each of the victims the medical examiner had labeled the stab wounds perimortem —at or about the time of death. No way to be absolutely certain. Why this brutal conclusion to his ritual? What significance did it hold for him?

Boldt backed into the corner of the room, drained. In his imagination the monster was still at work. He now positions the head so she is looking toward the door. Every victim the same. He collects himself, most certainly covering himself up in a coat—or a dress—and then calmly leaves by the front door, the same way by which he entered. Does he walk down the street, rejoining the society he feels no part of, or does he steal through the shadows at the back of the houses, stealthily covering his retreat?

Boldt found himself now standing on the front landing, a steady drizzle falling onto his shoulders and hair. His stomach felt inexorably knotted, the bitter taste of bile threatening at the back of his throat. He tried to imagine the killer walking away.

Then Kramer honked the car horn, and Lou Boldt was back on the steps of Croy's small house on Seventy-fourth Street.

Absentmindedly, the detective looked down, his eyesight zeroing in on the first concrete step. He crouched down.

There on the step, a brightly colored speck lay floating in a small puddle of water. He bent down further, making his knees wet, and touched his fingertip to it and it clung eagerly to his skin. He drew his finger in close to his eyes, his vision shifting focus, the speck becoming clearer.

A single red fiber.

3

LIEUTENANT PHILIP SHOSWITZ had eyes shaped like sunflower seeds and a dark bristly mustache that helped to hide his rabbitlike front teeth. It was his nature to move quickly, nervously, always fidgeting, rubbing at his chronic tennis elbow or scratching at his scalp. Boldt sat in the only other chair in the lieutenant's cramped but ordered office space that was defined by five-foot sound baffles, the dull clattering of typewriters spitting out arrhythmical reports from somewhere on the other side. When Shoswitz had weighed 250 he had been indolent and lethargic, now he was an entirely different man, wired and restless. Boldt remembered him from those early years when the two had played a weekly game of poker together, long before wives and mortgages, back when a policeman's pay had seemed decent enough. Boldt hadn't played poker in years.

"So how was Portland?" the lieutenant asked in his high, strained voice.

"Interrupted."

"Kramer tried to switch things around while you were gone."

"So I heard."

"He told you? I'm surprised. He was careful about it. He gave it his best, which for him isn't too good, is it?

Right? I told him we would leave things as they were. I think he knew my answer before he even asked. Right? I have to give him credit for trying." Shoswitz had long since adopted the annoying habit of asking, "Right?" in the middle of any conversation, as if expecting a reply—as if needing the reassurance. His apparent insecurity was nothing more than the lieutenant's way of making a statement. It was as if he believed himself always in the know, always right.

Boldt didn't play the game, not even nodding. After years of the rhetorical question he let it pass. But ignoring the query only made Shoswitz more persistent.

"So what's up?" Boldt asked.

"I need a pinch hitter." Shoswitz was devoted to baseball. The game continually crept into his conversations and Boldt was often annoyed by the tired clichés and useless statistics.

Boldt waited.

"I'm being interviewed. Correction: We're being interviewed. *Right?* A graduate student in journalism at the University is doing a term paper—the topic of which, he's quick to point out, concerns the inappropriate influence of the press on our legal system. He referred to the Gary Hart disaster as an example. At any rate, it would seem the Jergensen case has caught his eye, and my wonderful friends down in Public Information," he said sarcastically, "arranged for him to interview me. And I'm putting you on deck. If I swing and miss, then by all means correct me and set the record straight. I'll do the same for you. It's safer with two of us. Right?"

"Why not the captain?"

"He wants to distance himself from Jergensen. The fallout from that one continues to be intense. It's off-limits. Be thankful for small favors. You missed last night's news. They were less than kind. We're to make it perfectly clear that Jergensen's low-level and not at all the sort of thing that would have crossed the captain's desk. Notice is served. Keep in mind, Lou, our necks are on the line here. This is game seven—and we're behind.''

"There isn't much to tell this kid, is there?"

"Short and sweet, then. That's fine with me. If you can end the interview politely, then by all means, be my guest.'' Shoswitz rubbed his elbow, his face showing curiosity as he peered over Lou Boldt's shoulder. ''I think he's here. I'll grab a chair. Remember, you're my expert. Act like an expert. Right? And for God's sake, tuck in your shirt. You're looking a little bit ratty these days, Lou, for Christ's sake.''

Boldt grunted, moving his chair in preparation for the interviewer. A minute later Jerry Kline was seated, notebook in hand. He looked nervous. Boldt was glad for that. Kline combed his knotted hair out of his eyes with ink-stained fingers and began, ''Let me make one thing clear, gentlemen. I'm on your side in this, if sides exist in such matters, and it is my contention not only that they do, but that the lines are sharply drawn. My interest is in developing a factual foundation to support the theory that misconduct of the media can have devastating effects on law enforcement, and therefore society as a whole. That said, I should also explain that the reason for this seemingly biased attitude is that I have conducted interviews and research into the other side of the story—not this particular story, mind you, though I plan on that—and therefore am looking for substantiation of the opposing viewpoint. If I do a good job, this may run in our *Journalism Quarterly*, which enjoys a limited national circulation.'' Shoswitz threw Boldt a meaningful look.

Kline continued, ''There are plenty of examples where so-called thorough investigation on the part of the press reaffirms the First Amendment and weeds out corruption at the highest level. I am not an advocate of censorship. However, if I understand the Jergensen case correctly, a hungry press may essentially have been responsible for an innocent man's death—''

"Not an innocent man," Boldt interjected.

"Good. Okay. Fine. Let's start there, Detective."

"Labor Day weekend Jergensen was arrested on a B&E, breaking and entering, charge. A patrol caught him in possession of a stolen television set. Irrefutable evidence. 'Red-handed' you might call it. He stole the set and we caught him. That's how it all began."

"Exactly," Shoswitz contributed, hand working his elbow. "And from there it got out of hand."

"Not right away," Boldt corrected. "It wasn't overnight. It was a logical progression of events, really. It just backfired on us."

"Can you explain that, please?" Kline requested.

Boldt shrugged. "Jergensen was brought here, downtown. Standard procedure. He was booked on B&E and grand larceny. Jergensen couldn't afford an attorney so a public defender was assigned."

"But is it not the department's contention that the media and printed press directly interfered with the judicial process?"

Boldt looked over at Shoswitz, who nodded slightly and said, "I think the best response to such a question is 'no comment.' You may draw your own conclusions, Mr. Kline. Right? That's a pretty sweeping statement. Off the record . . . we have a relationship to maintain with the press, and a responsibility to the public not to get into name-calling. Why don't we just take you through it and you can make the call. Such a decision is better for you, anyway. After all, we were direct participants."

"The people I interviewed in the press were less considerate, Lieutenant. I had hoped—"

Boldt interrupted, "Our job is to arrest criminals, okay? Keep the streets safe. The city safe. We are not practiced in baiting and goading. What Lieutenant Shoswitz is telling you is that we'll give you the sequence that led to the Jergensen shooting. Drawing any conclusions, forming any opinions is better left up to you."

Kline looked a little puzzled. "I thought your department was upset about this."

"Off the record?" Boldt wondered, making sure to wait for an acknowledgment.

"Yes. Sure." Kline raised his pencil ostentatiously.

"My *personal* opinion is that the press overstepped their bounds. They created an atmosphere of a witch-hunt and a man died as a result. One thing important to remember is that, as cops, we read the papers. We watch the TV news, too. We're an integral part of the society we serve. If the press puts forward an idea, there are many of us on the force who are caught up in it as well. That's often overlooked. People think of us as uniformed men in an ivory tower. They forget that cops go home to a wife and kids, feed the dog, turn on the tube and pop a beer. In or out of uniform a cop is the guy next door."

"But that's off the record?" Kline complained.

"Absolutely."

"That's good stuff. I'd like to use it."

"Put it into your own words, then. I won't be quoted on opinion."

Kline nodded. "I get the picture."

Shoswitz said, "Jergensen was apprehended approximately thirty-six hours after the discovery of the eighth victim—Robin Bailey—of what the papers are calling the Cross Killer murders. Same neighborhood. By that time the Behavioral Science Unit of the FBI, the BSU, had drawn up a psychological profile based on the limited evidence we had. Only a few of us here in Homicide were privy to it."

"Could we go over the purpose of the profiles please? All I have is what I've read in the papers."

Shoswitz explained that the profiles draw on past case histories and present evidence. They give the police someone to look for. "The BSU interviewed convicted murderers and learned a great deal about what makes these guys tick, what motivates them, how they felt at the time, et cetera. They have amassed an enormous data base and as professional psychologists and psychiatrists—some of the sharpest minds in the country—they attempt to create a picture of the man we are after.''

"I've read about this, but I find it hard to believe such a profile can actually help.''

Boldt said, ''There are many people in our department who would agree with you. As an investigator I can tell you that the BSU profiles are invaluable. Their track record is uncanny.''

"For instance?''

"For instance, a series of murders was uncovered in a major West Coast city. The BSU profile stated that the suspect was between twenty-eight and thirty years old, lived alone within a mile of where a victim's station wagon had been found, and, believe it or not, that he wore a double-breasted suit most of the time. He was believed to have been previously institutionalized and released. BSU sent the police a map with a circle drawn on it, within which they believed the suspect would be found. The police started on the dot in the center of the circle. The very *first door* they knocked on was opened by a gaunt man in his late twenties wearing a double-breasted suit coat. A subsequent search of the premises revealed they had located the killer.'' Kline registered disbelief. ''That city was Seattle, Mr. Kline. I was a part of that investigation. It makes a believer out of you. There are dozens of similar examples. But that's the most dramatic I've ever been connected with. That's why we call the BSU efforts uncanny. It's a lot more than guess-work, which some people would have you believe.''

"I could never use that. It's far too fantastic.''

"Nonetheless,'' Shoswitz said, ''it happened. It's nec-essary you understand our faith in the BSU profiles, if you are to understand the Jergensen shooting.''

"Go on.''

Boldt explained. ''That profile arrived on a Wednesday morning. It's critical that it isn't released to the media. If it is, suddenly everyone is seeing the killer everywhere and

we're flooded with false reports. Running down false leads
wastes our limited manpower. We have a staff psychologist
—our resident expert—who helps narrow our beam. It's
a team effort. The profile is integrated into our investigation. It's not the most important thing, because our
physical evidence and our victims are our most valuable
asset."

"The profile is merely further grist to our mill," Shoswitz
said.

"So you received the profile."

"And someone leaked it to the press," Boldt explained.
"And that's when we ran into trouble." The silence in the
small space was heavy. Kline studied both men and resisted
asking a question. He scribbled something in his notebook.
Boldt wondered what he could be writing. Boldt continued,
"As we've said, the profiles themselves are not enough to
go on. With the profile leaked, however, all it took was one
clever reporter. I won't mention any names but he works
the crime beat. He had seen Jergensen in here the day before
and he made the connection to the physical description in
the profile. Mind you, to us the physical description is but
one facet of the profile, and the profile but one facet of the
investigation. This reporter made a series of what have now
proven to be erroneous jumps in logic. A equals C, B equals
C, A equals B. It may work in math, but not in logic or
police investigations. One thing to keep in mind, Mr. Kline:
a good investigator assumes *nothing*. We base our investigations on fact alone, which is not to say we don't make
educated guesses, but we differentiate strongly between an
educated guess and an assumption. It's something the press
should learn."

"The paper made an assumption," Shoswitz said, taking
over. "That was their mistake. They pointed out the uncanny physical similarity between Jergensen and the BSU
profile of the Cross Killer and *implied* the two were one in
the same."

"What we continue to ask," Boldt added, "is why we

allowed ourselves to bend to public sentiment. There's no question we began to believe that we had caught the Cross Killer. The killings stopped, after all. And although they had stopped for long periods before, we had never had someone in custody. One and one makes two, even in law enforcement. In hindsight, there came a time when this department was determined to link Jergensen to all the killings. Why? Because we wanted it over as much as anyone. You see, Mr. Kline, this is where the pressure of the media comes into play. I guarantee you there were law-enforcement officers who were convinced Jergensen *was* the Cross Killer. Did we allow ourselves to be swayed by the media?''

Shoswitz said, ''The killings stopped. Right? Suddenly we had ourselves *believing*. And this is where the real damage to society occurs. Right? We backed off on our investigation. We *scaled back* in order to accommodate a lot of other urgent investigations.''

Kline asked, ''Did Jergensen actually fit that closely?''

Boldt glanced at Shoswitz, who nodded. Boldt explained, ''As with any criminal, Mr. Kline, reliable witnesses are nearly impossible to come by. To this day we still can't connect Jergensen to any of the death scenes. Neither, however, can we substantiate any kind of alibi for him. In fact, he was robbing the same neighborhoods where the killings took place. The press emphasized that as well. He was a drug user, which fit the profile. He lived alone. And he even had prior history of being institutionalized.''

''Good God.''

''So, you see our dilemma. The man closely fit the profile. The crime scenes were—are—exceptionally clean, making physical evidence sparse, and therefore a match extremely difficult. The press knew we couldn't tie him to the murders. They harped on the fact that all we had Jergensen on was a B&E, and *implied* a mass murderer was about to 'slip from the jaws of justice,' '' Boldt quoted. ''That's how they put it.''

''Which infuriated the father of the second victim,'' Shos-

witz continued. "He read about the omnibus hearing—
that's the third and final hearing before trial in this state.
He decided to effect his own brand of justice. Two weeks
later, in the middle of September, he shot and killed Jergensen in that open courtroom. With Jergensen dead and
the killings ceased, we were convinced the Cross Killer had
died in that courtroom."

"Until yesterday," Kline suggested.

"Yes," said Shoswitz. "Until then."

A little while later Kline was gone. Shoswitz went to the
can. Boldt fetched fresh coffee. When the lieutenant returned Boldt asked, "So where do we stand? Do I get the
same crew back?"

Avoiding an answer, Shoswitz said, "You come in here,
hand me a list including dog shit, Marlboros, blue nail
polish, dates of yogurt cups, piss on a toilet, a paperback
receipt, and another damn red fiber, and you ask me where
we stand? *I* was about to ask *you*."

"The dog shit is from a neighbor's terrier," Boldt explained. "The Marlboros are an unknown. I need people
for that. I found a blue nail-polish bottle in her bathroom,
so that's handled. Took the urine sample to the lab. They
tell me you can't get squat from dried urine unless the person
is passing blood because of something wrong inside. They're
checking. But we do know it was a guy because it was on
the rim. Bad aim," he said, drawing no response from
Shoswitz. "Abe has the paperback and the receipt. He's
dusting for prints. But, as you can see, pulling all the strings
together on this is going to take one hell of a lot of manpower. I want to know where that paperback was purchased.
I want to know which of her friends, if any, smoked Marlboros. Or do we have a peeper on our hands who likes to
smoke while he watches? If we do, he's been watching her
for weeks, months maybe. A few of those butts were real
old. Lots of questions, Phil, and they won't get answered

without a hell of a lot of help. You wanted my help with Kline. I need yours on this.''

The lieutenant waved the sheet of paper in the air. They were back into business as usual, as if Kline had never been there. "We had a whole crew out there. Didn't catch any of this shit. Am I right?"

"I need more men."

"What'd you expect?"

"A fight."

"Not this time. Captain's on our side. Like I said, he wants this thing cleaned up. We're going to continue to take a lot of shit from the press until we have this wrapped. So we take what we need. We're short on detectives. We both know that. I'm told we can borrow a couple of base runners—some girls from Special Assaults. We'll use them for the door-to-door work."

Shoswitz paused in thought and then continued, "We do this the same way as before: everything goes through you guys and then through me. We take it nice and slow, Lou. No hurry. The press still has the BSU profile, of course. That's going to screw things up if we bring in any suspects. I'm working out a deal with the FBI to help with security in that event. They're cooperating, as always. BSU is willing to try and update the profile if we want them to. They haven't tried since number three. What do you think?"

"Based on what I've just seen?"

"Yeah."

"I'll write it up and give it to Daphne. Let her make the call. If she sees something new, something worthwhile, maybe it's worth a try."

"You don't look so good. Am I right?"

"That's the second time you said that, Lieutenant. Am I supposed to look so good?"

"Lou, you thought that scene out front was a mob scene? You ain't seen nothing." Boldt had been accosted by the press as he had arrived. "Most of them were waiting for you at the garage entrance. The press corps is huge on this one. Bigger than before! They're going to crawl all over us. Especially you. Count on it. A lousy physical appearance isn't going to help anything. You look like someone ran you over. You hear what I'm saying?"

"I hear you."

"You sure?"

"I hear you!"

"You look like you could use some sleep."

"Phil . . ."

"Just so I get my point across. There's been a lot of pressure on us from the Mayor's office to change the team. I'm sure you understand that. Personally, I think it's a stupid idea. We've come this far and it's worked out okay. We rearrange things, we have to start all over. That's absurd. At the same time—"

"I get the point."

"Right. Good. As long as I've made myself clear."

"Perfectly."

"So what's next, besides running this stuff down?" Shoswitz waved the sheet of paper again.

"We get a couple guys moving on that stuff. I have a talk with Daphne. I go back to Croy's tonight and try again."

"The captain is thinking about using that psychic."

"Oh, Christ."

"The man helped out in California."

"They raise psychics in California as a cash crop. He had the home-field advantage," he said, using an analogy he thought Shoswitz could understand.

"Just warning you."

"God, no. Fight that one, will you please? Talk about a circus. What about the FBI's help?"

"Same legal problems exist as before: until we have a state-line violation or something like that, they have to remain as advisers."

"Crazy system sometimes."

"Can be. Get a haircut too," Shoswitz said.

"Which one?" Boldt asked sarcastically, thinking it funny. Lou Boldt only knew old jokes.

"Hi there," Boldt said, knocking on the open door. *Come in, we're open*, was painted on a wooden placard that a small ceramic Charlie Brown held in plain view from the corner of her desk. "Hi there, yourself," she said. Daphne Matthews looked like a human version of a Kentucky thoroughbred, which was exactly what she was: well-bred, aristocratic, and naturally healthy. She had the disposition of a patron saint and the charm of a Southern girl, a trait inherited along with her dark coloring from her maternal grandmother, who had been born and bred bluegrass. Daphne had an easy way with people, which accounted in part for her success as a clinical psychologist and an extremely full social calendar. "Shut the door if you want," she added, seeing his worn look. She stood up and caught the door before he closed it. They were standing quite close, though she didn't seem to notice. She asked, "How about a cup of tea? You look like you need it."

He knew better than to ask for coffee. Daphne didn't approve of coffee, despite the fact that her breakfast tea contained more caffeine. "Sure," he said. "No—"

". . . cream."

"Right."

"Sit. Please. I have something just in from Quantico that will interest you."

"You must be a mind reader," he said down the hall after her. She raised a hand over her shoulder in acknowledgment and moved gracefully and powerfully toward the lounge. When he looked away from her he noticed Kramer, across the office area at a desk, staring him down with obvious disapproval. Kramer went back to work, the damage already done. His expression was not lost on Boldt. *What's a happily married man like you . . .* the man's eyes said. "Shut up," Boldt hissed, only to be overheard and misunderstood by a passing secretary.

"Jeez," she snapped, "same to you," looking back at him curiously and hurrying on.

He apologized to her—evidently unheard—and returned to the warm, spotless office. He felt comfortable here.

There were rumors about Daphne Matthews, like there were rumors about everyone who worked on the force. It wasn't enough to be a cop, or to work for the department —people seemed to believe your motivations for becoming a cop were their business, as if this was an elected position. Some were third-generation cops. Some were like Boldt— college cops—men and women attracted to the profession by courses or professors. And then there were the people who generated dramatic rumors, some eventually proven out, some never uncovered, some becoming legends that circulated through the hallways long after a cop had retired.

The rumors Boldt had heard about Daphne were remarkably varied, as rumors often are. One said that her interest in psychology had resulted from her younger brother being beaten badly by a group of blacks, and that, in turn, he had shot and killed a black. This rumor was proven false when a look through her records revealed that Daphne didn't have a younger brother. Another, the most cruel, insinuated that Daphne had once had a lesbian lover who had later flipped out after being jilted. There had been an era, Boldt recalled, several years past now, when gay rumors got the most lip service. At one point or another, everybody in the department had been accused of being gay. He didn't know Daphne's sexual preference, but he knew she was about the most feminine woman in the entire department, and he knew she dated many different men, and he assumed this to be the cause of the rumors. Interdepartment jealousies were the cause of more rumors than anything else. Just when someone started to excel, a rumor would surface that would shed doubt on him or her. And these doubts, however unfounded, would linger in even the most well-intentioned mind for weeks and months to come.

Daphne, being witty, womanly, and charming, and the

only member of the force who could act autonomously, was
the target of many rumors. Especially those generated by a
few envious women.

She never spoke of why she had chosen public service
over a private career that would easily be five to ten times
more lucrative—and it was her reticence that gave rise to
so many unfounded rumors. Privacy has its cost in any
fraternity.

She shut the door upon her return. Because of Kramer's
suspicious look, Boldt considered asking her to leave it
open, but didn't. She placed the mug of tea in front of him,
pulled a folder from one of her many file cabinets, and took
the chair next to him, crossing her fine athletic legs. Her
hosiery whistled. She smelled sweet and tropical. She maintained an upright spine and fine posture that emphasized her
full figure; she did this without seeming pompous or vain.
"How's Lou Boldt accepting all this?"

"He's not doing too well."

"When I heard . . . You were the first person I thought
of."

"You and half the city it would seem."

"I don't mean like that."

"Thanks."

"You blame yourself?"

"Wouldn't you?" He looked her in the eyes over the rim
of the cup and added, "I take that back. Wouldn't most
people?" he rephrased, drawing a quick grin from her.

"What makes you so special?" she asked somewhat
harshly.

He was taken aback. He leaned away from her, nearly
spilling tea and adding another stain to his tie. He reached
down and inspected it to make sure it was unsoiled.

She continued, "What makes you think you should have
foreseen what no one else foresaw? Are you filled with some
prescience or divination you haven't informed us of?"

"Point taken."

"I don't think so," she said, studying him.

"Don't start in with me, Daffy, okay? Truce."

"Okay." They sat in a calculated silence for a moment as each sipped their tea. She continued to look over at him with her penetrating eyes. He avoided her, choosing to look at Charlie Brown instead.

"What's this about Quantico?" he asked.

She opened the folder. "When I heard about Croy's murder I telexed BSU and asked for anything they could give us on our suspect's past other than the profile information we received earlier. They wired me this, along with all sorts of qualifying statements. You'll notice how they point out this shouldn't apply to the investigation, et cetera, et cetera, and that it's a result of a recent limited study with no qualified control group. They surveyed thirty-five inmates deemed clinically insane. Ten of them were lust murderers. You can understand their concern given these small numbers. Still, it's ground we haven't covered before, and I thought you might be interested in knowing where a man like this might have come from. It may not help any right now, but *when* you catch him, I think it's important you consider this kind of information."

"You don't miss a trick," he grinned, noting her use of "when," not "if."

"We've covered some of this before—you and I." She looked at him briefly, and for a moment something passed between them that had nothing to do with police work. She'd been flirting with him—he thought—for quite some time. And now that he thought about it, Kramer was right: it had been heating up lately.

"Like we talked about, he's quiet. Isolated. His preexisting —before crime—personality would be schizoid. He's given to preoccupations like study. He was, or is, a bookworm. He spent much of his adolescence reading either political or religious material or both—Nazism perhaps. He had or has adolescent sexual tension depending on how old he actually turns out to be, probably has unusual attitudes about pornography and prostitution. These concerns are troublesome to him. And here's the new ground," she said, looking up for a brief moment, serious and pensive. "His mother may have done unusual things to him. She may have dressed him in dresses as a young child, allowed his curls to grow too long—"

"They're working with the transvestite theme," he interjected.

"To my knowledge no one has run that by them. No, in fact, they're working only with evidence and death-scene reports." She seemed bothered by his interruption.

"Jesus."

"They're specialists," she reminded.

"I'd say so."

"His father might have been alcoholic—a *drunk* says it better. The father would be employed, but move from job to job. Verbally abusive, cold and distant from the young, sensitive boy that was emerging. His mother may have interested him in some girlish pursuit, or other, in order to 'sophisticate' him. Sewing perhaps. Ironing. Flower arranging. Cooking. Things like that. Knowingly or unknowingly this gave him a problem establishing a sexual identity. He can't identify with his father, who is an obnoxious, half-absent drunk, and yet he can't fully identify with the somewhat seductive mother, reinforcing his feminine traits." She continued to read. "He probably went through a Peeping Tom phase—voyeurism. But each time he would venture out, he would return and do something punitive to himself: burn himself with an iron—"

"Oh Christ."

"Something like that." She paused, traced across the page with her long red nail and continued, "A lot of guilt and tension developed around his sexual behavior. Similarly he may have gone through a stage of stealing his mother's underclothing and wearing them or violating them." Again, she looked up. "This may carry over into his souvenir collecting, may help to explain why he takes a piece of clothing from each victim." Boldt nodded, clearly uncomfortable.

He didn't want to know anything more about this man. He didn't want to feel sorry for him, but he found himself inclined to. He knew this was one of Daphne's intentions. In her professional opinion, which she shared with him constantly, this man was himself a victim, a man with an illness, rather than an animal. Boldt saw her efforts as twofold: one, to convince him he *would* catch the killer; two, to remind— to instill in him—that once caught, the Cross Killer should be treated as a sick man, not a calculating killer. Both of these thoughts remained with Boldt as he asked, "Is there more?"

"If we accept this as his past, then it's likely he misperceived an early sexual encounter. He thought a girl was interested in him, but she and the others turned out to pity him. This would have happened sometime in his early twenties. Five or six years ago. It's been building up in him ever since. He may have tried a homosexual relationship since then. Perhaps immediately before the killings began. As we've discussed, he's become an insomniac. He's back to reading all the time—probably the more obscure sections of the Bible. He's hearing voices, misinterpreting reality. I might add, he may perceive himself as a kind of fundamental Christian. Nothing could be further from the truth, of course. His is a fantasy world, and he probably thinks the voices he hears are from Christ himself. Perhaps that's why he marks them with a cross. Something triggers the need to kill. Until we know more . . . Are you all right?"

He couldn't hear her clearly.

"Lou?"

He raised a hand and laid his head back. He didn't like hearing this stuff. "I'm fine," he said. "It's that damn tea." He exhaled heavily.

"Anxiety attack?"

"Caffeine," he insisted.

"I'm a friend, remember?"

"You're a head doctor," he reminded. "It's nothing."

"You can talk to me, Lou. You know you can. What's wrong?"

"Drop it!" he shouted, hurting her. "Thanks for the report."

"Lou?"

He rose out of the chair, refusing to look at her, and headed for the door. Daphne called to him again. He wouldn't turn around. He said to the wall, "I'll draw up a full report on Croy and leave it up to you whether it's worth yet another try by the BSU people. Sound okay?" She didn't answer him. She waited him out and he finally turned around, forced to face her. "Okay?" he repeated, looking quickly away. *What's a happily married man . . .* chimed through his head.

"Fine," she snapped. "Wonderful. Leave it open."

He pushed open the door, checked his watch, and hurried from her office. "Almost noon. Got an appointment," he said. He spotted Shoswitz ahead and reached for his comb. Tightened his tie.

4

TECHNICALLY LUNCH HOUR fell under private time. He parked the unmarked car across the street from the Rainier Bank Tower, and turned on his KJZZ jazz station, avoiding news radio at all costs. The departmental radio occasionally growled intestinally from beneath the dash, the dispatcher's unfailing monotone summoning patrol cars by number. Boldt devoured two Tums like candy.

The Rainier Bank Tower appeared to rise from an inverted pyramid. Perched atop a meager support, it seemed delicately balanced and vulnerable, as if a strong gust of wind might topple it. The effect was disconcerting to Boldt. No doubt the winner of several architectural awards, he thought.

The woman came out a few minutes later, wearing her tan raincoat over a lavender dress, and walking briskly in shiny black heels. She had none of that haughty passive gait that accompanies many women of the business community. He waited briefly and then locked up the car, following behind and across the street on foot. He proceeded slowly, allowing her to gain distance on him.

They continued this way, she in the lead across the street, for a few short downhill blocks, until she found her way to the Four Seasons Olympic. She went in through the hotel's side entrance. Boldt crossed the street, approaching cautiously, and pushed through the heavy doors slowly, inspecting the lobby before entering. She disappeared up the flight of stairs and was gone.

The Four Seasons lobby was a throwback to the grand hotels: towering marble columns, lots of brass and luxurious carpeting. Boldt approached the concierge, withdrew his badge, and placed it in view. "A woman in a raincoat and lavender dress just entered. You couldn't have missed her."

The man, soft-featured and in his mid-thirties, looked Boldt in the eye silently.

Boldt said, "I'd like to know when she leaves the hotel. A gratuity is involved."

"Official business?" the man wondered.

"I'll be in your Garden Lounge," he answered, retrieving his badge. He padded silently around the corner and into the magnificent lounge. The room was like a giant greenhouse. Flowers, plants, and mature trees abounded. It was split-level, and in the far corner, an unattended concert grand as black and polished as Chinese enamel begged Boldt to play. The waitress was refreshingly young, polite, and courteous. When he ordered a tall milk, she made not the slightest indication of surprise or disappointment as some waitresses did. She thanked him, placed a logo-embossed napkin before him, and hurried away. A few minutes later she returned with the cold, cold milk. He drank it ungraciously without pausing, and wiped away the resulting mustache. A couple chatted in the far corner. Quite old and quite happy, they seemed. He hoped he might end up the same. The thought brought images of Cheryl Croy's frightened face to mind. In color. His stomach turned. He chewed down two more Tums.

He was anxious to read the autopsy protocol to see if there was anything different about Croy. Doc Dixon was one of the best medical examiners in the country. Like Boldt, he had taken a personal interest in the Cross Killings. As in any homicide investigation, the Medical Examiner's role was as important as the investigating officer's. Not only did the Medical Examiner's office pursue its own investigation of a crime scene, secure and identify physical evidence, but pathologists and their assistants often served as chief witnesses for the prosecution.

Any and all evidence in a homicide case had to be collected in a certain way, reported and categorized in a certain way, stored, presented, and filed with the courts in a certain way, or it became inadmissible. Even if it was the proverbial "smoking gun," a piece of evidence was useless to the prosecution if not handled properly. This, along with the hundreds and hundreds of regulations governing investigations, made the job of homicide detective all the more difficult. It was one thing to reach the point of finally arresting a suspect, something else entirely to see him ever reach jail. One minuscule mistake by the police in their investigation could negate reams of damning evidence. Boldt had no intention of allowing that to happen with this case.

He scribbled some notes on the fancy paper napkin, and reminded himself to talk over his ideas with Shoswitz and Kramer. This being the largest departmental investigation in years, Boldt was well aware of the chance of mistakes and oversights. A multiple-review system involving all three detectives would increase their chances of catching any such mistakes. Boldt's plan called for each detective to regularly check the other's work. It would increase their workload but might reduce the chance of losing a court battle. When the napkin had filled with notes, arrows, and asterisks, the soft gray pants appeared by the table's edge.

"Excuse me, sir," said the concierge. "She's leaving."

Boldt stood quickly, fetching the napkin and sliding a ten-dollar bill into the man's hand. "Just now?" he asked.

"Yes, sir."

Boldt walked into the lobby just in time to see a glimpse of her profile as she reached the street. He debated following her but decided against it, electing instead to take a seat in the far corner, hidden partially by a group of insurance salesmen collecting for a group lunch.

An attractive man came down the stairs alone only a few minutes later. He was about thirty-five, blond and broad-shouldered. He crossed the lobby, heading straight for the side doors. Boldt followed.

When, a few minutes later, this man entered the Rainier Bank Tower, Boldt wasn't too surprised. He climbed back into his car, checked in with the dispatcher, and drove away, heart pounding from the gradual climb uphill. Or so he tried to believe.

5

CHERYL CROY'S BOYFRIEND, Craig Marquette, worked as a butcher in a Safeway five blocks off of Forty-fifth Street. Boldt arrived at fifteen minutes past one. He found Marquette on the loading bay just lighting up a cigarette. A Marlboro, Boldt noticed, introducing himself. He could scratch that off his list. The young man nodded but didn't offer his hand. Boldt was put off by the sight of bloodstains on the man's apron.

"I already talked to you guys, didn't I?" complained Marquette.

Boldt explained his position on the case and his need to hear some things firsthand. "You understand," he finished explaining, "that in these cases the victims are all we have. It's up to the victims to tell us who did this."

"That's a little bit tough, isn't it?" Marquette sniped.

"Now you're getting the idea," Boldt returned in an equally condescending tone. At this point, Boldt couldn't rule anyone out as a suspect—even a boyfriend. Physically, Marquette didn't fit the BSU profile—he appeared healthy and strong—but he was an apprentice butcher by trade, a man accustomed to the sight of blood, a big man, and he didn't seem too fond of the police.

Marquette turned and peered at Boldt through squinting

red eyes. "If you assholes had arrested the right guy in the first place, then this whole thing would be different. Cheryl had stopped jogging because of the murders. She had become security-conscious. She'd done a damn good job of things. But she relaxed after the killer was nailed in court by that guy. Everybody did. This whole city relaxed. And now look at how things turned out. Shit."

He seemed younger than Boldt had first guessed. "Friday night was the last time you saw her alive?" Boldt asked, purposely avoiding any implication in his tone of voice.

"Yeah, Friday. That's right."

"You had dinner at Guido's?"

"We ate a pie at Guido's, went back to her place, and watched some tube."

"Anything unusual happen while you were at Guido's? Strange guys, anything like that?"

"You think this guy hunts them in restaurants?"

"It'll go quicker if I ask the questions," Boldt commented. "We both have a lot of work to do." Boldt's bedside manner differed according to whom he interviewed. With guys like Marquette—he had seen a hundred Marquettes—he preferred to cut through the shit and get the job over with. The image of this guy dropping a cleaver down onto raw meat didn't sit well.

"Nothing unusual," Marquette answered, lighting another Marlboro.

"You've been seeing Cheryl for how long?"

"Couple of months. We met at a friend's house in the middle of summer. I wasn't always a butcher, you know. I worked for Boeing up until eighteen months ago. Assembly crew. Laid off along with twelve hundred others. Couldn't find any assembly work except in southern Cal and I grew up there, no way I'm going back. This was the best I could find. Cheryl, being a vegetarian, wasn't too fond of my change in employment." He looked down at his apron. "And politicians have the nerve to say the economy is healthy again. What the fuck do they know?"

"How did she spend her time when she wasn't with you? You know anything about that?"

"Some. Sure. Her job took up most of her time. That lawyer worked her butt off. Sixty-hour weeks sometimes. She did some stuff with her girlfriends, shopping, that kind of thing. She took a cooking class—"

"Remember where?"

"University. One of those night things for people already through school."

Boldt took a note.

"She read a little. Liked movies. She was normal, as normal as anyone you've ever met. We had a good thing going. You catch this guy and I'll save the state the cost of a trial."

"It would be prudent to withhold that kind of comment, Mr. Marquette. That's not going to get you anywhere. Okay?"

"Yeah, sure. I got it." He took a long drag on the cigarette.

"Did she use the facilities at Green Lake? The jogging track, anything like that?"

"Sure. Everybody who lives around there uses that stuff. We went on walks, that kind of thing."

"Had she, or had both of you together, been at the lake in the last week?"

"I'm sure she had. She jogged there every day."

"I want you to think about this real carefully."

"I told you, I'm sure."

"She shop regularly at the same stores?" Boldt asked, thinking about the paperback he had found under her bed.

"For food?"

"That's right."

"Last few months she shopped here whenever I pulled a shift. I don't know. She had a couple of stores nearby her place. There's a small grocery up on Greenwood. Got ice cream there, things like that. You know how it is. She shopped the neighborhood like anybody else.''

"I'm making a list as we go along. When we're done I'd like you to go over it and fill in any specifics when you have some free time. You mind doing that?''

"I'm up for catching this guy—same as everybody else. You want me to fill something out, I'll fill something out.''

"She had bought a new paperback on Saturday. Any idea where she might have done so?''

Marquette shrugged and smoked some more. "Can't say. Like I already told you, she liked to read.''

"Think a little harder on that, would you please, Marquette? Where would she have bought a paperback? Any place in particular?''

"I'm thinking.''

"It's important," Boldt reminded.

"I hear ya, okay? I'm thinking.'' He took a deep drag on the cigarette and shook his head. "I don't know. I'd say here, but she didn't come here last Saturday.''

"You're sure?''

"Sure, I'm sure.'' Another drag. Long exhale. "I don't know, a drugstore maybe? You're the cop. She do any other shopping on Saturday?''

Had she? Boldt made himself a note. "See, you gave me an idea," he said.

"Gee whiz, ain't that swell, Mr. Detective.''

Boldt pursed his lips.

"You know what she might have done? Anything favorite she like to do weekends?''

He shook his head and exhaled a cloud. "Listen, I stayed with her Friday night. Had to be here by eight on Saturday. We had another date for tonight.'' He turned and faced Boldt fully, his bloodied apron screaming out. "How do you like that?''

Boldt looked away into a crate of rotting produce and then back at Marquette. "What can you tell me about her home life? Her habits. Did she draw the curtains at night?''

"Yeah, sure."

"How about windows? Was she in the habit of leaving windows open? We found two open upstairs."

"That house is tiny. It has a way of getting too hot upstairs when the heat kicks on. She was paying four bills a month, utilities extra. She shoulda had a roommate. She held back because she wanted the roommate to be me. Anyway, the heater had a mind of its own. You have to open a couple of windows to keep the place balanced. Downstairs needs more insulation."

"She shut them when it rained?"

"Wouldn't you? Shit! 'Course she did. Listen, she only turned the heat on now and then. Said when I wasn't there she had trouble keeping warm. Maybe I'm to blame for all this," he added.

Marquette's tone of voice bothered Boldt. "You nervous?" Boldt asked.

" 'Course I'm nervous. You're a cop, aren't you?" he replied. "Listen, Lieutenant, last time I was with Cheryl, we were in bed together watching the tube." Boldt didn't bother to correct the mistake in rank. "Next thing I know I'm reading about her in the papers." He paused, examined the short cigarette, and then crushed it with the toe of his boot. "A couple of weeks back she asked me to move in with her, like I told you. I turned her down. She knew things were rough for me, financially, and I wasn't sure what her motivation was. I didn't want charity. I'm divorced. My wife ditched out after Boeing laid us off. I liked Cheryl a lot. I'm not sure I loved her. Not in the commitment sense of the word. She felt the same way, I think. We were working on it, testing it out. But I couldn't see moving in with her. It wouldn't have been fair to either of us. But if I had . . ." He shrugged again. "What the hell. Who knows?"

Boldt waited a few moments before asking, "Did she wear a nightgown to bed? Did she wear a robe?"

"You're all heart, eh, Lieutenant? I know, I know, you've got a job to do. Don't let me slow you down." Marquette fished his last cigarette from the pack, and lit it before answering. "She had a nightgown hanging in the bathroom I think, but to be honest, I didn't see her in it too much." He smirked.

"We found a glass of milk by her bed."

"Her snack. She ate a bedtime snack—cookies and milk—every single night. A real routine for her."

The word *routine* caught Boldt's attention. "What time? Any time in particular?" Boldt could hear the excitement in his own voice.

"Bedtime. I don't know. Why?"

"She eat it in the kitchen or up in her room?"

"She'd kind of nibble on a cookie, you know? Drag it out, chase it with some milk. Up in bed usually. What's the big deal?"

Boldt tore the handwritten list from his pad and handed it to Marquette. "Fill in anything you can, will you? If you can do it tonight, that would help us out."

"Sure, no problem."

"Give us a call. Someone will stop by and pick it up."

"What's so important about the snack, Lieutenant?"

"Sergeant," Boldt corrected, reintroducing himself. He shoved out his hand. Despite a quick attempt by the butcher to wipe his hand on his apron, as they shook hands, Marquette's felt greasy and warm.

The smell of dead meat remained with Boldt for the rest of the day.

6

THE KING COUNTY Medical Examiner's office was housed in the basement of the Harbor View Medical Center. Boldt had been here often enough. He didn't like coming here. More often than not it was to oversee an autopsy, or discuss gruesome details of a case. And since the start of the Cross Killings, he had left here time and time again with no more than he had arrived with—empty hopes.

Doctor Ronald Dixon, chief pathologist, owned a deep, powerful voice but spoke softly and casually. He was a big bear of a man, with large, clean hands. A fastidious man, Dixon took great pleasure in constantly cleaning his nails. He wore gray pants and a white laboratory coat with his ID badge clipped to his pocket. The two men shook hands and Dixon sagged into a chair that seemed to swallow him. "Damn tough luck," he said, locating a small screwdriver in his middle drawer and going to work on his nails.

"Yeah," said Boldt.

"Not a hell of a lot to tell you about Croy. She died of suffocation: strangulation, same as the others. I've listed the stab wounds as perimortem. More this time—seventeen. I'd like to be able to tell you for certain when he inflicted those wounds, but I can't. Time of death was sometime Sunday night. That's about the best I can do. We didn't get the body for two days, you know. No way to really narrow it down very well. We sent the hand bags over to the lab, didn't pick up anything on the fingers or the nails.''

''No red fibers?''

''Not on her.'' He paused. ''Abe tells me he lifted some of that same mud from her doormat.''

Boldt nodded. ''Oil and gas mixture embedded in the mud. Probably from an outboard engine. Could be from a hundred different marinas. Doesn't help us much.''

''We found some sperm inside her tubes. Nothing vaginal. I assume from the report that it's the boyfriend's.''

Boldt made a note to check Marquette's blood type. ''I think she ate a snack—some cookies—right before the incident. Any way to tell how long before? It may help us with the timing.''

Doc Dixon excused himself and when he returned a few minutes later he said, ''We'll know shortly.''

''Anything new, Dixie?''

''No. Nothing new. Same as all the others.''

''Could it be the work of a copycat?''

The question caused Dixon a moment of thought. ''Hard to say, I guess. Depends. In my opinion we've got the same guy as before. I've been to what, nine of these now? You and I both know that two, maybe three of them looked a little bit different, but not enough to raise any kind of suspicion. A person could read about some of this in the papers, but not all of it, not the specifics. They would know about the cross, but not exactly what it looked like, how deeply it was cut, the angle of incision. They would know about the eyes being taped open, but that's not an easy thing to do, and this guy does it the same way every time. Same with the ropes, the timing of the stab wounds. I don't think so, Lou.''

Boldt nodded. Among other things he had been testing whether word of his discovery of a red fiber on the porch step had reached the Medical Examiner's department. He was glad it had not. One of the big problems with this case

was the press leaks. He and Shoswitz had tried to close
down the communication conduits in an effort to reduce the
leaks, and it seemed to be working.

Dixon said, "We do have one promising lead, but we
haven't gotten the lab results back yet."

"What's that?"

"Royce, one of my autopsy assistants, had the bright idea
that the killer might have used his teeth to tear the duct tape
from the roll. We removed all the tape very carefully this
time and sent it over to the lab. If we're lucky, they may
pull some facial hair."

"Lab should have thought of that. That was good thinking."

"I'll pass that along. These new guys need the strokes.
They need something. This department has been turning
over personnel at a ridiculous rate. Pay's lousy, working
conditions minimal, and they've got me for a boss."

"That's one out of three in their favor, Dixie. They're
batting three hundred."

"You've been around Shoswitz too much. You're starting
to talk like him."

"Tell me about it," Boldt said. "I have to listen to that
baseball shit day in and day out."

"Have you heard the new Hamilton album?" Like Boldt,
Dixon was a jazz enthusiast.

"Didn't even know one was out," Boldt admitted.

"You feeling all right, Lou?"

"Tired."

Dixon nodded. Tired was one thing he understood. "I
wish I could give you something new. Not much, I'm afraid.
He wore latex gloves, same as before. No prints anywhere."

"Still no indication as to why he ties them facedown
first?"

"No. Not from me. Not my department. We did find
indication of torn hair. We don't have the other bodies, so
we can't make comparisons. We could exhume, but Jesus

. . . It may be he ties them facedown and then pulls on their hair. Something like that.'' He shrugged his shoulders. ''Don't know if that helps you any.''

''No sign of rape?''

''No bruising. Nothing vaginal, as I said. I wish I had more.'' He paused. ''Incidentally, Croy's family is already screaming for us to release the body. I know you want us to hold each body a month, but I don't see any reason to hold on to this one that long. I told them another week at least. What do you think?''

''She's evidence. I want to hold on to her.''

''Medically speaking, there's no reason for it. We've been over her. But if you want it that way, that's okay with me. Just don't make it too long, will you? We've got limited space here.''

A knock on the door preceded a head poking inside. The man had narrow-set blue eyes and a heavy five o'clock shadow. He had a pair of headphones from a Sony Walkman slung around his neck, a Mozart concerto issuing forth. He looked as tired as Boldt felt. The man said, ''Mike checked on that for you. Food was still in the stomach. Couldn't have been eaten more than twenty or thirty minutes before death.''

Dixon nodded and thanked him. ''Lou Boldt, James Royce, the guy I was telling you about.''

''Good call on that tape,'' Boldt said, standing quickly, shaking hands enthusiastically, picking up on the hint Dixon had dropped. ''That's the kind of heads-up thinking we could use more of.''

Royce thanked him. He seemed embarrassed. ''No way to tell exactly what she had eaten,'' the man added. Boldt feared a lecture was forthcoming. ''Too much decomposition. But we're fairly sure of the time.''

Boldt nodded, thankful the man had not gone into detail. Boldt didn't like the work of the Medical Examiner's office.

''That help you out any?'' Royce asked Boldt hopefully.

"Everything helps at this point," Boldt admitted.

Royce nodded and shut the door, leaving the two alone. Dixon was working on the nail of his little finger.

On his way back to the office Boldt tried again to reconstruct the various possibilities. Had Cheryl Croy occasionally left the bedroom curtains parted while she changed? Had a voyeur spotted her, crawled in the open downstairs window, and then followed her upstairs after her cookie run? Or had she been spotted through the curtainless kitchen window while getting her midnight snack? That would have given her enough time to eat her cookie and climb back into bed before the killer caught up to her. Had he entered through the window and not the front door, and if so, why was a single red silk fiber found on the front steps? Did the killer know she ate a snack every night? Had he established her routine well enough to plan the kill? Had the other victims had similar routines that Boldt and his detectives had failed to uncover? Was there a common link they had missed?

Or had Craig Marquette killed Croy? Due to the discovery of the red silk fiber, Boldt knew this was improbable unless Marquette was the Cross Killer and had murdered his own girlfriend in an effort to hide himself from the police. It wouldn't be the first time such a ploy had been used. It was well documented that some psychopaths tried to get as close to the police investigation as possible, following the progress in the newspapers, often returning to the crime scene while the police were investigating. For many, the public notoriety and the "game" of the chase were as important as the killing itself.

Around and around he went, painfully aware that the killer's clock had started again. Except for the September hiatus following Jergensen's death, no more than a few weeks had passed between each of the previous killings. No apparent schedule to it. Somewhere out there the killer, still at large, was susceptible to an unknown psychological stimulus that would trigger another murder. He would select his prey somehow, stalk her, and then kill her.

Like any homicide detective, Boldt usually worked well under pressure. But he was unaccustomed to the worry he now carried with him. How soon until his phone rang announcing the discovery of another victim? The photographic images of the "crossed" victims flashed across his eyes. His heartbeat increased. How many more? If he had been a drinker, perhaps he could have drunk his worry away. But he was not. His father had died drunk. Boldt avoided liquor at every turn. He found himself wanting the investigation to move more quickly. It felt like slow motion at times—like a nightmare where his legs weighed a thousand pounds. Did he really have anything more to go on than a vague psychological sketch and a few red fibers? Not enough, he thought. Not nearly enough.

John LaMoia worked a plainclothes beat and wore his dark, curly hair long. He had a matching mustache, a square chin, and chocolate eyes. At thirty-three he was young for Homicide. Boldt had used him ten months earlier on a homicide case, borrowing him from Vice where his talents had been overlooked. He had helped Boldt break that case, and had been working Homicide ever since. Tall, strong, and fit, proud of his Italian heritage, he was in the habit of treating every woman in the office like a current or former lover. He came across as cocky and sure of himself, and he was.

The two men met in Boldt's partitioned office area, two stalls down from Kramer's. Boldt handed LaMoia a photocopy of the small cash-register receipt. "I want you to find out what store this came from. I.D. pulled a good thumbprint from it. I wrote down the title of the paperback alongside of it there. Any questions?"

"You want *me* to chase this down? Listen, we've just brought on a couple skirts from Special Assaults. Why not

put one of them on this? Me and Tommy are still working
Croy's neighborhood. That's a lot more import—''

"Any *other* questions," Boldt asked.

"A paperback? You know how many stores could have
sold that?''

"We have the receipt. We know where she lived. Get a
list from the publisher of the wholesalers who distribute it.
Find out from them what stores they distributed to. It's a
best-seller so there are bound to be a couple dozen at
least—''

"Couple hundred is more like it.''

"He may have spotted her there, okay? He may even
work behind the counter. This has to be handled just right
or we could scare him off. I chose you for a reason, John.
I don't want you asking any questions of the store personnel.
I want you to play it like a customer. Mark all the stores
on a map and work your way out from her house. Find out
from our boys what kind of registers make this kind of
receipt. That'll save you a lot of time. If the store has this
kind of register, then buy something cheap and get a receipt.
See how closely they match the one we've found. We should
be able to knock this thing down to a fairly small list of
stores with a little legwork. You see what I'm after?''

"I just don't see why me.''

"Don't give me any trouble on this, John. We have to
determine how he spots his victims. They all lived in roughly
the same neighborhood. They may have shopped the same
stores. The paperback is where we start.''

LaMoia nodded. "Can I take one of the skirts along for
company?''

Boldt shook his head. "No. Do it alone. It's got to look
perfectly normal. I want you to keep an eye out for anyone
who fits the profile. Okay?''

"Yeah. I got it.''

"Put Browning on the families and friends of the victims.
Make sure they each get a copy of the list you compile of

the possible stores. I want to know if any of the victims shopped any of the same stores. You follow?''

"I'll handle it.''

"Good. Sorry to do this to you, John, but it's got to be done right. This could be the connection we've been looking for. Check out all the angles. This is the kind of thing you're good at. He spots them somehow, okay? So where? How?''

"You don't mind me saying so, you don't look so good, Sergeant.''

"I *do* mind,'' barked Boldt.

I ought to start a club, he thought.

7

BY NIGHT, Seventy-fourth Street was quiet. The overhead wires formed a net of glittering black threads. The streetlamps disturbed the darkness, glaring down onto the puddle-stained pavement. Boldt entered Croy's house through the back door. In darkness it seemed even more empty. For Lou Boldt the peacefulness of the silence was a lie. *He* was still out there somewhere, unchecked and out of control.

He tested a variety of combinations of house lights. He switched on lights in the kitchen, the living room, the second-floor hallway, her bedroom, and her bath. He went outside again and circled the house slowly from a variety of distances, patiently studying each and every view of the residence. He concluded that it would have been easy to see her going after a snack in the kitchen. Had she worn a robe that night, or had she forgotten to, wearing only a skimpy nightgown instead, her lithe body silhouetted by the refrigerator's bright interior light? Boldt didn't put himself into the mind of the killer. He couldn't do that. He simply approached it from the *logistics* of a killer. How would a person have entered the home without Croy's knowledge? Where might the killer have spotted her from? It seemed the front of the house offered many less opportunities for a voyeur.

Had the killer simply selected Croy at random? Earlier in the investigation he might have believed this, but he no longer could. Each of the victims was a single woman, dissimilar in appearance but similar in age; each had a boyfriend or lover who occasionally spent the night at the victim's house or apartment. Yet each woman was attacked while alone. So the killer apparently planned his kills. He placed his victims under surveillance, formulated a plan, and then carried it out.

This was the fine line the killer crossed between psychotic and psychopath. Although his killings showed signs of violent, eruptive, psychotic spontaneity, the method of selection seemed to indicate premeditation and extensive planning, behavior attributed more to the psychopath. This combination of personalities made him more formidable, more unpredictable.

Boldt returned to his car, climbed inside, and switched on the interior light. He reread the reports collected by his various detectives. None of the neighbors recalled seeing any regular deliveries at Croy's house. No laundry services. No pizza delivery. Nothing to draw attention to the house on the night of the murder or any other night. He grabbed a pair of low-power binoculars from the glove box and shut off the light and went back to walking the neighborhood, looking back repeatedly toward her house. He walked up the hill hoping it might provide an unusual vantage point. Behind him he heard the faint offerings of an Oscar Peterson cut that made him think of his earlier years spent in piano bars working the ivories for fifty bucks and tips. He wondered what his life might be like now had he stayed with that occupation. There existed a serenity and simplicity to the life of a musician. The work was ethereal, lasting only as long as the notes resounded in the room. Variations on a theme. For years he had managed to keep it up as a hobby, yet now he couldn't remember the last time he had played. Too long. He stood on the sidewalk, Oscar vamping behind him, the familiar whine of tires in the distance, the regi-

mented uniformity of homes tucked neatly along Seventy-
fourth Street, and he returned to the work at hand. As he
walked on, the piano music faded slowly behind him, and
to him it seemed both symbolic and disturbing.

A few more houses up the street he lost sight of her house,
just as he had earlier in the day. He cut across to Seventy-
third and worked his way back down its hill, unable to catch
even a glimpse of the back of Croy's house until down on
the flats, where, between houses, he caught a good view of
her bedroom window. But as before, the low angle allowed
him only a view of the ceiling's light fixture. Still, from
here the killer could have seen the bedroom light go off.
He could have cut through the adjacent backyard, vaulted
a low fence and been in Croy's backyard. Boldt would return
and check this route by daylight.

The patrol car caught him by surprise. It pulled up behind
him before he realized it was even there. Someone had
alerted the police to Boldt's presence. He cleared it up
quickly and the patrol car moved along. Boldt had heard
about the renewed enthusiasm in the Neighborhood Watch
program. His being stopped was proof, as were recently
released crime statistics. Robbery, citywide, was down a
whopping eleven percent in the last two months, attributed
solely to police-assistance programs.

As difficult as it was for him to accept, he knew there
existed a greater chance the public would catch the killer
than he and his men. Perhaps he was out there right now.
And perhaps a watchful eye had just fallen upon him. . . .

His lap around the block completed, Boldt reentered the
house. He sat down at the kitchen table and imagined the
scantily clad Cheryl Croy opening the refrigerator, pouring
herself a glass of milk, taking a cookie from the cupboard,
and heading upstairs. He followed her, shutting the lights
off behind himself as she would have. He climbed the stairs,
the same stair singing out under his weight. He moved down
the hall and switched off the light. The sight of the bloodstained bed stopped him momentarily, but he followed through

with this exercise, pretending to place the milk down on the end table, and actually climbing up onto the mattress, avoiding the bloodstains and chalk, and leaning back against the wicker headboard.

Had the paperback been on the end table? Had the killer caught up to her here, surprising her, or had he caught her downstairs? Boldt sat up, noticing for the first time that the small front panel of the television was open. He jumped off the bed and hurried over to the TV. He looked back and forth between the pillows and the television. There was fingerprint powder on the set. Something wasn't right, and it took Boldt a few seconds to realize this was a remote-controlled TV without a remote-control device. He searched the end table, and the floor behind it. He searched under the bed. He carefully patted the stained sheets, hoping to feel the small box, but didn't. He looked around the television itself, checking behind the VCR and the set, on the floor, against the wall. No sign of the device. Perhaps this explained why the front flap was left open. She had lost or damaged the control and this was her only way to operate the set: manually from the front panel.

Again he knelt in front of the set, and again he began his search, methodically repeating each step. When he reached the end table, he eyed it from all angles, and then his focus shifted and he spotted the black edge of the control box where it was lodged between the mattress and headboard. He took a pen and a comb from his pockets and climbed up onto the mattress, moving the pillows out of the way. Without touching the device, and using his pen and comb as tools, he fished it from between the crack and placed it on the sheet. Like other detectives, Boldt always carried a handful of paper evidence bags in his coat pocket. He removed one and bagged the remote control.

As he was closing the bag, he glanced up momentarily and looked out her window. There, between a gap left by two houses on Seventy-third Street, illuminated in the ambient flood of a streetlamp, stood a solitary electrical pole, like the highest mast of a tall ship, its pinnacle overlooking Croy's house as a crow's nest towers above the giant swells of the ocean. A vantage point!

A minute later he was walking briskly up the hill, anxious to cross over to Seventy-third and locate the pole.

Something drew him to the pole as he approached. It rose on the far side of the street from a hill that briefly leveled out before climbing again. It stood separate from the others, and taller by a good two or three feet. A dozen wires ran from its cross, half of them feeding houses on the other side of the street. Metal climbing grips protruded from its sides, like the short legs of a centipede. Just as Boldt began to cross the street, a glint of white light winked from a second-story window in the house behind the pole. The spark caught his attention, and he backed up to see what had caused it. Again, the small oval orb of light appeared in the window, and for a moment he thought it might be from a flashlight. He looked more closely but could not see clearly. The street-light reflected off the window as well. He moved nearer the house. It wasn't a flashlight; it appeared to be the end of a telescope. He glanced quickly in the direction the telescope was aimed. A one-story house blocked his view of Seventy-fourth Street. But the telescope was on the second floor. His heart beat more quickly. He ran to a gap between the houses, looking first toward Seventy-fourth Street, then back at the telescope. He hurried to the end of this driveway and into a backyard. Across a fence and slightly below him— directly in the line of sight of the telescope—was the home of Cheryl Croy.

He rushed back to the street. The light pole showed evidence of a recent climb. The treated poles tended to weather into a dark brown; but this pole showed long scratches of ocher on the sides leading to the first hand grips. There was no doubt in his mind that the pole had been climbed recently, and from up there a man would have a clear view of Cheryl Croy's bedroom. Boldt smiled with a certain degree of self-satisfaction as he stared up the tall pole. We all make mistakes eventually, he thought. So few of us are able to do anything perfectly.

He felt tempted to wrap his arms around the pole and hug it to his chest. He bounded up the steps and rapped loudly on the front door. A curtain parted to his left. The worried expression of a man's face filled the quickly fogging glass. A moment later the chained front door opened a crack and the same partial face appeared.

"What is it?" the man inquired.

Boldt introduced himself showing his shield, and asked to use the phone.

The man demanded to see Boldt's identification more closely, asked for the phone number of the police department, and then shut and locked the door, leaving Boldt outside. Several minutes passed before the door reopened and the man admitted him, apologizing and excusing his precaution. Boldt congratulated him on his thoroughness.

He placed a call downtown and requested an I.D. technician meet him. The man he spoke with was not thrilled with the idea of attempting to lift prints from the rungs of a wet phone pole at nine o'clock at night and told Boldt so in blunt language. But Boldt was equally blunt—causing the housewife to blush. The I.D. man acquiesced.

Boldt was offered a seat in the modest living room. Mrs. Levitt, a prim woman in her middle-to-late forties, switched off the television and joined her husband and Boldt. They discussed the fear the murder had instilled in the neighborhood, and when Boldt had finally established a degree of rapport he asked about the pole. Had they seen anyone working there recently? Anyone from City Light or the cable companies? Anyone out of the ordinary? Any unusual noises heard on the night of the murder? To each question they shook their heads nearly in unison.

Boldt reminded himself that nothing is easy. Nothing is handed to you in this line of work.

She was a curious woman. She wore her vivid red hair

long for her age, and despite her good looks, she exuded irritation and animosity. An unhappy woman, she was tight and tense and concentrated heavily on every word her husband uttered, which were few. Boldt was clearly unwelcome. She wanted nothing to do with the police. She feared "becoming involved," and even said so. She wanted the door locked and chained and the television set back on.

"Our son's room faces the street," Mr. Levitt said. "Maybe he can help out."

Mrs. Levitt bristled at the suggestion, her spine suddenly stiff as her fingers bit into the sofa's cushions. "Doug, I hardly think that appropriate!" she argued.

The two of them went at it for a moment, both displaying hot tempers, and when all was said and done, Douglas Levitt had won out. He sent his wife upstairs to retrieve Justin and she did so with utmost unwillingness. Boldt fully expected her not to return at all—certainly without the boy who would be conveniently "asleep." Much to his surprise she reappeared quite promptly with the young man in tow.

He was a young weed with his mother's hair and his father's drawn features. He had size-twelve feet that he had only partially grown into, long spidery arms, and sloping undeveloped shoulders.

"Justin, this is Mr. Boldt from the police department. He'd like to ask you a few questions if that's okay."

Justin shrugged and remained standing.

Justin appeared to be about thirteen, heading into some of the most difficult years of his life. I wish I had one like you, Boldt thought. I wish the situation was reversed, and I was part of a moderately happy, middle-income family with two children and an eye on a motor home. The grass may always be greener, but right now it looks positively emerald.

"I'm curious," Boldt began, eyes locked on those of the young man. And indeed he was curious. Boldt's wife, Elizabeth, had gone off in search of her career, denying him—in his way of looking at things—the opportunity to have children. Had things been different, he might have had a son of his own, a son this same age, the first inkling of manhood seeping into the stalk and coloring the leaves. I'd play basketball with you on the weekends, and go trout fishing in the summers way up into Alaska where the rainbows run several pounds and fight like banshees. We would argue and I would secretly complain to Elizabeth, all the while loving every minute of it.

He wondered if Douglas Levitt knew how lucky he was.

"Yeah?" asked Justin.

"I wonder if you've seen anybody on the phone pole. The one in front of the house."

"No," the boy replied harshly. "Why should I have?"

"He might have been dressed like a phone man or an electrician or—"

"I told you I didn't."

"Justin!" his father scolded.

"Douglas," interjected the wife, "leave him alone."

Boldt had seen the boy blush. He had seen him check both parents before answering. You're nervous as all hell, he thought, and it's not just because I'm a cop. You saw something, or you know something and you're afraid to say so. "You didn't see anyone? Anything? Don't you have the room facing the street?" Boldt guessed. "The one with a telescope in the window—"

"I don't have a telescope."

Douglas Levitt sat forward, studying his son. "Sure you do, Just. We gave you one last Christmas."

"Justin," the mother said sympathetically, "you should think carefully before answering. Mr. Boldt's a very busy man, a *policeman*," she said childishly, "and I'm sure he has other things he needs to tend to."

Answering his father the young man said, "Oh yeah. I'd forgotten all about that thing. That's in my closet, I think. Remember, Dad? We tried it out but the light from the city screwed everything up."

"Watch your language, Justin," his mother scolded.

The young man's eyes darted nervously between Boldt and his father.

"But that *is* your room?" Boldt asked. "Facing the street," he added.

"Yeah."

"And the pole."

"Sure."

"And you haven't seen anyone at all on the pole? No one? It would be a tremendous help if—"

"No one," the kid interrupted. "This is about that lady getting killed over there," he said, "isn't it? You think the killer used our pole?"

Boldt didn't want to scare the kid. "Probably someone from the utilities. It was a long shot." To Douglas Levitt he said, "We go after anything. Anything at all. I hope you understand."

"Certainly, Lieutenant," Levitt said.

Everyone calls me by the wrong rank, Boldt thought. They watch too much TV and don't listen carefully enough when I introduce myself. If I was getting a lieutenant's pay, I'd have a new jacket and a graphite fly rod. I'd have extra cash for everything I don't have any extra cash for, and my wife wouldn't be the one who pays for dinner every time we go out. If I was a lieutenant, I'd give this case to a sergeant and point my finger a lot when things dragged down.

"You didn't have that telescope aimed out your window a few minutes ago?" Boldt asked Justin quickly.

The kid blushed and his mother stepped in with, "He answered you already, Lieutenant. Really! Do you think he's lying, or something? He told you the telescope's in his closet. Isn't that right, Justin?"

"Is that all?" the kid asked with the same strength of conviction Boldt might typically see in a prosecuting attorney.

"Did you ever see the woman over there?" Boldt asked.

"Cheryl Croy, the one who was killed? Did you ever see her in her backyard, maybe with a boyfriend or something?"

Justin blushed again, and again his mother objected, but Douglas Levitt barked back at her and silenced her, giving Justin a chance to answer.

"I've seen her before, sure. I know who you're talking about."

"Justin," the mother said, surprised and disconcerted.

"Mom, we're up on the hill. I see lots of people from my window. What's a window for, Mom? Jeez, so I look out my window now and then. What now?" he asked. "You don't want me looking out my window? Give me a break, would ya? You treat me like a goddamned five-year-old!"

"You watch your mouth, young man! You won't speak that way to your *mother*!" Justin Levitt fled the room, thundering upstairs, and slammed his door.

"Sorry, Lieutenant," Douglas Levitt apologized.

"It's sergeant. That's all right. I understand. I'm sorry for the inconvenience."

"You certainly should be," complained the wife, attempting to force a sprig of hair back in place.

Just then several cars pulled up outside the house. Lou Boldt noticed them and apologized once more before excusing himself. He put the I.D. man to work and then headed back down Seventy-third Street, alone, still wondering what it would have been like to have children. He told himself not to think about such things. What's past is past. Except that for Lou Boldt the past kept coming back around like the brass ring on a carousel. Young women dead, their eyes taped open. And he missed that damn ring every time. It was not in his nature to dwell on what might have been. He concentrated instead on Justin Levitt's blushing face. He wanted to speak with the boy again, to get him away from his doting mother. He intended to organize an extensive house-to-house—or pole-to-pole—investigation of all the prior victims' streets and neighborhoods in case his people had overlooked something. The discovery of the light pole had given him a second wind, a renewed optimism, a reminder that the killer was as human as his victims.

Boldt saw a car stop at a stop sign and watched as the driver lit a cigarette. It triggered a vision of Craig Marquette standing alongside rotting vegetable matter and wearing that bloodstained apron, and he wondered if it could be that easy.

Was anything ever that easy?

He didn't think so.

8

LOU BOLDT didn't head home that Tuesday night. Didn't call. His wife wouldn't expect him home from Portland until the weekend, and he convinced himself he needed the quiet. He took a seedy room on First Avenue and charged it on his MasterCard.

For the next three days Boldt oversaw the second search of Green Lake's surrounding neighborhoods, including all phone poles. He was working eighteen-hour days in an effort to keep up with the dozens of reports streaming across his desk. Kramer was living at the office too, and for the same reasons—he and Boldt had split the victims into two groups, and despite Shoswitz's objections to the increased overtime hours, each was running a thorough recanvassing of the areas. The same element of conflict between the two sergeants returned. Boldt wished Kramer had never been assigned to the task force; he was quite certain the feeling was reciprocal. He remained at his desk for days, swamped with paperwork and scheduling demands.

The press was kept at bay. Yet the leaks had begun again. KING news radio was already "theorizing" that the Special Task Force was withholding new evidence. The local papers carried it a step further, suggesting to their readers the police were close to apprehending the Cross Killer. It was pressure no one needed.

Kramer cleared his throat and stepped into Boldt's office area uninvited. Boldt was on the phone and unable to stop the man. Kramer slid his butt onto Boldt's desk and in doing so knocked a pile of papers onto the floor. He collected them absentmindedly, randomly, slapped them back onto the desk in a scattered heap and sat back down on them. Boldt waved him off the desktop and indicated in a crude sign language that he should get a chair. Kramer stood impatiently. Boldt hung up.

"Jesus, John. What the hell?" he complained, attempting to sort out the pile.

"You ought to keep your desk neater." Kramer's office area was typically spotless. Too clean for a cop who was supposed to be busy, as far as Boldt was concerned. Kramer stuck too close to regs. Triplicate this, duplicate that, everything in on time. But worthless most of the time. Void of any substantial content. Kramer was best at moving paper. He would have made a perfect IRS agent, Boldt thought. As a cop he lacked ideas and initiative—prerequisites for good detective work. To everyone but Kramer it was no wonder he was behind a desk.

"What is it, John?"

"I got the most recent I.D. report." He handed a copy to Boldt. "Just came across my desk. Yours is probably here somewhere," he sniped, leafing the papers on Boldt's desk. "Some other things I want to go over with you, as far as assignments."

"I read it," Boldt said, handing the copy back to Kramer. "We bagged red fibers from the throw rug inside the front door and from the carpet beneath the chair in her bedroom. The crumbs in the sink were from the chocolate chip cookies she had stashed in the cupboard. They pulled a trace amount of powder from the duct tape Dixie supplied. The powder's from the latex gloves. Same make as the other hits. Where do you want to go with all of it? What's next?" Boldt tossed out, puzzling Kramer. The man's face bunched in on itself. He looked as if he might cry.

Kramer whispered childishly, "I want some of the field-work, Boldt. You and Shoswitz are burying me in god-damned paperwork and I'm sick and tired of it. I'm just as competent—"

"John, it's out of my hands. You know that. This is absurd. You're going to have to talk with Shoswitz."

"Bullshit. A couple hours on this receipt thing, something like that—"

"Out of the question," Boldt interrupted. "That's LaMoia's baby. We've been over this . . ."

"I outrank LaMoia, dammit!"

"Rank has nothing to do with it. It's LaMoia's baby, and that's that. Are you going to get a chair, or am I going to get one for you?" With Kramer towering over him, Boldt felt uncomfortable. Kramer was essentially unpredictable, which made him all the worse for field-work. Although no one seemed to know about Daphne Matthews's past, everyone knew John Kramer's. His father, who had held a seat on the State Supreme Court until his death two years before, had peddled his influence to assure son John a place on Seattle's finest. The same influence had been used to obtain a series of undeserved promotions. John LaMoia deserved that office space a few paces down the hall, not Kramer, and Boldt still bristled every time he thought about it. Injustice within the ranks of those hired to serve and protect. What kind of system was that?

Boldt found him a chair and returned to his office. Kramer was gone. He wheeled the chair next door to Kramer's area and found the man at his clean desk. A nudie poster calendar hung on the wall. The woman—about eighteen—had breasts the size of healthy eggplants. She was sitting naked on an elegant buffet table, her legs wrapped around a huge bowl of fresh red cherries. "That's revolting," Boldt said. He hadn't seen Miss October yet.

"Each to his own," Kramer replied.

"Listen, John, team effort, right?"

"Stuff it, Boldt. I don't need it from you. I thought you might understand."

"You're whining. You're actually whining, John."

"Fuck off!" Kramer barked.

"I didn't make the assignments."

"Oh pleeease!"

"You want to go over the report or not?" Boldt said bluntly.

"Not."

"There are things we should cover."

"Later," Kramer insisted pathetically.

"Where have I been for the last three days, John? Answer me that? I'll tell you. I've been stuck to my goddamned chair just as you've been. Well, haven't I? Haven't I?"

Kramer shrugged, not looking at Boldt.

"We're running what, ten, twelve cops on this, you and I. We don't do it right, we waste time. We don't work together, then we don't do it right. I can't change our assignments, and I wouldn't if I could. Here's what I want you to do. You listening?"

Kramer was red in the face, rage in his eyes, holding himself stiffly upright, like a child expecting to be struck. "I have my friends," he said. "I know people you couldn't wish yourself onto. You're pathetic, Boldt. Look at you. You look like a fucking bum. You shouldn't be seen in public."

Boldt ignored it. When Kramer got on the defensive he made references to all his late father's connections. But Kramer was not his father's son. He had none of the spine of Judge Kramer. He was soft and seemed almost frightened most of the time. "I want you to put someone on the psychiatric hospitals, or handle it yourself if you have time. I want a list of any and all patients admitted voluntarily or otherwise into state or private institutions for the weeks immediately following Labor Day, and who were discharged anytime prior to last Sunday night."

The idea sparked Kramer's attention. For once, Boldt

thought, he reasoned quite well. "You're thinking that's why nothing happened in September," Kramer said.

"That's what I'm thinking."

"We put him away for a few weeks."

"It's possible."

Kramer nodded. "Jesus, God, can you imagine that? Can you imagine the irony if we had him at some point and let him walk?"

"Stranger things have happened."

"Okay, I got it."

"I don't want you going anywhere with this until we have all the data in, okay, John? And don't go spreading it around this office."

"With the leaks we've been having?" Kramer said. "No way."

"Speaking of which, you said you'd check with your press contacts and try to find the source that's been compromising us. Any luck along those lines?"

"Jury's still out," Kramer replied. "Haven't made any headway at all."

"I want a name, John. Whoever it is was indirectly responsible for Jergensen's death. And that cost Croy her life. Find me a name."

Kramer nodded.

"Keep me in mind for some fieldwork," Kramer reminded.

Boldt didn't nod. He purposely avoided any acknowledgment. "Keep me up to speed, John."

"Oh, one other thing, Boldt," Kramer said, stopping the detective at the door. "I did like you said and checked out the 911 call that ended up getting you stopped on foot over on Seventy-third."

Boldt nodded. He had asked Kramer to find out if the caller had left a name, curious whether or not this had anything to do with Neighborhood Watch programs as he had suspected. "And?"

"Caller didn't leave a name. I checked the tape myself."

All tapes containing 911 calls were filed and archived for ninety days, before being bulk-erased and recycled into the system again. "Our operator asked the kid for a name, but he chickened out and hung up."

"A kid. A boy?"

"That's right."

"You still have the tape?" Boldt asked.

Kramer pulled open a drawer. It was so neat it belonged in a mail-order catalog. "Right here," he said.

Detective John LaMoia pulled up a wheeled office chair and waited for Boldt to finish listening to the cassette. Boldt chewed vigorously on a fresh bear claw and washed it down with hot coffee. "What have you got, John?" Boldt asked, turning the machine off and removing the headphones.

"The Krantz paperback is available at sixty-two stores within the city area. The make of cash register has narrowed it down to just five. I haven't seen my woman in four days. She's been working the split shift at the hospital. I wonder if I could have the afternoon off—our schedules overlap today."

Boldt glared at the man.

"Hey, I was only asking. Okay. Fine." He continued, "I've been working on the other victims, cross-checking their checking accounts and credit-card records to see if they shopped any of these five stores. No luck so far. Of course, we wouldn't know anything if they paid cash, which means a lot of shit could slip through the cracks."

"So?"

"So, I checked out what they were up to. Like you said, we had tried that back around the Saviria kill, but we have a lot more data now. Not just stores—not just where they spent money—but what they were doing. Paul and I both have cauliflower ear from all the phone calls. We reinterviewed everyone. Boyfriends, family, co-workers, and we got ourselves a list of what these women did on the day the killer did them. Where they were. It's a shitload of stuff, Sarge. But it's something.''

"I'm listening.''

"Okay, here's what we got. We stripped it down to the area of the BSU profile. Threw out the places outside the three-mile radius. We know these babes spent time at a beauty parlor, two health clubs, several department stores and gas stations, a car wash, six different supermarkets, a toy store, a bookstore, and a pair of video-rental stores.''

"And a partridge in a pear tree.''

"You got it.''

"It's good work, John. I don't mean to put it down.''

"Thanks. I wish we had something a little more concrete.''

"So essentially these women were all over the place on the days of their murders. But no matches.'' Boldt paused and then said, "I want you to start again, John. Go back four days from each of the kills this time. Try to find where they might have gone, where they might have shopped. Let's find a connection between several of them. They all live pretty close to each other. Chances are they may have frequented the same places. Maybe stores that sell paperbacks have something to do with it, maybe not. But a store could be where he spots her. Try those malls. Maybe our boy spots them in mall parking lots and gets a look at their vehicle registration while they're shopping.''

"You want me to handle the malls too?''

"Put someone else on it. You have enough to do.''

"Amen.''

"You say today's the only day you two can get together?'' Boldt asked.

"This afternoon. She's working nights for another ten days.''

"When does she go off?''

"Eight in the morning, right as I show up here. She sleeps past noon and goes back on early evening.''

"So take a long lunch, John. Three hours. Even for an Italian stud like you that should be time enough to wake her up. Fair enough?"

LaMoia thanked him profusely and checked his watch.

"Don't daydream this morning, John. Give me some good hours."

"You got it, Sergeant. No problem."

Boldt leaned back in his chair and smiled as LaMoia charged through the office, flirting with every woman along the way. He rubbed his eyes and went back to his bear claw and lukewarm coffee. LaMoia had left him with a hand-written list of the various stores. There had to be some connection between these women, some way the killer chose these particular women out of the tens of thousands in Seattle. Was it the jogging path at Green Lake? A lineman for City Light? A poleman for Pacific Bell? Did the killer simply walk the streets until he noticed someone that fit his needs? Or did he spot them in a store?

I need to know how you choose them, he thought. I need to figure out how you select them and how you find their addresses and how you gain entrance to their homes. I need you to make a couple of mistakes—and that's a hell of a thing to wait around for.

He moved the newspaper out of the way and went about reorganizing his desk.

He called back City Light and spoke with a desk jockey. Following Boldt's request, they had searched their files for any repairs or installations that might have involved pole 6B423, the pole in front of the Levitts' house. None had been discovered. No servicemen had been in that area for months, not since a transformer had blown out in a summer storm—and that had been six blocks from the Levitts'.

This call prompted him to remind Miss Jenny Wise at Viacom Cablevision that he was still waiting for a similar report from her. After three transfers, he reached Miss Wise, who claimed to have tried to contact Boldt several times. She told him that their crew records had not showed any recent service in the area, but that because of Boldt's inquiry she had dispatched a crew to check for possible pirating. Subsequently, the crew discovered an unauthorized black-box connection on pole 6B423. Normal procedure required she take immediate legal action, but because of police involvement she had decided to wait until she had spoken with Boldt. "If it's okay with you," she said, "we're going to disconnect and file our complaint through proper channels. People don't realize there's a thousand-dollar fine for pirating. We intend to prosecute."

"Is that the Levitt home?"

"Yes."

"And there's no question about the pirating?"

"None."

"Can you tell if all the sets in the house are receiving the signal?"

"We know it's an illegal connection at the pole. That's all."

"Would you hold off for a few days, please? This may be of some use to us."

"I'll need something in writing. We've got a standard procedure for this, and I'll need something in writing if you want me to delay."

"Delay. By all means, delay. I'll send something over this afternoon. Nice and official," he said.

Daphne was doing a crossword puzzle at her desk, leaning on an elbow, finger-combing her hair, her painted nails disappearing into her chestnut mane. Her red dress had high, padded shoulders and short sleeves. Her arms were tan and exceptionally well-defined. Each time her hand moved to comb her hair, Boldt watched various muscles in her forearm contract. She was indeed a thoroughbred.

"Busy, I see," Boldt said from the doorway.

"Come in."

He took a chair, leaving the door open this time. "Sorry about the other day. I've been a little uptight lately."

"I hadn't noticed." She placed the pencil on the desk and folded the paper. She crossed her arms. "That's a lousy thing to say. My turn to apologize. I'm here to help, you know."

"Yes. I know. Maybe one of these days."

"All I do is listen. No pins. No dolls. No needles. No Pentothal. Pretty harmless, actually. You ought to try it sometime."

"Is that an invitation?" he asked, intentionally obscuring the meaning of her offer. His turn to flirt.

She replied bluntly. "Anytime."

"I need some help with a thirteen-year-old boy."

"Okay."

"He knows more than he's letting on. He told me he never used his telescope. I have him on tape reporting to our 911 people that he had spotted a 'suspicious-looking person' over on Seventy-fourth. I recognized his voice. The person he spotted was me. He described to our people what I was wearing. He had to be using the telescope to see that kind of detail at night at that distance."

"That's not all of it," she said wisely. Daffy was like that.

"No. There's more. I need to loosen him up, get him talking."

"More?" Persistent. Part of her trade.

"At first I thought he might have seen someone on a phone pole out his window. Now I'm thinking *he* was up the pole, not the killer. He blushed a couple of times when I was asking him questions about Cheryl Croy, our most recent victim. He lied about that telescope being in his window."

"Voyeur?"

"You tell me."

"At his age it's not uncommon. More typically you find young boys stealing their father's *Playboys*."

"From his room he would have a nearly perfect view of Croy's house. I'd like to put a little pressure on him. I wonder how I should approach it. I have a nephew about his age. He's bright as all get out. I have a feeling this kid is just as bright.''

"And how would you deal with your nephew? What would you say to him?" Unconsciously, she began to finger-comb her hair again. There was something sensual about the way she did this that Boldt found unsettling. He shifted uneasily in his chair and tried not to be mesmerized by it. It wasn't easy.

"I treat my nephew pretty much as an adult. He's very mature for his age, though. I don't know Justin at all. No way to know how to deal with him."

"If you're considering threatening him with legal action, that's up to you. Hard to say how a boy his age would respond. He might open up if the threat is strong enough; it might shut him up completely. If you make him feel he did something wrong, you won't get a word out of him—and just by showing up you may *imply* he did something wrong." She made a note to herself—he couldn't read it upside down—and then slipped the cap of the pen between her lips and began spinning it around. Her lips were moist and red. The pen seemed very happy.

"He did. I think he pirated a cable hookup."

"So maybe I'm wrong. Maybe you treat him as an adult and bargain. Kids like to be treated as adults. What do you think?"

"I thought I might tell him how tough my job is. You know, hand him the old sob story and try to soften him up. Then I'd hint that I know about the illegal cable hookup and see how he responds. If I get a rise, then I press for some cooperation, promising to keep his parents out of it, and telling him that I might be able to get the cable company to back off. If he denies it, then I lay it on him. I tell him the cable company is going to prosecute and it's going to cost his parents a grand, which is true incidently, and I walk away."

"I'm impressed." She pulled the pen out and set it down, folded her hands again, and sat cherublike before him.

He couldn't tell if she was coming on to him, or if this was her normal routine. He was absorbed in her—dangerously absorbed—and she seemed like the kind of woman who knew it. "How would you do it?" he asked.

"I like to take my time," she said, looking him in the eye. She wasn't talking about interviewing children. Then she added, "That approach sounds good."

"What's another approach?" he asked quickly.

"I like your way better than what I was first thinking of. I thought you might try an approach that makes him feel like every boy who's ever lived has tried to see naked women. Either that or the Boy Scout approach—you know, 'we all need to work together on this.' But I like your way better than either of those. You might alienate him my way. Teenagers are very difficult to second-guess."

"I don't have any kids. If I did, I might be better at this."

"Not for lack of trying, I hope."

He couldn't look at her then; he glanced at Charlie Brown. He felt thirteen all of a sudden—Justin Levitt's age. His palms were sweating. He wasn't any good at this kind of thing. She was simply teasing him—he could tell that by her tone of voice—but his imagination was running wild. What would an evening in the sack with Daphne be like? Like hot-buttered cornbread and honey.

"You think he saw something?" she added, taking him off the hook.

"What if he did? What if he saw the actual killing?"

"Then you have one scared boy. He may resist opening up to you in order to maintain his denial. As long as he can keep denying he saw anything, then he can avoid the pain and the guilt associated with it." She paused and then said, "You want me to come along, is that it?"

"I thought you'd never ask."

"I think it's a mistake at this point. I will if you want me to—no problem—but I think it's a mistake. If he was watching her, he won't admit it in front of a woman. Especially a stranger. This has to be man-to-man. You might ask the father. He may be able to help. I think it's best if you try it first. If he's going to open up to anyone, you have as good a chance as anyone. Try your approach. I like it the best.''

''If you insist.''

''I don't insist. I suggest, and only when I'm asked to.''

''Lucky you.''

''Let me know how it works out.''

''You'll be the first to hear.''

''Lucky me,'' she said, unfolding her newspaper and watching him leave her office.

He stopped and looked back at her, but she didn't notice. Her fingers were worming through her silky hair again, and the cap of the pen was slipping between those lips.

As he passed Kramer's office area, the sergeant said repugnantly, ''Another closed-door session, eh, Boldt?''

''What's your problem, Kramer?'' Boldt said, stopping. Towering above the redhead.

''You are,'' Kramer said, jumping up out of his seat. ''So do something about it.''

Boldt was well aware the first man to throw a punch would go on report, would risk his position on the task force. Kramer taunted him, waving him in seductively. ''Whatsa matter, Boldt. Liz not putting out these days?'' Kramer asked. Boldt stepped closer, his face scarlet, fists flexed. ''Gotta chase Daphne's skirt to feel like a man?'' He and Boldt were nose-to-nose.

A pair of detectives had stopped in the corridor. The Asian, Kim, encouraged, ''Nail his ass, Lou. We'll cover for you.''

Kramer looked suddenly frightened.

Boldt shook his head and continued on, ''Not worth it,'' he said.

''Big badass Homicide dick,'' Kramer said to the man's back.

Boldt stopped.

Kramer added, "You may have all of them fooled, Boldt. But not me. It's a nice show you put on, but where the hell's the beef?"

Boldt's blood pressure soared. He felt his face flush red. Children's games. Always Kramer. He forced one foot in front of the other, eyes trained on the toes of his scuffed shoes, and found his way to his office.

"Not worth it," he muttered to himself.

"What's this I hear about some sparring between you and John, Lou?" Shoswitz rested his shoulder gently against a baffle. His knee moved involuntarily, as if keeping time to a song.

Shoswitz could sense trouble on his section of the floor, and he pounced on it like a hungry mountain cat on carrion. Any unrest among his ranks would indicate to his superiors an inability on his part to manage people, and that in turn would reduce his chances at a captainship—an opportunity that would present itself in less than six months when one of the captains, Bill Gardner, retired. Shoswitz and two other veteran lieutenants were in the running for the job. The success of this task force would play heavily on his possibility of promotion.

"Same old shit, Phil."

"I don't need it in my dugout. Not now. Not ever."

"And I do?" Boldt spun around and glared at his boss. "He's begging for it, Phil."

Shoswitz raised his hand. "Don't go climbing onto a white horse, Lou. That wouldn't be healthy for either of us."

"Meaning?"

"I think that's clear enough."

"He's all over me about the fieldwork, Phil. And look at his record. What the hell is he even doing on this team?"

"We all have our cross to bear. I did what I had to do."

"Had to?" Boldt suddenly saw the bigger picture. Two words and it all became clear. There were still allies of

Judge Kramer out there. The review board? Perhaps the chief himself. "Politics, Phil?" Boldt asked incredulously, wishing he hadn't said it quite so naively. Internal politics entered every corner of the force, every wing of city government. This department was no exception. A Special Task Force was subject to public scrutiny and therefore the appointments were even more political than usual. The task force gave Shoswitz a direct connection to the Prosecuting Attorney's office as well as the Mayor's office. It provided all three men, Shoswitz, Boldt, and Kramer, with high visibility. Boldt was no newcomer to the possibilities the task force offered. If Shoswitz moved on, then his chair was open, and Boldt, as a second-in-command of the task force, would be the most likely candidate for that promotion.

"Don't push, Lou. We've all got shit riding on this. Right? You hear me? And we're all tired. People do and say stupid things when they're tired."

Boldt pinched the bridge of his nose and closed his eyes. He *was* tired. He felt exhausted.

"Besides," Shoswitz said. "John's not all rocks between the ears. Did he tell you about his plan to search all the private and public institutions?" He didn't allow Boldt a chance to answer. "It's a damn good idea, one I should have thought of myself. Or you. Am I right?" Boldt was so dumbstruck he didn't get out a word. "Team players," Shoswitz said. "That's what we want around here. Team players with some imagination and creativity. John's doing just fine. Fights in the hallways I don't need. Think about it." He turned and walked away. "Think about it, Lou," he said over the baffle.

Kramer hurried past Boldt's office space, folder in hand, as if he was going somewhere with it. He'd been listening in on their conversation. Again. Kramer made a habit of other people's business. Eavesdropping went entirely against regs. It increased the chances of the wrong people receiving partial or misunderstood data. And that in turn generated supposition, speculation, and rumor.

But Boldt wasn't about to do anything about it now. Unwittingly, Shoswitz had played right into Kramer's hand. Boldt was pinned. He brushed lint off his lapels using a loop of Scotch tape and made an attempt at combing his hair. Time to get out of there.

9

LOU BOLDT STOOD in the junior high school awaiting the end of class. The bright, tile corridor reminded him of the Medical Examiner's autopsy room, which in turn reminded him of the six dead women, and he felt frustrated to find himself waiting. Always waiting. Much of this job consisted of waiting, and on this day it annoyed him. On the other side of these doors a few hundred kids were impatiently waiting as well. It's something we're taught to do from the time we're very young, he thought. It was seldom enjoyable.

Boldt had liked school, and this hallway was really not much different than the hallway at Yakima High. If he listened carefully, he could almost hear echoes of his own footfalls. If he glanced out the window, perhaps he could see the junior varsity football team—number 35 working through calisthenics, one eye on the varsity cheerleaders. His childhood home was only a couple of hours away, but he hadn't been back in years. Not since his father died of liver failure and he had returned to pick up his mother and drive her down to his sister's place in southern California. That had been the last of Yakima. He had too many bad memories to want to return.

The bell sounded. Kids flooded through the doors and into the hall. It came alive with the familiar sound of lockers slamming and shrieks of nervous laughter. Nothing like a Friday afternoon. Boldt spotted Justin Levitt. The boy came out of the classroom, saw Boldt, and stopped cold. The girl behind him bumped into him, actually hugging him to maintain her balance and, embarrassed by the physical contact, berated him for being such a tweeb—whatever *that* was.

"What do you want?" Justin asked.

He could be my son, Boldt thought, seduced by a painful memory he would not allow. "A couple of minutes is all," he said.

Justin scanned the area. A few of the curious were watching, obviously wondering who Boldt was. "Outside," Justin Levitt hissed. "Those doors down there. It'll have to be quick. My mom's waiting in the car."

Boldt nodded and moved down the long hallway, drawing curious looks.

Justin appeared shortly and moved Boldt out of the mainstream of departing students. Boldt wanted to rub his hand into the boy's hair and mess it up. How had the greaseball fifties' look come back in style? He asked, "Do you understand what I'm up against?"

"What do you mean?"

"You're old enough that I don't have to screw around with you." He had decided some quasi-adult vocabulary might help loosen up the boy. "A guy has killed several women. Cheryl Croy was one of them." The boy flinched and switched his books to his other arm. "My job is to find him and stop him before he does it again. This isn't TV, Justin. I think you know that. In real life, eighty percent of all homicides go unsolved. This kind is the worst kind because the guy keeps doing it over and over. He frightens the public. He frightens the police—"

"Are you scared?" the boy asked somewhat incredulously, and in a tone of voice that implied he was also unnerved.

"You bet I am. It's us against one guy—only he knows we're looking for him, and we have very few clues to tell us who he is. One guy, you understand? It's exactly like a big puzzle—a jigsaw puzzle—only most of the pieces are missing. On television, everything fits together within an hour and the killer is in custody—arrested. In real life I've been working on this case since last April and I have very few pieces of the puzzle. The guy is still out there somewhere and for all I know he may try and kill another woman soon. I have to live with that. Do you understand?''

The boy nodded. ''I already told you I didn't see anyone on the pole.''

''I'm going to be straight with you, Justin, because I think it's the best way—I think you can handle it.'' Boldt paused to let the boy think about this. ''The other night, when I came by your house, before I got there I was stopped by a patrol car because someone had called the police and told them I was walking around the neighborhood in a rainstorm. It was smart thinking to call the police. Why the hell should someone be walking around in a rainstorm?'' The boy blushed. He shook his head and the red hair above his ears ruffled in the wind. ''The person called our emergency 911 number.'' He paused again. ''Part of police procedure is to tape-record all 911 calls.'' Boldt waited and then withdrew the cassette tape. ''The voice on this tape is yours, Justin, and you describe in detail what I'm wearing.'' The boy shook his head again. ''I was on Seventy-fourth Street at the time the report came in. I know that because I keep a log—like a diary—'' he explained, ''of where I am at what time, and what I'm doing. My boss requires it. It just so happens that I was at Cheryl Croy's—the house of the woman who was killed—at the time the 911 call came in. It's also the only possible place you could have seen me, even with a telescope. The houses across the street block your line of sight on the rest of Seventy-fourth. So you see, I *know* you have a telescope, and I *know* you've been using it. There's nothing wrong with that. Keeping watch on the neighborhood is a good idea. But there is something wrong about lying. Especially to the police.''

The boy nodded, unwilling to look Boldt in the eye.

Boldt gave him a moment to think, then he asked, "Do your parents know about the cable hookup?"

Justin Levitt blushed and looked away. "What are you talking about?"

"I'd rather work *with* you, Justin. I'd rather work *with* you than against you. Help me. Please."

The boy shook his head. "I don't know anything about it."

"We pulled a palm print about your size from the metal rungs on the pole. If you want us to print you, we can."

"Oh shit," the boy said. He dragged the toes of his shoes nervously across the cement. "My mother will *kill* me."

Boldt found the expression sadly ironic. "The telescope."

"I'm a member of the Neighborhood Watch program. Anonmous," he said, mispronouncing the word. "I reported that car accident a couple of weeks ago. That was me," he said, as if Boldt would know which accident.

"We appreciate that," Boldt indulged him. "But at the moment I'm interested in Cheryl Croy. Did you ever check out her place?"

"Maybe a few times . . ."

Boldt could feel his chance now and he was nearly lightheaded with elation. The boy *did* know something! "How about the night of her murder?"

The boy blushed again.

"Justin—"

"I didn't see *anything*," the boy shouted.

"Justin?"

"I'm telling you, I didn't see *anything*! Oh shit. Now I'm cooked. She hates it when I keep her waiting." He was staring off toward the road and when Boldt turned around he saw Mrs. Levitt approaching quickly, her red, fiery hair leaping with the wind.

Boldt prepared himself. "I can handle it," he said, wondering if he could.

"Just what is going on here?" she asked, still several yards away. "Lieutenant," she hollered angrily, "what is the meaning of this?" She stopped and faced Boldt, eyes squinting. "Justin," she scolded without taking her eyes off of Boldt, "go to the car." Justin glanced at Boldt, shook his head where his mother couldn't see, mouthing, "Don't tell her," and then hurried off. She waited until her son was out of earshot and bitched loudly, "Since when do the police have the right to question a thirteen-year-old boy without his parents' consent?"

"Good afternoon, Mrs. Levitt."

She looked toward the road, her boy now well away from them. "Don't hand me that B.S., Lieutenant! You have no right to be questioning my boy."

"I'm afraid I do, Mrs. Levitt."

"Not without my permission, you don't."

"Yes, I'm afraid I do. I'm conducting a murder investigation. I think your son may be able to help me."

She turned scarlet. "The department will hear about this. You can bet your badge the department will be hearing from my husband on this!" She hurried away, turning around at the last second. "Don't you *ever* try this again!" She moved like a machine, with none of the grace of a woman. She glanced over her shoulder several times, past her fiery red hair, to make sure he wasn't following.

Boldt noticed that the schoolyard had quickly emptied. The last yellow bus pulled from the parking lot. A crosswalk attendant, a woman with blue-white hair wearing a fluorescent orange vest, stood on one leg, a bird at rest, a hand-held stop sign dangling by her knee. Traffic moved past slowly.

He had been close. Justin had been on the verge of telling him something. Can it be that the key to this case lies inside the mind of a thirteen-year-old boy? Is there any way to get it out of him? Months of painstaking work had led him to this point, and yet he seemed as far away now as he had ever been. It was as if the closer he came, the further it moved from him, like chasing a ball you keep inadvertently kicking away.

I'll arrest him if I have to, he thought. I'll arrest the boy and turn him over to juvenile, if they leave me no choice. Or better yet, he reconsidered, I'll arrest the mother. He smiled at the thought.

Shoswitz scratched his head and some dandruff cascaded to his shoulders. "I tried to set her straight on this. She doesn't seem like the easiest woman in the world to deal with. Right?"

Boldt said, "I think the kid knows something. I don't know what it is. Maybe he was peeping at her through his telescope and he's afraid to admit it. Every time I mention her murder he blushes. Daphne says if he did see something he may not be able to face it. We have to go gently with him or we could lose him. His mother could screw it all up for us."

"It's a long shot though."

"I don't think so. I think he knows something. I think we have a witness. Maybe I should turn the boy over to Daphne."

"No. That's a lousy idea. That gets us into some gray areas I would just as soon avoid. It's one thing to have a Homicide detective talking to the boy. Right? It's another thing entirely if it's our staff shrink."

"So what are you saying?"

"I'll be the cutoff man, as far as the mother's concerned. We're within our rights if we suspect the boy is a material witness. We can always use the phone pole if we need it. How about the husband? Will he help us out?"

"He might."

"You handle it. If you can communicate with the kid, you can try my teenager next."

10

THE TENTH BODY was discovered deep within a copse of trees Saturday morning by two teenage boys taking a shortcut to Green Lake. Boldt, who had arrived to work early, was the fifth person to appear on the scene, after the two boys and the two responding patrolmen. He immediately established a large crime scene, including the six residential houses nearest to the body. The entire area was roped off with fluorescent police tape. All the neighbors cooperated. It kept the curious well away from the death scene, and secured any and all possible entry points to the site, including the wooded area to the south. Detectives began house-to-house interviews immediately, before people got away on Saturday outings and became difficult, if not impossible, to locate.

The victim was naked, and was lying face up with lengths of nylon rope tied to her ankles and wrists. Boldt felt a tremendous wave of grief flood through him, a familiar reaction to an all-too-familiar sight. Unlike single-victim murder investigations, the inability on the part of the police to solve these crimes came at the *ultimate* expense of others: their death.

In May this assignment had seemed like a big step forward. Selected from a dozen sergeants available, Boldt felt

this promised a certain degree of upward mobility. Prior
to this case he had been fortunate to have an enviable
record among homicide detectives—he had the single highest
percentage of solved cases among all the force. Twice he
had been part of special task forces—once on a Special
Assaults case, a serial-rape case that he and Doc Dixon
were able to solve within twenty-four hours; once, earlier
in his career, as part of Vice sweep of downtown illegal
drug merchants that received national press. It only made
sense—even to him—that he should be part of the Cross
Killer investigation. At that time he had hoped for an early
solution and subsequent promotion to lieutenant. A promotion would mean a better office area and higher salary,
perhaps closing the gap between his level of success and
that of his wife.

He had hoped, in fact, that the assignment would be a
remedy for many of his then-problems. He had hoped a
promotion would give him more time to spend with Elizabeth, more control over his schedule, and a chance to piece
back together a relationship that was troubled. His marriage
had not endured the demands of two careers. In late June
he had decided to keep a record of the hours he shared with
his wife. For three weeks running he was unable to tally
more than a single hour a day of waking time spent together.
She was traveling more and more, staying at the office late,
and leaving early. He was working seventy-hour weeks. He
gave up trying to keep track. Lately she had been arguing
that with her salary they could now afford a better house.
Boldt wondered what they needed a house for at all—neither
was ever home. He didn't like the idea, in part because he
knew it would be his final surrender to her controlling the
family finances—he could not budget his half of the mort-
gage payments on his sergeant's salary and she damn well
knew it. He would end up "in debt" to her, and his ego
couldn't stand that. He had no doubt that a move to a new
house would be the end of them.

He kept everyone back, away from the site, even his own people, allowing only Doc Dixon to join him.

"A new twist," the pathologist said as he appeared through the closely grown trees. "Haven't had one outside yet." He was dressed in khakis and a thin white shirt stretched at the buttons. His undershirt showed through; Boldt didn't know anyone else who still wore undershirts. The sight of the body didn't seem to affect Dixon in the least. Boldt wondered how a person could grow accustomed to such things.

"I want to take it carefully," Boldt explained. "We've established a huge crime scene. That's something new for us, something in our favor."

"Agreed." The pathologist placed two cases by the corpse and, opening one of them, prepared his camera.

"She fell down," Boldt observed.

"Hmm?" replied Dixon.

Boldt pointed out the deep impression in the mud next to the body. "She fell down there, face first. He rolled her over. She had to be running hard to land like that." Boldt looked back in the direction from where she had come.

Following the picture-taking, Dixon slipped on a pair of latex gloves and touched her legs gently. "Will my pictures do, or do you want your people in before I examine her?"

"Did you get all the angles we'll need? I'd just as soon not bring anyone else in for a while."

"I'll take a few more and bracket them, just to make sure."

"I'll be right back. Wait for me before you begin, will you please?"

"Sure."

Boldt retraced her path carefully, staying well away from where he guessed she might have run. The nearest building, a locked house, was about a hundred yards through the trees. He already had a man working on getting a court order to allow them entry. He reached the puddle she had run through.

A shoe print was filled with muddy water. Boldt studied the print and then looked up and saw the swath of broken vegetation cut through the thicket. He assumed this was the killer's footprint and that he had chased her from the house.

He put himself into the role of the victim. He could feel her fright. Something had gone wrong for the killer. She had broken free and even managed to get clear of the house. For some reason—a sudden worthless flash of modesty, or the killer's sudden appearance—she had fled into the trees rather than into the street. And here he had caught up to her, and here she had died.

Boldt was cautious not to leave his own footprints anywhere near the puddle. He stepped lightly and forged his own path through the dense growth reaching the pack of reporters, cops, and eager onlookers a moment later. The press aimed cameras at him and ran off dozens of shots. He disliked his celebrity status, despite the fact that during his early musical career he had once hoped for such notoriety. He spotted LaMoia and signaled him over.

"I want our boys to drain a puddle over by that house. It's about ten yards into the woods. I want a plaster cast made of the shoe print left behind, and anything else that shows up once the puddle is drained. I want photographs —whatever you think we need. I don't want anybody—I mean *nobody*—to use the route she took from the house. I cut my way out. Use my path, over here, see? In there. You and one other guy. No groups, no gawkers, no screw-ups. Clear enough?"

LaMoia had quite obviously been asleep when the call had come in. He nodded and finished off a Styrofoam cup of coffee. "Same MO?" he asked.

"It's him. Let's not screw it up."

When Boldt returned, he found Dixon examining the corpse, the camera equipment all put away. To Boldt it looked the same as all the others: eyes grotesquely taped open, the gaping wound of the cross on her chest. Boldt's

stomach turned. When he heard the roar of the pump, Boldt
returned to the puddle to oversee the work being done there.

The I.D. technician looked up at Boldt. "It's from an
office shoe, Sergeant. A Rockport. Vibram sole," he said.

"How clean is it?" Boldt asked.

"We'll get a beauty. Got two others as well. Barefoot.
Got to be hers. I think I'll take 'em together. It'll give us
a better picture of weight if they're lifted in perspective to
each other. That okay?" the technician asked. LaMoia saw
Boldt's expression and answered "yes" for him. Boldt went
back to Dixon.

"Well?" he said.

"Nothing new. She appears to have died of suffocation,"
he said, pointing to her throat. "No bruising to indicate
rape. I'll do the usual tests. Couldn't find any torn hair this
time, and though the lacerations appear nearly identical to
the others . . ." he trailed off. He ran a gloved finger over
one of the deeper wounds and Boldt felt his stomach twist.

"What's bothering you, Dixie?"

"Look here," Dixon said, lifting a limp wrist and holding
it in his gloved hand. He pushed back the knotted nylon
rope. "No bruising. None whatsoever. That's not right,
Lou. If she was tied up while she was still alive we'd see
bruising here," he pointed. "And look at this knot. It's not
nearly as tight as those we found on the others. You're the
detective, but if you ask me he tied these on *after* he killed
her."

Boldt moved carefully to the far side of the impression
in the mud. "No blood," he noted.

"No," Dixon said. "She was stabbed out here. Not enough
bleeding on any of these wounds. She escaped uncut. Had
to have. He must have caught up to her and finished her
out here."

"So he's finally made a mistake," Boldt stated.

"Looks like it. This sure didn't go according to the ritual
we've seen before. Almost like a different guy did it. He
wanted her inside. She got away. Did she already have her

clothes off? Did he catch her that way, or did he accomplish that out here? You've got a lot of questions to answer on this one, Lou. I can tell you right now that the body isn't going to answer many of them.''

''I know that.''

''I wish I could.''

''*Could* it be the work of a copycat?''

Doc Dixon studied the body again, then shook his head. ''I don't see how. No, I doubt it. My guess is that it's the same guy. You know as well as I do that you can never rule out a copycat completely.'' He paused. ''I'll say this much. If it *is* the work of a copycat, he would have to be close to the investigation. Really close. One of your police colleagues I'd have to think. But let's not forget, this is the third victim that has struck you and me as being somewhat different. No two kills are ever identical. The detail evidence here matches too closely, Lou. It's got to be the same guy.''

Boldt nodded.

''One thing that might interest you . . .''

''What's that?''

Dixon pointed. ''I found an abrasion on her upper lip. At first glance I thought it had been caused by her fall. But the ground's too soft, eh? And if you look closely,'' he said, forcing Boldt to drop to a knee and look along with him, ''you'll notice missing facial hair and the faint evidence of a gum residue here and here.''

''Tape?''

''Ah! It might explain why she didn't scream and alert the neighbors, mightn't it?''

''We haven't seen that before, have we?'' Boldt asked.

''Not to my knowledge. But to be quite honest, we never looked for it either. One swipe of alcohol across the mouth and we'd never pick it up. I'll check with my assistants. We use alcohol to clean up the cadaver before autopsy.''

''If he does clean them up, it opens up another possibility,'' Boldt suggested.

''What's that?''

"She may have torn the tape off during her escape. He may have used it on the others but removed it more carefully. Perhaps he kills them in a fit of rage and then changes personalities entirely and cleans them up. We can't rule out anything."

Following the work by the I.D. technician, Doc Dixon, impatient to bag the body and return to his office, suggested that two of his men be admitted to the area to hand-carry the body bag to the vehicles. Boldt agreed but wanted no others in the crime area until he had a chance to walk the site once more.

Starting at the back of the house, Boldt retraced the victim's steps. He edged his way around the area of the puddle where the I.D. technician was still busy with the plaster cast, and continued toward Doc Dixon, now thirty yards ahead.

He found the piece of gray tape stuck to a bare branch of a bush. Boldt knelt down and examined it. It meant her mouth *had* been taped shut, and she *had* removed it herself. "Dixie!" he called out to study the effect of yelling in the thick woods. "Dixie!" he tried again, more loudly. He heard the doctor's faint reply and realized sound carried poorly here. So perhaps she had screamed. Perhaps her final call for help had gone unheard.

A few minutes later Dixon helped Boldt secure the sticky piece of tape in a clear plastic evidence bag. They returned to the victim. At the request of the I.D. technician, Dixon had placed paper bags around her hands and had taped them at her wrists, containing any fiber or trace evidence that might contribute to the investigation. With fresh paper bags at the end of her arms she appeared even more tragic and helpless. Boldt apologized to her under his breath. It was an indecent way to die, an indecent way to leave this world: zipped tightly inside a black plastic bag. A songbird sang. To the bird, he thought, this day was no different from any other. It was a nice day, in fact. The overcast sky was

clearing to the southwest. Boldt wondered if the songbird
had witnessed this woman being murdered.

And then he realized that he didn't even know her name.
So it's come to that, he thought miserably. She's become
just another number. Number ten.

11

ON THE FOLLOWING Monday morning, October tenth, Lou Boldt was called into Shoswitz's office. Outside it was forty-eight degrees under partly cloudy skies, intermittent rain in the forecast. He tucked in his wrinkled shirt and straightened his tie. It was knotted improperly, the tail hanging longer than the front. He told the lieutenant, "I've started to think of them as numbers. Before I knew Katherine DeHavelin's name I was thinking of her as number ten."

"These things happen," said Shoswitz, spinning his chair to face the seated Boldt. "I talked to a coach once. He used to think of all his players in terms of hitting percentages. Never called them by name, he called them two-eleven, or whatever they were hitting. I've begun seeing this thing in terms of budget. As the monkey said while pissing into the cash register, 'This is running into money.' "

"Are you trying to tell me something?"

"Nothing you haven't heard."

"I don't need the extra pressure, Phil."

"None of us do. I'm getting it from up above, so I'm passing it on to you. Fair is fair. We're using too much personnel on this. We'd be better off if we could generate some good publicity. Right? The public is more forgiving of big budgets when we keep them informed of our progress.''

"You know as well as I—''

"Save it, Lou. This isn't up for discussion. We've reached a point where we *need* to leak a thing or two. We have to show them we're getting somewhere. The public is scared to death by this thing. It's getting out of hand. John is buddies with the press. I'm putting him on it.''

"Getting? This thing's been out of hand since April. We're doing everything we can.''

"That's what we have to keep telling them.''

"So tell Public Information to dream something up. That's *their* job.''

"I want to give them the footprint information. We know the guy is around a hundred and sixty pounds. Giving up that can't hurt us at all.''

"No way!'' Boldt demanded. "We give them that and the subject will toss the shoes. Those shoes could be a major part of our case. Absolutely not.''

"Then what?''

Boldt tried to think, but Shoswitz's demanding tone and the added pressure worked against him. He had not slept well for the past few nights, kept awake by an angry stomach and a heavy conscience. Sleep meant dreams, and the dreams weren't worth it. His dreams were of killing the Cross Killer. He tried to think: what was insignificant enough to feed the public but not jeopardize the investigation? "I don't see a whole hell of a lot.''

"That's the point.''

"I know you won't like this, but I say we continue as we have been. We've picked up a lot of information this last week. It's a new investigation. If nothing else we've gained a whole new set of questions that need to be answered. Little by little our man seems to be slipping up. Christ, we may have a witness in that boy.''

"Have you spoken to him?''

"No. Not yet. Later today. Daphne didn't think it prudent to try to speak to him in front of the parents. I agreed."

"And what about Katherine DeHavelin, our number ten? What do we know?"

"It's not a perfect fit, Phil. If nothing else supports my suggestion to keep a lid on this, I think DeHavelin does. Only a few of us know the profiles of the victims, right? If the press had it, the killer—or killer*s*—might be more careful. In DeHavelin's case there was no clear boyfriend in the picture, and she happened to live with two other women who were away for the weekend. That goes against everything we know about the others."

"Killer*s*?"

"I haven't ruled out a copycat killing on Kate De-Havelin."

"Oh come on, Lou. We both read Dixie's report. This one is identical!"

"Not true. There's the tape on the mouth, the fact that she got away somehow, and the lack of bruising on the wrists. No red fibers, don't forget. I don't go along with that."

"I sure hope you don't tell *that* to the press. That's all we need!"

"If you give anything to the press, it's with my objections. I'm going to put that in a memo, Phil. It'll undermine the investigation."

Shoswitz looked at Boldt skeptically. "Jesus, Lou."

"I protect my investigation."

"I'm glad to hear you call it *your* investigation," Shoswitz said.

"You know what I mean."

"I'm serious. I've been trying to make that point all along. That's the most encouraging thing I've heard you say in weeks. Just do me a favor. Stop coming to work looking like you slept in a chair. It doesn't help anything. Even the captain commented on it."

From behind them came the sound of a throat clearing.

They both glanced toward the entrance to Shoswitz's small office area. Kramer, his face flushed, his lips drawn white, said, "I thought it was *our* investigation, or did I miss something?"

Boldt looked over at Shoswitz and scrunched his eyes. The lieutenant bit his lip and tried to think of something to say.

"You bastards," Kramer said, and stormed off.

12

THE SCHOOLYARD also reminded Lou Boldt of his early days in Yakima. It reminded him of a beer-drinking father always down at the shop working behind the counter of the Volvo/White Truck service and parts shop. It reminded him of the sweet cinnamon smell of his mother's kitchen. It reminded him of the long walk home down roads straight as arrows—quiet roads with good people inside the houses, people who knew and trusted each other, people who looked out for one another.

Behind him the bell rang, and the first children—or were they young adults?—began to stream from the doors. That bell echoed back thirty years and shook Boldt's inner core. So much had changed since then. And yet, so little. The faces he saw were no different from the faces of his friends back when. He was transported back in time for a brief, fleeting moment—a passing instant during which he experienced the heedless joy and freedom of youth.

Justin Levitt recognized Boldt immediately. He made no attempt to look away or avoid him. He walked over and thrust out his hand, which Boldt shook.

"Thanks for not telling my parents," the boy said.

"No problem."

"My mom's waiting."

"Let's talk a minute."

The boy nodded.

Boldt immediately launched into what Daphne might have called phase two. "I remember one time I dropped a quarter in the bathhouse out at the town pool. It fell through the cracks in the floorboards and I crawled underneath the bath-house to get my quarter back. In those days it was a lot of money. On my hands and knees, on my way over to get the quarter, I found myself beneath Tina Chutland's booth. She was older than I was, she had all the stuff, you know —man!—and she happened to be undressing as I passed beneath her family's dressing room. I could have stopped looking and moved on, but I didn't. I stayed there, right below her, and watched every minute of it. She stripped clear down to nothing and I could have tickled her bare feet with my fingertips I was so close. She took her time getting into her suit, spreading suntan oil all over her first. I mean *all* over." He paused and then added, "That wasn't the end of it. I left that quarter down there, and I kept my eye on Tina Chutland from then on, and whenever she went to that bathhouse locker, I went after my quarter. Me and a buddy of mine spent most of that summer getting to know Tina Chutland real well. Even now, I could tell you every mole on her body. After a while the thrill wore off and we finally gave it up. What I'm trying to say is, there's nothing unusual about guys trying to sneak looks at naked women. It's been going on for a million years, maybe longer. You don't want to make a lifetime habit of it . . . but few of us do," he smiled genuinely. "It's the kind of thing you outgrow after a while. That's what you were using the telescope for, isn't it, Justin? You had a perfect view of Cheryl Croy's bed-room. I went back and checked."

The boy was bright red and studying the dirt at his feet. He swallowed once and nodded faintly. He choked out, "It just kind of happened by accident."

Boldt felt a warm rush of relief. He placed his hand on the boy's back and walked him over to a bench where they sat down overlooking the school's playing fields. The grass was still as green as summer, the sky still as threatening as it had been earlier in the day.

"I never saw her undress or anything like that," he said in a voice that was unconvincing. "Mr. Chambers said I could be part of the Neighborhood Watch, and that stupid telescope was worthless on the stars with all the city lights, and the clouds and everything. I could see clear down to the north end of the lake, could even see the bike path. I didn't think up using the telescope. I saw a movie where this guy watched a women undress using a telescope, and I don't know, it just gave me the idea, so I started checking out houses at night and seeing if I could see anything."

"And you saw Cheryl Croy."

"That lady over there. Yeah. Didn't see her undress or anything, I swear. I saw a lot of things in a lot of houses. People leave their curtains open a crack and with that telescope I could see a lot of things. None of them dirty. Just people eating dinner and watching TV and things."

"Tell me about the night she was killed."

Justin Levitt blushed. He started to talk but stopped himself.

Boldt wanted to wrap his arm around the boy. He said, "The truth never hurts, Justin. It's good to get it out. You don't need to make anything up."

Boldt could feel the boy relive it. "I did see her that night. Nothing dirty. I just saw her, that's all." Boldt didn't hear the conviction in the boy's voice he had hoped for. He looked at Justin quizzically, the boy staring out at the field. "I didn't dare say anything. You don't know my mom. She'd freak out if she knew about any of this."

"You saw him, didn't you, Justin? You saw the killer."

"I didn't know!" The boy swung his head around. He was in tears. "I swear to God I didn't know. I would have called the police, I swear I would have."

"It's all right. It's all right."

He shook his head. "No. Don't you get it? If I had called . . ."

Boldt moved his arm toward the boy and cut himself off, resting it on the back of the bench instead. He found it hard to swallow. Come on, boy, he felt like saying, get it out in the open.

"I didn't know what to do. How was I supposed to explain it?"

"What did you see, Justin? Did you see him?"

"My God!" Mrs. Levitt thundered on a fast approach, "I don't *believe* this!"

"Oh shit," the boy said, standing.

Boldt rose too.

"You have a lot of nerve, Lieu—"

"Get out of here, Mom," Justin Levitt hollered, stopping his mother dead in her tracks. "Wait for me in the car."

Mrs. Levitt's jaw dropped.

"I'm talking to Mr. Boldt. I'll be done in a minute. This is private, Mom. Private. You're always talking about respecting my privacy, so how about it?"

"Justin?" She was appalled, the rejection clearly overwhelming, but when he didn't answer her, when he stood there waiting, she finally rose to the challenge and turned away, surprising Boldt.

"I'll explain later," the boy shouted at her receding back, regret filling his voice. "Shit," he hissed again, loud enough only for Boldt to hear. "I *did* see him," he said, to Boldt, quickly looking back toward his mother. His voice hovered between a boy's and a man's. "He came in through her backyard carrying something. I couldn't see what it was. He went around front and I lost him. She was up in her room," he said uncomfortably. "She had her snack," he said without realizing his choice of words indicated a familiarity with Croy he was trying to sidestep. "I think she must have heard the doorbell or something . . ." He paused.

Go on, Boldt willed.

". . . because she left the room. She wasn't gone long.

I should have known," he said, looking into Boldt's eyes. "I knew what her boyfriend looked like. I didn't see this guy—not his face—but I knew it wasn't him. And I didn't realize what was going on until a few days later when you guys found her."

"She returned to the bedroom?"

"I think they both did. I don't know." He shook his head. "She fell down onto the bed, and then the curtain closed. That's all I saw, honest."

Boldt was silent for a long time. Some birds landed on the roof of the school. Lights in a few of the classrooms went off.

"I'm sorry I lied to you," Justin said.

"You didn't lie. You waited to tell me, that's all. What made you change your mind, Justin?"

"Not that shit about the bathhouse. Was that true?" he asked, wiping away tears.

"No."

"I didn't think so." The boy forced a grin.

Boldt maintained his work face.

He shrugged. "I don't know why. You have a job to do, right? That's what you told me the other night. I thought about that. If I had done something that night"—his face tightened—"she would still be alive."

"You don't know that."

He burst out crying. "You don't know what that feels like." He reached toward Boldt, but then balled up on himself, sucking his knees into his chest and wrapping his arms around them.

Boldt reached out reluctantly and stroked Justin Levitt's back. He looked up. In the far distance Mrs. Levitt was standing, watching. "Let it go, *son*." That word came painfully for him. "If it helps any, I know exactly how you feel." Justin shook his head, still bent over, still sobbing. "You see, if I had done *my* job right the first time, you never would have seen that man that night. It never would have happened, because I would have caught him. But I didn't. And I'll tell you something. As much as that bugs me, there's nothing I can do about it. You and I are in the same boat: we wish like hell we could do it all over again, but we can't, can we?''

The boy stopped sobbing and slowly sat up. "No, I guess not," he said.

"We're all tested in strange ways, son."

The boy nodded.

"I can't tell you that what you did was right. You'll have to think about that. But I can tell you this—there's no way to change it now, and thanks to you we may catch this guy after all. You may come out of this thing a hero, Justin."

"I don't want to be a hero."

"That makes two of us, but sometimes we're stuck with it."

"If I had called . . ."

"Listen, you had no way to know, okay? Don't be so hard on yourself. There are a hell of a lot of 'ifs' in life, Justin. No shit," he said, trying to grab the boy's attention and succeeding. "But very few of them are worth a damn. Let it go. I think you know what I'm trying to say."

The boy nodded and dragged his sleeve across his eyes.

"I'm going to need your help, son. I'm going to ask you the same questions a hundred times. You're going to hate me by the end of this. About the only thing good about it is that we'll probably keep you out of school for a couple of days." The boy was amused. "We may even fly a guy all the way out from Washington, D.C., just to talk with you."

"No kidding?"

He had the boy now. "It feels better, doesn't it? You feel better, right?"

"Yeah."

"I think you better apologize to your mother."

The kid took off across the schoolyard at a run. He was

swallowed up in his mother's forgiving arms. When Boldt finally reached her, Mrs. Levitt forced an apology through tears, Justin still clinging to her. "Forgive me," she said.

Boldt nodded. "Likewise," he said, and then escorted them to their car.

13

LATER THAT DAY, following a two-hour session with Justin Levitt, armed with the boy's description of the killer's approach, Boldt returned to the home of Cheryl Croy and scrutinized the property once more. He stood at the backyard fence wondering how the killer might have approached. If Justin was right, the killer must have vaulted the fence, entered the backyard, and then cut around to the front of Croy's house. Boldt avoided touching the posts that supported the low chain-link fence—he would have I.D. print them later—and vaulted over. The nearest building was a locked garage. He tried the house, but no one answered. He walked around the house, wondering if the killer could have parked on the street and come down this driveway. Too risky, he thought. A FOR SALE sign called out from his left. It was planted in the tiny overgrown front-lawn yard of the adjacent house. On the far side of this next house over, he came upon a carport conveniently shielded from view of any neighbors. If you were to cut your lights out on the street as you rounded the corner and pull in here quickly enough, your chances of being spotted were low.

Although the recent rain had washed any tracks from the sand-and-gravel driveway, the area under the carport held two clear tire impressions. A few feet back from where the tire tracks stopped, Boldt found a single paper match, half-burned and curled at the end. He did not touch it. Leading away from the tracks, headed directly for where Boldt had just come from, were two near-perfect impressions from basketball sneakers, one headed away from where the car had been parked, one returning. He realized he'd been holding his breath only when he exhaled forcibly. Sneakers had been mentioned in the BSU profile. The Cross Killer had been right here.

When he left the carport Boldt noticed the commotion up the street at the Levitts', and knew immediately its cause. There had been a leak, and Justin's story had made the papers. He shook his head in disgust but compelled himself not to enter into their problems just yet. This was more important.

He placed a phone call from Croy's and directed his people to park between Seventy-third and Seventy-fourth so the press wouldn't see them. Twenty-five agonizing minutes later he finally had the charred match in a paper bag on the way to the state lab, and a group taking photographs of the tire tracks and sneaker prints. The exact distance to her house was measured twice. Boldt timed himself both walking normally and walking quickly: no less than two minutes, no more than four.

Boldt theorized the killer might have waited to put on the latex gloves until inside the house, so he made the print team busy. An hour later the crew lifted a partial palm print from the corner fencepost. There was much celebration among the men for this was their first hard evidence—evidence that could be used in court to link a specific individual to the scene of the crime.

Boldt purposely avoided the Levitt house. There was nothing he could do there, and in all likelihood he might be put in an embarrassing situation by being asked questions he didn't want to answer. He had the on-duty officer at headquarters dispatch a patrol team to keep the press from trespassing and tried to reach the Levitts to apologize, but the line was busy—off the hook, he was told.

Back at the office, he left one of his detectives to begin a search of all citations and parking tickets issued on the night of Croy's killing, hoping for some good luck. Luck and chance often turned the tide of an investigation.

Nothing materialized. He ate a turkey sandwich at a deli on Second Avenue and was beginning a cup of coffee when Shoswitz caught up to him. The two men discussed the newly discovered evidence and then Boldt said, "I think we should protect the kid from the press. This is horrible for him."

"In a couple of days the press will have forgotten all about him. They can't milk this for much more than they already have. From what I've heard he and the family are sticking to their earlier promise. They aren't telling anyone anything."

"Still—"

"You've done good work, Lou. We're starting to make some real progress. Finally! And Kramer, too. He worked up a darn good list of institutional releases. None of them appear to fit the profile. But we haven't given up on that. LaMoia has pieced together a good look at where the victims shopped on the days before their deaths. We know more about these women now than ever. It's all being fed into the computer. With any luck at all the computer may kick out something we've overlooked."

Boldt's pager sounded. He reached down and silenced it. He normally would call in, but being only a few blocks away he decided to go back to the office. He waited for Shoswitz to get a coffee to go—the office coffee this time of night was strong and bitter.

The two men walked sluggishly, both overtired. They trudged up the hill, crossed the street, and entered the Public Safety building. They rode the elevator in silence. As they entered the offices Shoswitz said, "Use Interrogation. It'll give you some privacy."

Boldt had been so dazed he didn't understand what the lieutenant was talking about until his eyes changed focus and he saw Elizabeth sitting in a chair by his desk, looking at him angrily. He felt panicked by the sight of her. What a strange sensation—panicked by the sight of his own wife!

There had been a time when Lou Boldt couldn't wait to get home and see her. She had always been a strong and handsome woman, and in their early years, while she worked on her masters and he paid his dues as a detective, they had shared a strong, physical attraction to one another. He had made every effort to switch shifts and change schedules in order to find free time to be with her. She had done the same, often studying well past midnight and into the wee hours of the morning in order to accommodate the ill fit of their lifestyles. In those early years of their marriage most of their free time had been spent in bed, or any other convenient place they could find themselves in each other's arms. Their moments of passion often gave way to a blissful physical fatigue that made for the deepest rest. These "naps" had sustained each of them and the word had become a code to use when they wished to skip out on a social engagement early and get back between the sheets. Elizabeth had been a sensual, attractive woman who demanded and returned an enormous amount of physical love. He recalled the dozens of times she had initiated their lovemaking, keeping the honeymoon alive years into their marriage.

Then graduation, the bank job, the promotions, and the slow change in her personality. She began to dress up for any occasion, spending thirty to forty minutes in the bathroom each and every morning putting on her face, a face that only hid the true Elizabeth he had grown to care for and to love.

The interrogation room smelled of cigarette smoke. Smoking wasn't allowed in here, but no one ever obeyed the rule. Elizabeth fanned the air and pulled a seat from the bare table, quickly locking her fine legs and tugging her tight skirt. She looked even better now than she had a week earlier when she entered the Four Seasons Hotel wearing her lavender dress and tan raincoat. She had her dark hair pulled back sharply. Her mouth was pouty, with soft kissable lips.

He noticed her jaw muscles flex and he knew this mood. If they had been at home he would have made up an excuse and left the room for a few minutes to allow her time to cool off.

How can I feel this way, he wondered, when it's she who is at fault? Why do I still let her do this to me? Is she feeling as smug as she appears, or is she scared to death, frightened and alone and fearful of me?

"For a few days I allowed myself to believe you were still at the seminar. I read about Croy in the paper, wondering if you were still handling the case." She looked away for effect. "Then I thought maybe you had tried to call and the machine had screwed up. You were out of town— Washington, something like that. Tell me you tried to call, Lou."

He was silent.

"What the hell is going on?"

He debated a number of different angles, but his mouth beat him to it. "I followed you last Monday. Lunchtime. I've been staying at a downtown motel ever since."

"On your salary?" She glared at him and then laughed, though it was forced and sad. "It would help if I knew what you were talking about," she said.

"The Four Seasons."

"That?" He could see her mind whirring—could almost hear it. "That was a business meeting! Is that all? You think . . . Oh, God, Lou, grow up! You think I'm sleeping with someone on my lunch hours? You think this is 'Dallas' or something? You're just jealous. You never have understood my career, have you? Business meetings take place in hotels all the time, for your information."

He crossed his arms, sighed, and stared at her, obviously waiting. If she hadn't looked so absolutely stunning he might not have been so mad, but he *was* jealous—she was absolutely right. He hated it when she was right. She spread her hand out on the table and he noticed her gold watch and the ring she wore in place of the one he had given her a long time ago.

"Is that all?" she tried again.

"Yes. That's all," he echoed, altering the meaning with his tone of voice.

She winced and her eyes became glassy. "I don't *believe* you!"

"Try."

Elizabeth forced another laugh and pried inquisitively with her eyes. "You thought I was sleeping with someone?"

"I didn't think you were sleeping with someone," he corrected. "I assumed you were fucking the guy. I *know* you were fucking that guy. I've lived with you for ten years, babe. If there's one thing I know, it's how you look after an orgasm. Granted, I've failed you in that department lately. I suppose I shouldn't be surprised. But I am. Surprised, hurt, and even humiliated. I want to blame it entirely on you, but I suppose I'm responsible too. I didn't fully understand that until I saw you tonight. I wanted to hate you. For the last week I've tried really hard to hate you, but I can't. I feel sorry for you, I think. And for me."

Her face tightened. "You want it over, don't you? Jesus." She rose and began to pace, touching the edges of her eyes with her index finger.

Was she crying, or just pretending? Her accusation stung him. He hadn't considered this possibility, but the more he did, the more he knew she might be right. "I hadn't thought about it that way."

"No, I didn't think you had."

The interrogation room, he thought. Here I am in the interrogation room doing a melodramatic imitation of what I'm usually very good at. You know how to make me impotent in everything, babe. "How many have there been?"

"Oh, *really*!"

"Well?"

"Go to hell."

"Let me put it another way: Do you love him?"

She glared. She started to speak but stopped herself.

A few years ago she would have spoken her mind, not considered the repercussions. He liked the old her. He *loved* the old her. But she had changed. Or had he?

"You don't get it, do you?" she asked. "I messed up. I see that now, okay? I messed up. But do we let it wreck everything?"

"What is there left to wreck?"

"It's children, isn't it? That's not my fault. You *had* your chance!"

"That's part of it, I admit. But it isn't any *one* thing, Elizabeth. It's the whole mess we've made of it. When I saw that glow on your face something snapped. That was something dear to me. I couldn't go home after that."

"Oh, Christ. You make it sound so *permanent*." She was crying now. Real tears.

"I don't know," he said. "It feels permanent to me. I don't know you."

She crossed her arms tightly and tucked her chin in, spinning away from him.

Her shoulders shook and he felt tempted to comfort her. It had been a long time since he had held her. "Maybe we can work it out," he offered.

"I don't hear that in your voice."

"Right now is not a good time for me. This isn't the best time."

"Terrific, Lou. Really great," she snapped. "Let me know when it's *convenient*." She snatched up her purse and hurried from the room.

Boldt drummed his fingers on the desk imagining himself at a piano. Up until now he hadn't fully faced what a separation or a divorce—is that where they were headed?—would mean to him. He tried to stop thinking about it. Now wasn't the time. Right now he needed an escape.

He found temporary escape in the washroom, where he spent five minutes splashing cold water on his face, talking to himself, and looking at himself in the mirror. He reviewed their discussion, reflecting on how he might have approached it differently, much as he often used hindsight to review a case. His heart was still pounding, and that ache lingered. He still had a great deal to work out.

He reached his desk and placed a call to Carl Berensen. The Bear was one of the only reminders of Yakima here. He and Boldt had been high-school buddies together. Bear had started a comedy club nearly fifteen years ago. It had grown in popularity and had expanded twice since then, once in '74 and again in '81 after Bear's mother died and left him some money. But the bar still had the same cigarette-scarred, Yamaha baby grand in the corner, from which Bear occasionally entertained customers. It was the only piano available Boldt could think of, except for the ones over at the University, and they weren't accessible this time of night.

As he picked up his phone to dial Berensen, another line rang. He punched a button and said, "Yeah?"

"Sergeant Boldt, please."

"Speaking."

"This is Bill Yates calling back about your Neighborhood Watch inquiry."

Boldt had placed an earlier call to the leader of the community patrol program in the upper Green Lake area, inquiring about the night of Croy's murder. "Oh, yes, Mr. Yates. Any luck?"

"I think we may have something for you. Ned Farley remembers seeing a yellow van at the Fairmont home. It's up for sale, so real-estate people are always in and out, and the guys have gotten kind of lazy about writing anything down, but Ned swears he remembers seeing a yellow van that night. I just got off the phone with the man who owns the real-estate company and he says none of his people owns a yellow van. Sorry it took so long, but I had trouble reaching him. He volunteers his Monday nights to the Boy Scouts. That do you any good?"

"Lots of good. Did your people see anyone?"

"Not a soul."

"Nothing unusual?"

"Nothing. I have a hunch Ned wouldn't have seen it at all, except you got lucky. The Fairmont house, being empty and all, is on what we call our hot list. Vacant houses, people who are on vacation, anyone with recent trouble— they all go on our hot list and we try to pay particular attention to them. That's all I've got. No plates. Sorry about that. Ned should have written down the plates. That's part of his duty as shotgun rider."

"Time of day?"

"Oh yeah, got that too. Ned's sure it was before ten because they were listening to the Mariners game on the radio, and the game ended just after ten."

"Before ten. Got it. And what time did his patrol start, just so I can put a time on the other end of this?"

"Evening patrol begins at eight and runs until eleven. But they start in the Seventy block and work their way up to Eighty-five. A patrol consists of two full passes, and it must have been on the second pass because it was nearing the end of their shift, so that would make it what, around nine-thirty? Say, that's a little closer than we had it, isn't it?"

Boldt took down Ned Farley's phone number, and thanked Yates for calling back. It wasn't the first time a simple nudge to a person's reasoning powers had netted results. People were often amazed at what they could remember or deduce when given the chance. Encouraging a person to remember only made him forget all the quicker.

He phoned Ned Farley and pried him away from the National League playoff game that ran loudly in the background. The man offered no more than what Yates had relayed to Boldt: yellow van under the carport; he hadn't written down the plates.

"Were the lights on in the house?" Boldt asked. He

waited through a long pause as Ned Farley thought about it.

The man finally said, "I'd like to tell you one way or the other, Mr. Boldt, but the fact of the matter is, I just don't remember. The van being there didn't strike me as odd at the time. I just plain didn't pay much attention."

Boldt left him his direct number—in case he remembered anything—and hung up. So close . . . he thought.

He was dialing his friend Berensen when Shoswitz called him into his office area. Boldt's mood was still sour. Like his stomach. He passed on the information Yates had given him and the lieutenant agreed to make note of it at tomorrow's roll call. Shoswitz said, "Take a day off tomorrow. I think you could use it, and God knows you deserve it."

"No thanks. I'll be in at seven. I'm scheduled for seven."

"You need the rest, Lou. You're the only one who doesn't seem to realize it."

"Too much breaking too quick. A day off would only frustrate me."

"How's Elizabeth?"

Boldt shrugged.

"Problems?" He awaited an answer and then said, "I'm gonna be honest with you."

"Good. I could use a little honesty."

"We talked about your appearance the other day. And I don't see a whole hell of a lot of improvement. You don't look so good, Lou. In fact, you look sick. You're working too hard. If that's why Elizabeth—"

"It's not."

"I know this case has been hard on all of us—especially you—and it's not likely to get much easier. We're public servants, Lou. I'm not going to harp on that, but you get my message. I appreciate the long hours, the extra effort you've been giving this. I checked your card. I know you aren't applying for half the overtime you've worked. I thought you were trying to hold down the costs at first, but then I realized it wasn't for that reason. You're filling out your cards that way so you won't be caught turning in seven eighteen-hour days in a row. I don't need a basket case, right? I need you to be thinking clearly. You're my starter, Lou, and I don't have much in the bull pen.''

"You offering me a forced vacation, Lieutenant? You want me off the case?"

"Lou."

"You son of a bitch—"

"Lou! I'm not taking you off the case. Jesus H.'' He stared at Boldt. "What the hell's going on? Is it Liz? You want to talk about it?"

"No!" He held up his hand to stop Shoswitz. White spittle had collected at either side of his mouth. His eyes were badly bloodshot from fatigue. "Sure, we've got to be methodical in our pursuit. Systematic. But it isn't going fast enough. We've got to try harder, Phil. We have to go after every damn lead like it's the last one we'll ever get. We need a complete change of attitude on this!'' he hollered.

Shoswitz was not the kind of man who liked to be told what he needed. He collected himself and then said, "Get some rest, Lou. Go home and get some rest. Take tomorrow off. Believe it or not, we'll get along fine without you. Anything breaks, we'll give you a call."

"A call!" He barked out a laugh. "Lot a good that'll do," he said under his breath. He had lost control of himself, and for a brief moment he understood this and tried to correct it, but the combination of total fatigue and the emotional upheaval brought on by Elizabeth's visit overwhelmed him. He rose from the chair and glared at Shoswitz. "After everything I've given this," he said, feeling insulted and betrayed. An overpowering headache descended on him, swelling inside his head, heating up his eyes, pounding rhythmically in his ears. He pinched his temples. He wanted to scream. For once he wanted to let out a tremendous scream. He found it hard to breathe, that familiar balloon swelling inside his chest.

He was on the street now, walking down First Avenue past the bars with thumping rock music emanating from their dark entrances. He pressed his back against a cold brick wall, sweating despite the chill in the air, and watched the cars lumber past. The headache still remained, though the anxiety attack had passed.

For a minute, he was disoriented. Then he realized where he was: only two blocks from the seedy hotel he had been using as home for the past week. He'd been walking home, that was all—though the thought of home recalled images of Elizabeth, and this instilled in him the disquieting realization that he was alone, utterly alone, for the first time in years. He heard himself begin to pant, and felt his throat constrict, then swallowed it away, not allowing himself to cry. He wouldn't cry here.

A few minutes later he entered the hotel's dingy hallway, passed the registration desk manned by a young Asian with poor teeth and distrustful eyes, and reached the tiny elevator. The hallway smelled like Pinesol. Wonderful place you chose, he told himself. All the amenities of a refugee dormitory. And all this for thirty-two dollars a night. What a country!

The clock radio was permanently fixed to the chest of drawers, as was the television. Lou Boldt tuned in his jazz station and sat down on the bed. He pulled off his socks and washed them in the corner sink with the complimentary bar of Ivory. He removed his shirt and tie and then washed the armpits of the shirt and hung it on a hanger, along with his socks, above the radiator by the window. No wonder it looks as though I've been sleeping in my clothes, he thought. He slung his coat and tie over the tired chair and climbed into bed, utterly exhausted.

But he did not sleep.

He stared at the pulsating neon-orange light bouncing off the curtains, listened to a wailing tenor sax, and wondered where the Cross Killer was at this very moment.

And what he was doing.

14

WHEN LOU BOLDT awakened that Tuesday morning, he realized Shoswitz was right. He also knew the man well enough to know he would take whatever steps were necessary to maintain control of the investigation. If that included removing Boldt from the case, then Shoswitz would do it. He changed back into the shirt that he had left hanging over the radiator to dry, collected his things, and checked out of the dreary hotel. He walked back up to the office, hanging bag in hand, signed out his car, and drove home, knowing full well Elizabeth would be at work. Once there, he took a long hot shower, shaved, and changed into fresh clothes. He spent an hour and a half with the classifieds and the telephone searching for a rental and ended up with a list of three possibilities. As he packed up three suitcases of clothes, he was surprised to feel no self-pity or sorrow. He knew this was something that had to be done. They both needed time to think. Going through the motions now only served to fuel his self-confidence. Things suddenly seemed brighter.

He took some spare checks and his address book and wrote Elizabeth a short, curt note, explaining that their separation had officially begun. He made it neither sentimental nor accusatory; he simply stated that they were on their own now, that they both knew how to reach each other, and that if and when a talk seemed in order he was willing to participate. He signed the note and pocketed the pen.

The second rental he looked at seemed fine. It was a small two-bedroom house—more than he needed—furnished, slightly overpriced, but what wasn't? The landlord agreed to wave the security deposit because Boldt was a cop, believing Boldt's presence might reduce the incidence of crime, which was quite high in most parts of the city. The phone company promised to give him a line within the week. He hung up a dozen shirts and stored five pairs of shoes in a closet and then consumed an hour wandering around the two bedrooms, living room, and kitchen, pulling out drawers, opening and shutting closet doors, and familiarizing himself with his new environs. He finally came to rest on the edge of the firm double bed, patting it absentmindedly, finding himself a bit more depressed than he had hoped.

He drove across town and spent forty minutes straightening out the post office on forwarding his mail and then shopped at the local grocery store on his way home, buying mostly staples and spending more money than he had intended.

Back "home" he inspected himself in the mirror, feeling and looking like a new man. He took a leisurely walk around the neighborhood. Interlake North, his new address, ran perpendicular to the canal. He walked along the canal, alone, and felt the temptation of self-pity nag at him. A heavy front of storm clouds blew in off the sound quickly, bringing with it a cool drizzle.

He returned home at a clip and spent the early evening trying to figure out what to do with himself. At six-thirty he did the only thing that made any sense: he called Daphne and asked her out.

They met down by the waterfront where a dozen ferry companies shuttle thousands of people out to the islands and where tourists collect to sightsee and shop. She looked real good to him and he told her so.

"You look a whole lot better, Lou. Shoswitz told me he
was worried about you." There was still the faint, light lilt
of a Southern accent hidden behind her words. Its musical
nature charmed him. Her chestnut hair, caught by the offshore breeze, blew across her face, momentarily obstructing
her vision, and she finger-combed it back behind her ear,
pink from the chill.

"Nothing to worry about. Just going through some changes,
that's all."

"Such as?"

He noted that she made no attempt to tease him, and he
felt himself relax some. He wasn't emotionally prepared for
an evening of verbal fencing. He didn't intend to tell her
about Elizabeth; it would make this look all wrong. "We've
made some headway on the case. Can't be sure it's worth
anything, but it seems to be."

"You did well with the boy."

He nodded. "We lucked out there."

"It wasn't luck and you know it."

A long silence. He felt the truth bubbling up to the surface, and he could neither suppress it nor contain it. His
inability to stop it had something to do with Daphne. She
had what amounted to a spell over him, some kind of emotional magnet that reached down inside of him and drew
things out. "I left Elizabeth, Daffy. As of this moment
we're officially separated. I wanted some company and you
were the first person who came to mind." He looked over
at her. "But not like that. I don't mean it like that."

"It's okay, Lou." She hung her head and they walked
in silence for some distance. Hordes of people streamed
past as they approached the market and then they found
themselves out of the crowds. The sun was down, a final
stain of color lingering over the sound, and it was growing
colder.

"I'm supposed to say 'I'm sorry,' Lou. But that would
be less than honest."

"I wasn't going to tell you."

"I'm glad you did."

"I didn't want it to influence things. I didn't want you to get the wrong impression."

"And what's the wrong impression?"

"Don't go getting professional on me. I don't know how to play those games. You know very well what I mean."

"Answer the question."

He looked down into her eyes. There was a silent depth that drew him in, like the darkness of a well. If I drop a penny in there, will I hear it land? "We're friends, right?"

"We're more than friends, Lou, and you know it. We were friends once. But that was a long, long time ago. We're beyond that now. We have been for some time." She stopped him and took him by the shoulders. The surge of pedestrians parted around them like river water around a rock. Her grasp was firm yet tender. She looked intently at him and for a moment he thought she might kiss him and he wondered what that would be like. He didn't think he was ready for that. "I'm really glad you called. I'm nervous, and I'm even a little frightened, because you and I have been playing games with each other for a while now. I'm being anything but professional at the moment. One thing you learn in my line of work is to leave the office behind you. If I couldn't do that, I wouldn't last long. I don't mind talking about the case. Not now. But when we get to dinner I think I'd like to shut that door, if that's good with you. I'd like to spend some time with Lou Boldt—just me and you, you know? The detective-psychologist thing works better in the office." She released him and placed her smooth, warm hand on his cheek and said, "How are you holding up under all of this?"

He nodded, not wanting her to take her hand away, which she did. Her touch changed his attitude completely. It had been weeks since he had felt anyone touch him, many long months since he had experienced any form of physical tenderness. A wave of comforting relief passed through him, coinciding with the lazy slap of water on the seawall below them, and he suddenly felt purged of his anxieties. In that instant he knew she was his answer. She could get him going again. "Okay, I guess," he replied. "It's nice to see you outside the office, Daffy. You know that?" He closed his eyes and inhaled loudly through his nose, the cold, damp breeze stinging his face and lungs, lifting his hair wildly. He exhaled in a long, controlled sigh.

"Of course I do," she said, taking him by the elbow and guiding him along.

They walked this way for a few minutes. A street musician played "Mister Bojangles" on an out-of-tune harmonica.

"Let me ask you this," he said as they continued along, "before we get to dinner," and winked. "What are the odds the killer would tape the mouth of one victim, but not the others?"

"It might be dictated by circumstance. I suppose you're referring to the Kate DeHavelin case. She was found outside, indicating the possibility that she attempted to escape. It creates an entirely different set of circumstances."

"That aside."

"That aside? I would say unlikely. He has a set, established ritual that means something to him. It gives him purpose. He believes he's doing this *for* someone—something—probably God, probably in response to voices he hears. Nonetheless, it is an established ritual. We've seen the same evidence enough to know that, though we don't yet fully understand all the elements or his rationalization. More than likely he goes in and out of conscious thought when he's with his victims. He's controlled yet spontaneous, well planned yet impulsive. Even given this irrationality, I believe it's unlikely he would deviate from his ritual. In all probability the ritual is the only thing holding him together. If his ritual goes bad, Lou, he may come apart on us."

"What if I'm dealing with a copycat? And what if that copycat's one of us?"

She stopped. Again the tourists streamed around them. She stared into his eyes intensely. "You want to ask that again?"

"You heard me."

"One of us?" Shaken.

"Dixie says he would have to be. He knows too much."

She clutched her arms tightly to herself, as if suddenly colder. They began walking again. She stared straight ahead now. It was a long minute before she said, "How certain are you?"

"Three of the victims have been handled just slightly differently, Daffy. There's not much hard evidence, but I feel it. And I think Dixie does too."

"Jesus," she said, the full weight of the implication sinking in. "If you're trying to scare me, you're doing a good job."

"I'm not. I've only discussed it with Dixie. No one else. Unfortunately," he said, pausing briefly, "I have to consider all possibilities. That's part of the job." He waited a minute before saying, "You're our people expert. If I'm looking for someone inside our department, then I'm better off knowing as much as I can about him."

"Okay. I'm listening," she said in her best Dr. Matthews voice.

"What would *motivate* him? What makes him tick?"

She thought long and hard before telling him, "More than likely, you're talking about a psychopathic personality if you're talking about a copycat. He's a premeditated killer, most likely killing for the challenge—for the *fun* of it. Psychopaths are complex individuals. It's impossible to lump them together and make some kind of gross statement."

"But if you had to . . . what motivates him?"

"A copycat could be motivated by anything from some kind of personal thrill—real or imagined—to the challenge involved."

"Meaning?"

"Meaning it could be he simply gets a rush from attempting perfect duplication of the crime. If he *is* a cop, then it could be a kind of game. He may be challenging you to notice a difference between the various murders."

"Then it could be aimed at me personally?" Boldt asked.

"It *could* be. But it could be almost anything. What are you driving at?"

"Just thinking out loud, that's all. I have to consider all the possibilities."

"So you said." She glanced over at him with a furrowed brow. "I don't like the thought of any of this. I don't think I'd like having your job."

"That makes us even." He glanced over at her. Perfect profile. Slightly upturned nose. Just right. Thoroughly thoroughbred. "What you're saying is that someone could be putting me through the psychological ringer, duplicating the kills while at the same time working by my side."

"It's a horrible thought."

"But it's possible?"

"Yes." She waited a second before saying, "There's something else, isn't there, Lou?"

"Yes there is."

"Do you want to talk about it?"

"I suppose I must want to."

"You don't have to. Only if you want to."

He had been avoiding this. It had been lurking back there, always just out of reach. Nagging at him. But he had had no desire to face it. It was bad enough just acknowledging it. "It's Jergensen," he told her.

She said nothing.

He spoke more softly. "Kramer and I talked about it a little, and it's been bothering me ever since. The thing is, I've had to deal with a lot of different pressures, a lot of different things on this job . . . but the whole Jergensen thing stays with me."

"I'm listening," she said in that soothing, slightly Southern voice of hers.

"But the thing of it is . . . What's really bugging me is that we let ourselves be swayed. We went along with public sentiment.'' They had walked a good distance and now he turned and waited for a light.

She studied him with her milk-chocolate eyes. Daphne said, ''Okay.''

He glared at her, ''But it's not okay.''

''Why?''

''Why?'' he asked incredulously as the light changed and they crossed. ''Why?'' he repeated, looking away. ''Don't you understand? Jergensen was innocent.''

''Was he?''

''He wasn't the killer.''

''But was he *innocent*?''

''You're talking semantics.''

''Yes.''

''No, he probably wasn't innocent.''

''And could you have stopped it? Could one person have stopped it?''

He took her elbow and steered her around some construction, following behind her. When he was alongside he said, ''That's what I keep asking myself. That's it exactly. I wasn't convinced. We had no hard evidence. None. But I wanted it over as badly as anyone. I shouldn't have slowed down. My inaction got a man killed. Can't you see that?''

''So, it's your fault Jergensen was killed? Your fault alone?''

''I'm not saying that, dammit! I know it's not that simple—''

''It's not,'' she said, interrupting, ''it's only as complicated, it's only as involved as you want to make it. There are those in my profession who maintain that everything is made-up. We can choose to create whatever we want out of things. What do you think of that?''

''I think that's too simplistic. There's plenty that's beyond our control. If it's all made up, then why can't I just solve the murders, if that's what I want?''

''Because he's involved too. He's making it the way he wants it, which only makes it more complicated. You're at

cross-purposes. I'm not suggesting your job is easy, Lou,
or that there's a simple solution to this case, only that the
way you *approach* it—the way you feel about it—is left
up to you. You can carry Jergensen's death with you, or
you can let it go. It's up to you to make that decision."

"You make it sound so easy."

"Maybe it is."

After the climb they rounded a corner to the left and
walked down Third. The avenue was in disrepair because
of a mass-transit construction project that had been going
on for years now. Downtown was quiet. "Yes," Boldt
finally said, "maybe it is."

She looped her arm through his and asked, "Do you
mind?"

He shook his head and squeezed her arm in his grip.
"The hardest thing about this case has been the knowledge
that he's still out there. It gets in under your skin and festers.
Solving a single homicide is one thing—it's hard enough.
Preventing another death is something else entirely. We're
not really trained for that. Each time we discover another
victim I feel as if I failed. I've never really felt anything
quite like it. I keep thinking I should be the one he gets.
It's me who's failed, not the women he kills. I wish he'd
come after me."

She shivered. "Don't say that, Lou. What a grisly thought."

"How am I supposed to cope with that sense of failure,
Doctor?"

"Is it your fault he's still out there?"

"Isn't it?"

"For one thing it isn't your case alone. That's a mis-
conception. There must be twenty or thirty people on this
case, statewide. And I happen to believe that if there was
enough evidence, you would have caught him already. None
of us likes to relinquish control to another. One of the great
human drives is to remain in control—to dominate a situation. Is it failure that's eating away at you, or lack of

control? Could it be that what's really bothering you is that it's *his* game, not yours?''

He stopped at the door to The Brass Grill and looked over at her. He grinned, ever so slightly. ''I knew you were the right person to call,'' he said.

''I'm glad you did,'' she admitted.

''No more business?'' he asked, yanking open the door.

''From here on out we're just two people out for the evening.''

Classical music came from inside. Huge windows overlooked the harbor dotted with the lights of ferries, freighters, and tankers. He teased, ''I'm not sure I remember how to be a 'people.' It's been a long, long time.''

''Oh, I think you do,'' she said. ''And what you don't remember, I'll teach you.'' She pursed her lips and cocked her head at him, suppressing a grin.

''That sounds nice.''

''It can be.''

The glass doors swung shut. Lou Boldt glanced over his shoulder at his reflected image. For a brief moment, he saw himself not through his own eyes, but through hers.

She tugged on his arm, ''We're inside,'' she said. ''There's no escape now.''

''No,'' he said, turning to face her, ''I don't suppose there is.''

''Two?'' the headwaiter asked.

Lou Boldt nodded.

15

FOR THE NEXT THREE DAYS Boldt thought about that evening with Daphne. He wondered if his urge to ask her home had been stimulated by his warming affection for her, or by some subconscious desire to punish Elizabeth for her affair and her wearing down of their marriage. He wondered if his failure to do so had been out of consideration for Daphne, or had stemmed from fear of his own sexual inadequacy, a condition that had plagued him for the past several months. He couldn't picture himself unable to get it up with a woman like Daphne lying naked beside him, but he couldn't be sure either, and the embarrassment of such a failure loomed ever-present in his mind. I'd curl up and die, he thought.

Once again he felt stymied by the investigation, despite the fact that he was armed with a wealth of new information: (a) Cheryl Croy's cooking class had been taught by a woman and attended by all women, ruling it out as a place the killer had spotted his victims; (b) Croy's television's remote-control device had yielded only her prints, and no others; (c) the dates on the milk products in Croy's refrigerator indicated she had shopped either on that Friday or Saturday, no shopping receipt had been found to confirm this; (d) the paper match found in the carport behind Croy's house bore a partial thumbprint—possibly the killer's; (e) the partial palm print, lifted from the fence behind Croy's house; (f) photographs of the sneaker prints and tire tracks from the van spotted in the neighboring carport. I.D. estimated that the man wearing the sneakers weighed in at between 128 and 134 pounds, far less than the weight indicated by the Rockport shoe print found in the mud at Kate DeHavelin's death scene. The carport shoe prints were from a pair of size-eight sneakers sold at K mart. The Rockports were size nine and a half, meaning evidence at the DeHavelin site had been either "negated" by an unknown stranger, or her murder was the work of a copycat. Boldt was becoming increasingly convinced he had two killers on his hands. He had yet to share that theory with anyone but Daphne or Dixon. Without further proof of a copycat, the conflicting evidence would make building a court case against a suspect more difficult: Boldt would have to move very slowly now or find himself with inconsistent evidence that might defeat his efforts once he reached the courtroom.

Boldt felt increasingly frustrated. Absolutely nothing new had been uncovered in the last three days. He had tried to make an appointment with Justin Levitt to go over his statement again, in hopes something new might be jogged loose from the boy's memory as often happened with material witnesses. But the boy's parents had insisted the boy be allowed a few days to "become a boy again," and Boldt had not argued the point. He could not prove any kind of pressing need for another interview.

The clock continued to tick. Boldt had no way of knowing exactly when or where the next killing would take place. Any moment the phone would ring and another victim would be added to the list.

He drummed his pencil impatiently against his desk, studying the list LaMoia had prepared that catalogued the hundreds of items sold at the various stores where the victims shopped on the day prior to their deaths. He placed check marks by items appearing on two or more lists. There was a connection between these women somewhere. Somehow the killer had come across each of them. Was it something they had gone shopping for? Someplace they had eaten? A gas station? A repairman? A delivery man? A peeper? He looked forward to seeing LaMoia's list covering the four days prior to the victims' deaths.

A uniformed woman rounded his office baffle and glanced at her clipboard. Her face was freckled and sunburned. She told him, "Lou, an unidentified female Caucasian has washed ashore at Alki Point. Doctor Dixon is waiting for you. He thinks you ought to have a look at it. Something to do with your present case. He didn't say what." Boldt snatched his coat from the back of the chair. "Who's on it?"

"Browning and Bobbie Gaynes. Bobbie's been moved up from Special Assaults."

"Dammit! Pull Browning and put him back with LaMoia. I want him to *stay* on canvassing. Make that clear to him, would you?"

"But who'll—"

"I'll take this for the time being, and figure out what to do with it later," he said, rushing past the woman.

It was a gloomy day, and the shoreline of Alki Point was randomly consumed by shifting patches of thick fog blown in off the water. The fog swirled in like ambling gray tumbleweed, blanketing the large gathering of police personnel. Boldt tugged up his coat collar and crossed the stone beach to where the body lay.

Or what was left of it.

"Gaynes?" he called out, expecting one of the men to turn around, surprised when a pretty blonde about twenty-five approached. But then he recalled Shoswitz saying that they were pulling in temps from Special Assaults, the rape division, and the on-duty officer had said Gaynes was from SA.

"Lou Boldt," he said by way of introduction.

In this light, she had olive skin and moist lips. "Yes, I know. We met last year at one of the Christmas things."

He nodded, but didn't remember. Too many faces at those Christmas things. Too many faces and too much booze. He never said anything much at those affairs; he ate a couple of reindeer cookies and sneaked out early. "I pulled Browning from the case. For now, I'm going to handle it with you."

"You?" she said stunned, but recovered quickly enough to add, "Yes, sir."

"You can skip the sir shit, Bobbie. Your name is Bobbie, isn't it?"

"Barbara, actually. Everyone calls me Bobbie."

"I'm Lou."

"Fine. Why you? You're on the task force, aren't you?"

Boldt liked her immediately: casual and sure of herself, yet cloaked in femininity. "I've taken a special interest in the case. What have we got?"

"It's ugly," she said. They were standing a good thirty feet away. Even at this distance the stench was nauseating. Gaynes said, "The sea life's done away with the flesh on her hands and feet, as well as most of her face. Hair's gone. She's a mess."

Boldt walked over to take a look. He pulled out his handkerchief and pressed it to his face. He'd seen colorless, decomposed bodies before. Ugly was being polite. The sea had its own way with cadavers.

Doctor Dixon was examining Jane Doe. Her hands and feet were white shiny bone. Her swimsuit was caked with mud. "What have we got, Dixie?" Boldt asked.

Dixon glanced over his shoulder, a paper mask covering his lower face. "I've been waiting for you. Our sea friends seem to have been busy." Dixon poked what remained of the face with his gloved hand. Boldt looked away. Dixon was far too casual around rotten flesh. What a job.

"Cause of death?"

"Can't say for certain, Lou. Don't mean to make your job any tougher than it already is, but look here. This is why I thought you better come down."

Boldt bent down by Dixon, holding the handkerchief firmly in place. The pathologist pinched the soft, spongy tissue of the woman's throat. "Too much flesh gone to be absolutely certain, but look at the way the fish life fed on this neck." He indicated a line around the woman's throat. "Bruises fill with blood. The skin decomposes and the blood in the bruises seeps through the epidermal layer. Sea life is attracted to these areas first."

Boldt tried to maintain his professional attitude but felt on the edge of vomiting. How many similar bodies had he seen? Why did they still bother him? "What's your guess, Doc?" he asked, his voice muffled by the handkerchief.

Dixon pinched the gray-white cartilage of the trachea. "What this damage tells us, Lou, is that consistent pressure was applied from behind."

"Strangled?"

Dixon looked up at him. "Won't know for sure until I get her on the table. I think this one's worth your bother, Lou, or I wouldn't have called you."

"It's not much, Dixie."

Dixon said firmly, "What are the chances a boating accident would do this good a job of strangling her? This is *my line* of business, and I'll tell you there's no chance at all. Someone did this to her. Now listen, there may not be a cross on her chest; she may not look like a pincushion, like the rest of them, but how many young female strangulations do we get in a year? How many with this particular look to it? See the area back here?" He pointed. "This guy had her choked down hard, Lou. Same trademark as I've seen on some others recently, if you follow me. I *know* you. You like doing things right. Well, you had better take a good long look at this one then. How good a job is a transfer from SA going to do?"

So that's what it was about. "You don't like her," Boldt said, raising his head and looking over at Bobbie Gaynes.

"She's green," Dixon said. "She asked a bunch of stupid questions."

"I'll talk to her. And I'll pay extra attention, Dixie. Promise."

"You asked me to notify you if any of my guests showed similarities to your case. This woman qualifies." He pointed at the bloated cadaver.

"That I did."

Bobbie approached, pulled on Boldt's arm, and drew him away. She half-whispered, "Did you notice that her wetsuit is a rental?"

Boldt cocked his head. "What makes you think so?"

"I'm not positive. But that red nail polish along the collar. What else would that be for?"

Boldt didn't buy it, and he told her so. "Could be any number of things," he said. He had to weigh her comments with a degree of reservation. She was a young detective, probably in her first year in plainclothes, and she would try to impress him. Women rarely got a chance at a homicide case. She would want to make the most of it. "Okay," he said, "so what if it is?" If she was going to be gung-ho then he intended to test her at every chance. In all likelihood, he would have to turn much of the investigative work on this one over to her. For a brief moment he regretted having reassigned Browning so hastily, but he would not change things now.

"It may tell us something about her. Maybe help us identify her."

Boldt looked at Bobbie's moist face. She had a small slender nose, soft blue eyes, and rosy cheeks flushed from the chill. She showed a slight gap between her two front teeth, reminding him of Lauren Hutton. Pretty without being pretentious. "We take things kind of slow in Homicide. Slow and methodical. Step by step—"

"Lou?" Dixon called out.

Boldt walked back over to the man, returning the hand-kerchief to his face.

Dixon said, "Here's something for a curious mind like yours." He pulled back the thin wetsuit. "I unzipped this thing to get some preliminary photos. These water cadavers tend to fall apart on you, like chicken left too long in the broth. Best to get photos while they're still intact. Take a look." He had unzipped the wetsuit to her crotch. He opened it further. Two wrinkled, waterlogged, ink-stained pieces of pink paper were stuck to the woman's swimsuit just above her pubis.

"What the hell?" Boldt asked.

"I'll be as careful as possible with them. It's best if we lift them as a unit. The lab can freeze-dry them, remove the moisture, and then separate them later. Best chance of retaining anything written on them," Dixon said.

"What's your guess?" Boldt asked him.

"Some sort of receipt," Dixon offered.

"Same here," the detective agreed.

"A little weird to go swimming with some receipts stuffed down your suit, wouldn't you say?"

"I'd buy that." Boldt couldn't stand being by the cadaver another minute. He left Dixon to deal with the receipts, and went over by Bobbie.

Boldt led her away from the commotion, toward the stairs that led up to the parking lot. He said quietly, but sternly, "Between you and me, Detective, this case may be related to the Cross Killings. That's all you have to know right now. If I hear it from anyone else, I'll know you leaked it, and your ass will be in a sling. You follow me?"

"Yes."

"I just thought you should know, so you understand its importance. Okay?" he said, regretting his condescending tone. Why did he always treat every rookie detective like every other sergeant did? What gave sergeants the right to be so hard on them? He answered his own question: it's how they treated us, that's why.

"So what's our next step?"

She looked over as two men struggled awkwardly with the heavy black bag containing the corpse. "Missing persons, I'd say. Once we have her vitals, we go through all the water accidents and look for a match."

"And what's this case at the moment?"

"Death by suspicious causes."

"That wetsuit may help us keep this case open after the body is identified, but don't count on it. Same with those receipts Dixie found, although they look in pretty poor condition. If you're at all normal, you're eager to be involved with an active homicide case." She nodded her agreement. "And that's good. That's what I need. I'm plenty busy without this case. You'll handle most of it. But don't let your enthusiasm show too much, okay? We move slowly in Homicide. We can't afford to lose suspects in court because of sloppy police work. I have to trust you to do a good job. First off, we try and find out who she is. Wetsuits and whatever else come later. Okay? We move carefully. I'd like some progress by this afternoon." He smiled at her, and she smiled back. "We both stay in business that way, okay?"

" 'Cuse me."

They turned around. James Royce, Doctor Dixon's autopsy assistant whom Boldt had briefly met at the ME's office, was laden with equipment, and the two detectives were blocking the stairs that led up from the beach. He stared a little too long at Bobbie Gaynes and she blushed. Boldt introduced her to him as "the cop in charge of the case." Royce smiled and moved on.

Bobbie followed him with her eyes.

"Get going on those missing-person files. I'll ride over to the ME's with Dixon and wait for his initial report."

She hurried off toward the parked car, caught up to Royce,

and chatted briefly. He loaded the gear into the station
wagon marked KING COUNTY MEDICAL EXAMINER.

"Hey," Boldt called out, "get going."

"My car's blocked," she said, pointing. "Or would you
prefer I walk?"

Royce stayed out of it.

Spunk, Boldt thought. He was impressed.

16

LOU BOLDT WAITED in Doctor Dixon's office. The big man returned with two coffees and handed one to the detective. Dixon dragged a folding chair from a table across the room over to where Lou Boldt was seated. Here was a man who shunned the pretense of holding court from a chair behind a desk. Before Dixon could sit down, an assistant knocked and poked his head through the door.

"The mother of that one from the hotel is on six-five: Mrs. Malthaner, calling from Fresno. She wants to know what's going on."

Dixon nodded and the assistant closed the door. "Excuse me a minute," he said to Boldt and moved over to a sideboard where he picked up the phone and depressed a button. He spent five minutes explaining politely to the woman that her son had been found dead in a hotel room, and that the cause of death was an enlarged heart that had simply quit working, that his body was being held in order to complete the prerequisite tox-scans for alcohol and drugs, and that yes, it was an unusual condition for someone forty-one years of age but not unheard of, and that her son was sixty pounds overweight and the heart disease could have been caused by any number of things, and that they would know more by the end of the day. He hung up, removed his glasses, and rubbed fatigue from his eyes. To Boldt he said, "Found a guy dead in a hotel room. Couple thousand miles from home. No sign of violence. He had an ugly heart—twice the size of yours or mine. It killed him. I have a feeling he was into both booze and drugs. His liver didn't look good, and neither did his nasal passages. So we run the tests and this afternoon I speak with that woman again and tell her that her son abused himself chemically, and in the end it cost him his life.''

"Nice job you have."

"It has its moments." He returned to his seat. He carried his size casually. His eyes and his voice still held the tenderness of a young boy, but he had the intensity and the intelligence of a top doctor. He was the kind of man Boldt had always thought would make the best possible friend because he was so sincere. He was even-tempered and respected for the quality of his work.

"When do we get to Jane Doe?"

"We're cleaning her up for the autopsy. Shouldn't be long."

"How long had she been in the water?"

"I'd say two weeks, give or take a week. It depends how deep she went, how cold the water was. At least a couple of weeks. It takes sea life a while to strip them down to the bone like that."

"How would she have sunk with a wetsuit on? That doesn't seem right."

"Have to check with someone else on that. I've got a buddy I can refer you to. But this is one of the real thin suits. They aren't as buoyant as some of the others. But I see what you're chasing, Lou. My guess is that once she became water-heavy she went down. It would have been up to water temperature and currents then. At some point she touched bottom long enough for the crabs to get to her extremities. And to pick up that mud."

"Can the mud help us?"

"I doubt it," Dixon said, adding, "It's possible, I suppose."

"Can we hold on to some of it?"

"Sure." Dixon left the office and returned a few minutes later. "Too late for any kind of good sample. She's washed clean, almost ready for us. But we've got the swimsuit, and it's impregnated with the mud in places. For that kind of thing your best bet is to speak with Byron Rutledge over at the University. He's been studying the sound for years. Friend of mine. If anybody will know where her body has been, Rutledge will." After taking some coffee Dixon asked, "So what do you think? Am I wasting your time?"

"I appreciate the tip. Let's see it out."

"The lack of flesh on her wrists and ankles would keep us from seeing any bruises from ligatures. All we have is the damage to her throat, and those receipts. Sent them off, by the way. Know more after the autopsy."

Boldt explained. "If this is *his* work, then it's a whole new program. Two weeks ago he does this one and dumps her in the water. A week later he does DeHavelin. In between he does a clean job with Croy. Who knows what we'll see next? If it isn't him, then maybe there's no connection at all."

"I can hear it coming."

"What's that?"

"The copycat. I wouldn't bet too strongly on that."

"It's a possibility, Dixie. What we're doing here is considering possibilities."

"I'd like to have her out of here as soon as possible, Lou. We've been busy—ten guests last week—and there's no more room at the inn."

"How long will you hold her?"

"Ninety days, or until we know who she is and have someplace to send her. We'll need dental records, if you come up with a likely candidate. Without that, identification won't be easy. Which brings me to a delicate matter."

"I'm listening."

"It's about your Miss Gaynes. Before you arrived at Alki,

I had the opportunity to meet her. Don't misunderstand me, she's charming, attractive, and obviously quite bright.''

"But . . ."

"She's a little overeager, don't you think? She evidently called in while we were still on our way over here and asked for the cadaver's *exact* measurements. Now you and I both know, Lou, that measurements—as close as we can get them—are part of every report. We also know that after two weeks in the soup, we couldn't give you *exact* measurements, even if she was in perfect shape, which she isn't. You know what gases do to a body. We'll be lucky to even get close. My point is, we're plenty busy around here without redundant requests from Miss Gaynes. I'd prefer all requests come through you and that you filter whatever you can for us."

"Agreed."

"Thanks. I don't mean to be an old fart on this—"

"No problem."

"Okay," he said, rubbing his eyes, "okay, Lou, fine."

Royce knocked and entered. "She's all cleaned up, Doc. Should I set her up in room one?"

"Please. We'll be there in a minute."

Boldt heard Doc Dixon's use of "we" and he began to calculate how he could avoid the autopsy. He would never get used to them. He stood, slapped Royce on the arm, and said, "Keep up the good work." He left the office quickly. Two hours with a faceless corpse he didn't need.

Especially before lunch.

17

BOLDT RETURNED to the woods where Kate DeHavelin's body had been found. He had too many questions to answer, and the solitude here would help him. How had DeHavelin managed to get away, even briefly, when none of the others apparently had? And why had the killer taped DeHavelin's mouth shut, yet apparently none of the others?

He spent several minutes trying to figure out what the killer had done after the kill. Had he returned to her house, or had he cut through the woods? If Boldt could determine this, he might be able to reverse the strategy and determine how he had approached the house. At Croy's, the killer had approached from the backyard, but had gone around front before entering the house—this according to eyewitness Justin Levitt. He had been carrying something. But what? Women's clothes, including a hat with starched red fibers? Boldt no longer gave much credence to the transvestite theory. Justin Levitt had seen a man in blue jeans, and by the timing of events, how could the killer have had enough time to change his clothes? So he'd been carrying something. A hat? A bonnet?

He could find no additional evidence, other than the one print of the Rockport shoe. Toward the lake, where the earth in the woods was muddy and would have definitely shown footprints, none were to be found. Had the killer come through the dense woods? How had he left the area?

He searched the entire two-block area for tire tracks, hoping to connect the tracks behind Croy's to this kill, but again found no evidence. He wondered if the van spotted behind Croy's was as important to this investigation as it seemed to be. How many thousands of vans were there in the greater Seattle area?

Since his discussion with Daphne about the possible motives of a copycat killer, Boldt kept picturing a fellow cop lurking in the background. Looking over his shoulder. Angry. Jealous of him. The idea seemed absurd, but nothing could be completely ruled out. The only person Boldt *knew* was innocent of the crime was himself.

He drove back downtown, his mind still whirring. As he crested the hill on Aurora he saw the city below him. To his left, Interstate 5 was crammed with automobiles. Today he didn't notice the cheesy plastic signs. He saw instead the dockyards along the canal, the rust-colored hulls of fishing vessels languishing in the black water.

A few minutes later he parked in front of Bear Berensen's comedy bar, The Big Joke, and went inside. The windows needed cleaning and the sidewalk needed sweeping. A few construction types were eating clam baskets at the bar, drinking beer, and watching a silent music video on the overhead television. Boldt didn't recognize the bartender. It was like going home and finding a different mother in your kitchen. The bartender, a birdlike woman in her early forties, looked at him curiously. "Bear around?" he asked.

She had a husky voice and a wide, unattractive mouth. He found himself comparing her to Daphne—not Elizabeth —and a pang of guilt twitched somewhere inside him. "In the office," she tried to say politely.

"Tell him Monk's here, would you please?"

"Monk? As in Thelonious?"

"As in."

She shook her head in annoyance and picked up the phone.

Boldt lifted the keyboard cover on the baby grand and lovingly looked down at the ivories as a father looks into the cradle. He heard her mention "Monk," and heard her hang up the phone, but didn't take his eyes off the keyboard until she said, "Go ahead. One song is all, unless you're any good."

"Rusty," he said into her squinty eyes.

"That your real name?"

"No," he told her, giving up on conversation. The bench was wobbly and needed attention. The plastic on the low F had been chipped off. High C and high E showed cigarette scars. Inexcusable. He walked his fingers through the opening riff of "Blue Monk" and dropped a chord in with his left hand as a cushion. He closed his eyes, missed a note, and glanced back down at the keys to avoid butchering his attempt any further.

The melody brought back a flood of memories, as melodies often do. He could feel himself in a dozen different bars all at once. He could remember a few faces, and even one wild night with a redhead from somewhere in Nebraska.

The Bear had always been a little loud and a lot funny. He was one of these people who was too bright for his own good, far too sophisticated for Yakima High, and far too unworldly for the rest of the world. He and Boldt had teethed on jazz together and had both come over to college here, seeking fame, fortune, and women. Boldt had started out in agricultural sciences, having worked on plenty of orchards and thinking he had an understanding of farmers' problems. But his freshman year psych class had gotten him interested in the human mind. This, in turn, had led him into a course on criminal behavior. Then criminal sciences. And then he was hooked.

Bear dropped out of school, enlisting in the Army. Within six months he left for his first and only tour of Vietnam. He stepped on a land mine while sneaking off a trail to take a crap, and blew a piece of his right foot off and took

shrapnel in his left arm. They sewed most of his foot back
on, but were unable to find two of his toes, so Bear was
discharged and mailed a check every month of his life for
his disability. He claimed to have gained quite a reputation
as a comedian while overseas, though Boldt thought the
availability of strong pot had had something to do with that.
The last time he saw the Bear, the man was still chain-
smoking joints and guffawing at horrible jokes from the
back of his club. Still, the Bear had carved out a scene for
himself. He had a strong club that the college kids were
willing to travel downtown for, and a loyal lunch crowd
that helped cover costs. He leaned his weight on the piano
and said, "I'll be damned. If it isn't Dick Tracy. You've
been getting more press than a pair of cotton slacks. How's
the witch-hunt going?"

Bear had grown a beard that made him look tired and
older. He still had his penetrating brown eyes and black,
bushy eyebrows, of course, but his teeth weren't as white
as they had once been, and his eyes remained permanently
bloodshot. "Hey, Bear."

"What brings you by, Monk?"

"I miss the keys," he said, continuing to play.

"They've missed you. We all have. Check with me before
you go. I'll be the guy in the corner with the good buzz
on." Bear nodded and turned away, making a slow limping
trip through the bar. He must have signaled the bartender
for a milk, because a minute later one appeared on the piano.
Boldt played for forty-five minutes, ordered a clam basket,
and when it arrived joined Bear at a corner table away from
the scene.

"You want your old job back? I could use someone for
Happy Hour."

Boldt found himself toying with the idea for a moment.
"Can I take a raincheck?"

"Offer stands."

They stared at each other for a minute. Boldt went back
to the clam basket. "Good fries," he said.

"Got to change the oil regularly. Tricks of the trade," Bear said with a touch of self-pity in his voice.

Boldt couldn't imagine what it would be like to keep this place going, day in and day out. Nights until two or three. Days starting at nine or ten. Employees trying to cheat you. Customers trying to cheat you. Living your life in a place that smelled like stale beer and old cigars, where windows to the outside world were considered an intrusion, and conversation was tedious. No thanks. It made his life look pretty damn good.

That's what I came here for, he thought. This happens every time.

"How's your who-done-it going?" Bear wondered.

"Still don't know who-done-it."

"Why do they pay you?"

"Because nobody else took the job."

"Makes sense."

"We've got a crazy on our hands. Likes to tie up women."

"Who doesn't?"

"I left Elizabeth," Boldt told him. It took a moment to register.

"You what?"

Boldt nodded.

"Oh, Christ. That's a hell of a note."

"Speaking of notes, your piano needs tuning."

"Don't go changing subjects on me. You want to talk about it?"

"The piano or Elizabeth?"

"Don't turn this into an audition. I'm serious. You want to talk?"

"No."

"Oh. You came down on account of the good food."

"Sorry. Not much to talk about. She's been on my case for months. We lost total track of one another. She's into money. I don't know what I'm into. My job, I guess. Finding shooters. She wants to work her way up until she has a house in Broadmoor and a yacht at Shilshole."

"So what's wrong with that? A person could have worse dreams."

"She's been screwing a guy."

"Oh."

"At the Four Seasons, no less."

"Why not? The guy probably writes it off." Bear looked over, hoping to get a rise out of his buddy, but realized he had failed. "I used to be funny," he said.

"So, there you are."

"And where are you?"

"I'm renting on Interlake—over by Stone Way—behind the Allied Van place. Little two-bedroom house tucked back in behind an overgrown hedge. Porch smells like cat piss. Know anything you can do about that?"

"Burn it down." Failed again.

Boldt nodded. "I'm in the thirty-five hundred block if you're in the neighborhood. It's the only house you can't see from the road. Look for the jungle. That's me."

"Tarzan."

"Right."

"Sorry about Liz."

"Me too."

"Is it reconcilable?"

"I don't know. I love her. I must still love her, or I wouldn't hurt so much. I suppose most anything is reconcilable if you have the desire to make it right. I seem to be lacking in desire at the moment. It's only been a few days. That could change."

"Damn right. Go get yourself laid. That'll make you feel nice and guilty and then you'll be less angry with her."

Boldt smiled. "Is that how it works?"

"Damn right."

"I haven't been so good in that department lately. Know any remedies?"

"Kathleen Turner always does it for me. Her and the opening credits to the old James Bond flicks with Sean Connery. Naked fluffs swimming around with lights behind them. Rent yourself a couple of movies, and buy some sesame oil, the rest will come naturally. Try your left hand for a change.''

"You're disgusting sometimes, you know that?''

"What do think pays the bills? Kathleen Turner in *Body Heat*. I'm telling you, she can wake up the dead in all of us.''

Boldt couldn't resist chuckling. Bear would remain forever fifteen.

"You own a VCR?''

"No. I mean yes, but not any longer.''

"So rent one. *Body Heat*, I'm telling you.''

Boldt pulled out his wallet, but Bear stopped him, insisting he put it away. "One set of music equals one clam basket and a milk. We're even.''

"Is that how you're paying these days?''

"Happy Hour. Five to seven-thirty. Twenty bucks a set and all the milk you can drink. Keep me in mind.''

Boldt was standing. "I do that anyway, Bear. But I'll consider the gig.''

Without getting up, Bear reached out and the two shook hands. They held each other's hand and then let go. "Good to see you, Monk. Make it more often.''

"Now that I'm single, I'll probably live here.''

"Make a habit of it.''

On the way to the door Boldt closed the keyboard cover and rubbed the smooth surface of the piano's finish gently and thoughtfully, pausing briefly. Then he walked out.

18

BOLDT PHONED the office. Nothing cooking. A moment later he was patched through to Bobbie Gaynes, who asked him to meet her at a pastry shop on Northwest Market in Ballard.

She wore no raincoat today. She was dressed in black tapered slacks and a maroon-and-black—checked shirt with padded shoulders. She carried a big bag of a purse slung heavily over her shoulder and a black sweater over her arm. Her thick blond hair had an intentionally ruffled look about it. She was somehow sensual without that dazzling, synthetic beauty—the kind of woman to have a large appetite, a loud voice, and, judging by her walk, unerring self-confidence. She climbed onto the stool next to Boldt and wiggled to get comfortable.

Boldt felt himself stir. An encouraging sensation.

The central focus of the shop was a glass display case loaded with ordered rows of confections. Next to it was the cash register and a counter that seated six. This is what heaven must smell like, thought Boldt. He ordered a weird-looking thing with cherry filling in the cracks, and a de-caffeinated, with light cream. Gaynes ordered coffee, black, and a chocolate chip cookie with white frosting, telling him she shouldn't do this. He told her she didn't appear the kind of woman who had to worry about such things, assuming it was what she wanted to hear, and, judging by her reaction, decided it was. He stared at a wall that held a list of signs hooked in place, which presumably changed daily depending on what was fresh. A basket of day-old bread—*1 Bag, $1,* the handwritten note said—sat to the left of the cash register, two baguettes aimed at Boldt like the unwelcome end of a double-barrel shotgun. He glanced at them occasionally, annoyed by their intrusion.

"Sorry to bother you," she said.

"No problem. I want to be kept up to speed on this. You know that."

"You told me to call."

"Listen, Bobbie, no problem. Really. What's up?"

"I've located three possible candidates for Jane Doe," she began. "That's out of two dozen missing-person reports. I.D. didn't get squat. The ME says she was about five-ten and one thirty to one thirty-five. Three water-accident victims matched those stats. If a report wasn't water-related, I didn't bother with it."

"Good."

"No sense in making this more difficult than it has to be."

Keep this up, Boldt thought, and we'll get along just fine.

"The three are Lidestri, Norvak, and Banduci. I think we can scratch Lidestri off the list, though. I spoke to her mother. She was sailing with some friends and went overboard in a squall. She was wearing white pants, sneakers, and a mackinaw. Couldn't swim." She paused, clearly uncomfortable with the thought. The waitress, a tireless woman with a face like the Wicked Witch of the West, absentmindedly refilled Boldt's cup with real coffee and he slid it aside.

"Tell her," Bobbie demanded, noticing the mistake.

"Nah . . ."

"Excuse me," Bobbie said, rising off her stool.

Boldt reached out and pulled her back down.

The waitress turned.

Bobbie told her, "You poured real coffee into his cup. He's drinking decaf."

The waitress puckered her lips, then asked Boldt, "Is that right?"

"Decaf," Boldt said. This woman's annoyed expression made him feel awkward about being right. Shades of Kramer.

"He'd like a new cup," Bobbie informed the woman.

The waitress was not happy.

"Please," Bobbie said artificially.

Boldt began to object, but Bobbie squeezed his forearm to stop him. She had a lot of strength for her size.

The waitress brought a fresh cup of decaf. "Sorry about that," she apologized.

"No problem," said Boldt.

When the waitress was out of earshot, Bobbie explained, "I waitressed in college. There's no excuse for that." She nibbled on her cookie.

Boldt sipped the piping-hot decaf. Yes, you've got spunk, he thought.

She said, "Betsy Norvak was reported missing by her boyfriend last Wednesday. Her van and windsurfing stuff are gone. She was a 'fitness fanatic and sailboarding freak'—his words—and her physical characteristics are the closest match we have.

"Our last bet is Karla Banduci," she added. "Struck by a boat while waterskiing, her husband at the wheel. I called his work number. They suggested I try his favorite watering hole, which is a bar across the street from here. He hasn't been to work for ten days and likes vodka. I know you've got better things to do, but regs recommend a partner on this kind of thing, and I guess we're partners. I could have gone it alone but—"

"No problem. Have you established he's in there?"

"Yes. I phoned before we spoke. Bartender says he's there but in no shape to talk to the cops. I told him to keep our conversation private and he said he would. So I guess I should say he *was* in there.''

"Let's have a look." Boldt wiped his chin, slurped down his decaf, and left a fifty-five-cent tip.

Bobbie snatched up a quarter and handed it back to him at the door. "Don't encourage that kind of service," she scolded, and opened the door for him. "Besides, yours wasn't fresh.''

"How'd you know that?''

She tapped her temple. "Power of observation.''

"Oh." He motioned for her to go first, and she obliged.

Good, he thought. At least she's willing to yield now and then.

Joe Banduci was on a barstool at The Salt & Wind. He and the bartender and two others were watching TV with the sound off. The jukebox pounded out a Z. Z. Top song.

Lou Boldt introduced himself and Detective Gaynes to Banduci and asked if they might sit away from the bar where it was more quiet. Banduci had coloring much like John LaMoia—black hair, persistent beard, and brown eyes— but his beer belly gave away his hobby, as did the dazed look in his glassy eyes. "Sure," Banduci said, having no trouble with balance as he led them to the far corner by the silent jukebox. "This about Karla?"

"Yes, sir," replied Gaynes. Boldt nodded to her, signaling her to continue. He sat back and listened.

"We're here to ask you some questions," she told him.

"Surprise," Banduci said.

"You filed a missing-person report—"

"No. I notified the Coast Guard that I lost my wife waterskiing. She was down, you know. All I was doing was going back to pick her up. It was my turn next . . ." he trailed off, engulfed in a drunken sadness. "Next thing I know . . . Jesus.''

"You signed a missing-person report.''

"I filled out all sorts of forms. Big deal. It didn't bring her back, did it?"

"You reported your wife as five-foot-eight-and-a-half-inches tall, about one hundred and thirty pounds."

He wasn't listening clearly. "I turned away. I cut it hard to starboard and kicked it into neutral." He closed his eyes. "I heard it, you know. I heard it hit her. And I felt it in my legs . . ." He opened his bloodshot, jaundiced eyes. "What do *you* want?" he asked, as if seeing her for the first time. "You a cop?"

"That's right," she said, looking over at Boldt, who simply nodded back at her.

"You're fucking gorgeous," Banduci slobbered. "You're a cop?" he asked incredulously.

Her tone grew more aggressive. "Wasn't it a little cold to be waterskiing, Mr. Banduci?"

He shook his head. "We were out on Lake Union," he said. "Fucking beautiful afternoon. Hot September day."

"In the report it said she was wearing a wetsuit. Would you tell us please what your wife was wearing at the time of the accident."

"That day?"

"Just at the time of the accident, please."

He closed his eyes and rocked to one side. "The accident?"

"That's right. What was she *wearing*?"

"Wearing?" He opened his eyes and swayed some more. "Wetsuit top and her bathing suit, same as always."

"What make of wetsuit?"

"Make? Oneil, same as mine. I bought us both vests for Christmas, last . . . no, year before last."

Bobbie shook her head at Boldt, indicating they didn't have a match. "And her swimsuit? What kind of suit was it?"

"Fuck, I don't know. Blue I think. Tiny little thing. You know, like everybody else wears."

"Was it a one-piece or—"

"Hell, no. A bikini, you *know*. A blue bikini. Nothing to it, really. Tiny little thing. She saw it in my *Sports Illi*. Lots of leg and cheeks, you know."

"A blue bikini," she repeated, writing it down on a small pad. "And how was it cut? Was it cut high or low? French-cut or brief?"

"You know," he said, drawing a line on himself. "Like this here. Like everybody else wears. She saw it in my *Sports Illi*."

"It doesn't check out," she told Boldt.

He nodded and asked, reading from the report she had handed him, "Mr. Banduci. Can you describe any wounds you might have spotted?"

Banduci nodded but didn't say anything. He began to weep and then dragged his forearm across his eyes.

"You did, or did not, see her after the accident?" Boldt repeated.

"She must have tried to dive when she saw me coming. Her head and neck were a mess," he said. "If I thought we were going to have any trouble, I would have had her wear the belt. You know, the belt that keeps you up. She was floating for a second. I *saw* her floating. I thought the wetsuit would keep her up. Maybe she came out of it, I don't know. I should have been able to find her. But she wasn't anywhere."

Bobbie said, "Mr. Banduci, a lot of women who wear high-cut swimsuits have to shave more than their legs, if you follow me. The suits are cut pretty narrow in the crotch. Did your wife trim herself? Her pubic hair?"

He looked at her puzzled. Then over to Boldt.

"Answer the question, please," Boldt suggested, not having thought of it himself.

"Whatever you say, lady. How 'bout you? You shave your pussy?"

She blushed.

"Watch your mouth . . ." Boldt warned.

"Yeah, yeah."

". . . and answer the question."

He shrugged. "I don't know. Maybe she did. I suppose she did. You say she did, then she did. How 'bout a drink?"

Boldt looked over at Bobbie Gaynes and cocked his head, indicating they should leave. She nodded, and a moment later they were back out on the street, squinting as their eyes adjusted.

She didn't look at Boldt but she said, "Well, Jane Doe's not Karla Banduci. The woman we found was wearing a Body Glove wetsuit and a Speedo one-piece."

"Who's the other one?"

"Betsy Norvak. The windsurfer."

19

BETSY NORVAK'S PROPERTY, five minutes northeast of Carkeek Park, bordered the south shore of Haller Lake. The house was red brick with white trim. The trees caught the wind, leaves rustling noisily overhead. Further to the east droned the incessant insectlike traffic on I-5.

"It's quiet," Bobbie said, her ears accustomed to such noises.

The house was well hidden by dense landscaping, and removed from the nearest neighbor by a good fifty yards. A wooden picket gate leading to the backyard banged intermittently against a white painted post. A calico cat dashed from a hedge toward the woods, across Boldt's path. He was thankful it wasn't black. "I'll check the back," he told her as he walked through the gate and latched it shut behind himself.

He passed a propane barbecue cooker as he rounded the corner onto a brick patio. The barbecue was partially protected from the elements by the overhead deck, which was supported by roughhewn columns. A wheeled wooden cart sat next to the barbecue, a pair of long tongs resting atop it, and a garden hose hung from the wall. Across from him, on the other side of the house, was the continuation of the driveway leading to a small brick garage, its doors open. He peered through a downstairs window into a room occupied by a Ping-Pong table, a dart board, and two stereo speakers. The next room over appeared to be a narrow laundry room, housing a washer and dryer and a long curtain rod filled with empty hangers. Boldt's curiosity got the better of him, and he felt tempted to break in and have a look around. The last room on this lower level had the curtains drawn.

Using his handkerchief as a glove, he opened the first of three trash cans. Several flies flew out immediately, and the smell of garbage caught his attention. He wondered why all garbage smelled the same. Resting on the top of the bulging black plastic trash bags were two paper plates, folded in half. He left the lid off and opened the next can, and then the next. More black plastic bags.

He tried to feel fear. He wanted to experience a victim's fear, but he could not. He didn't feel anything. So much for psychic power, he thought, for he had already decided something was amiss here, but he couldn't put his finger on it.

The redwood stairs from the deck turned at a single landing and ended at two oversized posts that supported big pots of flowers. As he climbed toward the deck, he looked out on the backyard and grew envious of the landscaping. Boldt had once been a weekend gardener, and Norvak's place was a showcase. The grounds were immaculately kept. Two kidney-shaped flower gardens opposed each other with a circular garden/birdbath between their far ends. Of the fifteen fully mature trees he could see, no two were of similar species. If there was one thing Seattle was good for it was gardening, and Norvak had taken full advantage of the variety of flora that thrive in the climate. Beyond the birdbath was a manicured stretch of lawn dotted with trees, and slightly behind the garage he saw a vegetable garden plot —square-foot method—that appeared to have been pampered for years. The berries had been in at least ten years by the size of the patch, and the entire plot was bordered with tall mint that introduced itself in the breeze. He could smell it from where he stood. She had a lovely view of Haller Lake. He could imagine Betsy Norvak strolling out onto her deck, a cup of hot coffee in hand.

A dart of pain needled him, for he suddenly understood that this was what Elizabeth had wanted. This was the house and the lawn, the privacy and the prestige. It made his rental look like a tract house—which thirty years ago it probably had been. He stood there trying to forgive Elizabeth and found it difficult if not impossible, and this failure hurt him greatly for he knew forgiveness was a virtue. He wondered now if he had compromised and agreed to a new home if he would have been happily married at this moment. Had his own ego prevented the marriage from working? Was it his fault, not hers? He looked back out to the yard feeling as dazed as if someone had struck him. Could the marriage be saved?

There was no way one person handled grounds like this alone, so Norvak obviously had help. The lawn had been mowed within the last two days. Boldt made a note of that.

"Sergeant," Bobbie called out from the garage, standing beneath a rusted basketball hoop and faded backboard, "you might want to look at this."

The plate-glass doors behind him revealed a magnificent kitchen. He stared through the glass in awe for a moment, thinking again about Elizabeth. He could almost see the two of them working together in the kitchen like that, he prepping vegetables, she orchestrating the actual cooking—their routine a long time ago.

"Sergeant?" she repeated.

"Coming," he acknowledged.

When he caught up to her he was facing the interior of the garage. Norvak used the far wall for gardening and lawn tools. A door had been added to access these from the back. A short sailboard was fastened to the right wall with padded black right-angle brackets, two sails stored below it. An area for another board was empty, and its sails missing. Judging by the twin tracks of mud and pebbles, her car had been parked to the left. A ten-speed bike leaned against the left wall, and some beach chairs and odds-and-ends were hung up there as well. She pointed to the void on the wall and said that the car and the windsurfer were missing, thus confirming the missing-person report. She was about to step inside when Boldt blocked her with his forearm.

On the dusty cement of the garage floor, amid countless faint impressions left by meandering shoes, he spotted the outline of a large shoe and two words stenciled in the dust: *Vibram; Rockport.* "Call I.D.," he said. "Talk to Chuck Abrams. Tell him we've got another Rockport print. He'll know what you mean. He'll need a search warrant. Have him meet us as soon as he can."

She looked at him curiously.

"Now," he barked, immediately regretting his tone of voice.

He studied the scene carefully. The shoe print was aimed toward an empty section of wall where a sailboard had hung. He knelt to try and catch the light differently to see more of the floor. It seemed to him that a set of rounded toes made a line from the wall back toward where the car had been parked.

When Bobbie returned, he left her as a sentry and decided to circle the garage once, looking for other prints. But a brick path led to the back, removing the possibility of finding any. As he approached the garden he glanced at the building. To the left of the door he noticed a burn barrel, and he went over to it. The rusty fifty-five-gallon drum was riddled with drill holes to aid combustion. On top of the pile lay the charred remains of several thick paper sacks. Boldt couldn't locate a stick—the place was too damn clean. He resorted to pulling up a small wooden stake from the garden and, after banging the mud from it, used it to leaf through the ashes. Beneath the layer of charred paper he discovered a pile of incinerated fabric, well stirred.

His heart beating rapidly, he withdrew the stake carefully, preserving the evidence as best he could for I.D. He knew it might be nothing more than a pile of rags. But then again . . .

On the far side of the garage were two more fifty-five-gallon drums, tall fenceposts packed into them. On closer inspection he found they were soaking in a reddish chemical that smelled horrible. Several of the treated posts were stacked alongside the wall. The leaves had been scraped up here. He studied the area for several minutes. Then the others arrived.

Chuck Abrams, the best I.D. technician Boldt knew, was a short, balding black man in his mid-forties with a wide forehead, big ears, and sparse graying hair. He caught up with Boldt outside the garage, and set down the two heavy bags he had brought with him. He handed Boldt a folded piece of paper. "You haven't gone inside there, I hope?" Abrams was a stickler for detail. It was what made him such a good I.D. tech, but his adherence to regs could be frustrating to a detective. Boldt and he were good friends, but on the job that didn't count.

"Waited for you," Boldt explained.

"Can't get inside the house. The warrant permits me, and me alone, to go inside the garage in order to shoot the shoe impressions. But that's as far as it goes. The door was open, I take it?"

Boldt nodded.

"Lou?" Abrams looked at him skeptically.

"I promise you, Abe. This is how we found it."

"Good."

"One other thing," Boldt said. "I found something in a burn barrel out back. Can we bag it?"

"Anything outside the buildings we're okay on. It's 'crossing the threshold' we're concerned about," Abrams explained. "If I can match these shoe prints to the ones at DeHavelin's, we've got a different story. But that'll have to be done in the shop. Until then we don't touch anything inside the garage and we don't kick the house. There's more than one pair of Rockports in Seattle. That's the point, Lou.

We can't go kicking a place because some guy wears Rock-ports.''

Abrams had his bag open. He placed a piece of white tape along the bottom of a metal ruler. ''What's the case number?'' Boldt had Bobbie retrieve her paperwork from the car and give Abrams the number. The man wrote the number on the tape. ''I'll shoot these and blow 'em up one-to-one. Then we'll compare 'em with the plaster we took from the DeHavelin site.''

Abrams spent fifteen minutes taking the photographs, after which Boldt led him back to the burn barrel. Abrams dug down below the burned cardboard. ''You're right,'' he said. ''It might be clothing. But people often use old cloth-ing for rags. Don't forget that.''

''But not synthetics, right? They don't hold the dust.''

''Right. State lab should be able to tell you what kind of fabrics these were. You're thinking maybe you found a specific piece of clothing? You're thinking that shoe impres-sion will match the one we found at DeHavelin's—not that my opinion's worth a damn.'' Abrams had a habit of putting himself down. His opinion was worth plenty. Many a time his testimony alone had swayed a jury. He started to fill another bag. ''Those shoe prints are a different story. We haven't got much there. No full prints, that is. But we can probably give you a size, and by the lack of definition on the letters—that indicates wear—we may be able to tie them to the ones my people casted at the DeHavelin site. That would be nice, right?''

Boldt was aware that some detectives in the department occasionally made it clear to Abrams what they needed from I.D., in hopes of expediting their findings. Abrams was on record as being annoyed by such practices. ''I want whatever you find. Let's put it that way.''

''Good.''

''And you found prints on the paper plates in the trash?''

''Yeah, and on the barbecue tongs, too. We dusted the shit out of that cooker and the handles on the glass doors, but they were clean. Maybe too clean, if you hear what I'm saying.''

He finished bagging the ashes and dug down further. ''That's it. Anything else?''

''Sooner than later would be nice.''

''I'll see what I can do.''

Bobbie was standing by the corner of the building. Boldt hadn't noticed her. ''You want to talk with the boyfriend? He filed the report.''

''Set it up,'' he said to her. As he reached her, he patted her on the back and told her, ''Nice work, Detective. You're right on top of things.''

''Thanks, Sergeant,'' she said.

''How about calling me Lou?''

''How 'bout it?'' she asked, crossing in front of the car and looking over at him with a grin.

20

ON MONDAY MORNING, Boldt and Gaynes interviewed David Montrose. He was a French-Canadian linguistics expert on loan to the University through some kind of cultural exchange that he explained but Boldt tuned out. His teeth resembled headstones in a poorly maintained graveyard, twisted and leaning and of different heights. Unlike some irregular sets of teeth, his served to enhance his character and give him a kind of swarthy look that worked well with his wild hair and fiercely blue eyes. He had a soothing, hypnotic accent and manner of speaking—he professionally avoided inverting his prepositional phrases and misplacing his modifiers—and Boldt noticed that his young detective couldn't keep her eyes off him. Boldt distrusted him immediately, for he was far too sure of himself and was well practiced in first-impression performances.

"It is true. I filled out the report for the police. But please, do not jump to any conclusions," Montrose looked at Bobbie and glowed. "Our romance was all but over. If I may speak frankly: she is the kind of woman who does not accept rejection well. She has too much money and has had her way for far too long. Mind you, I did not see this at first, but this is exactly the way it is. We had a fight, and so I spent the night alone."

"What night was that?" Bobbie interrupted.

Montrose thought about it. "Friday."

"The date?" Boldt asked.

"Two weeks ago, last Friday."

Boldt looked to Bobbie, who said, "September thirtieth."

Montrose continued, "However, this was not the first time such a thing had happened, and she would, most often, call the next morning and apologize. Call it intuition. Perhaps it is more the male ego." He looked over at Boldt. "When I did not hear from her I telephoned and was unable to make a connection. I tried again a few evenings later—that would have been Tuesday, I think—and then drove my automobile to her house and waited for her. Her board-sailing equipment was absent from the garage as was her minivan and so I presumed she had gone sailing, though I must admit this surprised me some."

"Why's that?" Boldt interrupted. Montrose struck him as the kind of man who never stops talking. He was impressed with himself and would be comfortable dominating a conversation for hours. It was fine for a professor of linguistics, but not ideal for police questioning. Boldt was glad they were standing, thinking it might have turned into a filibuster had they been seated.

Montrose was annoyed by the interruption. "She is something of a fitness fanatic. Yes? Aerobics, weightlifting, this sort of thing. But the board-sailing most of all! This is her love."

"You said it surprised you." Boldt cut him off again and gave him a look that said he meant business. He nodded for the man to continue.

"She's had a bad elbow for quite some time. From the board-sailing, I think."

"Was she seeing a doctor about it?"

"Yes. A bone doctor." He glanced at the ceiling for help. "The term is . . ."

"Orthopedics," Bobbie filled in.

He smiled, flashing those ragged teeth. "Yes, thank you. I do not know his name."

Boldt made a note of it. Montrose had unusually short feet and was wearing black leather Italian shoes. Even so, Boldt asked him if he owned a pair of Rockports. Montrose appeared insulted by the question. He looked himself over. He said, "Please, Lieutenant. Do I look like I would own a pair of *Rockports*?"

Boldt then asked him for a *brief* history of their friendship, and Montrose claimed to have met her while pumping iron at The Body Shop, that they had initially enjoyed a casual relationship together that eventually developed into something more "dynamic," and that until a few weeks ago he had been seeing her "regularly."

Mention of The Body Shop grabbed Boldt's interest. LaMoia had mentioned health clubs when listing places the victims had frequented prior to their murders. There was no room for coincidence in police work. At least not in Lou Boldt's opinion. A health club would make as good a place as any to spot a victim.

Bobbie asked, "What would she have worn windsurfing, and where would she have gone?"

Montrose grinned and touched the edge of his lip as if a mustache were growing there. Or was he hiding his teeth? "She wears a wetsuit, Miss Gaynes."

"What style swimsuit?" she asked.

"No, I do not think you understand me, Miss Gaynes. A wetsuit. That is all. No swimming suit." He looked to Boldt and explained, "She likes the way such a suit feels against her . . . skin. Yes? No suit."

"Are you sure?" she asked, puzzled by the contradiction.

"Listen, *this* is something I should know about. Is it not? For instance, she sometimes works out in one of those plastic suits—nothing underneath. Nothing at all. She likes this very much. Other things too. Take my word for it. She is very unconventional in most every way. She does these things to be different, to pretend she is not the spoiled rich girl she is. I think she will outgrow these things in time. Some day. Inside of the child there exists a delicate, tender woman waiting to blossom. You have met similar people?''

"She wouldn't go windsurfing in a Speedo?"

He shook his head. "Are you listening?" He looked at them both. "A leotard for working out, certainly. Sailing? Never. Take my word for it. This was one reason for buying the minivan, I think. She would drive over to Lake Washington, park, and change into the wetsuit in the back of the van.''

"What color was the van?" Boldt asked.

"Dark blue," Montrose answered.

"Why Lake Washington?" Boldt wondered. "Why not the sound?''

The man shrugged. "I do not think she sails the sound. What exactly is this about, Detective?"

Boldt didn't answer. Instead he asked him to further describe the van. Montrose did so in detail, down to the antenna that had been torn off by a vandal. Bobbie took notes. Montrose sounded like a used-car salesman in need of a commission. Boldt's initial distrust subsided. It wasn't distrust now so much as dislike. Montrose was full of himself. It didn't surprise Boldt that a woman would look elsewhere after a few months with him; yet at the same time, he could understand the attraction. Montrose had the frenzied look of a Left Bank artist, that cool soothing accent, and a hard body he packed into designer clothes. He was a Canadian who fancied himself a Continental European. He moved over to the wall, obviously expecting the detectives to follow, tugged open a window, and lit up a nonfilter cigarette. He inhaled so deeply on his first drag that no smoke escaped when he said, "She has a very good tan. She spends a few minutes every day beneath the lights—you know, one of those machines. She bought one for herself, put it in the downstairs workout room.''

Boldt recalled the lower-level room with the curtains pulled and asked if that was what he was referring to, and it was.

Was this another opportunity for a voyeur to spot a potential victim? Boldt wondered. Croy with her midnight snack, Norvak with her tanning machine. This pattern of voyeurism seemed to fit the most recent killings. DeHavelin was the exception. She and her roommates had kept their bedroom shades pulled at all times because of a blindingly bright streetlamp, and had no known habits that would have had allowed a voyeur an opportunity to peep. But of course there were always opportunities. In a city, no life was perfectly private.

Haller Lake was far from Green Lake, yet within the BSU's three-mile radius. His heart sank, once again reminded of what a huge job it was. There had to be tens of thousands of people in that three-mile radius. Only one was the Cross Killer.

"You said your relationship was . . . isn't working out. Or did I misunderstand?" Bobbie Gaynes asked him.

"Betsy is a flirt. A tease. All the time I find her at The Body Shop, wearing next to nothing, showing herself off. What am I to do? These places . . . You see what I mean? Men go there to find the women. Women to find the men. I am afraid I do not appreciate a woman throwing her affections about in such obvious ways. You offer the correct bait, the fish will bite every time. Is it not so?" He pinched the cigarette between his lips and brushed his hands together. "Let her flirt all she wants now," he said maliciously, the cigarette bobbing, and then he sucked down more of the smoke. "She is nothing to me."

The interview continued for another fifteen minutes. Montrose explained that because of her financial independence, Norvak did not work. She was the daughter of a Philadelphian banker and had no family west of Chicago. He provided the detectives with a rough schedule of her typical day, which consisted mostly of windsurfing and

workouts at The Body Shop. She had three close friends
that he knew well. Bobbie took down their names, assuming
Boldt would have her contact them and arrange interviews.
Boldt questioned if Norvak would continue to windsurf,
given the cool fall weather; but Montrose said the wind was
terrific this time of year and that the "sailboarding addicts"
sailed whenever the wind was good.

"It doesn't match," Bobbie said when they were back in
the car. The sidewalks were cluttered with the usual variety:
young girls trying to look older, tenured professors trying
to look younger. For the most part they traveled in pairs
and trios, talking furiously and shifting stacks of books from
one arm to the other. A double-section bus took the corner
in front of them, bending in the middle, moving like an
inchworm. The billboard on its side advertised Boldt's favorite jazz station. He switched on the radio, and turned
the volume down. She continued, "If Montrose is right
about her wearing nothing underneath the wetsuit, then Jane
Doe probably isn't Betsy Norvak either." She hesitated.
"You want me to start all over with missing-person reports?
I swear to God I went through those things carefully, but
I'll try again if you want me to."

"I think he was talking through his hat. I don't think we
can go strictly on what he said. We have shoe prints in her
garage that may match a Cross Killer site. We have some
burned clothing. No car. We keep going on Norvak despite
Montrose. You want to go through the files again, that's
fine, probably a good idea. But I want you to check out
Jane Doe's wetsuit also—whether or not it's a rental."

"I thought you weren't interested in that." She sup-
pressed a smirk.

"Don't start with me," he said. "I want to find that
minivan, too."

"You didn't ask him if he had had a barbecue with her."

"No. I thought it better to wait. Abrams lifted a thumbprint from the paper plate." He paused, giving her a chance to see the connection, then said, "You remember when I handed Montrose my I.D.?"

"Yes."

"Do you recall how he took hold of it?"

She appeared puzzled.

"He placed his thumb directly on top of the plastic window."

"So you have a thumbprint."

"Exactly."

"I saw you fooling around with that on the way over—wiping it with your handkerchief—and I didn't get what you were up to."

"Now we have something to match against the print on the plates. We don't even know if the paper plates are significant. We may not have to involve Mr. Montrose at all, depending on what we find."

"Are you always this devious?"

"I don't consider it devious. It saves I.D. time and it saves Mr. Montrose time, and it saves the taxpayer money. We also don't have to tell Montrose more than we want to. I prefer to call it efficient."

"What about the health club? The Body Shop?" she asked.

"You think like a detective, Detective. That's good."

"You want me to look into it?"

"No. I want you to find her minivan. I'll drop you back at your car and you can try Lake Washington first. Call it in downtown and get her plates. See if it's been cited or ticketed in the last two weeks. See if it's been impounded."

"Lake Washington? We found her in the sound."

"Check the hot spots on Lake Washington first. Windsurfers are cliquish; someone may know her. They may be able to tell you where the good spots on the sound are. Or you could check the stores. Maybe they know her. That would give you a chance to nose around about wetsuit rentals. I don't care how you do it. Check Alki first if you want. Her van is our top priority, that's all.''

"We're looking for a pile of clothes in the back. Something like that.''

"When you find it," he said, trying Daphne's technique of implying success. "Look, but don't touch. We'll want I.D. to go over it.''

"What's going on, Lou? Norvak's not Jane Doe, nothing matches.''

"I don't know *what's* going on. I want a positive I.D. on Jane Doe. I want to know who she is. That's where we start. But I'm not giving up on Norvak, not until Abe tells me there's no connection.''

"What about The Body Shop?''

"I'll handle that," he told her.

21

DAPHNE MET HIM by the elevator. She was sitting on a bench in the hallway and she jumped up when she saw him. Her hair was full and lightly curled and her eyes intense. He didn't need to ask if something was up, because she rushed across the sterile corridor to intercept him. "Lou," she said, and he realized that somewhere, a week or so ago, she had stopped calling him by his last name. He considered that progress, though he didn't know toward what. His gut hurt and he resisted his Napoleonic stance as she continued, "He's here. The Levitt boy. He and his mother." She was excited, and like everything with Daphne it was contagious. He felt his skin prickle and his stomach turn again, and he had to lay a hand on his belly now because if he didn't, whatever was crawling around in there was going to bore a hole through and stain his new shirt. "He evidently remembers something about the killer and wants to tell you. John tried to help out . . ."

"Kramer?"

"Yes, Shoswitz pulled him off. The boy is obviously in a fragile condition. I would have questioned him, but it's you who should see him. You've established a bond with him and he wants to speak with you."

"How about the mother?"

"Extremely cooperative. Not at all the person you described. I gave them my office because it was quieter and I have that television, and he has an afternoon show he likes to watch, so that's what he's doing." She checked her watch, and then ran her fingers through her hair nervously. "The show ends in ten minutes. It's best if you let it finish and then speak with him. You can use my office. I'll keep the mother busy. Bad, huh?" she asked, noticing his hand on his abdomen. "You really should get that looked at."

"Bad doesn't begin to describe it," he said.

They both went back down in the elevator and he got a cup of coffee at the stand at the back of the building—just what his stomach needed—and then returned to the office and sat down at his desk, awaiting the end of the damn television show. Seven minutes had never dragged on so long.

Justin Levitt looked nervous. He greeted Boldt with a hearty handshake and the two sat facing each other. The boy looked tired and Boldt felt responsible. I've done to your life what the Cross Killer has done to mine, he thought. And at some point I'll have to come to grips with that.

"How you doing?" he asked.

The boy shrugged. "Okay, I guess. You were right," he said, hesitating, "about the hero stuff, I mean. Everyone wants to know what I saw. I haven't told anyone," he added, "just like I promised. But it's weird. I haven't been sleeping so good. We had to disconnect our phone, or change the number, or something."

"Why are you here, Justin?" Boldt asked. He had dealt with the boy as an adult before. No reason to change a winning formula.

"I know what he was carrying. It was cool. My dad came through the kitchen door last night, and I knew right away.

You told me some things might come back to me. You were right.''

"What was it, son?" Boldt was on the edge of his chair. He couldn't stand the tension. The little bubble began to build inside his chest and he closed his eyes and held it back.

"Flowers," the boy said. "He was carrying a bouquet of flowers. My dad brought my mom home a bouquet of roses last night and the way he was holding them— something—it just sort of connected all of a sudden. I could see the guy again. It was *rad*. For a second I could see the guy again, you know, crossing the backyard, and he was carrying flowers. I know that's what it was."

Silk flowers, Boldt thought. Red silk roses. What better way to get a woman to open her door for you than to pretend to be delivering flowers? She cracks the door . . . The killer steps inside . . . And then he pushes the door closed. . . .

He leaned forward, took Justin's small head in his hands, and pulled him to him, kissing him on the forehead. "God bless you!"

"Does it help?" the boy asked, blushing.

"You bet!"

The boy became caught up in Boldt's enthusiasm and began to ramble on about how his father came through the door and how he saw the bouquet, and how he knew he'd seen that somewhere else before, and how he knew it was *that* night—he claimed he could almost see the killer, could almost see the killer's face. . . .

"His face?" Boldt interrupted. "Justin, do you remember what he *looked like*?"

The boy seemed frozen in fear. He shook his head side to side slowly, eyes wide, staring at Lou Boldt. He cinched down his eyebrows and looked as if he might cry. "I can't," he whined. "I really can't. I want to. I want to help, but I can't remember. I just can't remember."

Boldt said calmly, "It doesn't matter, Justin. Don't sweat

it. You've been a big help. This is a big help. This is what we've needed.'' He stuck out his hand. "Thanks."

"Can I stick around a while, Mr. Boldt? You know, watch how you guys do things?"

"It's not very exciting, I'm afraid. If your mother says it's okay, it's okay with me, but all we really do is move a lot of paper around and talk on the phone. It's pretty boring, really.'' He heard himself say these words and he knew it was all too true. But someone has to do it, he convinced himself. And some of us do it better than others. "Stay here a minute, okay? I'll be right back."

He stepped out of the room and closed the door behind him, immediately approached by Mrs. Levitt and Daphne. Mrs. Levitt was a changed woman, demure and courteous. She asked, "Does it help you any? The flowers, I mean?"

He placed a hand on her arm and thanked her profusely, explaining it was the breakthrough they had been waiting for. He asked them to wait for him and hurried with the information to Shoswitz. He returned five minutes later and led them away from the door, from the boy's overhearing, and said to both, "I think there's a good chance he got a look at the killer and can't bring himself to recall the face. He so much as said so. It occurred to me," he said to Daphne, "that if the family agreed"—he glanced at Mrs. Levitt and offered a shy smile—"we might try putting him under hypnosis to see what he remembers. What do you think? Are you up to that?"

Daphne directed herself to Mrs. Levitt. "That's not for me to decide."

Mrs. Levitt studied them both. "Is there any danger to Justin?"

"No," Daphne assured her.

"No drugs or anything?"

Daphne smiled. "Nothing like that. I just help him to relax, to blank out any anxieties in the way of his memory and see what he can recall."

"I wish you'd do that for me," Boldt teased, drawing a smile from Mrs. Levitt, and a confused look from Daphne.

"It's fine with me, if Justin agrees," Mrs. Levitt said. "If it'll help . . ."

"Let's give it a try," Boldt said, "if you're game," he addressed Daphne.

She nodded. Their eyes met.

Something changed between them in that instant. He was reminded of her telling him that their relationship had long since passed the stage of friendship. He knew she was right, though he still resisted it. A single look between them and he sensed the rules had changed.

"I'll call you in when we're ready," she explained. "It's better that way . . . easier for him to relax."

Boldt turned around. Kramer was standing within earshot, pretending to be looking for something on an adjacent desk. Kramer said quite loudly, "He *saw* the killer's face?" Heads turned. Boldt took him by the arm and nearly dragged him into the firestair landing where they had some privacy. Kramer broke loose from Boldt's grip.

"What the hell, Kramer?"

"He saw the guy?"

"Tell the whole department, why don't you?"

"How 'bout keeping me informed?"

"You talk too much." Boldt immediately regretted having said it.

"Just what the hell does that mean?" Kramer's face was scarlet. He pushed Boldt. "Explain it!"

Boldt shoved him hard and backed him up. He pushed him again. Kramer gave ground. "Don't fuck with me, Kramer."

"I'm part of this investigation, damn it. I'm supposed to be included."

"You're a bullshit artist. You're a fucking bullshit artist who talked himself onto this task force with no damn qualifications."

Kramer took the first swing. He caught Boldt at the

base of his neck. Boldt delivered a hard right into the man's gut, bending him over, and then a left jab to the ribs. The effectiveness of Kramer's right arm was weakened by the blow and his left was useless. He didn't know how to fight.

The door swung open. It was LaMoia. "Shoswitz!" he spit out in warning.

The two detectives stood up. Kramer brushed his hair to the side. LaMoia came through the door and ran down the stairs out of sight.

Shoswitz pushed through the door. "Gentlemen?" he said. He stared glumly at them both. "Do we have a problem here?"

"No problem, Phil," Boldt said.

"Just comparing notes," Kramer acknowledged.

"Noisy notes," Shoswitz said. "Anything you'd like to share with me?"

"Got it handled," Kramer said.

Shoswitz held the door open for them. As they passed, Shoswitz said, "Use your heads, guys. I'd hate to toss you out of the game."

The two men passed in silence.

A few minutes later Daphne reappeared at her office door and ushered them inside and seated them in a businesslike manner. The boy, eyes shut, looked as if he was trying to take a nap.

Daphne sat down across from Justin; Mrs. Levitt and Lou Boldt sat in chairs to either side of her.

Daphne asked the boy to take her back to that night and describe what he was seeing. "You're up in your room," she said. "Can you see the house across the way?"

Justin Levitt nodded and said softly, ". . . The light's on in her room. I better lock my door . . . I'm setting up my telescope, same as always."

"You can see her now, Justin. What's she doing?"

"She's going over to her closet . . . same as always . . .

taking her clothes off. I can kind of see her shadow on the curtains. I see her ass as she goes into the bathroom. She's coming out. I see her tits, her pussy, *everything!*"

Mrs. Levitt tensed. Daphne interrupted, "Justin, can you tell me please, is she wearing a nightgown?" Boldt nodded—*good question*, he mouthed.

"No way! She's not wearing *anything!*"

"And now what?"

"She's going over to her bed. Shit, I lost her behind the curtains . . . oh, man . . . I can't see her . . . there . . . she's getting in bed . . . now she's turning on the TV."

"With the remote control?" Boldt wondered aloud.

Justin turned his head, his eyelids lifting slightly.

"Do you mind if Mr. Boldt asks you some questions, Justin?"

"No. I don't mind. I like Mr. Boldt a lot."

She nodded. "Then you can hear his voice now, can't you, Justin?"

"Hi, Justin," Boldt said.

"Sure I can. Hi, Mr. Boldt." He sounded half-asleep.

Boldt tried to think in present tense. It was disconcerting. They were talking about a woman who was lying naked in a refrigerator with a tag on her big toe. "Does she turn her television on with the remote control?"

"Sure. She always does."

"Always?" Boldt hesitated. "Do you watch her every night, Justin?"

The boy grinned. "Every night I can."

"Can *you* see the television?"

The grin uncurled on Justin's lips. "What do you think? Damn straight, I can."

His mother bit down on her lips. The lipstick stained her front teeth red.

"And what's she watching?"

"That stupid cable channel. Nothing *good* tonight."

"*Which* cable channel?"

"You know, the one with the weather and the ads and the music. She just uses it for background music, I think."

"Was—is she reading a book?"

"Maybe. I can't see her now. Just the TV with those stupid ads. Forget it."

"Go ahead," Daphne said.

Boldt felt himself cringe at the invasion of privacy. He apologized to Croy silently and listened as Justin continued.

"Forget the telescope. Nothing *good* tonight. . . . Hold it . . . someone's jumping her fence! A guy. Holy shit, I can't believe it . . . the telescope . . . can't find him . . . fuck, I can't find him. . . . There . . . there he is . . . his hand. He's carrying something . . . like a green funnel. . . ."

"The flowers," Boldt said.

"Yeah, flowers," Justin agreed. "That's right."

Daphne leaned over and whispered to Boldt, "Don't lead him on."

Boldt glanced over at the cassette recorder running on Daphne's desk. The red light was on and the hubs turning.

"His face," Boldt said anxiously. "Can you see his face?"

"Blue jeans. I lost him. . . . God damn, I lost the guy! I'm looking out my window now . . . he's going around the side of the house. . . ."

Boldt felt his heart beating faster.

"Shadows on her curtains. I'm back on the telescope now. She shuts off the TV and she's getting out of bed. I can see her tits and ass as she heads back toward the bathroom. She's putting her nightgown on . . . tying her robe. She's leaving the room. Can't see anything." He started shaking his head violently. Daphne looked over to Boldt and then back to the child.

"What is it?" Daphne asked in a gentle tone.

"Shh . . . Shadows. Oh, God . . . she's in trouble. I think she's in trouble . . . oh shit!" He sat shaking.

"It's okay . . ." she assured him. But the boy shook his head no.

Boldt sat stunned. He was there with the boy and Cheryl Croy and he felt cold, numb, and unable to help.

"He turned off the lights . . . don't pull the curtains, asshole! Let me see! Oh, shit. Mom. Dad? Should I tell them . . . shit . . . sure thing . . . that's a great idea. What am I gonna say? The curtains are blue now. Weird shadows bouncing on the curtains. I better pack it up . . . I'm putting the telescope away . . . I can hear Mom coming upstairs. Oh, shit . . . I run to the door and unlock it just as she knocks. . . ." Mrs. Levitt was crying, tears blurring her mascara and running down her cheeks. " 'I'm changing, Mom,' I tell her."

"Oh, God," Mrs. Levitt sobbed.

"Mom?" Justin Levitt asked in a different voice, opening his eyes completely and looking around with a puzzled and dazed look on his face. Staring at Daphne.

She asked him to close his eyes again and when he did she then brought him out of the hypnotic state slowly. It was obvious she had lost him to the sound of his mother's voice, and there was no sense in trying to go back.

Boldt turned off the cassette recorder and pocketed the tape. Daphne looked at him and indicated they should leave Justin to his mother.

"I wouldn't have had her in there," Daphne explained once she was alone with Boldt, "but he's a minor and I wasn't sure about the coercion laws. We were lucky to get her consent at all."

"You did fine."

"We could have had more."

"I'd like to try again."

"Not today. It wouldn't do much good today."

"You look tired," he told her.

"It's draining. It's a strange feeling, isn't it? He's back there and the rest of us are just sitting there looking on."

He nodded. "I felt it too. Yeah." And added, "It's good stuff, Daphne. We should have tried this sooner."

She shrugged and said fatalistically, "It happened now because it was supposed to happen now."

Boldt rolled his eyes. He hated comments like that.

"The truth is, Lou, it occurred to me last week when you came in and asked me about questioning the boy. I thought about trying light hypnosis then. But the patient has to be willing in order for it to work. All I really do is provide them with an atmosphere that feels safe. It wouldn't have worked the other day. He has to be ready or it doesn't work."

"I'd like to try again as soon as possible."

"We should get his parents' written consent and do it without them present. We should check with the prosecutor's office."

"I don't think we'll have any problems with his parents. She must have seen how much we can learn from him. Will you talk to her?"

She nodded and pinched fatigue from the bridge of her nose. "Sure," she said.

"Dinner later?"

"Thanks, Lou," she said, reaching over and touching his arm affectionately. "I don't think so. Not tonight."

"Busy?" he asked somewhat childishly.

She smiled at him with a patronizing look that offended him. "Later in the week?" she asked, not answering his question.

"Sure," he said, his disappointment obvious. "Later in the week." He held up the tape—"Got to run this by Shoswitz"—then turned, walking down the carpeted corridor past the dozens of office spaces that crowded the room.

Shoswitz said to Boldt, "Listen, while you were in there picking his brain, I've been going over this flower thing. This isn't going to be easy. Right? Most of the silk flowers

are made in Taiwan. What do you want to bet half the
distributors speak Pidgin English and aren't eager to talk
with the police? Probably don't have their green cards. Fan-
fucking-tastic.''

"How about the florists?"

"Kramer's on that. Try this out, we checked the yellow
pages: over one hundred ninety florists, more than sixty
plant shops, ten floral supply companies, another couple
dozen regional wholesalers—we're talking major-league in-
dustry here. Add to that the number of department stores
and gift shops that sell silk roses and you can see what we're
up against.''

"It's a start. How about the lab? All the flowers can't
be the same, right? Those red fibers may tell us something.''

"I'll ask. You may be right.''

"I'll talk to them,'' Boldt suggested. "I have to speak
with them about those receipts we found on Jane Doe anyway.''

"Anything new there?''

"We'll find out.''

"About this Jane Doe thing,'' Shoswitz said. "How come
you took that one?''

"Dixie wanted me to have a look because of the neck
wound. He's right, Phil. It's awfully similar. I learned my
lesson with Jergensen—I'm going after any and every lead
I get.''

"I don't know, Lou. I don't know.''

Boldt lowered his voice. "What would you say if I told
you we may be dealing with two killers and that one of
them may even be in this department?''

"I'd say you took a fastball in the head.''

"No joke, Phil.''

"Don't make this more complicated than it already is,
Lou. Rule number one. Right?''

"We have a sneaker print in the carport behind Croy's,
a different print at the DeHavelin site—different sizes, dif-

ferent weights. DeHavelin's mouth was taped, Croy's wasn't. Inconsistencies. Two different people.''

"Maybe. But as far as I'm concerned, we treat Jane Doe as an unidentified corpse. One step at a time. Right? Don't go swinging at bad pitches, Lou. Chasing down these silk flowers is going to take awhile. We'll be lucky to narrow it down to fifty or sixty stores. Christ, it could take us six months to do the paperwork on this. You go doing what you have to do. Who am I to argue? You're on a roll. Right? Keep it that way. Just don't get too sidetracked.''

"I'd like a warrant to get me inside Norvak's house. If we can get to her canceled checks, maybe we can find out who her dentist is and pull some X rays for comparison.''

"That's stretching it, Lou. We both read Abe's report. He can't match those shoe prints.''

"Not true. He's certain they're from the same shoe.''

"He can't prove it, Lou. Come on. We both read the same report. It won't convince a judge. We both know that. Abrams made that clear.''

"You could try.''

"I'll try.''

"Sure.'' Boldt hesitated. "Remind Kramer to keep all the specifics straight on this flower thing. We sure as hell don't want to lose that, too. That may be our only link to this guy. We don't want to blow it.''

"Point taken.'' He hesitated. "Do I want to know what that skirmish was all about?''

"Do you?''

"I think I do.''

"He was listening in again. He overheard me say the kid had seen our boy's face and he broadcast it to half the floor.'' Boldt thought twice and then said, "He's a liability, Phil. I don't trust him.''

"He's well organized and he's good at paperwork. You and I suck in that department. When was the last time you filled out a proper report? I pinch-hit for you all the time with records. He's good at what he does. We need him.''

"He's jealous of the fieldwork. He tries to involve himself in places he shouldn't. A secretary can handle the paperwork. LaMoia's twice the detective he is. If his father hadn't been—"

"Enough!" Shoswitz interrupted. "We're not breaking any new ground here."

"That's just the point, isn't it?" He turned and left the man's office.

22

THE YOUNG LAB technician wore wire-rim glasses and a white coat. He spoke in a low voice and kept his eyes trained intensely on Boldt. "We used the same procedure with these receipts that is used on valuable paperwork that has suffered water damage resulting from fighting a fire. The technique is to freeze-dry them, which removes all the moisture. We aren't equipped for that here, which is why this took awhile. Had to contract it out to an independent in San Francisco."

He led Boldt over to the counter where the two receipts were sealed between thick, clear plastic. "This particular paper—recycled—is air-sensitive following this procedure, so they've been hermetically sealed for protection."

"What are they?"

"We ran them through the mill, Detective. The paper of this one is recycled by Westvaco here in Washington. This stock is used as a carbonless insert in retail receipts. Unfortunately, the chemicals embedded in the carbonless paper are somewhat self-destructive, and in this case the ink has been nearly lost completely. We were able to pull a printed invoice number from the upper right-hand corner"—he pointed to a blank corner—"and the name of the company from here," he said, drawing an imaginary circle around another equally blank area. "The invoice is 1786 dash 45 and the company is Speedy Bee Dry Clean over on Fourth Ave. All the pertinent information is on here,'' he said, handing Boldt a typed piece of paper. ''We lost any chance at a name or items cleaned, I'm afraid, because of the ink, but, as you can see, we picked up the first half of the date: July seventh. No year. Got that from reading impressions.''

He pointed to the second piece of enclosed paper. It was torn and damaged. ''This did not fare nearly as well. It's a cheaper grade of paper, from somewhere in South America—we can't be sure which country, but we know from its composition that it's foreign stock—also packaged and sold as multiple receipts. Despite the apparent damage, we actually had better luck here, because the paper, though cheaper, is not embedded with inks. We don't know the store—but it's clearly not the same one. We lost the upper third of the receipt in the drying process. That's a fairly common problem. So we don't have a date or name for you, but we do have the item, a blouse, and a cost and tax.'' He pointed to the piece of paper Boldt was holding. ''The blouse cost a dollar seventy-five to clean and press, two dollars apiece for repairing two buttonholes. I know it isn't much, but this quality paper just doesn't hold up in saltwater. We were lucky to get anything.''

''Have we exhausted all our possibilities?''

''I'm afraid so. What you have there is as much as these things are going to tell us.''

Boldt thanked the man and requested that the receipts and reports be sent to the evidence room downtown, as always. He proceeded directly to Speedy Bee Dry Cleaning.

The man behind the counter was Vietnamese and spoke good English. It took him ten minutes to locate the store's copy of the receipt. The name on the invoice read *Johnson*. No address. The only item listed was a cotton sweater.

''What's this 'two' for? Two dollars?'' Boldt asked.

The small man turned the receipt around so he could read it. He looked up at Boldt. ''Two stains,'' he said.

"What kind of stains? Any way to know?"

The man pursed his lips and shook his head.

Boldt took the receipt as evidence with no complaints from the man.

For the hell of it he stopped at a pay phone before getting back in his car and leafed through the white pages. The listings for Johnson were a mile long. He slapped the big book shut and left it swinging below the phone.

23

THE BODY SHOP had once been an icehouse, used to supply commercial fishing boats with block ice for refrigeration at sea. In the early forties it had been duplexed, one half converted into a ballet studio, the other half into a furniture showroom. Now it was a three-story brick building with recently added Jeffersonian windows overlooking the harbor. The staircase leading to the desk was oak with a sturdy brass rail, Boston ferns overhead dangling their branches like green tentacles. Lionel Richie was pounding out "All Night Long" through small stereo speakers. A foxy woman wearing a turquoise Lycra body suit passed Boldt and smiled. The suit clung to her so tightly she might as well have been naked. Boldt stopped on the stairway stunned, and watched her ass shift back and forth as she continued down.

The woman at the desk had frosted blond hair, a drawn face, and a jutting chin. She wore a gymnasium-gray T-shirt torn above her navel, *Body Shop* silk-screened across small breasts. Her abdomen was a mahogany brown, flat and hard, and she wore pink, snugly fitting French-cut shorts that rode very high on her flank. "Hi, guy," she said in a slightly squeaky voice, straightening her already rigid posture so that her gray T-shirt nearly lifted off her.

"I'm considering membership," he explained. "I wondered if I might have a look around?"

"Sure!" she beamed. "I'd take you on a tour but Jan's sick with the flu and I'm stuck here alone at the moment." She looked at the wall clock. "It's almost six-thirty. I can show you around at seven, or you're welcome to just wander, or, if you'd like to work out you can pay a small visitor's fee and have full use of the facilities."

"I'll just look . . . look around, I think."

"Sure thing." She pointed, explaining that the lap pool and tanning salon were downstairs along with four Jaccuzzis: men and women's privates, and two coeds. This floor boasted three Nautilus rooms, one with a complete video setup—"all the latest stuff"—and a health bar. He was told he would find two aerobics rooms, personal trainer offices, a masseuse, and administration on the third floor. She handed him a brochure. "Everyone's real friendly. If you have any questions just ask."

He inquired about a rate schedule and she apologized, explaining that as a matter of policy, rate schedules were only made available *after* a tour.

A moment later Boldt saw why. He started out on the third floor where an aerobics class was underway. He could hear the thumping rock music through the glass and there were no speakers broadcasting Lionel in the halls up here, thank God. Nothing irritated him quite as much as the sound of two pieces of music playing simultaneously—except maybe cocktail parties, where ten people spoke at once. The thought of cocktail parties reminded him of Elizabeth, as everything seemed to these days. As her career had progressed, so had the necessity to attend cocktail parties. Boldt had avoided these affairs at every turn, often using his work as an excuse. No wonder she hated his work: it was always his most handy excuse. With each passing day he was feeling more responsible for the failure of their relationship. It takes two to tangle. A few days earlier it had seemed so blatantly her fault—she was *screwing* another man, for Christ's sake. But more recently he had begun to see things in terms of motivation—people do things for a reason—psychotics kill because they hear voices; psychopaths kill because they enjoy it; a wife finds a lover because she's lost one at home.

The sight of the aerobics class brought her to mind. In the early years of their marriage Elizabeth spent her mornings, seven days a week, working out to a television fitness show. Looking back on it, he realized how rough he had been on her, often not calling home at all, leaving her waiting for hours on end without word. In his particular occupation, lack of communication often meant trouble. *Officer down*—words they both feared. She had doted on Boldt like a worried mother, bending to the demands of his schedule, rarely complaining.

She was an intelligent, attractive, considerate, loving woman. All she had ever asked from him was a normal life—a home, maybe a family. But she had married into an abnormal life, a policeman's life. When he denied her these wishes, by virtually living at the office, she had eventually sought out a new life as a career woman. It all seemed much clearer now that they were apart. He had resisted any change in her, not overtly, but certainly subconsciously. He had grown accustomed to her waiting at home for him, focusing her world around him, as he focused his around the department. He took her growing interest in her career as a lack of interest in him. A threat. He sniped at her and cut her down in subtle ways, attempting to retain the control of her he had once had. He began to see another woman in her, and yet he wondered now if that woman had been real or simply a woman he had wanted to see. Had he only imagined the change in her?

These realizations came painfully to him. He could not put out of his mind the image of her flushed neck as she left the Four Seasons. Nor the various images of how that flush had gotten there. He knew only too well what she was like in bed—enthusiastic, hungry, eager. The controlled, demure housewife was someone, something, altogether different in the throes of her own pleasure. She threw herself into sex with a kind of limitless, wonderful abandon that he had always treasured as his own. Eager to find satisfaction, desperate for completion. And now she had shared it with another man, and he hated her for it. Absolutely hated her.

The thirty men and women who comprised the aerobics class were pumping, flexing, running, and leaping in unison to the sensual, thumping beat of the music. Boldt moved away from the window.

The other workout room was empty. He reached administration but the door was locked and business hours were posted as ten to five, Monday through Saturday.

The main floor's three rooms were filled with weightlifting equipment, floor-to-ceiling mirrors, indoor-outdoor carpet, and the bittersweet smell of physical activity. Grunting seemed to be an acceptable, if not desirable attribute, as did grimacing. No modesty here.

He had heard a lot of jokes about athletic clubs but had never bothered to visit one. Now he knew why. These kinds of body positions were meant for the privacy of one's home, or at the very least, in the sole company of one's own sex. It was too much for a bachelor. On a bench, not ten feet away, a frighteningly beautiful black woman was lying on her back, holding on to handlebars above her head and humping the air with severe pelvic thrusts, legs spread wide, feet flat on the floor. Boldt caught himself staring and moved on to the next room.

He caught sight of a hand waving at him. Mike Sharff, one of Doctor Dixon's autopsy assistants, motioned for him to come inside and join him. Sharff was balding and a few pounds heavy. He blinked a lot. Boldt weaved his way through the undulating bodies. Several women smiled at him, mid-flex. Boldt smiled back. He felt overdressed and out of place.

"What brings you here, Sergeant?" Sharff asked, his T-

shirt soaked at the armpits. "Never seen you around before."

"A case, actually."

"No kidding?" Sharff pulled Boldt away from the lifting
machine, allowing a heavyset man to take his place. They
stood near a mirror, and Boldt could see all the reversed
action over Sharff's shoulder.

"Mike, would you spot for me, please?" A petite woman
in a burgundy leotard had sneaked up behind them. "I'm
sorry," she said, suddenly connecting Boldt with Sharff.

"No problem," insisted Sharff, introducing her to Boldt.
Tina, he explained, was one of five people from the ME's
office who belonged to The Body Shop. She lay down
between them—it was disconcerting to Boldt—and Sharff
kept his hands ready to catch the weight bar she was pressing. Sharff explained that as a promo effort, the club had
offered offices group plans for five or more, and the ME's
office had signed up. "A bunch of your guys and gals work
out here too," he added. Boldt had wondered why the name
had seemed familiar, and now he vaguely remembered a
flyer crossing his desk last summer, and told Sharff so.

"Do either of you know a woman named Betsy Norvak?"
Boldt asked. "Five-foot-ten, blond hair?"

Sharff shook his head, " 'Betsy' doesn't ring any bells
with me." He glanced down at Tina's sweating face. "How
about you?"

She paused and looked up into Boldt's eyes. It seemed
to him the only time he looked down into a woman's eyes
like this was when he was making love with Elizabeth,
and the effect was both disarming and unsettling. Tina
explained, "You don't hear a lot of last names around
here, but I know a Betsy from aerobics. You know, Mike,
she's the one with the curly hair who wears the plastic
jumpsuits."

"That's her," Boldt said, remembering his conversation
with Montrose.

Tina told him, "A strange one, she is. Real serious about her routine. She's a competition windsurfer."

"Sure," Sharff said, nodding. "Sure," repeating himself, "I know who you mean."

"Have you seen her around lately?"

"Not lately," Tina replied.

"She have any close friends here that you're aware of?" Boldt asked them both.

Tina paused. "I think Sam's her personal trainer, isn't he?"

Sharff shrugged.

"Sam?" Boldt asked.

"Sam DeVito," she said. "If you can afford it," she explained, straining, "you hire a personal trainer. Betsy can afford anything." Her strained voice reminded Boldt of Elizabeth, when she tried to speak during their lovemaking. He wondered if he'd ever get Elizabeth off the brain. Did it mean he loved her, or had he simply developed a habit he now found difficult to break?

"DeVito is our resident stud," Sharff explained. "Chances are if he was her personal trainer he was probably more than that. You might want to speak with him."

"Mike!" Tina scolded.

"Well, it's true, isn't it?"

"Sam's a perfectly nice guy."

"And he jumps on anyone who looks good in a leotard," Sharff commented. Tina laughed, blushed, and shook her head. "Don't listen to him," she suggested. "All the guys are jealous of Sam."

"Jealous?" Sharff teased, though he appeared somewhat angry. "Not on your life."

"Where might I find this Sam?"

Sharff answered, "Personal trainer offices are on the third floor, but this time of night he probably is with a client. Try the next room over, or the lap pool. You can't miss him. He's a body builder—I mean a body *builder*. He trains all the serious body builders. He wears a red muscle shirt, gray full-length gymnastic pants, and a stopwatch around his neck. He has Frankie Avalon hair and a jaw that could take a baseball bat across it. Can't miss him.''

He also had beady dark eyes and a nose that had been hammered on a few times. Boldt found him in the humid, chlorinated room with the long, narrow pool. He was staring at the stopwatch. A gazelle of a woman was frantically swimming freestyle upstream against powerful jets that wouldn't allow her any progress. Her slight suit had slipped into the crack of her buttocks, exposing two finely tuned, glistening flanks. Sam studied the stopwatch. Boldt studied the woman. ''Harder,'' Sam yelled over the roar, and turned toward the wall, noticing Boldt for the first time and passing him to reach a panel there. He fiddled with a control and the jets suddenly roared more loudly. The lean woman lost some distance and then swam harder to keep up.

Boldt had to raise his voice to be heard. ''Sam DeVito?'' The trainer nodded. ''Sergeant Boldt,'' he showed his I.D. ''SPD, Homicide,'' he added for effect. He seldom mentioned his division, but it worked well if you wanted a person's attention. It had that effect on Sam. He forgot all about the stopwatch and directed his agate glare at Boldt.

''So what?'' he said, his arms flexing instinctively.

''I'd like to ask you a few questions.''

''Later.'' Sam returned his attention to the watch and screamed, ''*Faster*,'' at the woman. ''You want to develop or not?!''

''*Now!*'' Boldt corrected loudly, ''Not later.''

DeVito frowned at him, shoved out his jaw, and clicked the stopwatch defiantly. He went over to the panel and shut the machine down. The water stopped moving and the woman stood, adjusting her suit absentmindedly. ''What's the deal?'' she complained, nipples hard, pubic hair wildly escaping her crotch.

''Gimme fifty sit-ups,'' he said to her. She groaned. ''Back in a minute. Out here,'' he told Boldt.

He was short, maybe five-eight, but probably weighed close to two-twenty, and none of it fat. He had twenty-two-inch arms and equally developed thighs. He was disgusting. "I'm paid by the hour," he informed Boldt, "and I got a busy schedule."

Boldt recognized the accent as East Coast, maybe New Jersey. He'd met a couple FBI men with accents like that. He hadn't noticed it in the roar of the water jets. "Betsy Norvak," he said, and noticed DeVito's jaw muscles harden.

"What about her?"

"She's missing."

"You telling me? She's missed three sessions with me. Didn't bother to cancel. You know what that does to my bottom line?"

"Know where she might be?"

"Listen, pal. I got twelve regulars. Eighteen part-times this month. That leaves me just enough time to take a crap and tie my shoes in the morning. I'm not their nannies, though God knows I feel like it sometimes. They miss a scheduled appointment without canceling, I charge them half rate. That covers the house percentage and that's about all. Leaves me fucked, with an hour dead time, and no way to capitalize on it. You find Betsy, you tell her Sam is one pissed-off dude and that if she misses one more session she can find herself another P.T."

"You know her personally?" Boldt asked, recalling Sharff's comments.

"What's that supposed to mean?"

"Just what it sounds like. Personally. Get it?"

He hesitated too long. "No. No. That's not the way I do things around here."

"I hear she was pretty cute."

"They're *all* cute, pal. And they all got curves like Italian race cars—big deal—that doesn't mean I get *personal* with them."

"Not from what I hear."

His jaw muscles flexed again and he said, "That so?"

Boldt nodded. "I hear maybe you and Betsy were close."

"That's bullshit. Who told you that?"

"When was the last time you saw her?"

The muscle man seemed to realize this was more serious than he had initially thought, and he considered this question carefully. "I'd say about two weeks ago. I could check my book. My billings. I'd have a record of it."

"Would you do that?"

"Now?"

"Yeah, now."

"Shit."

"There are other ways we could go about this," Boldt explained.

"Okay, okay. Hold your water." Sam leaned his head back into the room. His voice echoed as he said, "Gimme two five-minute workouts. I'll be right back."

Boldt heard the swimmer whine a complaint but the trainer barked at her stiffly and shut the door. "Bitch," Sam said under his breath. Boldt followed him upstairs.

The trainer's records showed it as two weeks and three days since Betsy Norvak had kept an appointment with him, which approximately matched Doc Dixon's dating of the body. Boldt let him go back to the woman.

He asked around for another half hour, keeping one eye out for the trainer's departure. The man had struck Boldt as a liar and he wanted to keep an eye on him. A woman named Candy Langholf, no taller than five feet, with too much hip and thigh, claimed to know Betsy Norvak well. Boldt offered to buy her a fruit smoothie in the small health bar Coconuts. There were posters on the wall of oiled body builders, male and female. They turned Boldt's stomach. There were also shots from the *Sports Illustrated* swimsuit calendar, which Boldt found positively erotic.

"I haven't seen Betsy around here in a couple of weeks," she said.

He asked her when exactly and Candy Langholf said she

couldn't remember. Betsy had been having trouble with her elbow again—a recurring injury. Two men wearing muscle shirts entered the bar and ordered fresh-squeezed orange juice. They were talking loudly, and it distracted Boldt. One of them kept checking Boldt out with sideways glances.

"Did you ever meet a guy name Montrose, a Canadian from the University?"

"Her flame? Sure. He used to lift here. He made a real scene once. Came in looking for her. He was a little drunk and tried to literally drag her away. He had the wrong impression. It's a club, you know, and we all get to know each other, and it doesn't matter if a little hair escapes now and then or a boob pops out. We're all adults. We're all here for the same reason, most of us, and we all help each other come along. That crazy Canadian thought Betsy was trying to get laid all the time. Jeez! What an attitude problem. He didn't understand us at all."

"He made a scene?"

"Tried to take her home."

"And?"

"And Sam threatened to rearrange his body parts if he didn't vamoose. He took one look at Sam and hightailed it out of here."

"So Betsy didn't flirt?"

" 'Didn't'? Why the past tense? Say, just what kind of cop are you, anyway? Come to think about it, I better see your badge." She hopped off her stool and stood away from him. "After what's been happening lately . . ."

He fished out his I.D. wallet and opened it for her. The badge sparkled in the overhead light.

One of the guys at the bar saw the I.D., and a minute later the two were gone. Good riddance, thought Lou Boldt. "Homicide," he told Candy Langholf.

"Betsy?" she gasped in a whisper. "The Cross Killer?"

"No," he stated emphatically, and she seemed relieved. He wondered if it was the truth. "But we'd like to speak with her," he told her.

"She lives up past Carkeek."

"Yes."

"I really didn't know her all that well," she said, changing her story.

"How much truth is there in that she flirts a lot?" He changed the tense to reassure her.

"A lot of the girls come here for the guys. Vice versa too. But not Betsy."

"Meaning?"

"Betsy is real serious about her body, about her workouts. She races windsurfers. She wants to get on the international circuit . . . France, Hawaii, you know. She spends a lot of time at the Gorge during the summer months. Works out fall and winter here. But you couldn't call her a flirt. Not like some of the girls."

"Did Betsy have anything going with Sam?"

She chuckled. "You *do* get around."

"Is that a 'yes'?"

She shrugged. "Listen, Sam takes an interest in certain people. You hear all sorts of rumors, you know what I mean? Personally, I don't put much faith in them. Betsy bought herself some home gear. You know, tanning lights, a couple of weight machines. What the hell, she can afford it. So Sam has to spend some time over there setting up the stuff. He moonlights as a distributor, you know. That's how rumors get started. I wouldn't put much faith in them. There are enough rumors in a place like this to burn your ears off."

"But there *was* a rumor about Sam and Betsy?"

"It's inevitable. Sam comes to her rescue from the drunk Canadian. He drives her home. That's enough for most people around here. The truth is, since the AIDS thing, people are a lot less casual about sex. I'm not saying at one time there wasn't a lot of bed-hopping going on around here. Jeez, it was musical pillows for a while. But those days have passed. You can't be sure anymore. It makes for a lot less sex. There's a lot of dating still, but that's about it.''

Boldt thanked her and paid for the smoothies. The drink helped his gut. He thought it might be smart to stop at the store and buy some yogurt and fruit and try making one at home. He stopped in and said good-bye to Mike Sharff before leaving, thinking it important to keep good relations with the ME's office. Boldt's pager beeped, drawing the annoyed attention of nearly everyone in the room. On his way out the door he placed a call downtown. Bobbie's efforts had located Betsy Norvak's minivan at Carkeek Park.

Before he left, Boldt asked the receptionist when Sam was through for the night, and was told ten o'clock. It gave him a little over two hours. The woman stopped Boldt as he reached the door, her provocative torn T-shirt tempting his eyes as she bounced down the stairs and caught up to him.

She handed him a rate card.

The door jerked open. He stood face-to-face with Daphne Matthews, and behind her, John Kramer. She wore a pink velour sweatsuit and had her brown hair pulled back in a ponytail. With her hair back her jaw seemed stronger and her eyes bigger. She had tiny gold studs in her earlobes, which were red from the cold. Kramer was still in his office clothes, a flight bag in hand. Smiles fell from their faces and for a moment the three of them stood there in absolute silence. Boldt stared at her and felt the color drain from his face. What now? he wondered. Kramer mumbled, ''Hi, Lou,'' and tried to act casual, which was like a politician trying to sound funny. Lou Boldt didn't take his eyes off of Daphne. A smile finally twitched across her face, forced and unnatural.

''See ya,'' Boldt said. He brushed past, his bad knee bumping Kramer's flight bag in just the wrong place. He limped down the cement steps, feeling embarrassed, frustrated, and alone.

24

WIND HOWLED OFF the sound carrying a heavy salt mist, slapping Boldt's face, lifting his collar and finally untucking his shirt. Alongside the minivan, illuminated in profile by the blinding blue-white headlights from her car, Bobbie struggled to keep her skirt from flying. As Boldt approached, the back of the skirt jumped up around her shoulders and Boldt had a quick flash of her panty hose.

She slapped down the fabric and caught sight of him. She lifted her hands, showing him how her skirt danced in the wind, and said, "Wonderful night to be wearing a skirt. I was just headed out to dinner."

"What have we got?" he asked in an all-business tone of voice.

"It had been tagged here ten days ago. Was supposed to be impounded. We sifted through the paperwork and discovered it was still here. Towing contractor messed up. I've got a truck coming down to tow it into our garage."

Boldt called in on his radio and asked that Chuck Abrams meet him at the garage in thirty minutes. He got a flashlight from his trunk and walked back to the minivan. "Abrams'll meet us downtown," he said.

"You *do* have clout." He shrugged and shined the flashlight under the vehicle. She crouched down alongside him, gathering the hem of her skirt in a ball. "What are we looking for?" she asked.

"Keys," he said. He covered the entire area under the vehicle twice. Then he walked to the front of the van, slid underneath, and shined the light up into the bumper and suspension work. He climbed out and went to the rear of the van and repeated this. "Got 'em," he said. He fished a paper bag out of his coat pocket, opened it awkwardly, still lying down, and used his Bic pen to pry loose the magnetic Hide-a-Key box. It dropped into the bag. He climbed back out, carefully sealed the bag, and with Bobbie holding the flashlight, worked on forcing the small box open while it remained in the bag. It slid around like a wet bar of soap. He forced it into a corner and pushed with his thumb. "It's rusted shut, which means it's not where she kept her keys." He handed her the bag, took the flashlight, and crawled back under. He had her turn off her headlights—they overpowered the flashlight on the right side of the car—and he searched in vain for another hidden set of keys. He came out damp and dirty.

The tow truck's blinking orange light appeared in the distance. The driver was accustomed to working with detectives. He connected his towing rig without so much as brushing against the van, avoiding any chance of removing prints. Ten minutes later they were on the road.

The garage below the Public Safety building was a large indoor parking facility with rows of bright, overhead lights. Oil stains covered the smooth cement floor like spots on a leopard. Boldt looked through the side window of the van. "Nothing in there," he said to Bobbie. "No clothes, no sails, no nothing." He added, "Call Montrose. See if he knows what she did with her keys. Depending on what he says, check with the property room. See if that wetsuit had any inside pockets, any way we might have missed a set of keys."

"Now?"

"When did you have in mind? We've got his home phone, right?"

She hurried into the building.

Another car arrived. It was Chuck Abrams. He told Boldt, "You're aware it's dinnertime, I suppose." As Abrams went about the task of dusting for prints, he told Boldt, "Crime lab sent the report on those ashes over to us for some reason. I'm not sure those bozos will ever learn to read paperwork."

"And?"

"A blend of polyesters and a blob of neoprene."

"Meaning?"

"You're in a charming mood tonight."

"What's it mean, Chuck?"

"It means," Abrams said with an unusual harshness to his voice, "that you probably have a bathing suit and a wetsuit set afire with some of the Penta that was in those barrels."

"Penta?"

"Pentachlorophenol—the red stuff in the barrels. Wood preservative. In her case, it helps keep the wet ground from rotting her fenceposts. As far as the clothes are concerned, I asked state lab for an infrared spectrograph because I didn't think you'd know how to pronounce it. It may help narrow down the manufacturers, maybe even the original colors."

"Fantastic."

"And one other thing," Abrams said. "The paper on top of the burn pile was from two ninety-pound bags of dry cement. Portland cement, manufactured outside of Bremerton. Stuff's available all over the city."

"Cement?"

"That's right."

Boldt looked over at the empty van. "Oh, Christ."

"My sentiments exactly. It doesn't look good, Lou."

Boldt shook his head, still staring at the van. "Check the back for rust or cement dust, will you please?"

"You think he dumped her?"

"Those posts on the ground on the far side of the garage could have been in another barrel."

"We'll check the ground for Penta, too."

Boldt nodded. If someone had killed Betsy Norvak, burned her clothes, and stuffed her into a fifty-five-gallon drum which he then filled with cement and dumped, then who had washed ashore at Alki Point? And was it a coincidence that, in Norvak's backyard, a wetsuit and a bathing suit had been burned—the same two articles of clothing that Jane Doe had been wearing? What was the connection? More to the point, *who* was the connection? He said, "I read your report about the shoe prints."

"Sorry, Lou. I know you were hoping for something there. No way it'll hold up in court."

"Why not?"

"Only a partial impression; a photograph of a dust pattern on an uneven cement floor versus a plaster cast. Defense could tear us apart. But, as I said, it's as close to a match as you can get. Odds are they're from the same shoe. The same guy."

"But not for court."

"That's right."

"Damn." Boldt watched as the man dusted the windows with the black powder. I.D. used white or black, depending on the background color. The black powder was horrible; it always got all over everything and made a mess of your clothes.

"I've got a partial thumb on the outside mirror," Abrams said.

Boldt stepped closer and Abrams pointed. "It's a good partial," he said. "Left thumb, male. That's too bad."

"Why's that?"

"The print we lifted from the paper plate is from a *right* thumb. Same with the partial we lifted off that burnt match you found by Croy's. And we already know those two didn't match."

"Speaking of which. What about the prints on my wallet?"

"Your friend Montrose did not have a barbecue with Norvak, if that's what you're asking. The prints on the paper plates didn't match."

"My lucky day."

"What can I tell you?"

"You want to know where this stands, Abe?" Boldt answered before Abrams could reply: "I've got a corpse that washes up on Alki. The fingers have been chewed to the bone by sea life, so even if we could lift prints from her belongings, we've got nothing to match them with. Same with the feet. No way to match a baby record. So I have one of my people check out a missing-person report. We find a shoe print that may match an earlier death scene and a burn barrel that I find out contains clothes intentionally burned up. Now we locate the woman's missing van and it appears to have been wiped clean, only whoever was driving it last adjusted the outside mirror." His eyes lit up. "Do me a favor, let's estimate the driver's height from the angle of both mirrors. That may help."

Abrams liked the idea. He continued to dust around the outside of the van.

Bobbie appeared through a door at the far end of the garage, and a moment later was at Boldt's side. "Inside the gas flap," she said. "Montrose claims she left the keys inside the gas flap whenever she went windsurfing."

Boldt checked for himself. "Not there," he said. "I want you to speak with the Coast Guard in the morning and see if they have any reports of windsurfer debris off of Carkeek."

"No problem."

"And then I want you to make an appointment with a . . ." He searched for the name Dixie had given him a few days earlier. "Bainbridge . . . no, no . . ." He moved into better light and checked his spiral pad. "Rutledge. Dr.

Byron Rutledge over at the University's Marine Sciences department.''

"May I ask why?"

He nodded. "Dixie says Rutledge may be able to tell me what the sound had done with Jane Doe for the two weeks prior to our finding her. We've found Norvak's van at Carkeek, her body down at Alki. I want to make sure that makes sense.''

"You don't think it does. I can tell by your tone of voice.''

"Listen, Abrams came up with some evidence that suggests the possibility of foul play.''

"Like?"

"Like maybe Norvak's body is at the bottom of the sound in a few cubic yards of cement.'' He glanced at his watch.

"What is it?" she asked.

"I have a date," he said.

"So do I," she said, pointing out to him again that she was dressed up.

"Mine's with a body builder," he said.

"Mine's with James Royce."

He wasn't particularly surprised. "You be careful of him. I saw that look he gave you the other day.''

"Yes, Daddy," she mocked. "And I promise not to tell anyone about the body builder.'' She turned and walked away from him, giggling. "But I'd say you have more to worry about than I do.''

25

AT SEVEN MINUTES past ten Sam DeVito left The Body Shop. Boldt followed at a good distance. The body builder stopped first at his apartment, left the car running, and returned carrying something. He then stopped at an all-night diner that catered to the health-food set and picked up some takeout. Boldt assumed he had called in the order from his apartment, or even perhaps from the club.

As he turned north, in the direction of Carkeek Park and Haller Lake, Boldt knew where he was headed. He allowed him a good distance and followed patiently. When the man pulled to a stop at Norvak's a few minutes later, it came as no surprise. Boldt stopped a block away and approached on foot.

The night air was chilly. It cut through Boldt's jacket, stinging him. Boldt paused in a copse of trees as he neared the house, and rubbed his arms to keep warm.

Boldt edged his way to the fence, slipped through the gate, and stayed close to the house. He rounded the corner by the barbecue. He could hear the metallic clicking of tools. Through the cracks in the decking above, Boldt could see the thin yellow beam of light from a penlight. The man was holding it in his mouth, aiming it at the door.

Boldt withdrew his gun, suddenly regretting he had no backup. The trainer was nearly twice as thick as himself, certainly twice as strong. He held the gun aimed toward the sky and moved cautiously and quietly toward the redwood stairs on the far side.

He heard the sliding door grumble when it opened, and the light disappeared from overhead, making it more difficult for Boldt to see. The man was inside.

Boldt hurried to the stairs and climbed them nearly silently, reaching the deck quickly. From what he could make out in the darkness, the trainer had compromised the security device by unscrewing it from the wall and applying some jumper cables and a small battery. He had left the door open for a quick exit, if needed. Boldt reached the open door and stopped, listening intently. He couldn't make out any of the hollow sounds, couldn't tell if the man was five feet away or down a hallway. He stepped inside and opened his eyes wide.

He saw the play from the penlight as it barely illuminated a hallway that ran from the kitchen to points unknown. Boldt stepped forward in the darkness and continued on.

As he reached the hallway he saw the light again, this time coming from a bedroom at the end of the hall. Boldt moved silently toward the bedroom door and lowered his gun. The light caught his attention as it reflected in the medicine-cabinet mirror. The man was searching Betsy Norvak's bathroom. Boldt was willing to give him a few minutes to find whatever it was he was looking for. After several seconds DeVito's face appeared in the mirror, and, had he been able to see in the dark, he would have seen Boldt staring back at him.

Again he rummaged through the contents of the medicine cabinet, this time popping caps and inspecting the contents of the few pill bottles, the penlight held awkwardly in his mouth.

With a vial of pills open, he stepped toward the toilet, and that was when Boldt stopped him by switching on the bedroom light. "Don't move," Boldt said.

The man's eyes revealed he was still contemplating flushing the pills down the toilet, but Boldt waved the gun and stopped the man. He told the trainer to put the vial down at his feet and turn around, hands against the medicine-cabinet mirror.

"Were you waiting, or did you follow me?" the man asked.

"Followed," Boldt said. "What's going on, Sam? You want to tell me, or you want to take a trip downtown?"

"You're Homicide. I'll tell you right now, I didn't kill no one."

Boldt approached him cautiously and patted him down. The man had several screwdrivers and wires in his back pocket. Boldt removed them. "Pretty handy with those wires," he said.

"I put the system in for her after we installed her workout equipment. She's got five grand in that room downstairs."

"Jack of all trades."

"A man's got to earn a living."

Boldt kept him leaning against the wall. He switched on the bathroom light and picked up the pills. "What do we have here?"

"Maybe I better talk to a lawyer. You already got me on a B&E. I don't need no more trouble."

"I can read you your rights, Sam, or we can talk and see if maybe we can make a trade."

There was a long silence. "I don't know, man."

"You dealing drugs, Sam? That carries a stiff penalty in this town."

"Ah, man . . ."

"Talk to me, Sam. I'm losing my patience."

"They're steroids. You come in asking all sorts of questions about Betsy and I can just picture it. That broad wanted too much gain too quickly. I figure you're there because she fucked up and put herself down for the long count. That makes me an accessory, right? Like I said, I think it's time for a lawyer."

"I'm not going to stop you from seeking counsel if that's what you want, but I doubt Betsy Norvak died from steroids, if she's dead at all. That's not why I was there."

"Shit."

"Tell me about it, Sam, and maybe we can both go home without a lot of paperwork."

"What's to tell? A bunch of the people at the club are real into bulking, you know. They come to me all the time for beans—steroids—and I kinda got a little side business going. Listen, if it's not me, they'll get 'em somewhere else. I don't deal in anything heavy. No high-dose stuff. Betsy, a few of the other girls, were into a low-grade thing. Just enough to tone them up. A couple of the guys are into slightly stronger stuff. Nothing heavy. Thing about it is, this brand name . . . I'm one of the only dudes who can get hold of it. I got to thinking—you find that stuff here and it's only a matter of time till you connect it to me. I'm one of the only dudes, man."

"How long?"

"What?" He started to turn around, but Boldt kept him leaning against the wall.

"How long has Betsy been on them?"

"Norv? Shit, I don't know. Six months. Ten, maybe. This windsurfing thing, man, you gotta be strong. She's been coming along nice."

"Tell me about her, Sam. About you and her, I mean."

He looked at Boldt in the reflection of the mirror. "No truth to that, man. Swear to God. The lady got in a jam at the club and I bailed her out. All there was to it. Swear to God. I got nothing like that going on with her."

"I heard different. I heard you like the women."

"Some of 'em, man. Sure. I hear you. But not Norv. Norv was into training in a big way. Sure, she went out with a few of the guys at the club, you know, friends. I hear rumors same as everybody else. That place is full of rumors. We never talked about it. Norv likes to work her

bod. She's real solid for a girl, real good attitude. Attitude
is half the battle in training. You gotta have your head in
the right place.''

"Steroids stay in your system, don't they? I mean months?''

"That's right. That's why they've gone out of the pro
thing. But there's still a big market in fitness clubs. People
are crazy about their bods, man. Some people do about
anything to look better than the next guy, lift another fifty
pounds. You'd be surprised.''

"I'm going to bust you on the B&E." The man looked
shocked. "Got to do it. But I don't have to mention the
drugs. Not yet. I'll give you forty-eight hours to clean up
after yourself. Then I turn your name over to Narco. They'll
sit on you, Sam. You'll never even know they're there.
You're out of the business, but you're out of drug court,
too. Understood?''

"I hear ya.''

"They'll give you probation on the B&E. First offense,
right?''

"Right.''

"A year of probation and it comes off your record. Everybody wins.''

"Not quite.''

"I can't let you skate. I've got my reasons.'' Boldt began
to put his gun away. The quick move caught him by surprise.
The big man kicked straight back and slammed Boldt against
the wall, robbing him of his wind. Boldt sagged and took
a devastating blow to his stomach as the trainer turned and
struck him hard. He managed to hook the man's foot with
his own and he yanked hard, throwing Sam off balance.
Boldt ducked his head and charged. He heard the mirror
break and saw blood on the sink, but DeVito didn't seem
fazed in the least. He linked both hands and brought them
up under Boldt's chin. Boldt's head snapped back, and when
the man lunged at him, his head struck the tile wall.

Everything turned ugly and black and his head rang in a
dull surging pain. He vaguely felt himself sag to the floor.

He heard a reverberating thumping as the trainer ran from the house. Boldt fell forward, groping blindly. He dragged himself a few feet and vomited into the toilet.

He heard a car start up and knew the trainer was getting away. He felt like he weighed three hundred pounds. He vomited again and then managed to lift himself up and stumble into the bedroom to a phone by the bedside.

He dialed 911 and prayed he wouldn't get a recording.

26

AS BOLDT APPROACHED the overgrown path to his rental apartment, Daphne stepped out from her car. She was still in the pink velour sweats and her expression was grave. She had undone the ponytail, but sweat matted the hair at her temples and her eyes and cheeks were flushed. She noticed the ugly bruise on his forehead and gasped, "Jesus, Lou, what happened?"

He glanced over at her, didn't answer, and turned his back on her, walking down the short path to his front steps. He unlocked the mailbox and, to his surprise, found some mail that had been forwarded, amazed that the postal system had functioned so well. If only he'd been so lucky with the telephone. He kept getting calls for a pharmacy. He wondered who was getting his calls.

She caught up to him. "Lou?" she pleaded.

He turned around and glared down at her. He had quickly thought of several things to say and so was all the more surprised when he heard himself tell her, "Come on in if you like."

She followed up the porch steps and held the screen door while Boldt fiddled with the keys. "What happened?" she repeated.

"Had a little wrestling match. That's all. It's nothing."

"It doesn't look like nothing."

"Give me a minute to clean up. I'll be right with you."

"No hurry. Nice place," she called out.

When Boldt came out of the bathroom he looked better, except for a bruise on his forehead and a pink ear. He offered her a soda water with lime, and fixed one for himself, thinking that had he been a drinker he certainly would have poured a stiff one tonight.

"That was awkward tonight," she began. "I thought we should talk about it."

"No big deal," he said, rubbing his elbow and thinking of Shoswitz and his habits.

"That's it exactly. It's no big deal between John and me. We work out together now and then, that's all. It's nothing more than that."

"I don't own you, Daphne," he said, purposely avoiding his nickname for her. "You don't have to explain anything to me."

"We're friends you and I, and I could tell you were hurt tonight, whether or not you'll admit it, and I wanted to clear things up. That's all."

"So you cleared them up. Thanks."

"Oh, Lou!" She leaned back into the couch and huffed and looked around the room, carefully avoiding Boldt.

"Damn," he said, unfolding the paper and seeing another picture of Justin Levitt on the front page. He skimmed the article. It said the boy was the only material witness to the police investigation of the Cross Killer serial murders and that it was believed he had recently provided the police with yet another clue to help narrow the investigation. "Someone must have seen Justin and his mother come down to the office." He spun the paper around so Daphne could read it. "This pisses me off."

She told him she had already seen it and then said, "You're toying with me, Lou. Please stop. I'm here because I care about you. You know I care about you. You're more than a friend to me, Lou. You're an *interest*. Okay? I won't put any more pressure on you than that—I know you're going through some tough times at the moment—but the idea that seeing me with John Kramer could create a problem between us. Well . . . It's ludicrous.''

"I'm sorry if I was rude. There, does that help?"

"Oh, God." She slammed her drink down on the low coffee table and stood briskly.

"I didn't think psychologists lost their tempers."

She fumed, red-faced, fists clenched. The muscles and veins in her neck looked as taut as piano wires.

He didn't know why he felt driven to beat her down, but he couldn't help himself. As he spoke he wondered why he had to drive everything—everyone he loved—away from him. "How does Kramer react to this kind of tantrum?"

"You bastard!" she hollered. "You self-righteous bastard! You're not even hearing what I'm saying. You're interpreting it all so that it fits into some preconceived picture you have of how everything is. You want to feel sorry for yourself, you want to sit on the pity pot, you go right ahead, Lou Boldt. Get into it. Really get into it! Drive yourself down as low as you can go—''

"Look, you want to go out with Kramer, be my guest. Personally, I find the man vapid and banal, but maybe that suits your tastes. I can get along fine without the misplaced emotions of a woman psychologist. I'm not going to go blow myself away over this, you know. We had *one* dinner together. Big deal! Big deal!''

He saw her hair fly behind her, she was moving so fast. Her hips pumped nicely. She slammed the door so hard the curtain fell off the far wall and tumbled like a windless flag onto the television.

"See ya, babe,'' he said, using the nickname formerly reserved for Elizabeth, kicking his feet up onto the coffee table, and touching the rising purple lump on his head. He heard her car start up and rev loudly. He thought she might blow a rod. Then he heard contact as she hit something in her attempt to get out of the parking space quickly.

He would have gotten up to look, but his head hurt too much.

27

THE NEXT MORNING, Tuesday, the eighteenth, he carefully avoided Kramer and Daphne. He arrived early enough that he wouldn't have to pass either of them in the hall. A copy of an FBI pink sheet in his in-box explained why the trainer had taken off: his real name was Samuel Romanello, and he was wanted on a drug charge in Fort Lauderdale.

Bobbie caught up to him in the elevator. She jumped inside just as the doors closed. He pushed the *L*. "Morning," she said. "I hear you did a little wrestling last night."

"How about you?" he asked in a toneless, malicious voice.

She was stunned. "That's uncalled for," she said.

She crossed her arms defiantly and squinted. He thought she might cry. The elevator was too slow. It groaned as it descended.

"Sorry," he said. "Taking it out on you. It's not fair."

"No, it isn't. And I resent you implying that I *fuck* a man every time I go out on a date. That's insensitive and unforgivable."

"Can we start over?"

"No," she said angrily.

"Please," he pleaded, his resignation complete. "Please," he repeated.

"What's got into you?"

"A case of the bads."

"I'd say so."

"I didn't mean it."

The elevator stopped and they both got out on the ground floor. He turned toward the street. "Buy you a cup of decent coffee?" he asked her. She hesitated and then followed.

"What I was going to tell you was that I made some headway on the wetsuit."

He didn't seem to hear her. He said, "Norvak was taking steroids. I asked Dixie if they could do a tissue sample. He said it was no problem. Said he would send it over to the crime lab. Won't have any results for a couple of days. If there are no steroids in that woman, then we're one step closer to proving she's not Norvak."

"I found a rental shop down by the pier. They mark their rentals with red nail polish. Talked to a guy about defaults—nonreturns, you know. Are you listening?"

"Got a search warrant since he broke into her place. I knew Shoswitz wouldn't get it anyway. He doesn't give much effort to those things."

"I think that blow to your head knocked something loose. Have you heard a word I've said?"

"Do you have a name?" he asked, indicating he had been listening.

"That's a couple of weeks back, so he has to go through his records, but I'm going to go over there now and lean on him. I'm sure people rip them off, but there can't be that many women's wetsuits missing from two weeks ago. We'll get a name, a credit-card number, the whole bit."

"We're going through Norvak's checks trying to find her dentist. Nothing so far, and they've gone back over a year. She must have moss in her mouth."

"Some people can go years," she said.

They stopped at the corner and waited for the pedestrian light to change. When it did they moved across at a slow pace. Boldt was not moving quickly.

"I'm gonna skip the coffee. Thanks anyway. So, I'll check in later. You going to be okay?"

"Sure, I'm okay."

"You're not moving so well."

"Tell me about it."

"What's the other guy look like?"

"Not a scratch, I'm afraid. And I doubt I'll ever know for sure. He's long gone. By the time a patrol made it to his apartment, he had cleaned the place out. We won't be seeing him again."

"Norvak's really *not* Jane Doe, is she?"

He stopped on the sidewalk. A lady carrying a toy poodle bumped into him and issued a noise of discontent. The dog whimpered but wagged its tail.

"That's what we're trying to answer, Detective. And if it's not Norvak, then who the hell *is* Jane Doe? And where the hell is Norvak? And why was the same guy at Norvak's and Kate DeHavelin's?"

"Judith Fuller," Bobbie told him three hours later. They were seated close to each other in Boldt's office cubicle. "She rented a wetsuit, a windsurfer, and a car rack on Friday, September thirtieth. Didn't return any of it. The shop takes it as an insurance loss next week."

"You have an address?"

"She gave them Seagate Village. No number. Condominium apartments in a high-rise overlooking the sound. They're handled by Lyn Lymann Property Management. Super is a Chinese by the name of Chen Wo. I have calls in to both Wo and Lymann."

"Do we have a description?"

"No one remembered her, but they had a California driver's license listed. They require a license and a credit card."

"California?"

"Yes. So we'll get a photo. And I've asked LAPD's DMV to FAX us up a copy." She paused. "How about the dental records?" She waited. "Lou?"

He was watching Daphne. She was standing by her door looking in the opposite direction. She returned to her office and closed the door, never looking over.

Still staring off, Boldt said, "We've located the dentist. He had X-rays of some bottom molars. That's all. Not much to go on. They should be at the ME's by now. Dixie will let us know if they're any help." He stood slowly.

"What's up?"

"Following through on this Rutledge thing. He may be able to tell us where our Jane Doe has been, and therefore, where she came from. Did I tell you the Coast Guard called back?"

"No."

He nodded, though somewhat painfully. "A sailboard was found a week ago adrift in the Admiralty Inlet, just off Whidbey. We're cross-checking the board's serial number with the manufacturer's warranty list. We may be able to identify the board."

"Betsy Norvak?"

"Meet me at The Flaming Griddle at one for lunch. With Miss Judith Fuller's apartment number. It's over in the U section."

"I know where it is."

"I'm buying."

"One o'clock." She headed back toward the light.

"And Bobbie?" he called out, waiting for her to face him. "I really am sorry about what I said. Forgive me?"

She nodded reluctantly and pushed her way into the busy pedestrian traffic. She might forgive him—but she wouldn't forget for a while. He could tell by the way she had nodded.

He was pushing away anyone who dared try to befriend him, and he had no idea why. Daphne could probably tell him why, he realized. But that knowledge didn't help a whole lot.

28

DR. BYRON RUTLEDGE was head of the Sea Grant Program at the University. His offices were in a converted brick apartment duplex across from the Marine Sciences building. An innocuous wooden plaque marked the building. Boldt parked in a sticker-only parking lot. A single, chipped-cement path led between the two-story brick buildings; Rutledge's office was midway down the left side. An attractive secretary in her early fifties alerted the professor by telephone, and a few minutes later Boldt was shown inside.

Rutledge fit the salty sailor image perfectly: he had a black-gray beard, craggy teeth, and narrow-set, haunting blue eyes. His hands were thick and hard. He carried a pipe as a fixture in his left hand and had a confident, winning smile. His office was small, linoleum-floored, with a single viewless window. A busy blackboard occupied the inside wall. His desk was cluttered, though he clearly knew his way around it, and he sat in a chair that allowed him to tilt and to rock. He had a squeaky voice—like that of an old man, despite his forty-odd years—and the somewhat disconcerting habit of tapping the gnawed stem of his pipe against his jawbone and scratching his beard.

Boldt introduced himself and took a seat in a captain's chair. What else? The overhead fluorescent lights hummed loudly. Behind Rutledge were some pieces of cheap-motel artwork depicting sea scenes. "What I'm wondering," Boldt began, "is whether or not you can help me identify where a body entered Puget Sound, given where it came back out and how long it was in. I guess what I'm asking is how tidal currents affect a submerged body."

"I see. Homicide, you say? Okay. Well, a submerged body may be neutrally buoyant—that is, it is neither completely floating nor really sinking—depending on the amount of bone in the body, body fat, and so on. In a dead person, it also depends on how much gas has been generated. Any neutrally buoyant object, including a corpse, that's in the water occupies a space just as if it were a water parcel. And so it's embedded in the flow, and will go wherever that water parcel would go."

"We found the body on Alki Point. It had been in the sound for about two weeks."

"Alki, eh? Now that's not surprising really. Alki tends to catch a lot of debris that enters East Passage. Let me show you something, Detective Boldt." Rutledge had trouble lighting his pipe. He tried several times, blue sulfur smoke twisting in the air, and when he finally had it going, he rose and walked over to his blackboard, erasing a large area and picking up the chalk with the familiarity of a man who has been doing this for years. He drew several hard lines, and after a moment, Boldt began to recognize the outline as the lower half of Puget Sound, with Vashon Island in the center and Alki Point to the right, below a circle he drew for the city. He marked Colvos Passage, a narrow strip of water between Vashon Island and the Olympic Peninsula of western Washington, as well as East Passage, a wider body of water to the east of Vashon. "We look at surface flow versus flow at depth. We find that in the tidal currents, the net flow in the East Passage region is this direction—southerly. Now, I don't mean for one tide period or an average flood, but if you average over both ebbs and floods you find both surface and depth flows—especially depth—tends to run down the estuary and into this region. When your tide is rising to fill the Puget Sound estuary, water is preferentially taken from this side,'' he said, pointing to the east of Vashon Island. ''It's driven down through these lower narrows''—he indicated an area off his map, below the island—''and we get a lot of vertical mixing in here. When the flood is done and the tide starts to drop, then because of the way Point Defiance sticks out here, the water is directed this way, up Colvos Passage.''

Rutledge continued, ''Now, on the next flood, because Colvos Passage is such a narrow, restricted channel, and is very shallow, the tide moves more quickly, and as it reaches the north end of Vashon, it tends to hook around and begin the process again, in a kind of continual clockwise circular motion then, around Vashon Island. Actually, some of the surface water on the ebb coming out of Colvos Passage shoots across toward Alki. Some of it goes north with the surface currents, some of it south to recycle.

''In your case, Detective, you say you found a body on Alki. I'd say the body may have submerged initially over here in East Passage. After five days, a week—you'd have to check with a pathologist—the decomposition would generate some gases and the body would become neutrally buoyant. Remember, the water at depth here is extremely cold, slowing decomposition. Now, the body spends time in the water flow and moves through here,'' he said, once again pointing toward Point Defiance. ''It lifts with the water parcel that is pulled up from depth out of East Passage, and on an ebb it enters Colvos Passage. As it hits shallower, warmer water, decomposition accelerates. By the end of Colvos Passage it is buoyant from the gases. It begins to float and is carried by surface currents over to Alki Point.'' He stabbed the blackboard with the chalk. It shattered into several pieces. Sparks of white chalk cascaded to the tile floor.

Boldt asked, ''Then in your opinion, the body would have entered inside of East Passage?''

"You said two weeks?"

"Yes."

"Then I can almost guarantee it. If it had been four or six weeks, there is a slight chance it might have traveled from further up the estuary. Two, even three weeks, then it is more than likely the body entered below Alki, inside of East Passage."

"Not at Carkeek?"

"Carkeek?" Rutledge asked in despair. "Carkeek? I should say not! The surface and depth flow at Carkeek is much the opposite. Water is drawn toward Admiralty Inlet and out into the straits."

"Let's say," Boldt suggested, "that I put a surfboard in the water at Carkeek. Where would it end up, say a week later?"

"Ah, a surfboard is another thing entirely. Being entirely on the surface, it is carried not only by surface currents, but is greatly affected by wind. You would have to check the meteorological people for the time period in question and determine the force and direction of winds."

"Discounting the wind." Boldt felt revitalized. Rutledge's expertise seemed to be supporting the inconsistencies that Boldt had sensed.

"Discounting? Seven to ten days? I'd put it up off of Whidbey."

"That's where the Coast Guard found a sailboard. Whidbey. The deceased is believed to have been sailboarding at the time of her death."

"In the sound?"

"Yes."

"That's highly unlikely, Detective. Windsurfers much prefer the lakes."

"But if a person had an accident off of Carkeek, would the board go one way and the body another?"

"Different directions is possible. You're asking about surface currents versus depth, and there are too many variables on the surface. For your purposes, the thing to stress

is that given the two-week time restriction, it's highly unlikely that a body entering at Carkeek could find its way to
Alki Point. It *must* do this clockwise loop I showed you,
and if it entered clear up by Carkeek there simply isn't time
enough to make this loop.''

Boldt nodded. ''Is there any way I can corroborate that?
Anything that could confirm where a body entered the sound?
Saltwater in the lungs . . . anything like that?''

This seemed to intrigue Doctor Rutledge. He relit his pipe
and pondered the question. After a moment he spoke. ''Yes,
I see. Well, if the lungs were to contain water with a very
low degree of salinity, then in this region there would be
only two possibilities—obviously both freshwater rivers—
the Duwamish or over here at the Puyallup River—''

''Okay.''

''But the Duwamish is really too high, you see, clear up
here, to allow the body to become embedded in this southerly flow we're talking about, so I would say if you found
a low degree of salinity in the lungs it would have to be
from the Puyallup.''

''So, the Tacoma area is a possibility?''

''Sure. What we're talking about is what we call a distinct
label. A way to distinguish one source from another. The
Duwamish happens to have a higher mercury content, but
these kinds of toxicants don't tend to stay in the water. They
tend to adhere to particulate matter and fall out of the water.
I doubt the mercury would show up. Ah!'' he coughed out.
''There is a distinguishing label. The Puyallup is fed more
by streams that have glacier sources, like the White River.
This glacier water tends to contain very, very fine rock
particle. That might be a label for you.''

''There was some mud found on the body . . . mud caught
in her wetsuit. Can that tell us anything?''

''Mud? Why didn't you say so?'' Rutledge seemed to
come alive with enthusiasm. He was the detective now.
''Mud! That's it exactly.'' He moved back over to his crudely
drawn map. He spiked the blackboard with his stick of

chalk. White sparks flew to the floor. "As I mentioned before, the body would be quite low in the water at the southernmost region of East Passage, right before the water parcel is lifted up and into or through the Tacoma Narrows." He tapped the blackboard below Vashon Island. "That's the most likely place it will catch some mud. And we can tell whether or not it did. Years ago at Ruston, the ASARCO smelter operated a copper smelter. Arsenic is used in copper smelting, and it's a well-known fact that the seafloor in this area is still permeated with arsenic. The arsenic was discharged into the atmosphere through smokestacks and because of northerly winds, it settled into Commencement Bay and Dalco Passage, where it still remains today. If that mud contains arsenic, then you can prove beyond a doubt that the body passed through the Dalco Passage area, confirming what we've hypothesized here. And if it passed through Commencement Bay or Dalco, and was in the water two, even three weeks, then we know there's no way it entered as high as Carkeek Park. It would have had to have been somewhere in here." He pointed. "Somewhere in East Passage.

"I'll tell you how you can confirm it, Detective." He waited until Boldt looked up from his notes. Ever the professor. "There's a working model of the estuary at the Poly Pacific Science Center over in Seattle Center. Building number four, I think. We could use dye and neutrally dense wax to determine very closely what the exact progress of your body was. I could call over there and arrange for one of my colleagues to meet you, if you think that necessary."

"I'd like that very much, Doctor."

At one o'clock, Boldt picked up Bobbie Gaynes at The Flaming Griddle, explaining that they didn't have time to eat. His stomach penalized him for the neglect and he chewed down three antacid tablets, much to Bobbie's horror. On the way over she explained that her efforts had netted them

Fuller's apartment number. Boldt was pleased. In truth, he had expected no less.

The Seattle Center was an odd assortment of buildings and kiddy rides, set in a park atmosphere on the edge of the sprawling downtown business center. Its most famous resident was the Space Needle. A monorail from downtown led to the park. It passed overhead as the two detectives entered the Center and approached a directory.

The Poly Pacific Science Center charged an admission of two dollars and fifty cents. Boldt tried to bypass the fee, but the man in the glassed-in booth would have none of it. A group of sixty grade-school children were lining up behind Boldt so he went ahead and paid the five dollars and asked for building number four. He and Bobbie circumnavigated some reflecting pools and eventually came upon a steel door that looked like the side entrance to an auditorium. On the door in bold lettering was NUMBER FOUR.

Inside the open area were dozens of scientific user-interactive teaching modules. Some used computer screens and electronic cuing, others were reminiscent of science demonstrations from junior high. On the far side of the building, steps led up to a walkway that overlooked the model of Puget Sound. Retired Chief of Staff of the United States Coast Guard Richard Melnor was on hand, a nametag pinned to his sport coat. He was big man with a happy face and large hands he used to demonstrate every point. He was awaiting Boldt, who leaned over the rail to shake hands and introduced Bobbie as his assistant.

The model was twenty feet square, made of formed fiberglass. The water in the model duplicated the estuary's salinity, diluted in appropriate ratios by freshwater running from copper tubes that could be seen at the mouth of each of the dozens of rivers that fed the system. At the far end of the model, an electronic machine depressed a flat metal arm into the water out where the Pacific Ocean would have been. The tidal generator's plate then retracted, representing the ebb flow. Melnor said, "Every three seconds is an hour, every seventy-three seconds a day. In seven hours, forty-nine seconds we can duplicate an entire year. But from what Rut told me, you're interested in East Passage and Colvos Passage."

Boldt confirmed this with a nod.

Two teenagers came over and rang an ear-piercing nautical bell not five feet from Melnor. The one boy rang it three times and Melnor called out harshly, "Young man, if you ring that one more time, I'm going to ring *your* bell," and the boys backed away and wandered off. "Kids," he grunted.

"He said something about dye and pieces of wax," Boldt prompted.

"Yes," Melnor confirmed, picking up a bottle of blue dye marked SALTWATER. "Mind you, this model is so small, we only get the gross effects of net flow." He withdrew a bit of blue dye via a long eyedropper, inserted the device deep into one of the channels off of the bay, and squirted the dye into the model. "You can see," he said, "that at extreme depths there is very little flow. I'm using saltwater dye because Byron said you were interested in neutral buoyancy, and the freshwater dye would rise to the surface. Now, if I elevate this slightly," he said, squirting out more dye, "you can see that the net flow at depth is incoming. And here, at the surface, the net flow is outgoing. This is a general rule of the tidal system here. Since we are talking about a body, it is more than likely the body would initially go to depth."

"And the undercurrents would carry it toward Tacoma," Boldt stated.

"Tidal currents," he corrected. "Depending on where it entered. Yes."

"Could you show us the surface flow by Carkeek Park, please."

Melnor nodded, switched bottles, and squeezed another blue dye onto the surface by Carkeek's approximate location. The dye hesitated and then moved quickly, dissipating past Whidbey Island, drawn toward the ocean.

"And at depth there?"

Melnor used saltwater dye at a deeper depth and the blob hung in the deep channel, edging slowly to the south. Too slowly, Boldt thought, realizing Rutledge's explanation of time scheduling had been accurate. The blob had barely moved, even after three minutes—over two days.

Melnor said, "I've got some wax balls here we use to demonstrate the effect of the currents on boats, debris, and that sort of thing. Byron recommended we run them through the system starting at East Passage and clock their movements for a two-week period. We have a Polaroid here we use to record the actual movements. If you'll just give me a minute . . ." He hurried off.

"Nice man," Bobbie said. "Knows his stuff."

"Look there," Boldt said, checking his watch and pointing to the fading dye by Whidbey Island. "There's her windsurfer. That's where the Coast Guard found it. And there—that blob of ink. Her body has hardly moved. Rutledge is right. The body didn't enter at Carkeek."

Bobbie questioned, "So, even if Norvak had a windsurfing accident up by Carkeek, which someone evidently went to a great deal of trouble to make us believe, she couldn't wash ashore at Alki."

"Not in two weeks. The currents move too slowly."

"So Jane Doe isn't Betsy Norvak. She's someone else."

"At least there's a *possibility* the body isn't Norvak's. And there's a possibility someone wants us to think it is. And that leaves us with two conceivable scenarios." He caught himself about to lecture her, and instead asked for her opinion.

Bobbie thought aloud, speaking slowly and choosing her words carefully. "If the Jane Doe corpse isn't Norvak, then it's possible someone killed Norvak and wants us to believe the body we found at Alki is hers, when in fact it isn't. I suppose Norvak might not be connected to this at all"—

she noticed Boldt's skeptical look—"except that someone went to a lot of trouble to make it appear Norvak disappeared windsurfing, when, in fact, we now know it's unlikely she did. We have the burned clothing, the van with prints indicating it was last driven by a man, the Rockports in the garage. . . ."

"We may be able to confirm that the Jane Doe body is *not* Norvak's by the steroids, or dental records. But go on," he encouraged.

"So maybe someone killed Norvak and tried to make it look like an accident."

"There's another possibility you're overlooking," Boldt told her. "Think it through."

Her brow tightened and he nearly apologized for his tone of voice when she cut him off by saying quickly, "Or . . . I suppose the attempt could be to conceal a different murder. The body closely matches Norvak's. Norvak's accident seems plausible enough. Under normal circumstances, we would have simply assumed that Jane Doe is Norvak but she could be someone else—perhaps Judith Fuller."

Boldt smiled at her, confirming she had done well.

"But why?" he asked, testing. "Why go to the trouble of killing Norvak, and disposing of her body, when you could just as easily dispose of the other body—Fuller's, if that's who it is."

"I'll keep time," Melnor said, charging through the door, showing off the stopwatch he had retrieved as well. "Seven shots left, so we'll go every two days. If you have the time, it would be best if we ran a few tests before wasting the film."

"Fine. Of course. Rutledge said that as the body entered Colvos it would probably have decayed more quickly because of warmer water temperatures—"

Melnor interrupted, "I'm all set for that." He pointed to three different-colored balls of wax no bigger than BBs. "I have a neutral density, a rising, and a floating. That should about do it. Where would you like to start?"

"Two weeks is about the time period. You're more familiar with the model than we are. Where do you think it would enter in order to reach Alki two weeks later?"

Melnor studied the model. He used several experiments with the dye before committing himself. "I think this is a good place to start." He dropped the darkest ball into the East Passage and clicked the stopwatch. They all three watched intently as the ball undulated in corresponding motions with the tide generator. As predicted, the net gain was in a southerly direction. It edged around the southern tip of the island, hitting bottom.

Boldt asked, "Is that where the ASARCO plant would be?"

Melnor nodded, eyes on the ball. "Just about." He checked his watch. "Five days," he said. As the ball bumped once again into the rising shelf at Point Defiance, Melnor dropped the dark red ball in and said, "I won't go after the other yet, because it would disturb the model." The red ball edged slowly to the surface, drifting quickly north up Colvos Passage. By the time it reached the topmost western corner of Vashon, Melnor announced, "Eight days," and switched to the white ball that floated, better duplicating the density of the body at the time. This ball seemed confused as it vacillated in the surface currents. It tried to move into the clockwise motion again and Melnor had to move it by nudging it with his eyedropper. He explained, "I put in the floater too quickly. But this will give us an idea." The ball missed Alki Point by a matter of centimeters.

"Nine days," Melnor stated. "Too short. We'll try again."

He ran the twenty-minute test twice more, the last time with Boldt photographing the progress every few minutes. The closest they could come to a point of entry was an area just south of Piner Point, off Maury Island, which connected to the east of Vashon. Piner Point was nearly directly across from where the ASARCO smelter had once operated.

They thanked the man profusely. Melnor offered to help anytime and provided Bobbie with a business card where he could be reached. He also provided them with the name and number of the current chief of staff for the Coast Guard.

Photos in hand, Boldt walked silently back to the car, Bobbie at his side. He was thinking about the concept of tidal currents—layers of water moving in opposing directions at different speeds. Like hidden meanings, these currents could easily deceive. He thought that his own life was filled with such unseen currents; he was torn in a dozen directions at once by a dozen different elements—work, love, friendship, health, responsibility—all moving simultaneously, all determining the direction he would go.

"What do you think?" Bobbie finally asked, disturbed by his silence.

They were in the car, Boldt driving. "Makes sense to me," he said.

She looked at him curiously. "I mean, do you mind?"

"I'm sorry . . ."

"Weren't you listening?"

"I guess not." He tried to pay attention now; he had to force himself to concentrate because her question had been one often asked by Elizabeth. He didn't intentionally "not listen," he just simply didn't *hear* all the time, too easily absorbed in his own thoughts.

"I asked if it was all right if I got off at six tonight instead of working overtime."

"You have another date?"

"None of your business," she replied harshly.

"No, it isn't." He backed off the gas and turned on some jazz.

29

JOHN LAMOIA was waiting in Lou Boldt's office cubicle, nervously tapping a pencil.

"What is it, John?" the sergeant asked, checking a list of telephone messages. Among the stack of pink phone-call slips were two from Daphne, one from Abrams, and one from Doctor McClure, Norvak's orthopedist. An appointment with the doctor had been arranged for an hour from now.

LaMoia jumped up from the chair. "The computer kicked out the overlapping stores, Sergeant. We went back four days prior to the kills, like you said to do. We fed the computer all the stores the victims had shopped—this according to receipts we found—checking accounts and interviews. Of the dozens of possibilities we had it search for stores that at least three of the women had shopped."

"Okay."

"We've got eighteen stores, Sarge. Six gas stations, four supermarkets, three department stores, and one each of a beauty salon, a downtown parking facility, a toy store, a car wash, and a bakery."

"Eighteen is better than a few hundred thousand, eh, John?" Boldt added. "What about the flowers?"

"That list is together, but it's huge."

"Narrow it down to the radius."

"It is. It's still huge; they sell silk flowers everywhere."

"Of the eighteen stores, we'll start with the ones closest to stores that sell red silk roses. The proximity of the stores may play a role in this."

"Christ, we can't stake out eighteen, Sarge."

"I know that," Boldt said. "Hang on a second. Hear me out. He may drive a yellow van. Targeting the vans is a possibility if the killer happens to be an employee at one of these places. Let's say we have eighteen stores; each store has between five and, what, twenty-five employees?"

"Something like that."

"So we're looking at between ninety and, say, five hundred employees."

"It's a hell of a lot."

"Figure half, maybe more are female. That knocks it down to between fifty and two hundred and fifty."

"Still too big."

"So without letting on what we're after, we get a current list of employees. We involve only the highest manager or owner, keep curiosity to a minimum."

LaMoia caught up with his thinking. "And we run the employee lists through DMV, looking for an owner of a pale-colored van." He sat forward enthusiastically. "Shit, how many can there be?"

"Not many," Boldt said. "Our killer may not have worked in one of the stores, but if he did, I'd say we've got him. How soon can we put this together, John? I'd like to get right on it."

"You'll run it by the lieutenant?"

"I'll talk to Shoswitz. You lay out a plan to best use our manpower. Talk to Kramer. He'll help with scheduling."

"Oh, come on."

Boldt said forcefully, "Work with Kramer, John. That's how it has got to be. I don't like it either."

"A couple of days," LaMoia guessed, answering his earlier question. "If we could get ten or fifteen detectives, it would go faster."

"I doubt I can get half that, but I'll try."

"Couple of days isn't too long to wait. Not after all this time." A rare bit of optimism from LaMoia.

"Tell that to his next victim."

LaMoia shrugged.

Boldt was on his way out, but the call stopped him. It was Doc Dixon. In his affable voice the man said, "Lou. Do we have any reason to hold on to Norvak?"

"Jane Doe," Lou Boldt corrected.

"I spoke to Royce. He claims your young detective just called and went on and on with him about tidal currents and contradictions. She says you don't think it's Norvak. Is that true?"

"I'm still looking into it."

"Well listen, we talked about this. She's a rookie detective, Lou. You know how that goes. I got a full house, down here. You hear about the fire?"

"No."

"I've got seven new check-ins because of a fire over in the Madrona district. I've got a positive I.D. on your mermaid, Lou. I'd just as soon get her moving."

"Positive?"

"As near as we're going to get. Those dental X-rays are a good match."

"But they're only partials. Molars, I thought."

"But they're perfect, Lou. Royce and I just went over them a second time. I've got to do my job."

Boldt closed his eyes and attempted to control his voice. Doc Dixon had a job to do, and from his point of view the corpse was Betsy Norvak. Boldt needed to make it sound as professional as possible, but it wasn't easy for him. He couldn't keep the fatigue and his own personal involvement out of his voice. "It's true, about the tidal currents, I mean. It was *my* idea. I know it's nothing hard, Ron, but it supports our suspicions. I have an appointment with her doctor in a few minutes. That may give me some

more ammunition. I'm also waiting for a call from the lab
on that tissue sample.''

"Lou . . .''

"Give me until the end of the day, will you? Tomorrow
morning at the latest.''

"I need the space, Lou. I've got to have something to
justify the space. The end of the day, okay? She won't be
lost and gone forever, you know. We'll just get her
moving—let a funeral home hold her for a week or so. I
can ask the family to delay—something like that.''

"Have you notified the family?'' Boldt wondered, horrified.

"Not yet. Don't worry.''

"Don't notify the family, Dixie. I can't explain it, but I
think you'd be making a mistake.''

"You've got the rest of the day, okay? I'll see what I
can do about extending it.'' He hesitated. "Hey, what about
those pieces of paper I found? Any help to you?''

"Try this. Two pieces of women's clothing dry-cleaned.
One had torn buttonholes, the other two stains. The only
name we could pull was Johnson. No help there—no female
Johnsons missing that we know of. What it comes down to
is why would some woman go windsurfing with two dry-
cleaning receipts that don't belong to her, stuck between
her wetsuit and swimsuit? She's trying to tell me something,
Dixie, but I'm not getting it.''

"Stay with it, Lou. I'll try to make room for her. Maybe
I'll be able to come up with a less-deluxe accommodation.''

"Appreciate it.'' Boldt thanked him, hung up, and chewed
down two Tums. What he really wanted was a yogurt
smoothie.

30

DOCTOR MCCLURE'S waiting room contained a dozen blue padded chairs. Low white Formica tables between them held back issues of dog-eared magazines. The receptionist was dressed in beige slacks and a tight sweater. She was chewing gum and working furiously on the computer keyboard.

McClure saw Boldt in his office. Despite its small size, it tried hard to project the scholarly image a doctor deserves. Boldt had great respect for the medical profession and McClure was no exception. He was about Boldt's age, with graying curly hair and a natural smile.

"You wanted to know about Betsy Norvak." Soft-spoken.

"She was your patient?"

"Was?"

"Is."

"Is there something I should know, Sergeant? This isn't a medically related case, is it?"

"No."

"Nothing that in any way might involve malpractice?"

"No."

"Thank God for that. You understand my concern, I'm sure."

Boldt knew the good doctor paid more for insurance than Boldt earned in a year. "Yes."

"And how can I help you?"

"Her companion—a Mr. Montrose—mentioned a bad arm. We found a sling in her bathroom. It looked well used."

"Worn-out is probably more like it. Yes, that's right."

"Tennis elbow?" Boldt wondered.

McClure smiled. "Windsurfer elbow?" He seemed to tease. "We can't say what caused the arthritis. My bet is a number of factors contributed, but the windsurfing certainly didn't help matters."

Boldt asked about her condition as of two weeks ago and McClure described it as advanced something-or-other-itis. He suggested there was no way she could have windsurfed without extreme pain. The doctor pointed to a working model of the bones in an arm and directed Boldt's attention to it. He pointed at the elbow, rattled off some long medical terms, and bent the arm a few times.

"Would you recognize the elbow?" Boldt asked.

"Possibly. Not by sight as easily as by X-ray. Are you implying what I think you're implying?"

"How's that? About the X-ray, I mean."

"We hadn't operated yet. I'm scheduled to perform orthoscopic surgery"—he checked the file—"in about three weeks. Exploratory really, to see how bad the arthritis is."

"You mentioned X-rays."

"That's right. She has some calcium buildup in the joint. The question is whether to try and scrape it off or not. Sometimes that works quite well. Sometimes not."

"But you can see the calcium in the X-rays?"

"Of course."

"And you have X-rays of her elbow?"

"On file. Certainly."

Boldt sat forward anxiously. "Could I borrow those for a few hours, sir?"

"I'd like to help, Detective. But I couldn't allow that

without Ms. Norvak's permission, I'm afraid. That, or a court order. I'd be happy to cooperate if we can put it together properly.''

Dixon's confirmation that the dental X-rays matched began to sink in and Boldt felt further depressed. The discrepancies in the case had been building nicely—the dental X-rays had pulled the wind from his sails. An hour earlier he would have put money on the fact that Jane Doe wasn't Norvak. Now . . .

Boldt wondered: ''What if I brought you an X-ray of a woman's elbow and asked you to compare it with that of Norvak's? Could you do that for me?''

''That's acceptable to me. I have no problems with that.''

''Can you make time for me?''

''We can pull her X-rays in a matter of minutes. Happy to help.''

Already up and out of his chair, Boldt nodded.

''Have you had that looked at?'' McClure asked, pointing toward Boldt's forehead. ''That doesn't look very good.''

He didn't get an answer.

31

DOCTOR DIXON WAS in the middle of his third consecutive autopsy when Boldt arrived. Boldt entered the large, brightly lit room, his visitor's pass clipped to his lapel, and kept his eyes off the table. Burn victims were the worst. Dixon worked efficiently, a fire detective looking on. Dixon spoke into a voice-activated tape-recording system as he proceeded. When he saw Boldt, he asked his assistant to continue with an incision and handed him the knife. He went over to Boldt and spoke in a soft voice to avoid inadvertently tripping the tape system. Boldt was used to this precaution. He'd been here plenty of times before.

"I'd shake your hand, but you know . . ." He held up his blood-smeared gloved hand.

Boldt felt his ulcer complain. "I need to ask a favor."

"Shoot."

"I'd like an X-ray of Norvak's right elbow. I think we can settle this thing once and for all."

"Come on, Lou. We've already *confirmed*."

"Arthritis. Norvak had arthritis in her right elbow. There's some kind of deposit that shows up on X-ray."

Dixon nodded. Then he bit his lip. "Royce can get you the X-rays, but you don't need them. I went over them thoroughly. There's no arthritis in either elbow. Something's wrong here."

238

"You're positive about the arthritis?"

"Absolutely. And the teeth, too. One of us is wrong, Lou. Maybe we screwed something up. It happens in a place this size."

"I think I should run the X-rays by her doctor."

He nodded. "Talk to Royce. He, or one of the girls can pull her file. Just bring 'em back, will you please? And sign 'em out. Let's keep the damned paperwork straight. Okay?"

"Would you mind taking another look at her?"

"How's that?"

"Another look at her elbow. If we get you on the stand, I want more than an X-ray." He added, "Today, if possible."

"Lou, I'm knee-deep in burn victims. Two more after this. I'll be here till nine o'clock as it is. Besides, I've already done her."

"I'll give you access to my entire collection for a month. You can tape 'em all."

Dixon seemed to ponder this for a moment. Stunned. Like Boldt, he too was a jazz fan. Boldt prized his record collection, which included dozens of impossible-to-find albums. He forbade any borrowing. The opening up of his collection to a friend was tantamount to the opening of King Tut's tomb.

"A month?" Dixon asked incredulously. "That blow to your head must have dislodged something," he said, pointing.

"It'll give you time to tape them all."

"No arguments. You'll forgive me. I'm in shock. Just what the hell is so important?"

"Our second killer. The man in the Rockports wants us to think DeHavelin was done by the Cross Killer."

Dixon looked skeptical. "Don't put down Rockports, Lou. I wear them." He pointed. "Damn comfortable."

It caused Boldt to hesitate. Then he said, "You and I agreed it was possible someone else did Kate DeHavelin.

A copycat. Don't back out on me now, Dixie. DeHavelin's not the first one that's bugged us.''

"I said it was highly unlikely, Lou. There's a difference."

"But possible."

Dixon shrugged. "If you put me on the stand, I'd have to say the kills were identical. That's how close they are."

Boldt considered this a moment and said, "That may be the copycat's game. Still, you agree, it's *possible*. That's the only word I need to hear."

Dixon shrugged again. "I'll look over Jane Doe again, Lou. A whole month," he reminded him. "The full collection."

"By tonight," Boldt restated.

"It'll be late."

"My phone's been screwing up. If you don't get me, drive it over. Thirty-five-thirty and a half, Interlake North. I'll wait up."

"Got it."

Boldt glanced over accidentally at the charred body. "That's really awful," he said.

"Depends on how you look at it," Dixon said with a wry smile.

Boldt was told that James Royce was cleaning a body. Boldt refused to enter the room. He'd seen enough for a lifetime. He didn't understand how anyone could get used to this job. You either had to be numb or sick. Or both.

Royce snapped off his gloves and threw them into the trash. His white jacket was filthy and his handsome face looked exhausted. He rubbed the fatigue from his eyes. "Jesus, what a day."

"So I hear."

"You're my saving grace, Sergeant."

Boldt asked for Norvak's X-rays.

Royce inquired cautiously, "You heard that we confirmed her earlier?"

Boldt grunted. "Not exactly," he mumbled.

Royce led Boldt down a hall and into a file room. He pulled Norvak's large folder of X-rays from a drawer, and handed it to the detective.

"One other thing," Boldt said as they left the room.

"What's that?"

"There was some mud on Jane Doe when she came in."

"Sure was. I cleaned her up."

"How about her swimsuit? Dixie told me you'd hold it for us."

Royce furrowed his brow. "Yeah, that's right."

"Thanks. Have it sent over to the state lab, would you please?"

"What should I tell them?"

"I'll call ahead. Don't worry about it."

The two shook hands. Royce's was still clammy, the skin soft, from being inside the latex gloves for hours. The strange texture and temperature gave Boldt an odd sensation in his bowels.

After leaving his visitor's tag at the reception desk, Boldt headed straight to the john. A few minutes later he realized it wasn't Royce's handshake. It was the ulcer.

32

BOLDT DIDN'T LIKE the waiting. It did nothing to improve his mood. He was waiting for the tissue samples from the lab that might show traces of steroids. He was waiting for Dixon's confirmation of what he already knew—the Jane Doe corpse did not have Betsy Norvak's arthritic elbow. Now he wanted more: he wanted Judith Fuller's apartment number; he wanted LaMoia's efforts to yield something; he wanted I.D.'s report on Norvak's minivan; the lab's spectrograph of the burned clothing; he wanted to prove to the others what he already knew: Kate DeHavelin and possibly some of the other Cross Killer victims—and perhaps Betsy Norvak—were the work of a second man. Someone close to the investigation who was taking advantage of the sensational nature of the Cross Killings. A copycat.

In an effort to quell his impatience, he turned his attention to paperwork. Stacked neatly on his desk were two dozen manila folders, each thick with reports and computer fanfold paper. Boldt read through the most recent, which included LaMoia's lists of stores and the various items bought by the victims. He scanned the thick computer printout listing the scores of shops that sold red silk roses. The task before them was enormous and time seemed to be working against them.

He put these folders aside and opened the file on Kate DeHavelin. He didn't want to look at the photos. He was sick of the photos. He studied I.D.'s report on the plaster cast and was again reminded that the footprints found at Cheryl Croy's and those found at Kate DeHavelin's were made by two different men—and again he was reminded of his waiting. His stomach cramped and he had to close his eyes to relax.

Eyes closed, he saw Cheryl Croy's bloodstained bedroom. The vision was dreamlike, monotone colors, fuzzy edges. He tried his best to re-create the incident, as he had done dozens of times. He located the tape of Justin Levitt's hypnosis session and placed it in the machine, donning the lightweight headphones. As the boy spoke, Boldt could see the parted curtains, could picture Justin behind the telescope. Croy hears a knock on her door. She shuts off the television and quickly slips on her nightgown. "*Nothing good on tonight,*" Justin says. Boldt backs up the tape and listens to this again. And again. It had struck him oddly at the time and it stayed with him now as he pictured the faceless Cross Killer handing Croy a bouquet of red silk roses and forcing his way inside, forcing her upstairs and into her bedroom. He throws her onto the bed and pulls the curtain. ". . . *blue light on the curtains* . . ." Boldt stops the machine and rewinds. ". . . *blue light on the curtains* . . ." ". . . *blue light on the curtains.*"

"*Nothing good on tonight* . . ." He leafed through Croy's folder and found a Xerox of the VICAP report, thumbing several pages until reaching the inventory of the death scene. His finger slid down the list and stopped. He skidded the folder from the second murder atop this and dug once again into the stack, seeking the VICAP report. He located the death-scene inventory and his fingertip raced down the typed columns of items.

"*Nothing good on tonight.*"

As common as a home stereo.

Too easily overlooked.

The word just above his dirty fingernail read, "VCR."

The Levitts were just finishing dinner in front of "Wheel of Fortune." Boldt hadn't realized how late it was. They were pleasant enough to him, but when he asked if he could speak with Justin, the mother sent her son up to his room and asked for a few words with Boldt.

When the boy was out of earshot, she asked, "Did you see tonight's paper?"

Boldt had not. He told her so. Mr. Levitt stood by passively. He was the passenger in this marriage; she was the driver.

"They're claiming Justin knows what the killer looks like, calling him the only material witness. He didn't see the man's face, Mr. Boldt, we both know that. All this press, these claims that he does know, is upsetting to him. Why'd you people do this? He thinks he's supposed to know something he doesn't know. We've tried to explain why the press does what it does, but I don't think we got through. He feels like he's letting us all down. I really think it's time he got back to being a boy. We're thinking of taking him out of school. He has an uncle in Idaho. We've been thinking about sending him over there until Thanksgiving, until this all settles down somewhat. My husband's brother teaches school over there and he thinks he can arrange something."

"If there's a trial . . . anything like that, of course he'd be available on short notice," Douglas Levitt added. "It's just too much for a boy his age. Nancy would go over and stay with him," he said, motioning toward his wife. It was the first time Boldt had heard her name. "I'd make it on as many weekends as I could. We think he'd be better off out of the city."

"That's up to you," Boldt said. "There's nothing I can do about that. Oh, I suppose there is . . . But I'm not going to do anything, if that's what you're asking." He added, "We would like to try hypnosis one more time."

Levitt glanced at his wife. "We've decided against that," he acknowledged, "in light of what it's doing to Justin."

Boldt was in no mood to argue. "However you want it. We can't force you. May I speak with the boy a minute? It's *extremely* important."

Mrs. Levitt nodded her approval.

As he reached the stairs, Mrs. Levitt asked, "Mr. Boldt? He's not in any kind of danger, is he? I mean all this press?"

"My lieutenant thinks the press is your biggest concern."

Mr. Levitt nodded, put an arm around his wife, and squeezed.

Justin Levitt was sitting on his bed. "She tell you about the paper? I swear to God I didn't see the guy's face. That's bullshit."

It was strange for Boldt to hear a boy this age swear. He wondered if he would have tolerated such language from his own son. He thought not. "Don't worry about it. They'll do anything to sell newspapers."

"Assholes."

"I agree." He paused, collecting his thoughts. "Justin, what I have to say, what I have to ask you . . . I'm not saying you lied to me. I'm not accusing you of anything. I want you to understand how grateful I am, we all are, for your being so helpful. But I need to ask you some tough questions. And I need the truth, Justin. Anything said is strictly between you and me. Okay?"

Justin's face tightened. He finally nodded.

"You told me you could see her television from here, right?" The boy nodded apprehensively. "And what was she watching that night?"

"I told you. That radio channel."

"I mean the night she was killed."

"The *radio* channel. I already *told* you."

Boldt considered this a moment and then said, "Tell me about once they were in the room."

Justin Levitt sighed, clearly fed up with the repetitive

questioning. "She entered the room in front of him. She fell onto the bed. That's all."

"The curtains."

"He *pulled* the curtains."

"The lights."

"He *shut off* the lights. Jeez!"

"And then?"

"Nothing. I *told* you. Nothing."

"You told me you saw blue light."

The boy looked surprised. He thought about this. "So what?"

"Light from the television?" Boldt questioned.

The boy didn't answer. He looked puzzled.

Boldt left a long pause before finally asking, "Did she ever watch dirty movies?"

The boy blushed. "No way."

"Justin?"

"Maybe."

"With her boyfriend?" Boldt recalled Marquette explaining their last night together had been spent "watching tube."

"Maybe." He was extremely quiet.

"Was she watching one that night?"

"No!"

"Justin."

"No! I swear. The *radio* channel."

"You said she turned *off* the TV."

"That's right. She heard the guy at the door, I suppose."

"Did she turn it off at the set?"

"No. I told you. The remote control."

"From the bed?"

"Yeah. From the bed. She turned it off. Same as always. Then she got up, crossed in front of the window, and went into the bathroom. I *told* you all this."

"Did she watch dirty movies, Justin? I *have* to know. Did you ever see her watching dirty movies?"

He blushed again.

"Tell me the truth, damn it," Boldt said harshly. "A

woman's been murdered!'' He was close to the boy now, hanging on his answer. He said softly, ''You could see her TV from here. You could see the movies, too. Isn't that right?''

''My mom will *kill* me.''

Boldt shook his head. ''Come on. Come on!''

Justin looked up at Boldt with sad eyes. He nodded extremely slowly. ''She and her boyfriend, they *did it* on the bed while the movies were going. I watched.'' He swallowed. ''Not very often, you know. I didn't see them *that many* times.''

Boldt had not anticipated that the boy might have seen them in the act as well. No wonder he had been reluctant to mention it.

''When was the last time . . . the last time they watched one of those movies?''

''That weekend. Friday night, I think. Her boyfriend came over. I wouldn't have watched if they had pulled the curtains all the way. I *couldn't* have! They never pulled the curtains all the way. It's not *my* fault. They *always* left them open a crack.''

''A crusader,'' Boldt whispered.

''What's that?'' Justin Levitt asked, bringing Boldt back to the room.

He said, ''I'm going to need your help again.''

''I'll do my best.''

Boldt stepped forward and hugged the boy to his chest. ''That's all I ask, son. That's all any of us can ask.''

33

"WHAT'S THIS all about, Lou?" Shoswitz set down his flight bag. His first baseman's glove and blue aluminum bat were sticking out through the open zipper. He looked silly in his softball uniform and yellow cap. Number 9. "Top half of the second inning and my goddamned beeper goes off. What's going on?"

Boldt had ten folders open on his desk, their contents somewhat scattered. He knew Shoswitz loved a good game of softball, despite his bad elbow. It had not been all that long ago that he himself had taken time for sports and such things. But not lately. Lately, it seemed that work was all he knew, and he wondered how he had allowed it to come to this. No wonder Elizabeth had found someone else.

A shift change had occurred forty minutes earlier and the office cubicles were mostly empty. Shoswitz rolled up a chair. "No rest for the wicked, right?"

"The connection is porno films. Justin Levitt confirmed it. Video rentals. That's how he chooses his victims. I've made some calls. I only reached four of the boyfriends, but they all admitted that they had watched porno flicks with their girlfriends. And in every case it was the *woman* who belonged to the video store. It's just the kind of private thing a person would find a way to leave out of a police report. And if the killer took time to place the women under surveillance, then the movie could have been rented days prior to the killing—not an easy connection for the boyfriend to make. It's the pattern we've been missing. I've gone through this shit," he said, lifting one of the folders. "As far as I can tell, seven of the ten victims owned VCRs. Three of the others didn't. Right now we're concentrating on the four we *know* rented videos."

"Who's on it?"

"LaMoia."

"Good. What's he doing?"

"He's going to get the name of the video store or stores from the boyfriends. If they don't know, he'll go back through the victims' finances. Once we've got the stores, we'll get employee lists and cross-check them with DMV for yellow vans. We're moving as quickly as possible, but we've got to be real careful, Phil. We're close now. As close as we've been. One mistake and we could lose this guy in court."

"Agreed." Shoswitz thought for a moment. "You, me, and Kramer, my office tomorrow morning. I want to know the count on this, and I mean play by play—with color commentary. We work as a team. Right? Teamwork. Right?"

"Sure. There's something else I need from you, Phil. I need a warrant to search Judith Fuller's apartment."

"You're not going to try and sell me this copycat crap again, are you?"

"Did I miss something? I thought after Jergensen we all agreed we'd chase any lead—any lead at all. Are we going to let a thing like—"

"Okay. You've made your point."

Boldt handed Shoswitz a pink phone-call memo. Shoswitz read it over. "So? This only tells us what we already knew. Norvak had a windsurfing accident. It's not all that rare."

"What that says is that the sailboard the Coast Guard

found off Whidbey is registered under warranty to Norvak.
It says nothing about an accident. Try this one.'' Boldt
handed him Abrams's report.

"I already saw this.''

"Then you know I.D. found traces of both rust and Portland cement in the back of Norvak's minivan. They also
confirmed that the large spill of chemical by the stack of
fenceposts in back of her garage was Penta. *And*, using the
minivan's mirrors, they estimate the last person to drive
that thing was just shy of six feet. Norvak was five-seven,
tops.''

"Lou? You need another rest? You pulling for some time
off or something? Make some sense.''

"I want a search warrant for Judith Fuller's apartment.
And I'm not going to get it without your help.''

"We've been over this, Lou. We have a match of dental
records on Norvak. The woman who washed ashore at Alki
is Norvak, not Fuller.''

"But we *don't* have a match on the arthritic elbow. Even
Dixie admitted they screw up the paperwork now and then.''

"Give me a break, would ya?''

"Lieutenant, we have a bathing suit and a wetsuit dipped
in Penta and set afire. We have a missing fifty-five-gallon
drum.'' Seeing Shoswitz's disbelief, Boldt nodded. "That's
right, we do. The lawn man said there had been *three* drums
out back. You know how expensive Penta is. No one in
their right mind would dump twenty gallons. You'd pour it
into another drum at least. Save it. But somebody dumped
it. Somebody burned a Danskin and a wetsuit. Norvak never
wore the two together. This thing isn't totally assembled
yet, but the pieces are coming into place.''

Shoswitz rubbed his elbow. He waited a moment and
then said, "Well, are you going to tell me, or am I supposed
to be psychic?''

"You won't like it.''

"I'm still waiting.''

"Let's say for a moment that you're a man close to the

Cross Killer investigation. Close enough to know the details.''

"Go on."

"And you're also homicidal." Boldt waited for a comment from Shoswitz, but he had the lieutenant's attention now. "And you see a way to kill some women and have the murders blamed on the Cross Killer. Only you're more into the actual act of killing than the Cross Killer. A copycat could very well enjoy torturing his victims. This, according to Daphne, not me. He takes his time. He tapes their mouths shut so they can't scream and he strangles them like the Cross Killer does because he knows enough to do the job right. But he tortures them. Instead of a quick death, the copycat's victims are forced to endure an extremely slow death.''

"Are you going somewhere with this?" Shoswitz checked his watch.

Boldt raised his hand. "So let's say you enjoy the torture aspect so much that the more women you do, the more you really drag the torture out. And once . . . no twice, you actually lose your victim. She gets away. Maybe you're convinced she's passed out, but she isn't. Maybe part of the torture is letting her think you aren't looking—teasing —and you give her a chance at escape." Shoswitz was interested now. Boldt could feel it. "One of the women who gets away on you is Katherine DeHavelin. Only she's quicker than you thought, and by the time you get her again, she has the tape off her mouth and is running through some woods. Maybe she's screaming. And you kill her right there."

Shoswitz nodded. "I think you've got something going here, Lou."

"One of your other victims is a woman named Judith Fuller. Only Fuller gets completely away from you before you've even choked her down—maybe she fights back harder than the others, who knows? But the important thing is she gets away, her windpipe damaged and hemorrhaging.''

"She dives into the sound," Shoswitz said.

Now Boldt nodded. "And before you catch up to her, she's under. Gone. Drowned. You've lost this one completely."

"And you haven't had time to tidy the job."

"Just the opposite. The job's a mess. Remember, you're close enough to the investigation to know how it's being handled. You *have* to be or couldn't possibly duplicate the kills well enough."

"Oh, Christ."

"Remember, this is all essentially wild speculation. We only have a few pieces to put this thing together with, and they're all circumstantial."

Shoswitz nodded. "It's good work, Lou. I follow you. Stay with it."

"Okay, so what's your problem now? You've botched this job, you haven't had a chance to make it look like the work of the Cross Killer. In fact, maybe you're worried that *this* body could lead the cops back to you. You need someone for the cops to easily identify this woman as. Again, you're a cop yourself. You know what the sound does to a body. You know there's a good chance it will be basically unrecognizable when it washes ashore. And it *will* wash ashore. Where, you can't be sure. The chances of a body making it clear out to the ocean are next to none. So you hunt down a woman to take your victim's place. She has to be a windsurfer because you know your victim's going to come up wearing windsurf gear. You know what her face looked like, and you know her body type so you check out places where this time of year you can see body types—"

"The water."

"Exactly. Lakes, the shore maybe. You locate Norvak. She's perfect for your needs. Do you befriend her? Do you show her your badge out at her house and tell her you need to talk to her?"

"Jesus."

"You kill her. You stuff her into a fifty-five-gallon drum,

get some cement, and make her a steel coffin. You wait out most of the night. Before dawn the cement has set enough to move her. You roll the drum up into the back of her van. You take her sailboard and sails. But wait! You remember that the woman you lost was wearing a suit and a wetsuit. You need to balance the equation—Norvak can't suddenly have an extra wetsuit and swimsuit.''

''So you burn them.''

''Burn them down to a lump of nothing. Mind you, we never would be onto any of this if we hadn't connected the shoe prints. That was this guy's one mistake. A different pair of shoes, and we would have never connected it.''

''He drives her straight over to Carkeek,'' Shoswitz said, ''and dumps the body.''

''Maybe. A cliff somewhere would more suit his purposes. Maybe even one of the islands. We'll never find her, that's for sure, and that's all that matters. But he makes sure to leave the van where it will be found. He wipes it down and dumps the windsurf gear into the sound, assuming it will probably be found. Just like his victim, the chances of it getting out to sea are next to nil.

''But he doesn't know where the body is going to wash up. He doesn't know we can trace that body back from Alki to a point off of Vashon. Phil, the body wasn't anywhere near Carkeek. He didn't know about the undercurrents.''

Shoswitz sat in silence. The lights overhead buzzed. Down on the street a patrol car's siren kicked on and faded slowly into the distance.

''We have the teeth,'' Shoswitz reminded. ''I don't buy this switching records thing.''

''Two things I need from you,'' Boldt said.

''Surprise.''

''Abe lifted a male thumbprint from a paper plate behind Norvak's. If it is a cop, Phil, then his prints are in our files. I want to try for a match in our files.''

''Oh, Christ, Lou. You know what that involves? This

isn't Quantico, you know. We're talking hand-and-eye search, file by file. And to catch a single print, you're talking veteran expert, someone like Jimmie.''

"Okay, Jimmie then.''

"And what, Robbery and Narco take a two-month vacation? How long do you think it will take? Four weeks, six weeks, twelve weeks?''

"Someone else then. Not Jimmie.''

"Take 'em even longer.''

" 'No stone unturned.' That's what you handed me.''

"Okay. Sold, to the man in the ratty coat. One of Jimmie's assistants. But *one,* that's all. And no mention of why. He reports directly to me. Bad morale I don't need on top of everything else.'' He paused. "So what's number two?''

"Get me into Judith Fuller's apartment, Lieutenant. I've had Gaynes watching it and there's been no action whatsoever. There may be answers to this thing inside there. All I need is a warrant. I bust in there my way, and we can't use anything in court. The dental records could have been mixed up—Dixie told me it happens. And besides—I've already confirmed by X-rays of her elbow that Jane Doe is not Betsy Norvak. I'm waiting for a call now from Dixie. He's going to look at it personally—but I guarantee there's no arthritis in that elbow. That should be enough to get me my warrant.''

"Okay, okay. You'll have your warrant by morning. But don't leave me in the dark on this. I want to know the score, right? What you're implying here is that one of my men may be involved. I want to know what the fuck is going on, Lou.''

"Will do.''

Shoswitz stood and looked out at the empty office cubicles. "Gives me the creeps,'' he said. "You know what I mean?''

"I know what you mean.''

34

AT TEN MINUTES past eleven Dr. Ronald Dixon knocked on Boldt's front door. Boldt had been waiting for a call. He turned down the radio and answered the door.

Dixon stepped inside saying, "I called you a dozen times. Each time I get some all-night pharmacy."

"Phone company's working on it."

"Nice place," he said, not meaning it. Dixon had been over to dinner at Boldt's house a few times and this place didn't measure up.

"Thanks."

"Things any better with Liz?"

Boldt shrugged. "I miss her. I've got some beer in the box. Can I get you one?"

"Beer? You?"

"For my guests," he explained.

"Oh, I see. Been enjoying the bachelor life, have we?"

"It's not like that."

"I'd love one."

Boldt brought him a Miller in an aluminum can.

Dixon sat on the couch and patted it for feel. "Your porch smells like cat piss," he said.

"What's a fellow to do?" Boldt asked.

"Try tomato juice. Seriously. Buy a couple of quarts of

generic tomato juice up at the Safeway there, and mōp the corners with it. Hose it down. You'll notice a big difference. Works just like it does for skunks.''

"You didn't stop by to talk about cat piss."

"Who says I didn't? Has everything got to be business with you? We're friends, remember?" The men sat looking at each other. Their wives were good friends.

"I remember," Boldt said.

"And since I don't see your collection here, I'm assuming your offer of letting me borrow some was not based in truth."

"I'm moving it over here as soon as I have the time. The offer stands."

"Lou. Listen, Ginny and I talked about this. So Liz had a little fling? I mean, what marriage hasn't been through that a couple of times? You've been a wreck lately. You look like hell. Everybody says so. Liz has told Ginny everything, and if you ask me, I think she wants another go of it. She's not in love with anyone but you. You've been so buried in this damn case you haven't given any of us the time of day. It's not healthy. It's not good for anyone. Give it another shot, Lou. You're not the type of guy to be pigheaded about something. It's not in your nature. You know that as well as I. So why be pigheaded about Liz? She's your wife, for Christ's sake. And you *need* her, buddy. One look at you says that much. So how 'bout a little effort on your part?"

"You were going to look at Jane Doe for me."

"Lou."

"No promises, Dixie. We all handle this kind of thing in our own way. This is my way. This is how it has to be for me. At least for now. I go back now, nothing's going to be any different. A lot's riding on this case for me."

"Promotion? You think they base a promotion solely on case performance? You know better than that. What kind of leadership qualities does a man who can't even wear an ironed shirt have? I don't go along with that."

"My point is I'm too consumed to give Elizabeth any quality time. We'd be right back where we were, and that might wreck us for good."

"Ah! So there *is* some hope."

"Nothing's over until it's over. That includes marriages and investigations."

Dixon sampled the beer and smacked his lips. He was pale and his face oily. He appeared tired. "Why all the cloak and dagger on this?"

"Because we may have a copycat on our hands."

"But still—"

"And he may be in my department."

It silenced Dixon. He tried the beer again and kept the can in hand. "I thought you might say something like that. Then what I have to tell you is hardly going to make you sleep any better."

"No arthritis."

"No arthritis. Right. If Betsy Norvak's elbow looked that bad, then she's not Jane Doe, or more to the point, Jane Doe is not her. I went in and had a look. Clean as a whistle. Perfectly normal elbow."

"I thought so. And that will hold up in court, right?"

"It should."

"One other thing I'd like you to do for me, Dixie, when you get the time."

"Tonight? I can hear it in your tone of voice. Lou . . ."

"Whenever."

"What is it?" Dixon asked, resignation in his voice.

"I'd like you to compare two of the neck bruises."

"We did them *all*."

"I don't mean look them over, I mean compare. Really compare. Just the two of them against each other. Angles, amount of pressure. Anything you can give me."

"Who?"

"DeHavelin and Jane Doe."

Dixon shook his head, "No chance, Lou. Jane Doe's sponge cake. I can't get shit off of her."

35

ON A COLD Thursday morning, the twentieth of October, Shoswitz, Kramer, and Boldt sat down to discuss the case. The three men guzzled coffee and tugged on not-so-fresh donuts.

"These things suck," Shoswitz proclaimed, attempting to chew the rubber dough. "They hit bottom like a ton of rocks. Right?"

"White flour clogs the system, Lieutenant," Kramer announced merrily. "Try whole wheat."

"You're awfully quiet this morning, Lou," Shoswitz said.

Lou Boldt nodded. "Up late," he said.

He and Daphne had been sidestepping each other in the hallways. He thought it strange that their feud had actually brought them closer. He thought about her almost constantly. He kept hearing her tell him how he was "an interest." Her sulking bore that out. It was like a high-school infatuation. He knew it was time for an apology, but the situation had not presented itself—at least that's what he kept telling himself. Only now, at thirty-nine years of age, was he beginning to realize that situations don't present themselves, you make them happen. You create the way it is—isn't that what she had said?

"What do we have, Lou?"

"Yeah, Lou, what do *we* have?" Kramer whined.

"John," Shoswitz chided.

"Jesus, Lieutenant, I don't hear shit around here. I find shit out from my fucking detectives. Fuckin' LaMoia knows more about this case than I do. That's not right."

Shoswitz flashed Boldt a look. He said, "Listen to me, John. We're all on short fuses. We've all been stretched thin. Lou's put in some tough hours. He's done some fine police work. We *all* have. But let me make myself clear, here. This is a team. We don't need infighting. We've got plenty to handle without being on each other's cases. You got that?"

"What the fuck, Lieutenant? LaMoia knows more."

"My fault," Boldt said, attempting to calm Kramer, who seemed stunned by the comment.

"Damn right."

"Sorry, John. I needed some legwork done. I've been using LaMoia for that. My fault."

"Okay?" Shoswitz asked.

"Shit," Kramer spit out and settled back. "Fucking perfect."

"Lou?" Shoswitz asked.

"We have the match. LaMoia went back through Croy's finances. Eight months ago she joined a video-rental club —paid a one-time membership fee by check. The chain is called Market Video. Six stores in all, mostly along Market and in the U section. Three stores within the BSU boundary. The chain owns four plain yellow vans. They offer free delivery and pickup within their neighborhoods. We've confirmed that six of the other women were members as well. The computer never picked up the connection. It may be because the women rented the videos *days* before they were killed. We may have missed it because the women paid cash. Or it could be they called in their orders—did everything by phone. The computers would have missed that, too."

"The computers, or you, Boldt," Kramer criticized.

"John!" Shoswitz chided. "So we have three stores," he said. "Four vans. Any one of which could be the one spotted behind Croy's house."

"And we have tire impressions from that one," Kramer recalled.

"True," Boldt said, "but if we impound the vans we'll tip our hand. Scare him off."

"That's possible," Kramer acknowledged.

"We're jumping to conclusions. It's not necessarily one of those vans," Boldt said. "The problem is, it could be someone in the store. It could even be a *customer* who hangs around waiting to spot a woman renting a porno video. We can't be sure."

Kramer shifted uneasily in his chair, like he had a burr under his saddle. "So we need to put them under surveillance."

Boldt said, "I'm going to have LaMoia check the employee records of all six stores. Meanwhile I'd like to run three teams, one into each store. We use the girls from SA. One team assigned to each store. The woman signs up alone, we know his victims were members. We try different variations then: woman rents porno alone; woman and guy rent porno flick; woman calls in for a porno flick to be delivered. We're looking for a guy that matches the BSU profile—behind the counter or out in the racks. If we spot a suspect we put him under surveillance."

"A setup!" Kramer objected.

"Why not? Vice plants women undercover as hookers. We go after prostitution that way. Why should we let this guy get some innocent woman?" He pleaded his case to Shoswitz. "Maybe we can *control* where he hits. Besides, that's not the point. The idea is to keep our eyes open for a guy matching the profile. We have nothing on this guy, Lieutenant. We all know that. At *best* we can put him *near* one of the crime scenes—Croy's back fence. But we can't even place him inside the house. We haven't got squat. We need to find the bastard, follow him to his residence, search the place when he isn't there, and hopefully build a case against him. A partial palm print isn't going to take a jury 'beyond a reasonable doubt.' We have the courts to contend with. The Cross Killer could walk in here right now, and we couldn't hold him for more than twenty-four hours with what we've got.''

Boldt and Kramer exchanged glances.

"I don't know, Lou," Shoswitz said.

It pleased Kramer.

"He must be connected to one of the three stores. Maybe even all three. Two of the three victims we've linked to the chain shopped *different* Market Videos. Working there would give the killer access to the addresses. Listen, what I'm suggesting is that we run these pairs. They give the stores the *same* home address, three apartments in a building we choose. We stake out the apartment and wait for the killer to put it under surveillance. We *know* he cases these places. It's the only way he could possibly know the boyfriends aren't there. If we go in there as cops and scare him off, we may never have anything more than a palm print. It's *women* renting porn movies—that's how he selects his victims. He picks them out at the video store. When he's sure they're alone, he delivers flowers to get their doors open. We know what he does after that: he tapes their eyes open, holds them up by their hair, and makes them watch another porn movie while he kills them. Wonderful thought, right? He tortures them. Stabs them. What the hell? Are we going to let it happen again? It won't be long now until he hits again. And I, for one, can't see just sitting back and letting it happen.''

"Lou," Shoswitz snapped, "don't be an ass. That's a shitty thing to say." Again the men fell silent. "Your thoughts, John?''

"The single apartment building is a good idea. I have to go along with the suggestion. We need to have a hell of a lot of things fall into place if we're going to build a case against this guy. We can't just expect them to happen. As

Boldt pointed out," he said as if Boldt wasn't in the room,
"it's not like we're putting the skirts in a hell of a lot of
danger. This guy stakes them out; he delivers flowers; even
if it went to the extreme, we'd have the jump on him, not
the other way around. He'd be met at the door with a thirty-
eight in his face."

Shoswitz sighed and rubbed his elbow out of nervous
habit. "I don't know."

With Shoswitz, that was as good as a confirmation. "I'd
like to recommend Barbara Gaynes for the assignment, if
we go this direction," Boldt said. "I've been working with
her, and she's a good cop."

"I'll have to run it by the captain," Shoswitz pointed
out. "I want this to be a team effort, as tight as a gnat's
ass. Right? No more Jergensens. No way we let him get to
one of these women—and as far as Gaynes is concerned
. . . this is strictly volunteer. You hear me, Lou? I want
these girls to know the full extent of risk involved. This is
no vice operation—"

"These women are trained for rape investigations, Lieutenant," Boldt pointed out. "They're the logical choice."

"Volunteers. I want that made clear." He switched to
scratching his head. Boldt felt tempted to brush the man's
shoulders clean. "Set it up. Get it ready to go and wait for
the word. I'll take it upstairs."

"I'll get LaMoia going on those lists." Suddenly Boldt
felt wide awake.

36

"KNOCK, KNOCK."

"Shut the door," she instructed.

"I got your message," he said formally.

"Please," Daphne added.

Lou Boldt shut the door.

"Thank you."

"I owe you an apology," he said.

"Yes, you do. Accepted."

"I have this habit of driving people away from me."

"So I've noticed."

"I'd like to try again, if that's all right."

"I don't know. I don't think now is the time. We've got other things to discuss."

"Okay. May I?" he asked, motioning to the chair. He noted that she remained behind the security of her desk. She nodded, and he sat down.

She said formally, "We have several things to go over." Without pausing she continued, "First, I got your memo about the videos. I don't mind telling you the thought of that gives me the willies. Some guy behind the counter picking out his kills. Good God. But it fits. That's what you were asking me in the memo, and that's my professional opinion. It's a perfect fit, actually. . . . It tells us more about him. There may even be a specific video that precipitates his need to kill. I'd look into that if I were you—the names of the last porno videos rented. There may be something there. It may simply be that a woman rents what he considers to be a 'sinful' movie. There are all sorts of obvious implications here. But what it boils down to is that you have yourself his method of selection. The roses are symbolic, I think. They may mean something to him: his sweetheart, his bride. . . . To him it may all be connected to her death somehow."

"Oh, come on."

She paused, glaring at him. "I'm sure you're right about taping the victim's eyes open. He brings a film along with him. He restricts her—ties her facedown—and holds her head up by the hair, forcing her to watch. He brings her in and out of consciousness with the ligature around her neck." She hesitated to clear her throat. "I called BSU in Quantico and ran it by the doctor we've been dealing with there. He suggested something to me that I hadn't considered, and I think it's worth passing along to you. That is, there's a good chance he rapes them. I know. I know. We haven't had any evidence of that. But we've been overlooking something . . . something none of us has considered until now, and that is the possibility that he uses a condom. I haven't called the ME; that's your business. But I would if I were you. The agent I spoke with pointed out that an ME only swabs for semen. They wouldn't pick up a rape with condoms unless there was some bruising. And if he ties her down . . ."

Boldt recalled the paramedics mentioning a strange but familiar medicinal smell. It wouldn't be hard to check out. "To punish them?"

"Exactly. He considers them dirty—filthy. The condom keeps him 'pure,' while he punishes them. And it fits with a lust murder. We've thought he might be impotent all along. This, because of the lack of rape evidence. I think we better reassess. BSU is feeding the videotape information into VICAP to see if we get a match with any other serial killings. I doubt we will. This video business is a new angle—was new even to the agent I spoke with.'' She reached up toward her hair to finger-comb it, but thought better of it.

"Hell of a thing to be original at."

"I want to remind you of something. I realize my timing may be less than perfect, but I want to stress again that this man is more than likely both schizophrenic and psychotic. He is a very sick man."

"Daphne . . ."

"It's important you remember who and what you're dealing with. If we accept his profile, he's probably been under psychiatric care before and was subsequently discharged. He's probably been prescribed medicines that he not only can't afford but can't remember to take. Do we blame him for that?"

"You expect me to feel sorry for this animal?" he asked. "I have to live with his victims, Daffy."

"He's a human being, damn it! First and foremost he's a human being. Not, I repeat, *not,* some animal. Why is it that you cops insist on seeing the mentally ill as animals?" She was half out of her chair, and her face was scarlet. She sat back down and made no attempt at an apology. She began to work with her hair then, her eyes glued to her desk. Boldt had trouble with the textbook side of Daphne Matthews.

He waited for what felt like an eternity before saying softly, "He's a murderer. He murders women. Okay?"

"That's unacceptable," she told the desk.

He did not reply immediately. He waited before asking, "What about my copycat? Have you had any time to work on that?"

As if they had begun their discussion here, she said, "I've been working on that for you," hoisting a large reference book.

"And?"

"Your copycat is altogether different from the Cross Killer. He's more than likely a psychopath or sociopath, not psychotic. His childhood was a wreck. His behavior is amoral and asocial. He's highly intelligent. He knows no shame, and has no remorse for what he does. His crimes are premeditated—deliberate. For this reason, psychopaths are frightening. Don't misunderstand. It's not that he isn't ill —of course he is—he is more than likely *socially* ill, and therefore more dangerous, more unpredictable, much more difficult to treat than the psychotic.''

"And I'm supposed to differentiate between the two?"

"Yes," she told him, attempting tenderness in her voice. "You of all people, Lou. You're a cop."

"Anything else?" he wondered. "Anything *you* want to talk about?"

"There's one other thing, if you have a minute."

"Sure."

She rounded her desk, went over to the door, and pushed against it. She came over and knelt by him. She pulled him to her and hugged him. "Hold me," she pleaded softly into his ear.

He felt the warmth of her surround him. The comforting warmth. The sweet smell of her neck. The softness of her as she pressed against him. Her delicate hands stroking his back. Confusion built from the sour pit in his stomach. His arms began to tremble, his shoulders shake. He wanted tenderness. He was starved for it.

She didn't say anything. She pressed her face tenderly against his scratchy cheek and kissed him lightly.

Their lips met eagerly, and they both laughed simultaneously.

"What are we doing?" he asked.

But she didn't answer. She silenced him with another kiss.

37

HE LEFT HER OFFICE, drained but on the comeback. The emotional release he had experienced, coupled with the excitement of their shared intimacy, rekindled his energy and enthusiasm. He left Kramer to establish a list of women volunteers—reminding himself to leave room for Bobbie Gaynes—and headed off to find Bobbie.

Shoswitz caught up to him in the hallway. "For you," he said, handing Boldt a folded piece of paper. "Thought you might like something to do. Better than waiting around."

Boldt knew from the feel of it what it was: the search warrant for Fuller's apartment. "Thanks, Lieutenant."

"No sweat."

Bobbie was parked in a Pay & Park, across the street from the Seagate Apartments, well hidden but with a good view of number 321—Fuller's apartment. Boldt slid into the front seat and she said, "Nothing going. Dead as a doornail."

He explained the video connection in the Cross Killer case, and that the department was asking for Special Assaults volunteers to case the three Market Video stores that had been connected to the victims. He let her know there was room for her if she wanted the assignment. She jumped at the opportunity, eager to get out of a stakeout, and asked, "Why me?"

"Because you're good. Because you want to be the first woman cop assigned to Homicide. It won't happen overnight. We both know that. But you stand as good a chance as anyone else. You're a good cop, Bobbie. You think like a cop and you're willing to work and to learn, two keys to becoming a good homicide investigator. It's a long road in this division—but this is the ultimate in being a cop. Believe me. For all its rough moments, this is it."

"I know," she said. "I love it."

Chen Wo was tall and lanky with hunched shoulders and thinning hair. He looked to be in his fifties. When asked by Boldt, Wo mentioned that Fuller's car had not been parked in its slip for over three weeks. Fuller had sublet the apartment through a client of Lyn Lymann Property Management, and as a result, neither Lymann nor Wo had anything more current than what Bobbie had turned up at the rental shop—a California driver's license. Wo had met her once, two months before. He had not run into her since. He admitted them to Fuller's apartment without even looking at the warrant, asking them to check in with him before leaving, which they agreed to do.

Boldt removed two pairs of disposable surgical gloves from his coat pocket and handed a pair to Gaynes. They both put them on. "You should start carrying these," he said.

The door swung open. It was a plain, stark apartment, smelling of rug cleaner and disinfectant.

"What's your first impression, Detective?" Boldt asked before they were barely inside.

"It's new. It feels new and not lived in. Almost temporary."

Boldt shut the door and switched on the light. "Go on." He followed her.

"No photographs. No personal memorabilia." The living room was sterile and looked like a section of a furniture showcase. The kitchen clean, cupboards bare except for breakfast cereal, instant coffee, and Equal. The refrigerator held a quart of sour milk, two Dannon yogurts, and withered celery. "She eats out," Bobbie said, Boldt following behind. "She's single."

Her bedroom was equally bare, reminding Boldt of a motel. The bathroom sink was messy. The shower needed cleaning. "She's not domestic," Gaynes observed. "Strange that the desktop should be so clean." She checked the drawers. The top center drawer was bare. The two others were cluttered and brimming with paper. "Why the empty drawer?"

"That's good," Boldt told her. "I agree. Trash basket is empty, too."

Gaynes leafed through the top left drawer. There were two boxes, each brimming with receipts, one filled with those from credit cards, the other with what appeared to be cash receipts. A folder had careful accounting of dozens of entries—two columns, cash and credit card.

"She keeps good books," Bobbie noted.

"Agreed."

"So?"

"So, who keeps these kinds of books?" he wondered.

She checked the contents of the file folder. "Telephone accounting, too. Thorough."

"So?"

Bobbie Gaynes thought for a moment and then said, "An expense account. This goes beyond home accounting . . . she's kept track of every cent she's spent. She's on an expense account."

"Agreed."

"So she's working for someone." She beamed. "And that may tell us something."

"Or she *was*," reminded Boldt.

Seeing the Mobil Oil credit-card bills gave Boldt an idea. They went through the bills carefully, noting each date.

Bobbie said, "So she filled up at the same gas station once she reached Seattle—"

"Just around the corner," Boldt added, noting the address.

"And she filled up about once—sometimes twice—a week. Last billing date is over a month ago. There are still clothes in her closet, so she hasn't moved. But she may be away visiting. We can't say for certain she's Jane Doe until we cross-check these signatures against the windsurfing supply rental agreement."

"She's Jane Doe," Boldt said defiantly. "And according to these"—he pointed to the bills—"she stayed in Denver and Tucson, prior to here, but only for a week or so in each place. These stations in between show us the route she used to move between the cities, and they tell us that she relied on this card for, what looks like, all her gas. If we take that a step further, then if she's still alive, she's still using the card." He read a number from the bill, picked up the phone carefully, and dialed. Bobbie Gaynes roamed the room for ten minutes while Boldt spoke on the phone inquiring about current charges.

When he hung up the phone, she said, "All her dresses are synthetic. No iron. She travels light. No toothbrush in her medicine cabinet, no deodorant or toothpaste. I don't see a suitcase. It looks like she took a trip. But she left her eyeliner."

"So she left in a hurry."

"Or someone did her packing for her. I wouldn't leave my eyeliner, I'll tell you that."

"There have been no gas charges in the last three weeks on her account, though it sometimes takes several weeks for charges to be fully processed. It doesn't give us a definite, but it gives us a possibility."

"I have a feeling I'm going to be hunting for cars again," Bobbie worried.

"Unless you volunteer for the video stakeout."

"I'll volunteer. You *know* I'll volunteer. But it doesn't mean they'll pick me. There are others in Special Assaults who would love a shot at Homicide. The only reason I got this assignment was because everyone believed it was going to be gofer work."

"Live and learn," Boldt said.

"Indeed."

"We'll place her car on the stolen sheet, check citations, alert repair shops and parking garages. I'll notify State Police in Washington, Oregon, California, Idaho, and Nevada, and contact Canadian Immigration. We'll find her car.

"I keep all my current stuff in my top drawer. How about you?" he added.

Bobbie took the hint. "Someone cleared her drawer out. *And* they packed for her. I'll call I.D. and have them dust for latents."

He nodded. "We'll try and get into her bank accounts and search deposits. That may trace backward to an employer, which may tell us more about her. Someone has to know what she was doing here."

"Windsurfing?"

"Yes, I think we've already met Judith Fuller," Boldt stated bluntly. "I think Dixie's got her on ice down at the ME's."

38

THREE SPECIAL ASSAULTS DETECTIVES were selected from a list of nine volunteers for the stakeout teams. It was agreed that the women would sign up for membership at the three Market Videos within the BSU boundary. Bobbie Gaynes was assigned the Market Video on Forty-sixth Street. They would give the same address, but using different apartment numbers. The three apartment rentals had been arranged through Special Operations earlier in the afternoon.

The minute Gaynes returned from her first visit to the store, she headed directly to Boldt's office. Boldt and Kramer ushered her into interrogation room A, the same room in which Boldt had heard Elizabeth's voice for the last time. The door clicked shut and Boldt smelled the bitter afterglow of sweat and cigarette smoke he found so distasteful. Gaynes wore black pleated pants and a white pleated blouse and looked like anything but a detective.

"So?" Kramer asked as they all sat down.

She looked over at Lou Boldt. "The clerk was a woman."

"Terrific," Kramer complained.

"And we ran into an unforeseen snag."

"What's that?" asked Boldt.

"She didn't ask me for my address, she took it off my

driver's license. I wasn't able to give her the apartment address you wanted.''

"Damn," Boldt snarled. "That's no good. Stop the others. We'll have to issue them new driver's licenses," he told Kramer.

"I'll get on it." Kramer left the room.

"He's not so bad," Bobbie said to Boldt.

"He's like a chest cold that way: at first he's just a tickle at the back of the throat. He becomes a pain later on. Tell me about the store."

"It's huge, and very busy. They must have close to a thousand videos. Everything you can imagine."

"Did you rent anything?"

"Sure."

"But not porno, I hope. Not the first time."

"I know how to follow orders, Sergeant. I rented *The Thirty-Nine Steps*. Alfred Hitchcock. The only problem is, I don't own a VCR. I think I'm the last person not to own one."

"We'll get you one. That's no problem. Do you think you can get your address changed on the membership?"

"I'm sure it's possible to do, but the woman insisted I show her a state driver's license and a major credit card. If I change it, it may arouse suspicion—I almost corrected it while I was there—but the thing is, it may cause someone to remember the address, and the fact that the same address will be used at the other stores by the other girls made me cautious."

"You did the right thing. It does complicate things, but we'll put you under surveillance at your own apartment."

"What's next on the Judith Fuller investigation?"

Boldt looked at her curiously. "I hope you understood fully what this volunteer work entails."

"You weren't serious about me going home and sitting around all day, were you?"

"We'll keep you under surveillance."

"You have to be kidding! You guys were serious? I checked for any tails. All the procedures. It took me nearly two hours to make sure I wasn't being followed. Put me to work. I'm clean."

"No can do. This is your last briefing here. And since my mug has been in the papers so much lately," Boldt added, "we've assigned John LaMoia to be your contact and go-between. If we have anything to pass to you, John will do it. He's your new boyfriend. The apartments we've rented are set up to handle that. You'll have to improvise now."

"Meaning?"

"You know how we're running this, Bobbie. We have to act the whole thing out to the T. We *talked* about this. LaMoia's going to take you out to dinner a few times. Show up at the apart—at your place after work. He'll have to spend the night a few times."

"Oh, Christ. What have I gotten myself into? I have a one-bedroom efficiency apartment over on Eighth Avenue in the U section. The bathroom is the size of a postage stamp. If two people are in the kitchen at the same time, they brush fannies. This is not going to work."

"You're going to have to make it work. I assume you've had visitors before—"

"And that's another thing . . . What do I say to my friends, one of whom is not going to take kindly to John LaMoia coming over to watch X-rated videos with me. I'm assuming we'll have to do that as well. . . ."

"You know the routine. You have to act it out all the way. We don't know to what extremes the killer goes. He may try and peep on you while you're watching the show. Who knows? At the apartment building we chose, we had three units close together. It was much more easily controlled. Up until the lights go out at your place, you'll want to act it out as best you can. We'll be right there of course. We should know if he has you under surveillance."

She shivered. "I don't like the thought of that."

"Having LaMoia around may not be so bad after all."

"I'd rather it were you. I *trust* you."

You shouldn't, he thought. You're young, sweet, and quite beautiful, just the kind of temptation a recently separated man in his late, late thirties doesn't need.

"LaMoia's an animal," she continued.

"Enough," he said somewhat harshly.

She nodded, and then had an idea. "Listen, since what we're after is covering as many shifts as possible at these places, why don't I return later tonight and tell them my machine broke down and I've sent it off to be repaired and I'd like to rent one? It would definitely speed things up. Since LaMoia's my partner and he's on stakeout up there, I could just wait until he told me the shift changed, and then go back in. That's really how we're doing it anyway, right?"

Boldt nodded. "Sure. That's fine by me. Just remember, we don't know what this guy looks like. We think he wears sneakers and jeans. It doesn't give us much. You'll have to do all your communication with LaMoia by phone through the radio dispatcher. You don't want to direct attention to the stakeout."

"I understand," she said.

"Now get out of here. And don't come back. You need me, give me a call. From here on out you're Bobbie Gaynes, duly unemployed, attractive young woman with a thing for porno flicks."

"I've got a tight leather skirt that will fit that image perfectly."

"Don't overdo it."

"And black fishnet panty hose," she said, standing, smiling, and touching Boldt lasciviously on the hard line of his cheek. "That ought to get a rise."

"Bobbie . . ." he chided.

She stopped at the door and shoved out her hip, playfully.

It was a nice hip, and it fit inside her black slacks very well. "Later," she said, running her fingers down the molding and closing the door.

LaMoia was gabbing by the smoking room. Boldt pulled him aside and reviewed how he would team up with Gaynes. LaMoia complained about the overtime but shut up when he saw the look in Boldt's eyes. Boldt asked, "What about the employee lists at the Market Videos?"

"Hey, Sarge, I put in the request as soon as I could. The owner wouldn't take my call until an hour ago. I told him we needed it ASAP, but you didn't want me tipping our hand so I couldn't rag on the guy. He says he'll have a complete list sometime late afternoon. That's the best I could do."

Boldt nodded. Sometimes the pace of an investigation was stifling. "Keep on him, John. Don't let him stall us too long. He probably thinks it's IRS-related or something. We'll have to wait him out, but we don't want to wait forever."

"Okay, Sarge."

The officer of the day, a uniformed sergeant in his mid-fifties, spotted Boldt and came over. "This just in for you, Lou." He handed Boldt an interdepartmental memo. Boldt read it. "Keep me filled in, John. Got to run."

An airport security patrol had found Judith Fuller's Mercury parked in a long-term lot at SeaTac International Airport. The long-term lot was a favorite dumping ground for both stolen and abandoned cars, and a routine patrol cross-checked registration numbers against police lists. That afternoon, the sky smoky with ashen clouds and heavy with the noxious odor of diesel fuel, Lou Boldt slipped on a pair of gloves and used a police "speed key" to unlock and open the driver's door. The device, a favorite tool of car thieves, gained him access to the car in a matter of seconds. He left the door open and was careful not to touch anything as he leaned his head inside.

Abrams joined him twenty minutes later and said he had only agreed to dust the car because Lou was a friend and he had heard that Lou had offered Doc Dixon a chance to tape his record collection. Abrams wanted to tape three Charlie Parker albums. A deal was cut, right then and there, and Lou Boldt realized he had opened Pandora's box. The piranhas were on him now. So as part of the contingency plan he let Abrams know that all taping had to be done on his equipment, under his watchful eye. He didn't bother to explain that his albums and recording equipment were still with Elizabeth.

It only took Abrams a matter of minutes to determine the car had either been driven by a person wearing cotton gloves, or had been wiped down. The door and the steering wheel were clean, as was the interior rearview mirror. He was dusting the exterior mirror mounted to the driver's door when he suggested that Boldt might want to check what size person had driven the car last, as they had done with the Norvak minivan. He pointed out that there were cotton fibers on this mirror as well, indicating that it may have been adjusted. As Boldt climbed in and pulled the door shut, Abrams moved on to dust the gas cap and flap door on the side of the car.

Boldt came out of the car with a puzzled look on his face. "I could see in the mirror without any problem," Boldt confirmed. "Fuller isn't that tall. I'm a little over six feet."

"Look here," Abrams said, pointing to the gas cap, "I've got a beauty." Abrams had dusted the gas cap, yielding a large and perfectly formed print. "By the size of it, that's a man's thumbprint. Right thumb. That's what we've been waiting for."

"May I search the car?"

"Go ahead. And while you're in there, pop the hood for me." He saw Boldt's expression and explained, "If he got gas, chances are he might have checked the oil."

"It could be nothing more than a gas attendant's print, Chuck," Boldt reminded.

"True. My job's not to find out who the prints belong to, just to find the prints. Pop the hood."

Boldt climbed back inside the car and popped the hood for Abrams. As the hood came up, the inside of the car darkened. Boldt slid open the ashtray. It was littered with butts lying in a bed of dark gray ashes. He used his pen to stir the contents. Some of the ashes lifted out and floated down to the interior carpeting, and a moment later the car smelled more bitter. He tried the glove box next. Her papers were all in order: a current registration listing Fuller's Los Angeles address and an insurance voucher. Gleaning her home address from a credit card, Boldt had already tried Fuller's home phone number and had found it disconnected. He assumed the address no longer valid, the apartment or home sublet or rented out again. They had put in a request to the LAPD to check the apartment out for them, but Boldt knew it would take several weeks for the unimportant request to be handled, and it was not worth the taxpayers' money to fly down and have a look himself, though he was tempted to do so anyway. He opened the front page of the owner's manual and six parking tickets dropped into his lap—two from Denver, four from SPD's traffic division. Returning the manual to the glove box, he studied each of the tickets in detail, knowing full well they would tell him where Fuller had been and when she had been there. He ignored the two from Denver. The other four had been issued earlier in the month, within a time span of ten days. From what he could tell, all the addresses were in the general downtown area. He pocketed all four, like a miner pockets a land claim, and dug back into the box with the same enthusiasm a miner might use to force a pick into the hard earth. He pulled out a white envelope, another nugget worth weighing. Inside the envelope were a dozen receipts. He leafed through them briefly—more recent dates than those found in the apartment—aware they would require additional scrutiny back at his office. He would line them up by date and organize them according to category. The parking tickets and receipts both from the car and the apartment offered just the kind of puzzle he lived for. With any luck at all he would soon know exactly where Fuller had been, what she had been buying, and therefore quite possibly what she had been doing in Seattle.

"Nothing worthwhile," Abrams said, leaning his bald black head into the car. "How about you?"

"Hit a gold mine," Boldt said, waving the envelope in the air. "Receipts spanning nearly a two-week period, by the look of it. They should help."

"I'll take the gas cap back to the office. Need me for anything else?"

"Radio in to have this thing towed, would you please? I'll hang around until they arrive."

Abrams said he would, and a minute later, after packing up his gear, was gone.

Boldt began a thorough inspection of the car. He noted the rented roof rack for the windsurfer as well as sandy mud on the fenders that he also found evidence of on the accelerator and the driver's floor mat. He scraped some of it into the receipt envelope as a sample. Methodically, he searched every square inch of the car's interior, not knowing what he was looking for. This was nothing new to him. He wondered how many dozens of cars he had searched in this exact way—cars belonging to victims or suspects. A few of the boys from Vice ran a lecture once a year on new-model cars, pointing out easily accessed hiding places. Boldt hadn't bothered to attend for a few years, and realized now it was one of those things worth the time.

It took him several minutes to search the front-seat area thoroughly. In the process he discovered the radio's on-off knob had been left on. He used the speed key to engage the car's battery. Static-cluttered classical music filled the car. Boldt noted the FM station's call number and then pushed the radio's first preset button. The reception jumped and he was listening to an AM news station. The next button brought a similar news station, also AM. The third button switched the radio to the FM band—soft rock. The fourth and fifth gave two more rock stations. None of the presets—all tuned for Seattle stations, he noted—had produced classical music. It suggested that someone other than the car's owner had last used the radio—someone who liked classical music, not rock. It was an inconsistency that intrigued Lou Boldt.

"You gonna go for a ride, or what, buddy?" The man's face was acne-scarred and he had a devious delight in his eyes, proud of his comment.

Boldt had not heard the tow truck arrive.

39

DAPHNE MATTHEWS KNOCKED on Boldt's front door at just after seven that night. He answered it, surprised to see her, and asked her in. She carried a bag of groceries in her arms. She wore a white pleated blouse and black skirt. Jade earrings danced from her lobes. "Relief supplies," she announced. "I'm counting on the fact you haven't eaten dinner."

"Good guess."

"Show me to the kitchen and then stay out of my way." She whisked past him, well aware of where the kitchen was. She called out, "I know you're not a drinker, but I brought some wine along and I'm hoping you'll help me out. You can begin by opening it so it can breathe."

He was going to object to the wine, but didn't. He found himself watching her as she unpacked the groceries. Cork-screw in hand, he liberated the cork and set the bottle aside to breathe. It was a California Cabarnet, Robert Mondavi. She kicked him out of the kitchen a minute later and told him she had heard wonderful things about his jazz collection, and how about a sample? He explained he didn't have his collection here, but turned on the radio in the living room in time to hear that tonight's Spotlight featured Ornette Coleman. He returned to the kitchen. "I have homesteading rights,'' he told her. ''You can't kick me out of my own kitchen.''

''No comment,'' she said, going about her work studiously. She brought some water to boil and placed fifteen good-sized shrimp into it, leaving them only a matter of seconds. She then peeled them, deveined them, and placed them to one side. She instructed him to empty the pot, clean it, and bring about a quart of water to boil. He obeyed without comment. She was prepping some onions and green pepper when she said, ''You like pasta?''

''Love it.''

''Blackened fish?''

''Never had it.''

''Never had blackened fish? Do you like spicy food— hot, spicy food?''

He worried about his stomach and said anyway, ''Sure.''

''Good, because that's what you're getting.''

''Why the meal? Why the special treatment?'' he asked.

She turned and faced him. She had brought along an apron she was now wearing. It read: Kiss the Cook. She stepped up to him and kissed him on the lips. It was a long gentle kiss. She kept her eyes open and stared right back at him. ''That's why,'' she told him nervously. ''Because I liked that this morning, and I thought you did too.''

''Guilty,'' he said.

''Is that how it feels to you?''

''Kind of.'' He thought of Elizabeth. He liked Daphne, appreciated her presence, but she was not Elizabeth.

''It shouldn't.''

''I know.''

''You'll get over it.''

''Glad to hear it.''

She heard his cynical tone of voice and asked, ''Would you prefer I leave?''

''No.''

''Sure?''

''Sure.''

"Pour me some wine."

"Yes, dear."

She produced four metal skewers and went about thread-ing shrimp, onion, cherry tomato, and green pepper onto them. He marveled at how she turned a pile of food into a work of art. He found the color combinations and the shapes extremely attractive and appetizing.

He poured them each a glass of wine. It tasted great to him. "A toast to the chef," he said.

"No fair," she protested, "I can't drink to that."

"In this house you can."

"Splendid." She beamed and sipped the red wine, hum-ming her approval. "I should have brought white—with fish, that is—but white wine and I don't often agree."

"I wouldn't know the difference. I drink wine about twice a year: Christmas and Easter. Not a real connoisseur."

They remained silent as she melted some unsalted butter and brushed the skewered shrimp. She then sprinkled a red powder flecked with black spices onto the shrimp. The stove was electric. She moved the oven rack close to the top element, produced a small cast-iron skillet, and placed it beneath the broiler element. "This is an attempt to contain the smoke," she said. "It works at home." He had gone through his first glass of wine quickly, and he poured himself another, noticing she had barely touched hers. He encour-aged her to keep up.

The pasta and the Cajun shrimp-kebob were ready si-multaneously. Boldt set the table quickly and suddenly they were both facing each other at the dinner table. She retrieved a candle from her shopping bag, melted it to a saucer, and lit it, turning off the lights.

"Thanks," he said, preparing to eat.

She topped off their wines and sat down, staring through the flickering candle and returning his fond gaze. She blew lightly on the flame and it bent toward him briefly before standing strongly again. He returned the gesture. The flame pointed toward Daphne.

"We humans bend like that, don't we," she mused.

"How's that?"

"To the whim of the other."

"Sometimes," he said, thinking that lately he had been independent, not bending toward anyone; *lonely,* he thought they called it.

"It has been a strange couple of weeks."

"Yes, it has."

"For a while there I wasn't sure you would be able to handle it. A lot of pressure was heaped on your shoulders, not the least of which was Jergensen. How do you think that leak happened, anyway? I know some of the department blames me, but I swear—"

"I know it wasn't you, Daffy. Everyone who knows Daphne Matthews, knows it's not her style. Whoever leaked that information—first that we had apprehended a guy in that neighborhood, and then that he fit the BSU profile— is directly responsible for Jergensen's murder. He or she should be thrown off the force. I doubt we'll ever know who did it."

"That's the ugly side of being a cop: there are so many unanswered questions, unsolved cases. As a psychologist I understand the need for completion. Too many incompletes in one's life and the stress and tension become too much to bear."

"Tell me about it."

She stabbed at her food. Boldt consumed his voraciously.

"I've been thinking about your copycat," she said.

"Yes?"

"Yes. If you close in on him, I'd like you to do me a favor."

Boldt suddenly thought he was about to hear the reason for the special treatment. So you want something from me, he thought. Just like Rutledge's description of Puget Sound, there are things happening on the surface and there are things happening underneath. Nothing is as simple as it seems. "I'm listening."

"We, that is, people in my profession, seldom have a chance to work with a homicidal personality prior to arrest. We are brought in later to identify and quantify the degree of an individual's sickness. We're meat inspectors for the most part. And by the time we see the individual he is typically resigned to his own failure, to the permanence of his incarceration."

"What are you asking?" he wondered in a less tolerant tone of voice.

"Just thinking aloud, that's all."

"Daffy—"

"If you know who it is, Lou, and it works out, I would appreciate a few minutes with him prior to his arrest."

"My first reaction is, *impossible*."

"I was certain it would be. But a situation might arise."

He nodded. "Yeah, it might, I suppose."

"Let's leave it at that. Just keep it in mind."

"Okay."

"The thing about it is, it would be an incredible opportunity. A chance like that might not only help people in my profession but in *our* profession as well. It might give us some insight into motivations and rationales that elude us once a person is put in an unworkable situation."

"I said, okay. Okay?"

"Sorry I've upset you."

"It doesn't take much, these days. It's not your fault."

"I'm sorry, Lou."

"Really, no problem. Not your fault. There's a lot on my mind. Sometimes I'm thinking about so many things that it's hard to think. How's that for not making any sense?"

"It makes plenty of sense."

He sipped his wine. He felt pleasantly light-headed. "I'm lonely, Daffy." His face tightened. "I've isolated myself. Being a cop used to be one thing I did. Now it's all I seem to have. It's all I've left myself with. I've isolated myself but good. Being a cop is like a terminal disease or something: it consumes you, entirely, slowly but surely. I've allowed it to take everything out of my life. And I've suddenly reached the stage where I resent that.''

"That's understandable.''

"But I did it to myself. No one made me do this.'' No one but the Cross Killer, he thought. "What got you into this, Daffy?''

"You've heard the rumors?'' she wondered.

"There are rumors about all of us.''

"True enough.''

"If you don't want to talk—''

"On the contrary. I do.'' She paused.

He waited.

"I had a private practice for a while. Part of a clinic. Had my own patients.'' She put her fork down. "People are so complex,'' she said, and her voice trailed off. "I had in my practice a young woman. Not very pretty. Not particularly bright.'' He could feel that she was very far away. "She had been abused by a stepfather. Sexually abused. Repeatedly. For years. Made to do horrible things. She was too young at the time to know any better. It wasn't until a few years before I saw her that she began to understand the full weight of exactly what she had been through. She spent a lot of her adulthood thinking about it—looking back— and it was very destructive. We worked on that together.'' She seemed mesmerized by the candle. Boldt watched her eyes watch the candle's flame. As the flame wavered, her expression seemed to change. "Her stepfather had been a truck driver, and while she was in treatment with me, she began to seek out truck stops—hang around truck stops. I tried to steer her away from this. She wasn't certain why she did it, and she had several blackouts—total blackouts associated with the visits that worried me terribly. I debated institutionalizing her. Decided against it,'' she said painfully. The flame straightened. Black carbon rose in a steady stream. "Not long after,'' she said, "she was raped by a truck driver. Incidentally, he was later let off by a judge because he claimed she had come on to him. I don't believe that, for what it's worth. I told the judge so, but it didn't seem to help any, did it? Anyway"—she glanced at him—"I still resisted institutionalizing her." She sipped the wine. "On a Tuesday night—I remember it was a Tuesday— Mary Alice walked into a truck stop waving a handgun."

"Oh, God . . ." Boldt said. She nodded.

"She fired one shot into the ceiling. No drugs. No substance abuse. She had simply come undone. I had lost her, and I was too green to realize it. It was my fault, Lou," she said in a way he found impossible to contradict. "She never killed anyone. Never even wounded anyone." She continued, "He was a rookie cop. His partner was in the men's room at the time. Someone shouted, and I quote, 'She's *flipped out*, she's got a gun.' Mary Alice spun around and the patrolman fired four shots into her chest. She never knew what hit her." After a long hesitation she said, "After that, I began to look around and I saw a void in law enforcement that no one seemed to be addressing. The mentally ill are vastly misunderstood, Lou. Mary Alice didn't go in there to kill anyone. She was a sick individual who needed more help than I was giving her."

"You couldn't have foreseen—"

"You *never* can foresee. But you learn to anticipate. That's why I've been browbeating you over this case. I want to see that he gets help, not a bullet through his head. The only mistake that's unforgivable is a repeated mistake."

She came out of her chair and was standing next to him. She placed her warm hands on his head and pulled him against her chest. She was soft and good. She held him there, whispering something incoherent. He reached out and awkwardly hugged her around the middle, his big hands resting gently on her hips and the slick surface of her skirt. Her heart continued to drum, out of sync with the music. He sensed she was crying. She trembled in his arms. Crying for Mary Alice? he wondered. Crying for me? For herself?

No, he thought, just crying. Crying perhaps because she doesn't understand this any more than I do. None of us has it completely figured out.

He pulled her down to face him. He kissed the tears from her face, wishing he had tears of his own. She blurted out his name a few more times, shaking her head, her message obvious. Her message ignored.

He kicked away the chair. It tipped and crashed to the floor, evoking a giggle from her. She was unbuttoning his shirt. He worked loose the oversized buttons on the back of her blouse, and as it came free she slipped out of it, allowing it to gracefully slide down her long arms and cascade to the carpet in an uneven heap of peaks and contours.

He wanted to disappear inside of her, to meld into her and dwell there alone with her thoughts and her tenderness. Their bare chests touched and he sensed the first awakening within him. He kissed his way down her chest and felt her shiver as he took her into his lips. Her fingers wormed in his hair. Then their lips met again and she seemed filled with a renewed intensity. His thoughts vanished. He was nowhere but with her. Her sensitivity overwhelmed him, overpowered him to the point that all was lost but their mutual frenzied effort at intimacy. Their attempts developed into a kind of restrained wrestling, an awkwardly compassionate, aching bid at consonance. They rolled beneath the table and Boldt banged his foot against a table leg. Laughing, she pulled his pants off, simultaneously thumping her head and crying out. And then, free of her own undergarments, she spread herself atop him, drawing him into her warmth. For a moment they were awkward with the intimacy, but then it developed into a playful, empathetic rite, a private ritual not born out of love as much as from mutual need.

As they joined, Boldt was consumed by the smooth, luscious warmth that enveloped him. In their careless affection they had become one, however briefly, and nothing could ever remove that from either of them. She moved steadily above him, her head occasionally thumping the underside of the tabletop. She smiled down at him, and then bent to kiss him hotly as the timing of her efforts increased. He relished their physical exhilaration, and the delicious intensity of it. He encouraged her to join him now in his release, his tongue searching for her firm nipple, hands locked under her arms, lifting and dropping her heavily upon himself. He begged for her release, suddenly answered by rippling contortions that directed his senses to the deepest point of their union, drawing his heat from within, flowing into her as she cried out softly and clutched him firmly. They sang together briefly, an odd harmony at best. Soon —too soon, he thought—the moment passed; she sank peacefully into his arms, their skin damp and salty, their chests heaving in long, uncontrolled breaths, their hearts pounding out "Big Noise from Winnetka." And slowly— too soon, he thought—he returned to the somewhat embarrassing reality of their nakedness, of their joined bodies below a dining room table, of the silence left behind. Ornette Coleman was finished. They were finished.

How does one stay there? he wondered. How can one preserve that moment of tranquillity and bottle it for future use? Is it sex that makes us feel this good, or is it the fundamental knowledge that we are willingly participating in a shared emotion? That we are contributing.

"The latter, I think," she whispered tenderly into his ear. And he realized he had spoken his thoughts aloud. "You don't need to tell me you love me, if that's what's bothering you," she said. "And I won't tell you, if doing so will make you uncomfortable. Even if it is the truth. But what just took place between us transcended sex so completely, so totally that the word loses all meaning by comparison. I was so far gone from this room. I was off with you . . . well aware of you . . . lost in a combined fulfillment of *epic* proportions. That one was for Cecil B. De Mille," she said, drawing a laugh from him. "When we first began," she admitted, "I felt it was the wrong direction

to go. It was awkward and even frantic. But my God, Lou
. . .'' She wiggled on top of him and felt him stir inside of
her. "Good Lord, that was wonderful."

He kissed her lips lightly at first. Their hearts and breathing had slowed. Her fingers twisted in his hair, her breasts
slid moistly across his chest as she adjusted herself to en-
tertain his rekindled enthusiasm. Her skin was soft, her
buttocks firm, and her hips powerful as she began to respond
to his swelling and the delightful wavelike motions he offered her. He took hold of her rib cage and with a surprising
quickness inverted them in a single roll. She swallowed him
up with her thighs, trapping him so that each of his motions
transferred to her. She held to him tightly at first, then
surrendered, throwing open her arms and taking hold of the
table legs at either side. With an arched back he looked
down upon her flushed and glowing chest; he could not
move that she did not move; he could not feel that she did
not feel. Held so firmly, so deeply inside her, his movements
were minimal though wrought with power. He placed his
hands on the spikes of her hipbones and drove rhythmically
against her swollen lips, tiny circular motions, lifting and
falling, lifting and falling, her movements echoing and
countering his. Her chest glowed an even darker scarlet,
hands still clutching the table legs forcefully, her nipples
spiked and teasing him to kiss them, which he did. Her
mouth fell open and she coughed gutturally and he felt the
moment arrive. Her legs gripped his even more tightly, a
spongy softness as they rocked on her flexing buttocks. He
experienced the same dizzy delirium as before. The total
freedom. She threw her hips into him, harder and harder,
her sounds growing louder and more anxious, words and
emotions mixing in an incomprehensible language.

"Yes," he managed to wheeze.

"Yes, yes," she uttered behind gritted teeth. "It's perfect."

40

DAPHNE LEFT THAT EVENING nearly as quickly as she had arrived. After collecting herself, and offering to do the dishes, which he steadfastly refused, she organized the kitchen goods she had brought and was gone with a simple kiss to his cheek. No excuses were made. In fact—it occurred to him later—following a short time of nestling, and a hesitant return to their clothing, no mention of their lovemaking had been made at all.

He began the task of dishes—a small task at that—but abandoned it immediately. He felt too damn good to do dishes. Dexter Gordon wailed from the radio. Boldt leaned back against his rented couch. The tenor flowed lyrically from the speaker, soothing him. Images of Daphne's reckless lovemaking stormed his brain and assaulted his groin, and he wanted to catch up to her—wherever she was—and be with her again. He had not been this virile since his teen years and he wondered what chemical had renewed him so quickly and so completely. To him it seemed a miracle. Yesterday he had been impotent.

The guilt began to seep into him slowly, like groundwater rising after a storm. His time with Daphne had been fiery, too good for a married man to feel anything but guilty about. He knew how Elizabeth would feel if she was to find out about the tryst, and despite her own assignations he could not find the contempt necessary to exploit his situation.

The phone rang just as the sax took a solo. Boldt was so tired of receiving wrong numbers created by the phone company's ineptitude, that he nearly didn't answer it. He stared at the phone and moved over to it slowly, reluctantly. If it was for him, it was too late—nearly ten o'clock—for it to be anything but bad news.

As he lifted the receiver, he was startled by a pounding on his front door—Daphne behind the ugly, translucent drapes.

"Detective Boldt?" the voice asked over the phone.

"Just a minute," he said, hurrying to the front door, which he unlocked and opened gladly.

She threw her arms around his neck. He closed his eyes and sighed at the splendor of the sensation. He wrapped his arms around her tightly. "Oh, Lou," she moaned. He leaned away because he could hear she was crying. Tear lines marked her cheeks.

"Daphne?" He looked back at the phone receiver lying on the cheap tabletop. "What is it?" His heart began to drum forcibly.

She saw the phone now and glanced alternately between it and the dark, terrified eyes of Lou Boldt. "I'm sorry," she apologized. "I just heard it over dispatch . . ."

"Daphne?"

"It's the Levitts," she blurted out. "The Cross Killer. He killed the Levitts. . . . Both parents . . ."

He released her and stumbled back, turning to look at the phone and then quickly back to Daphne. "Justin?" he asked loudly, his face tensing. He shouted, "What about Justin?"

She shook her head.

"Justin? Daphne? What about Justin?" He took her by the shoulders and shook her. "Daphne!"

Tears poured from her eyes and she trembled. Her mouth opened, but the words would not come out. She finally managed to groan, "He's missing, Lou. . . . Signs of a struggle . . ."

41

AS LOU BOLDT stepped inside the Levitts' living room he cringed. Despite all the confusion, the noise and the commotion of the dozens of policemen and the background strobe of the patrol-car lights, he could feel the terror of the victims. On the wall, drawn in the darkened brown of drying blood, was the single word:

S T O P !

"Everybody out," the voice of Lieutenant Shoswitz called, and Lou Boldt knew the order didn't pertain to him. He stayed roughly in the middle of the room as the other detectives left. The brightly colored police-car lights continued to swirl about the walls of the room, giving the illusion of a merry-go-round. Shoswitz laid a hand on his shoulder. "Tough break," he said. The room was a horrible mess. Beneath an overturned chair he made out the bare leg of a man.

"The boy?" Lou Boldt asked sullenly.

"We don't know. Right?"

"Don't know?"

"There are signs of a struggle in his room. His body hasn't been found."

"Oh, Christ." Boldt took a step forward.

Shoswitz explained, "He disemboweled the woman. Kitchen knife. Raped her, we think. Evidence of cannibalism."

"Oh, Christ."

"He's flipped out, Lou. We think it has something to do with the boy having seen him. He thinks it has blown his cover—something like that. Daphne should be able to tell us more."

Boldt nodded in order to silence the man.

The boy's room was a mess. A struggle had occurred but Boldt saw no evidence of blood. "He's alive," he whispered.

"It's possible," Shoswitz agreed. "But I wouldn't count on it."

42

IT WAS NEARLY TWO O'CLOCK in the morning before Shoswitz, Boldt, and Daphne Matthews met in interrogation room A. Daphne's complexion was pasty and she moved slowly. She offered the men a hapless, halfhearted smile and took a seat in one of the chairs. She heaved an exhausted sigh and referred to her notes.

Boldt could not rid himself of the image of a frightened Justin Levitt in the clutches of a wild man.

"As for the boy," she said in a lifeless professional voice that reminded Boldt of prerecorded telephone interrupts, "we can assume he is still alive—this based on three similar hostage cases provided by the FBI's VICAP computer. A lust murderer's enemy is almost always the woman victim—"

"But the husband," Shoswitz reminded.

"Yes, I know." She nodded solemnly. Boldt could see the steady beat of her heart in a vein at her temple. She bit back the tension and swallowed noticeably. "I realize that killing the husband doesn't fit. The husband may have come upon the scene *after* the killer had arrived. Would he attack with a male present? I don't think so. His excessive violence may have even been triggered by the husband's arrival—his father catching him in the act, his own memories as a boy. On sight of the husband Mrs. Levitt became his mother—a target for his anger. It may help to explain the disembowelment.'' She went silent and didn't look up from her notes for several long, heavy seconds. ''The writing on the wall is also new. A warning, certainly. Your guess is probably right, Lieutenant: he's desperate now. He fears being caught. It's possible he's convinced himself that by holding the boy he will force us to temper our investigation—''

''He doesn't know us very well,'' Boldt blurted out.

She glanced up at him. Dull, dying eyes. ''No.''

''I didn't mean to interrupt.''

She said, ''He's unpredictable now. Obviously. It may occur to him that killing the boy is the safest way out. His killing the man—the father—may start a new pattern in him. His anger has been directed solely at the women up until now. I wouldn't count on that any longer. The disembowelment is evidence of an increased anger. What's next?—I can see it in your faces. He's near the end, I think. We'll see more violence, a change in the ritual. He's bound to see that things can only get worse now. The only sign of encouragement is the message he left us. He's communicating. That's new. That's a good sign.''

''A good sign?'' Shoswitz grunted. ''You weren't in that living room.''

''Phil,'' Boldt said.

''Well, she wasn't, dammit! A good sign?'' He addressed Daphne. ''Have you ever seen a woman's guts spread across a living room? This guy's out of his fucking tree, lady! As mad as a hatter! A *good* sign?''

''A man who has gone mad and a madman are two different people in my way of thinking, *sir*. This is a man who has gone mad, and as a professional I urge you to keep the distinction foremost in your mind.''

''Oh, Christ,'' Shoswitz interjected.

''Let's not forget that this is a sick man. It's my *duty* as a professional to stress this to both of you. I despise this man's *actions* as much as either of you—as a woman, perhaps even more so. But we mustn't confuse actions and deeds with responsibility. This man is no more responsible for what he is doing than you and I are.''

"I don't buy that," Shoswitz yelled. "He knows damn well what he's doing.''

"No, he does not.'' She looked to Lou Boldt for support. "My duty is to express my opinion.'' Suddenly indignant, she rose from the chair. "Is that all, Lieutenant?'' She refused to look at the man.

"Daphne,'' Boldt pleaded.

She left the room without acknowledgment.

"I like her,'' Shoswitz said innocently enough. "She's got balls.''

Boldt sat watching the door. He regretted their intimacy now. The hollow feeling of having made a mistake sank into him. He didn't fully understand Daphne. Had it simply been his way to get back at Elizabeth?

"So,'' Shoswitz asked, "what do you suggest?''

Boldt said dryly, "Suggest? We do whatever it takes to get Justin back, that's what! *Right?*'' he overemphasized. "If we negate some evidence, then that's what happens. Damned if I'm waiting around for the goddamned brass's approval—''

"Lou . . .''

"I'm serious, Phil. The captain is going to hand us the typical shit. . . . 'We have to move slow. We have to watch the evidence, protect the *investment*.' Well, no sale. We start kicking down doors as far as I'm concerned. He's thirteen years old, Phil. How old is William?''

Shoswitz glanced over at the family photo. The boy was holding a baseball bat. The lieutenant was speechless.

The report from the crime lab stated that the right thumbprint lifted from Judith Fuller's gas cap matched the print gleaned from the paper plate found in Betsy Norvak's trash. It did not match the print from the burned match found in the car-port behind Croy's. Although the driver of Fuller's car had "wiped down" the vehicle thoroughly, he had overlooked his own stopping for gas, leaving the opportunity for a print match. With the Rockport shoes connecting DeHavelin to the missing Betsy Norvak, and a thumbprint connecting Norvak to Fuller, Boldt now had a link between all three women and a killer, a man he believed to be the copycat. At last, Boldt's and Abrams's efforts to collect every shred of evidence had paid off. But he didn't have long to savor the moment.

He spotted LaMoia out of the corner of his eye. It didn't register at first, but then it struck him that LaMoia was supposed to be keeping an eye on Bobbie Gaynes. He hurried over and took the cocky young detective by the arm, from behind.

LaMoia bristled at the contact. He, like half the people in the office, had been awake for over twenty hours. He was on edge. "Hey, what the fuck!" he barked, spinning around to find himself facing Boldt. "Sorry, Sergeant," he quickly apologized. "Nerves."

"Why aren't you watching Gaynes's place?"

"Easy, Sarge. Back off a minute, would ya? Kramer spelled me. I can't work 'round the clock, ya know."

"Kramer?"

"As in Sergeant Kramer," the young detective said sarcastically.

Boldt hadn't seen Kramer all night. From the sound of it, Kramer had finally found a way to get some fieldwork. "What's her address?" he asked.

Bobbie Gaynes's apartment building was on the north fringe of the U section, east of I-5. He parked a block away and came on the building's main entrance from the west. LaMoia had assured him that the rest of the building's entrances were self-locking—only this front entrance allowed access. The apartment building was a large, nondescript, rectangular cement block painted a cream color. A jet silently broke through the scattered gray cloud cover overhead, aimed

toward the airport. A white light blinked from its belly.
Boldt wondered if Justin Levitt had ever watched the jets
in the night sky through his telescope.

He approached the apartment building's front door. It was
locked. He wondered how long it would take Kramer to let
Bobbie know that someone was at the front door. He pretended to fool with the lock, as if attempting to break in.
Then he walked fully around the building once and stopped
again at the front door. He buzzed the apartment listed as B.
Gaynes. No number. It took her several minutes to respond.

"Hello?"

"Bobbie, Lou Boldt. You okay?"

"Fine, Sergeant." She must have pushed a button because the door's lock buzzed.

"I'm not coming up," he told her. "Any calls?"

"Nothing," she replied. "What is it?"

"Call me tomorrow. I'll fill you in. Sorry to bother you.
Go back to bed."

"Good night," she said.

He looked around for Kramer's car and spotted it quickly.
He imagined he might hear Muzak playing. He crossed the
street. Kramer was asleep behind the wheel, leaning against
the door.

Boldt yanked the door open. Kramer caught himself at
the last moment, shoving an arm out and bracing his fall
to the pavement.

"What the fuck?" Kramer wondered.

Boldt dragged him out of the car onto the pavement. "I
could have killed her."

"What the fuck?" Kramer repeated, struggling to his
feet, blinking.

"Who makes the field assignments?" Boldt shoved him
into the side panel of the car. Kramer landed hard. "I ought
to bust your head open!" Kramer winced as Boldt pushed
him again, took hold of him, and stuffed him into the driver's seat behind the wheel.

"You're a desk cop, Kramer. You could have gotten one

of our best cops killed. What were you thinking? What the hell goes on inside of that head of yours? You try something like this again and I'll have you busted down to traffic. Get the fuck out of here!'' He slammed the door—dented the side panel with a hard kick and watched the car roar away.

Kramer switched on the lights a block later.

43

BOLDT RADIOED LaMoia and had him assign Paul Browning to keep Gaynes under surveillance for the rest of the night. Less than an hour later Boldt drove away, confident the job was in good hands. He met LaMoia back at the office as planned.

"Christ, it's past three, Sarge."

"What about that list?"

"The master list of employees is on your desk. Got it about eight o'clock. That asshole took his sweet time about it. Cost me a goddamned dinner date with my woman—"

"John!"

"I dropped all the girls from the list. That cut it down from thirty-eight to twenty employees. I put in a request with our computer people to pull licenses on those twenty. Stats on the driver's licenses will give us a look at the physical characteristics of these guys. That should knock it down to just a couple of guys who are close to matching the profile. That's how you wanted it, right, Sarge?"

Boldt nodded. "Have you heard back from DMV?"

"Shit, I didn't put the request in until after nine. No way we'll get that stuff back until tomorrow sometime."

"Lean on them."

"At three in the morning?"

"Someone's running those computers. How much can

they have to do at three in the morning? Better yet, why don't you go see them in person."

"Now?"

"Now!"

LaMoia turned tail and left the office at a brisk pace.

Boldt was thinking of lying down for a few minutes—the office floor was the only place available—when his extension rang. The exhausted voice of Chuck Abrams said, "Lou? You got a few minutes?"

Boldt had no desire to go down to I.D.'s offices, several floors below, but Abrams hated phones and always demanded this of detectives, even at three in the morning. Boldt knew better than to suggest that Abrams simply tell him whatever it was.

Abrams's office area was a ruin. The bookshelf was disorganized, his desk cluttered. Boldt sank into a padded chair. Its springs were shot and it was uncomfortable. Abrams was drinking coffee. He offered Boldt a cup and the detective accepted.

The black man sat down and sipped his coffee. He said proudly, "We just confirmed the tire tracks."

"Come again?"

"The tire tracks."

"Didn't know we got any."

"We lifted a set of beauties, right where you told me to look."

"Behind the house?"

"Yup. One block over from the Levitts'." He smiled broadly. "It rained earlier, so those tracks couldn't be over three hours old. The set we got matches the tire impression we lifted from behind Croy's. It matches perfectly. Just confirmed it. Same vehicle. No question about it."

"Any footprints?"

"Great minds think alike." He shook his head. "No. Not by the tire tracks. We struck out there. I was hoping for something too. The mud was along the curb—that's how we got such a good print. Whoever drove it away would have entered the vehicle on the driver's side, over by the pavement. No impressions.''

A few sentences over the phone would have had the same results, Boldt thought.

Abrams added, ''One more thing of interest. We lifted more of what appears to be that same mud from the Levitts' doormat,'' he said, grabbing Boldt's attention. ''Must have scraped off as he came through the door. Motor oil and gasoline mixed in. Almost certain it's the same. One of my people is checking it out now.''

''Outboard motors?''

''More than likely. State lab will be able to tell us the manufacturers, same as before. It'll take a couple of days. Listen, Lou, it's still circumstantial stuff. I know that. But I'm prepared to take the stand and say that the same vehicle that was at Croy's was at the Levitts', and that the same mud links the Levitt kill to the second kill—Reddick, I think it was. The red fibers connect another three, Bailey, Croy, and Shufflebeam, and we've got the palm print and the partial thumbprint off the burned match.'' He paused. ''I'm saying two things. One, you bring me a suspect or a good set of prints and I now have enough to link him, at least circumstantially, to several of the death scenes. Two . . . I'm willing to go along with your copycat theory. I can buy that. The shoes, the different prints we've got, the discrepancy in body weights between the sneakers and the Rockports—you've got yourself two different killers.''

''Swell,'' Boldt said quietly.

''I thought you'd be happy.''

''So did I.''

At seven o'clock that same morning he received word that the diving team he had assigned to search the waters off Carkeek Park had found no sign of Norvak's body. It came as no surprise. Nor did it spark much interest in Boldt. His attention was focused on finding Justin Levitt.

Shoswitz entered Boldt's office area tired and angry. "You had no authority to order that search team. Come with me."

"I know," Boldt said, walking furiously to keep up with the lieutenant, who was rubbing his elbow and scratching his scalp simultaneously.

The comment stopped Shoswitz, who paused briefly and then hurried on toward his cubicle. "Who's going to pay for it? It wouldn't hurt if you cleared a few things with me from time to time. Right? You left me all alone, Lou, and I don't appreciate it."

"Sorry."

"It would help if I knew just what the hell this department was up to. Right? Christ, you can be a pain in the ass."

Boldt sat down. The lieutenant paced the small office space, keeping his voice low. "The captain called me in. He wanted the Jane Doe connection explained to him. Right? He asked if I always allowed 'renegade detectives'—his words—to carry out their own investigations without my prior knowledge."

"Oh boy."

"He suggested my leadership is anything but noteworthy."

"My fault."

"You're damn right it is! So where the hell do we stand on this thing, anyway? My attention's been on the Cross Killings."

Boldt filled him in for what seemed like the fourth time. "We know Jane Doe is Judith Fuller. She rented the wetsuit; her car had the rented rack. Her car also held a fingerprint that matched one found at Norvak's. So DeHavelin, Norvak, and Fuller are all linked to the same man. He wears Rockports and is too big to be the Cross Killer."

"So we *do* have a copycat."

"Absolutely no question in my mind."

"And how do we flush him out?"

"I'm reconstructing Fuller's last two weeks through some receipts I found in her car. They take me up to September thirtieth, the same day Fuller rented the windsurfer. Early afternoon, she took a ferry over to Vashon, presumably to windsurf. Though I found a receipt for the way over, there was no receipt for the return ferry, and her car was found back over here at SeaTac, so I assume she didn't drive her car back, or she would have saved the receipt. Someone else did. He parked her car at SeaTac to delay us finding it and to suggest she had taken a plane somewhere. We think he probably got into her apartment with her keys, took some of her papers, and packed some of her belongings—again, probably trying to sell us on the fact she'd taken a vacation.

"Vashon checks with what the oceanographer, Rutledge, told me about the undercurrents," he added. "If she went in off of Vashon, she'd stand a good chance of washing up at Alki a couple weeks later." He paused. "No question it's Fuller."

"And who is she?"

"We're looking into it. Someone's been reimbursing her for expenses. Everyone's been cooperative so far. The credit-card people at Wells Fargo, her bank, have traced her payments to a checking account she has with them. Deposits into that account may tell us who she's been working for, which may or may not help us."

"I want to know who she is, what she does. I want to know if there are any similarities to DeHavelin. Anything like that. If this guy's in my department, Lou, I want him by the balls."

The phone rang. Shoswitz answered it, listened, and frowned. "Shit," he said and hung up. "Two more victims, Lou. A *man* and a woman this time. He crossed 'em both. Disemboweled her. Just like Daphne warned, he's flipped out."

44

THE HOUSE overlooked Green Lake. The couple were in their forties. He was wearing a blue terry-cloth robe partially tied at the waist and his throat was slashed. He had evidently taken backward steps, knocked over the five-foot ficus, and died, bent backward across the armrest of the couch. His chest was lacerated in the symbol of the cross—breast to breast, throat to navel. How many times had Lou Boldt seen that mark? He looked away, closed his eyes, and took a deep breath.

The uniformed cop at his side told Boldt and Shoswitz, "Member of the car pool found them. Back door was unlocked. The wife's upstairs," he said, pointing, stopping, not wanting to continue.

Shoswitz dismissed him. "Abrams and Dixon say it had to have happened before midnight. Somewhere between eleven and midnight."

"That's only minutes after the Levitts," Boldt said.

"He must have headed straight here. Abe's looking around for tire impressions. Street's too clean. We're not going to get any." Shoswitz stopped for Boldt to lead the way upstairs.

Boldt glanced up, hesitated, and then climbed the stairs slowly, heart pounding. What would it be like to open your front door and have your throat slit? He wondered now if the wife had gone to the top of the stairs to see who was knocking on the front door at eleven-thirty at night. Had the husband turned around to tell her it was a flower delivery? Had the Cross Killer gone in the back door and foregone the formality of his ritual? Had the husband gone downstairs curious about a noise he had heard?

Boldt reached the top of the stairs and stepped into the hallway, the bedroom door open at the end. Lights on. Scores of family photographs lined the walls, big and small, color and black-and-white, snapshots and professional quality intermixed. There was happiness here, and that blend of upper-middle-class Americana: picnics, ten-speed bikes, sporting activities, the history of raising a single child from baby to high school. Eastern prep school, Boldt noted. "We better notify the kid," he told the empty hallway before him. Shoswitz cursed from behind.

He stepped into the bedroom. He didn't want to do this. He didn't want to be here. He wished someone else would take the case. He wished someone else would take over his life for a while. He wanted a vacation from being Lou Boldt.

Her face was stretched by gray duct tape, her eyes open in that dead stare that Lou Boldt had come to expect. He couldn't look at the rest of her. It was worse now for Boldt, knowing the woman had been raped. Boldt lifted the sheet and covered the grotesque remains of her body. The sheet turned red. Boldt looked over at the television. Then he closed his eyes.

"You all right?" the lieutenant asked.

"Tired."

"When we finish up here, why don't you take a few hours? We've all been up all night. If I don't lie down for a few hours, I'm going to be useless." He dragged a hand down his face.

"I want the kid back," Boldt said. He moved over to the television and touched the on-off button with his pen. The screen remained dark gray but the speaker hissed. "He had it switched to the VCR, not the cable. At least that's consistent. That's still part of his ritual.''

"And we know where he works," Shoswitz added.

"We think we do. We can't be sure. He could be just another customer. We can't be sure of anything." Boldt intended to say more, but the bubble exploded in his chest like a horrible case of indigestion and he felt as if he were choking. He stabbed the button on the set again and the screen went black, the hissing stopped. His ears were ringing from fatigue.

"He drives the van. A customer couldn't drive the van," Shoswitz said.

"He drives *a* van," Boldt reminded. "We think. Until we cast the tires of every van operated by Market Video, we won't know for sure."

"I think that time has come," Shoswitz said. "It's what, seven-fifty? I bet the place doesn't open until ten, maybe eleven. We get a warrant and send I.D. over there ASAP. That takes what, another hour? They can ink them and photograph them in no time. We don't want to scare him off, I agree, but he'll never know if we get right on it."

"You won't get any argument from me, Phil," Boldt said, standing. "I can't go along with the delicate approach any longer. Not now. I know we risk losing the court case if we move too fast, if we're not careful. But if we move too slow, then we're going to be seeing a lot more like her, I'm afraid," he said, gesturing toward the red sheet. "Not to mention the boy. If we lose the boy, Phil—"

"Hey, I'm with you. So we go ahead with the tires? You're game?"

"I'm game."

"Good."

"And I'll personally run down the employees through DMV's computers if LaMoia isn't standing at my desk when we return. We have to move fast now, Phil. Real fast, or we're going to lose the boy. I can feel it, damn it all. The boy's alive, Phil. But for how long?"

"I wouldn't count on it, Lou," Shoswitz said, glancing toward the bed. "With a guy like this, I wouldn't count on anything."

LaMoia was asleep, arms folded on Lou Boldt's desk. He was snoring. Boldt tapped him lightly on the shoulder and LaMoia jumped.

"Shit," LaMoia said, rubbing his eyes, "bad dream." He rose and offered Boldt the seat. Standing, he told Boldt enthusiastically, "If he works for Market Video, he has to be one of four guys. Only four guys are close to the BSU profile. Two of them are drivers."

Boldt picked up the sheet of paper LaMoia had left on his desk and read from it. "Where do we stand on this?"

"Kramer and I have lined up four surveillance teams. It wasn't easy, given the way the department is stretched so thin. We got good people. We can milk about six hours out of it. After that—it'll take a miracle to put together four teams for a second shift. That is, unless you, Kramer, Shoswitz, and I pull singles. Something like that."

"Okay, okay. So what do we know about these guys?" he asked, lifting the paper from the desk.

"Two of the four are University kids. I was able to check that out right away. Drew a blank on the other two. No priors. No sheets on any of them. I'm waiting a few more minutes to try the state agencies. Food stamps, institutions, that sort of thing. Kramer's helping out, and he has a couple of skirts on it too. If the profile is right, then he's been institutionalized. We should know which guy if we get lucky at all."

"Meanwhile we just tail the four, okay? We're hoping this guy will lead us to Justin. But for God's sake let's not spook him. If we do, we'll have a hostage situation, and that'll mean that SWAT will handle it." SPD's Special Weapons and Tactics force had a miserable record in hostage situations. Department policy required SWAT to handle all such situations, and Boldt had no desire to have Justin Levitt end up like the last two hostages SWAT had attempted to rescue.

"I hear what you're saying, Sarge. I got to agree with you. So what do we do—get these guys under surveillance and kick their places when we know they're well away?"

"Getting the warrants may be a problem. We'll need more than what we've got."

"We have the partial thumbprint lifted from the burned match you found behind Croy's. We have the palm print. What if we dust the doorknobs, something like that? We get a possible match, we get the warrant and we kick the place."

Boldt nodded.

"Or maybe we dust a car or something."

"That gets us into some gray areas. We'd have to run it through the ranks to make that fly. I don't know, John." The two men were quiet as they thought. The coffee he had had in Abrams's office was full strength in Boldt's system now, and he felt jumpy and hot. His heart was racing. He felt the skin on his face stretch tight as he puckered his lips and swallowed. "I've got it," he said.

"Go."

"I want you to put the teams out. That's good. Let's follow these guys. But carefully. Real carefully. Abe is comparing the tire prints as we speak. That may help us out. Meanwhile I want you to get inside all three stores before they open—before any employees are around. I want you to go in with the owner. You think you can arrange that?"

"I can arrange *anything*, Sarge." He said it in his most cocky voice.

Boldt didn't doubt it. With anyone else he would have winced at such a comment. Not with LaMoia.

"What's the story?" the detective asked.

Boldt said, "The couple that he got last night—"

"It wasn't a single woman?"

"The pattern's blown. Completely blown. That's what

makes this so damned important. No telling what's next. No way to know. Where was I?''

"The couple . . ."

"Their name is Fabiano. Richard Fabiano. Wife's name was Glenda. What I want to know is whether or not they belonged to Market Video. Whether or not they rented a film—and when. Okay? Those places run sheets—they keep track of rentals. That'll help us all around. If you make headway, then see if they had the film delivered, or what the story is. Let's look for a connection to one of your four suspects. If we can tie the Fabianos to one of those guys, we're ninety percent there. That's good enough odds that I'd be willing to kick the guy's place and look for Justin. Without something like that, then we're blowing hot air.''

"I'll go call the guy. You want to tell Kramer the surveillance teams are a go, or should I?''

"You do it." Boldt had no desire to talk with Kramer.

45

THE REPORT from the state lab came in at half past ten. Boldt was into his third cup of coffee. He read it through and then copied it, placing one copy in Norvak's file folder, the original in Fuller's. He had trouble thinking about the copycat—his concern was for Justin Levitt.

The test for steroids in the tissue sample from Jane Doe had turned up negative, further establishing that Jane Doe was not Betsy Norvak. It still puzzled Boldt that the copycat—a man who had to be close to the investigation —had apparently attempted to kill a woman on Vashon Island, a ferry ride away from the city, miles outside the Cross Killer's suspected territory. Considering the degree of care taken in the earlier kills to perfectly duplicate the Cross Killings, the copycat had departed radically from the set "formula." Why take such a risk? Boldt wondered. Connecting this to the empty desk drawer in Fuller's apartment, and the hasty packing job meant to mislead police further, Boldt had to wonder what had prompted these additional risks. Was the copycat now killing spontaneously, too? Did Boldt have a second uncontrolled killer on his hands?

The answer had to be with Fuller. Why had she rented a windsurfer in Seattle and then taken a ferry clear over to Vashon? He reached for the phone, to call Fuller's L.A.

bank and give them a nudge, but set the receiver back on the hook as Abrams said from behind, "We've got a match."

Boldt spun around in his chair, his hand absentmindedly replacing the receiver. It was not unusual for Abrams to pay a visit to his office—it was unthinkable. "Abe?" was all he could gasp out.

"Vehicle three. They keep all the vans parked behind a store down near Ballard. The drivers report there around noon, and return around midnight. Number three was parked behind Croy's and was parked behind the Levitt house. Perfect match. No question about it. We've got the photos to prove it." He was grinning—something else equally strange for Chuck Abrams.

Boldt nodded. "No question about the van?"

"None. Number three in their fleet. That'll make your job a little easier. Won't it?"

Boldt didn't answer. He spun in his chair and picked up the phone.

"You're welcome," Abrams said, gleefully.

Boldt raised his hand and looked quickly over at his friend. "Any albums you want, for as long as you want. Standing offer."

Abrams hesitated for a moment. "Seriously?" he nearly whined.

"Anytime. As long as you want."

"You son of a bitch," he said enthusiastically as he left the office.

Boldt placed a call for LaMoia. Radio dispatch paged him on his Motorola, and less than five minutes later LaMoia phoned in. He was as cheerful as Abrams, and Boldt suddenly found himself wondering if they all weren't far too tired to be working effectively. Boldt filled him in, and asked that LaMoia check the previous night's schedule to see who was driving van number three. He suggested he check the schedule for the night Croy was murdered as well. He was in the middle of explaining the need for haste when LaMoia cut him off.

"It's all the same video, Sarge."

"Come again?"

"I looked up the Fabianos like you asked. They belong to the Forty-fifth Street store. That's where I am now. They rented a movie called *Hot Summer Knights,* it's a porno-horror picture. And get this . . . one of the chics gets laid by a guy who ices her and draws a cross on her chest with red lipstick."

Boldt sat in absolute silence. There was something about the icy casualness of LaMoia's tone that made Boldt uncomfortable.

LaMoia continued, "It's supposed to be a real erotic flick. Only a couple of gross-out scenes. So anyway, I went back through their lists. Back to around the time of the other kills. I can probably find more, but I've already located two matches. Croy and Heuston rented *Summer Knights* a few days before they were iced. It's got to be the connection."

"When did the Fabianos rent it?"

"Here's the kicker." LaMoia was shouting he was so excited. "They rented it last night, and the film is *here*, Sarge. It had been left in the night drop-off box. The way I figure it . . ." he said tentatively, waiting to see if Boldt would cut him off. "In the past the killer put his victims under surveillance—we *assume* that, okay? So he ended up taking a couple of days to get his act together. By the time he did the actual kill, the video was back in the store, no one wiser. But now he isn't waiting. He isn't setting it up the same way, isn't scoping out the scene. He's impulsive, okay? So after he does the Fabianos, he realizes they're in no condition to return the flick. He's fucked up. He has to cover his ass, has to get that thing back to the store, so he takes the flick with him and returns it himself, so it won't be noticed missing, okay? The store must have some sort of policy for tapes that are late. He can't afford a connection being made. Okay? So he takes care of it himself . . . uses the night drop-off box. Makes sense, doesn't it?"

"Have you touched it?" Boldt worried.

"No." LaMoia hesitated and then said in a whisper of a voice, "Christ, I hadn't thought of that."

Boldt was impatiently awaiting LaMoia's arrival when Shoswitz shouted at a run, "Lou, John, right now!" and ran toward the elevator.

Boldt made it into the elevator two steps behind Kramer, just as the doors were closing.

Shoswitz said, "Van three has taken off on us. We're in pursuit."

"Who the hell authorized that?" Boldt wondered.

"I did," Shoswitz said firmly. "It's raining like hell out, Lou, and traffic is a mess and the guy is on Aurora doing about eighty. You want me to let him run?"

"This could be a big mistake, Phil. There's a boy's life on the line here."

The elevator opened and the men ran toward the parked vehicles. "I'm going in mine," Boldt yelled.

Shoswitz and Kramer drove together.

The rain began to beat against the windshield. Boldt couldn't see the front of his car. He entered a kind of time warp. So many months had gone into this investigation that it seemed impossible they could be within minutes of apprehending the killer. The rain fell harder and the darkness increased because of the dense cloud cover. A location was barked over the radio and Boldt followed Shoswitz's car into traffic. The wipers slapped rhythmically. Boldt had often imagined how the arrest would go down. Typical of fantasies, what was now happening didn't fit at all. Somewhere, a few blocks ahead, was a speeding yellow van, a possible killer behind the wheel. Boldt had always pictured the arrest in a house—a home—the killer poised over one of his victims, about to kill. And in the fantasy Boldt pulled the trigger, killing the man.

He thought it ironic that after all their efforts to gather the necessary evidence to arrest the killer, after thousands of hours of police work, by breaking the speed limit the killer was essentially handing himself over to the police.

He knew they were taking a huge risk. If everything didn't go exactly right from here on out, they might never convict this man of anything more than speeding. But with Justin Levitt's life on the line, and the possibility of losing the van in heavy traffic, they were left no choice.

He wondered where the boy was at this moment, how great his fear must be, how hopeless his condition. Anger steeped into him. If the papers hadn't run a front-page story on Justin Levitt seeing the killer's face, Douglas and Nancy Levitt might still be alive. And someone had leaked that information to the press. Someone in his office. And that person belonged behind bars as much as the Cross Killer did. Hopefully Kramer was doing a better job tracking down the leaks than usual—it was the one area in which he had more contacts than the rest of them.

Boldt wondered what would happen to Justin if they now caught the killer and the man refused to acknowledge the kidnapping. Would the boy starve to death somewhere?

For the next seven minutes (which seemed more like several hours to Lou Boldt), the radio popped frantically as the attempt to pull the van over developed into a high-speed chase over on Aurora. Boldt followed Shoswitz, who constantly adjusted his route as the patrol cars tightened their net. Boldt found himself speeding, siren screaming, following Shoswitz by only a few yards.

Two roadblocks were established by SPD to keep the van out of downtown, where a speeding vehicle represented too great a threat to public safety. The van was forced off the elevated highway at the Kingdome. The driver made a last-minute attempt to avoid the second roadblock and met a highway support column head-on.

Two patrolmen were just prying open the van's rear doors as Boldt came to a stop. Another two doused the engine

with fire extinguishers. It wasn't raining under the protection
of the highway, but a heavy, cold mist swirled through the
air, cutting through Boldt's sport coat. He pulled it tight as
he, Shoswitz, and Kramer climbed up into the back of the
van.

"He's alive, Lieutenant," one of the two advance patrolmen told them. "But not by much." Shoswitz and Boldt
moved aside in the tight quarters and Shoswitz told the
patrolmen to get out and keep everyone else out until an
ambulance arrived. He took a long-neck flashlight from a
patrolman's hands. Dozens of video cassettes were spilled
about the back of the van.

"And not a word to anyone," Shoswitz admonished. The
patrolmen left.

The space was tight for all three men. Boldt hung back.
He had seen enough blood lately. The body was hunched
forward awkwardly. Shoswitz searched the man's bloodstained neck for a pulse. He nodded. "Almost no pulse,"
he said. The driver's wallet was halfway out of his back
pocket. Shoswitz removed it and opened it up. He shined
the flashlight down and sorted through some papers before
coming across the driver's license and photo. "Herman
Wykoff," he read.

"He's too big," Boldt said.

"What's that supposed to mean?"

"This guy's too big, and he's not wearing sneakers."

"He ran from us, Lou? What the hell do you want?"

"He's not right," Boldt said nervously.

"He looks right to me," Kramer said.

"Shine the light over here," Boldt demanded. He picked
up one of the video tapes. The label was crooked and poorly
printed. "Here's your reason for the chase," he said.

"What are you talking about?" Shoswitz was obviously
displeased with Boldt's attitude.

"Lou . . ." Kramer chided.

"Bootleg videos. *That's* why he ran from us. We've got
the wrong guy, Phil."

"Lou!" Shoswitz shouted, obviously confused.

"One step at a time, right, Lieutenant?" Kramer asked.

"Piss on it," Boldt complained. He hurried from the van. He had to push his way through the crowd of police and the curious. Some flash guns erupted in his face and several reporters called out his name followed by questions. The flashguns disoriented him and he raised his hands to shield his eyes, blindly stumbling toward his car.

"Lou!" Shoswitz called out from the back of the van. Lou Boldt heard, but he didn't hear; he was tempted to turn around, but he wasn't tempted—if he paused even for a second the press would surround and detain him. How had the press gotten here so quickly anyway? "Detective Boldt!" Shoswitz thundered. Boldt reached his car and opened the door. He looked up just once—time enough to meet the eyes of the lieutenant, who was joined by the paramedics at the back of the van. White, sterile flashes peppered them as the reporters shouted loudly. Shoswitz shielded his eyes against the agonizing glare of a television minicam. Boldt pulled the door shut and turned the key. The wipers squeaked on the glass.

He no longer had the color images of the killer's victims in his mind.

Instead, he saw the terrorized face of Justin Levitt, and the dead, colorless eyes of a cornered killer.

46

BOLDT CAUGHT UP to John LaMoia in the smoking room outside of I.D.—the caves. LaMoia looked as tired as Boldt felt. They were both drinking instant coffee Boldt had bought from a vending machine. It tasted like weak, lukewarm broth. Boldt set his aside and watched in amazement as LaMoia slurped his down.

"His name is Milo Lange," LaMoia said. "He was signed up for van three last night. He delivered *Summer Knights* to the Fabianos. He also drove number three on the nights Heuston and Croy were killed. He's got to be our boy. The address on his driver's license is out-of-date—the same address he used on his employment application to Market Video. No current address. No way for us to easily track him down. But get this. He's listed as one-forty, five-foot-seven. But the owner says he's thin as a rail."

Boldt asked, "Back up. What about the others?"

"Only dates I could remember were Heuston and Croy. Haven't checked the others."

"Do it."

LaMoia bumped into Abrams on his way out.

The I.D. man puckered his lips and asked Boldt, "You want the good news or the bad news?"

"I think I better have the good first. It's late."

"Amen to that," the balding black man said. "Okay.

Good news is that we lifted a partial thumbprint from the outside of the video box and a piece of it matches the partial we lifted from the burned match you found.''

"And the bad?'' LaMoia asked.

"Bad is that we have two partials. Nowhere near enough to convict. Add to that that this guy worked for the store, and there's a reason for his print to be on the *outside* of any video. Okay?''

"So we got, but we ain't got?'' Boldt said.

"I couldn't have said it better.'' Abrams nodded. "Sorry, Lou.''

"Enough to get a warrant though, wouldn't you say, Chuck? Would you back me up there?''

"I saw the Fabianos, Lou. I'll back you up as far as you want to take this.''

Shoswitz was frantic, but remained sitting behind his desk. LaMoia waited outside the office area.

"I have a plan,'' Boldt said.

"Let's hear it.''

"We know the news about the chase will hit the papers this evening. It will hit the radios in a matter of minutes.''

"I tried, Lou.''

Boldt raised his hand to silence Shoswitz. It was not a gesture he used very often. "And we have to assume Lange follows the investigation in the press. We should probably assume he listens to the radio as well.''

"Which means we may have lost him.''

"Not necessarily. Chuck says we don't have enough to press charges. Not yet. The palm print would help—''

"*Anything* would help.''

"We could bring him in. No question about that, but it could backfire on us. So anyway, I think we should try this. We offer the owner of the stores a trade. We drop the bootlegging charges if he'll cover the van story for us. We supply him a rental van to replace the one that got wrecked. We put a pigeon on it.'' (A "pigeon'' was an electronic homing device more frequently used by Narco.) "The owner makes up a good story for us, to cover the loss of his van. That should be agreeable to him."

Shoswitz nodded, less frantic now. "Go on."

"The van we give him happens to have a busted radio. We know Lange goes on shift at just after noon. We make sure he has a busy schedule. We don't give him much time to be out of that van. No time to pick up on the media's version of what happened this morning. We keep this bastard under tight surveillance."

"Agreed."

"And we gamble. A big risk, actually. Something you won't like, Phil, but it's the only way I—"

"Lou! Screw the sales pitch."

"We force his hand," Boldt said softly. "If the store can keep him busy enough we may be able to keep his nose out of the evening papers. No way we'll keep him from reading the morning papers. By then he'll know we're after him and we may lose Justin, may lose the chance at getting Lange on anything substantial. We've come too far to miss him, Phil. Circumstantial evidence isn't going to buy us shit with this guy."

"But . . . I can hear it in your voice."

"We can't abandon Justin. And we have to avoid a hostage situation at all costs. I can't go along with turning Justin over to SWAT. They'll get him killed."

"Lou."

"It's a possibility I can't accept."

"So?"

"Bear with me. What I suggest is that we wait until we know he's on shift and then Gaynes rents the video. The *Summer Knights* video. The one that triggers him. She has it delivered. He delivers it. We sit on her good and wait him out. And we hope to high hell he goes after her like he went after the Fabianos. Meanwhile I try and find where he lives. We search his place and see if we find the boy, see if we can't find something to tie him to the kills. If we can, then the Gaynes thing is moot. We only use Gaynes if all else fails. But we can't wait to put it in motion. Timing is the key. He has to deliver the video, has to see her alone, has to have all the pieces fall into place or he may not be suckered in. It all goes down this afternoon, and we work like hell to keep him away from the evening papers.''

Shoswitz sat silently and absolutely still, staring at Boldt. It was a rare moment. ''This is a joke, right?''

''Phil.''

''You know damn well what our departmental philosophy is on this kind of thing. If the federal boys want to sting and toy with entrapment, that's their business. Not us. We don't lure killers in. That simply isn't done here. Never done here.''

''We have extenuating circumstances, don't we? The boy for one. The press. I'm not suggesting we go ahead with the plan, only put it in motion. The question is the same one we faced before. Do we sit around only to find out that someone *else* has rented *Summer Knights* and we have an innocent he's after? I'd much rather *we* take control than leave it in his hands.''

''That's part of this, isn't it, Lou? He's had us by the balls for months, and now we have our chance. That's what's really going on here, isn't it?''

''Oh come one, Phil! I thought we had a better understanding than that.'' Boldt rose from his chair. His knee hurt and his head felt heavy. His ears continued to buzz and whine from fatigue. He had never used a tactic like this on Shoswitz. He had no idea if it would work or not. Two steps from the entrance to Shoswitz's office, he believed it had failed.

''I'll talk to the captain,'' the lieutenant said.

''I'll be in my office,'' Boldt replied, without turning around. He didn't want the lieutenant to see his smile.

47

LAMOIA AND BOLDT were sitting in Boldt's car across the street from Brett Hill Veterinary Clinic. Traffic was light. It was still raining heavily.

"You sure this is right?"

"This is what Market Video had as Lange's reference."

"Loiter for a minute. I'll go inside. You see him come out of the place, keep an eye on him, but don't tip your hand."

The two men climbed out of the car and Boldt went into the reception area. He had never liked the smell of a veterinarian's, and he hated to hear animals whine. He asked the receptionist if he could speak with Doctor Hill. She was a thick-faced woman with large eyeglasses and broad shoulders. She reminded Boldt of a boxer, a cartoon of which was taped to the cash register. Her voice sounded like she had swallowed sandpaper. She looked around for his pet. "Is this your first visit?"

An overweight woman came out of a room carrying an overweight lap dog. Boldt caught a glimpse of a lab coat.

"Is that the doctor?" he asked.

Hill was a black-bearded man with white teeth and a flat nose. He had a genuine smile.

Boldt pulled out his identification and introduced himself.

"Homicide?" Hill exclaimed.

"I need a minute of your time."

The two men stepped inside the examining room. There was a picture of a collie on the wall, a stainless-steel table in the middle of the room. "What the hell's going on, Sergeant?"

"You had an employee by the name of Milo Lange?"

"Had? Milo works our night shift. He cleans the pens and baby-sits any of our intensive-care animals."

"Night shift?"

"Midnight to nine. An hour off for breakfast."

"Midnight to nine?"

"A couple days a week when we need him."

"Are you sure about that?" LaMoia had told Boldt that Lange's schedule at Market Video was roughly noon to midnight, six days a week. If he worked nights here, then he never got a chance to sleep. Psychotics often suffered from insomnia—Boldt was well aware of that—but this degree of insomnia was so far from his experience that the thought actually frightened him. He knew what a single night of insomnia did to him. How would a person cope with weeks of no sleep? Leaving the profile and beginning to piece together an actual personality, Boldt began to see a living, breathing human being instead of a few descriptive paragraphs on a piece of paper. And despite Daphne's arguments to the contrary, the closer Boldt got, the more Lange seemed like an animal.

"Maybe that's why he worked here," Boldt said aloud, confusing the doctor.

"What's this all about, Sergeant?"

"Last night. Did Lange work last night as well?"

"If you're not going to tell me wh—"

"He's not here now?"

"No. He left around opening time. Same as always."

"Cleans pens?"

"And keeps an eye on our real sick animals."

"Skinny guy. Wears jeans and sneakers?"

"Is Milo in trouble with the police? I find that hard to

believe. Very hard to believe. He's a quiet man, you know. Very soft-spoken. And a good, hard worker."

"Answer it."

"Jeans and sneakers. Yes. That's Milo, all right. Always a white shirt, jeans, and sneakers. It's kind of a joke around here."

"Do you have an address for him? You're required to have an address for him, aren't you? I'd like to see any of your records that might concern Lange."

"Sergeant, unless you—"

"*Now*, Doctor. I'd like to see those files now. I'm bigger than a mastiff, I'm tired, and I'm running out of patience."

"And manners."

"That too," Boldt apologized. "I've been up thirty-plus hours, Doctor Hill. I'm working on a deadline"—Boldt grimaced at the double meaning—"and I need some answers I think you can provide."

"Now I've placed it," Hill said. "You're the one with the Cross Killer investigation." Then he looked stunned. "Oh my God, no . . ."

"I need your help."

The doctor nodded.

"Same address," Boldt told LaMoia.

"So what now?"

"I had them pull a couple canceled paychecks. Lange cashed them all at the Rainier over on Stoneway."

LaMoia nodded. Boldt called in by radio and checked on the surveillance teams. Still no sign of Lange. A team was waiting near the Forty-sixth Street store. Lange was scheduled to report for work within a few minutes. They hoped.

The bank's branch manager was a woman in her early fifties with a shock of blond hair streaked into her natural brunette. Her blouse was buttoned at her neck and she wore a man's tie, double Windsor. Boldt explained his position very carefully. It was the first time in a long while that he introduced himself as part of the Special Task Force dealing with what the media had labeled the Cross Killings. There was no time to go through proper channels and he needed her assistance immediately. She placed two phone calls and then they sat back and waited. She attempted some small talk, but must have sensed Boldt's fatigue, for she quickly gave it up in favor of silence. Boldt took a five-minute "nap," eyes closed, listening to the annoying drone of elevator music coming from somewhere high above them. Her phone rang. She listened carefully. She doodled a squiggly image of a flower arrangement—no talent whatsoever—and then hung up. "It's all okayed. I'm at your disposal."

A few minutes later Boldt had the same outdated address staring up at him. The phone number was crossed out, however, and one had been written in by hand. Boldt made note of it. He was about to leave when he thought of something. "You mail him monthly statements, don't you? You must have a more recent address."

"It's possible. The central office might," she said. "We're a branch office. Downtown handles all the statements, all our mailings, that sort of thing. We handle transactions. That's all."

"Don't you have it on computer?"

She shook her head. "No. We're in the process of going fully on-line with downtown right now. By Christmas the system should be up and running. Which is not to say that we aren't computerized. Of course we are. But only hard copy—printouts—and only in so far as account information is concerned. What you're looking for would be handled by downtown."

"Could you call?" Boldt asked, his impatience obvious.

She frowned and knitted her brow. "All right," she said. "If it's really *that* important. But you know, this is highly irregular."

"Please."

She placed the call, made the request, and curled the blond shock of hair around her index finger as she waited.

A moment later she pursed her lips and nodded, as if to say, "I'll be damned," and began writing. She hung up and handed the piece of paper to Boldt. "You were right," she told him. "It's a different address. I had better update our records."

"I wouldn't bother," said Lou Boldt.

LaMoia rolled down his window. The search warrant flew toward Boldt, who snagged it as word came over the police radio that Lange had just arrived at Market Video. It was five minutes past noon. Lange had been given his pickup and delivery manifest, and had driven off in the replacement van, seemingly unconcerned at the change in vehicles. A pair of patrol cars had followed, as did an undercover cop on a ten-speed bicycle who had been given a photocopy of the delivery manifest. Any problems with surveillance or inconsistencies in his timetable would be reported immediately. Lange was scheduled to pick up another manifest and additional tapes sometime between three and four. Bobbie Gaynes's request for *Summer Knights* would be among that batch.

The apartment building was more like a rooming house. There were five rooms for rent on the first floor and three on the second. Milo Lange's was on the second floor, overlooking the canal, not far away. The superintendent unlocked the door for Boldt and then stepped back. Boldt dismissed the man, and LaMoia accompanied him back downstairs, repeating the necessity to keep this visit secret. Chuck Abrams was only minutes behind. He entered the building with an oversized briefcase and stopped at the door to the room.

Boldt was standing in the center of the small room. In the far corner was a single bed, gray blanket, neatly made. The only artwork was over the bed: a reproduction of Jesus on the cross, a crown of thorns spreading blood onto his forehead. Legs and arms nailed to the crucifix. Beside the bed was a thumb-worn copy of the Bible. A single metal folding chair was positioned in the opposite corner by the curtainless window. An oilcloth window shade hung coiled above the closed window. The floor was bare. Abrams dusted the doorknob to the closet and shook his head. Lou Boldt turned the handle slowly, shyly, fearing he would find Justin Levitt balled up inside.

The closet was sparkling clean. Folded on the shelf were three pairs of equally faded blue jeans, a half-dozen pairs of Jockey shorts, and a pile of black socks. Hanging from the curtain rod were three permanent-press white shirts, two of them quite new. A raincoat hung alongside the shirts— plastic, sold by J. C. Penney. A sweatshirt hung on the hook on the inside of the door.

A bare bulb shone from the ceiling.

Boldt stepped back and let Abrams go to work. The I.D. technician spent nearly thirty minutes checking every logical spot in the room for a print. Then he tried the hard-to-reach places. Then he turned to Boldt and said, ''You're not going to like this, but this guy keeps this place so damn clean that I can't find a single print.''

Boldt had witnessed the man's thoroughness and had prepared himself for this outcome. How much worse could it get? he wondered. How much could Justin Levitt endure? ''The closet?'' he asked.

Abrams went to work on the closet. After another twenty minutes he said, ''No prints. Not even on the zipper of the rain jacket.'' His voice sounded hollow in the closet. ''Wait a second,'' he said, dropping to one knee. ''Here we go.'' He removed a thin, knifelike instrument from his case and dislodged a tiny bit of gray-brown dirt from between the cracks in the closet flooring. He deposited it into a plastic container and closed the lid.

''What have you got?'' Boldt wondered.

''Dust. Dirt. By the color of it, quite possibly dried mud.''

''Mud as in our mud?''

''As in. It's the right color for it.''

''That would be nice.''

"Yes. Any other ideas?"

Boldt looked down at the Bible, which was covered in print dust. "What about the pages?"

Chuck Abrams smiled. "Amen."

A partial thumbprint was gleaned from the upper right-hand corner of page five. It matched a cross section of the other partial print they had, and was enough to convince Abrams that whoever rented this room had most likely been in the carport behind Croy's. It was not enough to hold up in a court of law, he reminded. The prosecutor would want at least five matching ridge charateristics; Abrams could identify but three.

It took Abrams nearly an hour to clean the fingerprint dust and leave the room as they had found it. He convinced Boldt it was worth the risk of discovery to cut the page from the Bible, which is what he did. Boldt oversaw the superintendent relock the room, and then told the man to avoid Lange at all costs, warning that even a wrong look could negate their investigation. A two-man surveillance team would arrive shortly to wire and stake out the room.

Boldt had hoped to find Justin Levitt. Worry worked at his stomach. He reached into his pocket, but the Tums were all gone.

48

IT TOOK BOLDT'S, Kramer's, and Shoswitz's mutual efforts to arrange protection/surveillance for Bobbie Gaynes. The second floor of her apartment building was evacuated—hotel rooms provided compliments of SPD. In the apartments adjacent to Bobbie's, two teams of plainclothes detectives, one male and one female each, both dressed casually, waited as backup. Care was taken to stage them as couples in case the Cross Killer was more careful in his surveillance than they now believed him to be. There was no room for mistakes. In both of these adjacent rooms the male detective was equipped with a hidden radio receiver and miniature earphone, enabling him to receive instructions from outside the building, or to overhear activity in Gaynes's apartment, where an open-mic transmitter had been hidden. In the apartment directly across from Gaynes's was another detective in plainclothes. Like everyone on this floor, he was within two paces of a standard-issue shotgun. The Beretta 9mm was hidden on his person. He too could overhear the goings-on in Bobbie's apartment and the constant chatter of the rest of the stakeout. In all, some nine plainclothes detectives were committed to the stakeout, with another five patrol cars placed strategically in the surrounding neighborhood. When combined with the officers assigned to Lange's surveillance, it added up to the single largest operation Homicide had staged in three years.

At two-twenty, forty minutes before Lange was scheduled to return to the Forty-sixth Street Market Video, all officers in position, Bobbie Gaynes was given the go-ahead to request delivery of the film. She placed the phone call.

Chuck Abrams called Boldt on the phone. He confirmed that the mud found in the cracks of Lange's closet contained the same percentage of motor oil and gasoline that had been found at earlier death scenes. Again, it was only circumstantial evidence, but it could help link Lange to the crimes in the eyes of a jury, and Boldt was beginning to believe this was going to be a murder trial based largely on just such circumstantial evidence. Lange had covered himself well, and unless they could lure him into their trap, Boldt feared they would have to pick him up and book him with little to hold him on. The system was wrought with pitfalls, and Boldt feared Milo Lange would be able to wiggle through the cracks.

Daphne caught up to Boldt as he was putting on his sport jacket. She too seemed exhausted, her forehead lined with concern, her lips pursed.

"Hi there," Boldt said.

She grinned at him sadly. "How are you holding up?" He shrugged.

"Me too." She reached out and briefly brushed her hand against his, hooking little fingers and then letting go. "I need to bend your ear a minute."

"Nothing would give me more pleasure."

She led him to her office and left the door open. They both sat away from her desk. She said, "I've gone over the Levitt evidence again, and the Fabiano case in detail. I've just come from a twenty-minute meeting with Shoswitz where he outlined what you have planned and he wanted me to speak to you—he felt it important I speak to you."

"Okay."

"I have to be honest with you, Lou. I don't like it. It's

a bad plan. Let me explain why—explain from my perspective—and tell you what I told the lieutenant. You're crossing a very fine line here. I realize the law reads one way, but from where I'm sitting this is essentially entrapment. That's my concern as a doctor. You are creating a psychological stimulus that you *know* has the possibility of inciting the suspect to a violent act. Now, to my knowledge there's no legal precedence—I'm still looking into that, in fact we have Bob Shol over at the Prosecutor's office digging around for us—but this could very well backfire on you. What makes it worse is that you know he's likely to attack her. Incidently, I have to agree with you. From everything I can tell he has *changed* his ritual, not abandoned it. He is more driven than ever now to punish these women, and I think you can count on him going after Detective Gaynes. I'm almost certain of it. And therein lies your dilemma. You're certain of it, too. You're counting on luring him to another attempted kill, and a clever attorney may be able to turn that right around on you and get a dismissal.''

Boldt closed his eyes. He had not considered that he might be creating a psychological entrapment case, had not considered he might be establishing some kind of legal precedence, and the whole thing made him mad. ''Shit, Daffy, I don't know what to say.''

She reached out and touched his knee. ''I'm not trying to stop you, Lou. I know your concern is for the boy, and believe me, I'm with you there, but the lieutenant thought it added something to the case he had not considered and he wanted you to hear it as well. Lange's going to go after her, Lou. Count on it.''

She suddenly seemed young to him. Naive.

''Anything I can do?'' she asked.

He thought a moment. ''Yes, I think there is. Contact Quantico and run all this latest stuff by them. The mud, don't forget the mud, and the cleanliness of his rented room, the Jesus poster, the clothes we found in his closet. Give

them everything we have on the Levitts and the Fabianos
and let's see if they can give us any parameters to help us
narrow the search radius for Justin. You add up all this stuff
and it must tell us something.''

She nodded. She obviously didn't share his confidence.
''I'll give it a try.''

When Boldt received word from the mobile surveillance
team that Lange was presently at Market Video, he drove
to Gaynes's apartment, parking several blocks away, and
joined her. She was dressed in blue jeans and a white T-
shirt, no bra, and was barefooted. She looked positively
stunning—a real heart-stopper—like something from a Bruce
Springsteen song. Boldt thought of this because Springsteen
was pounding out a piece of rock from her home stereo.
Elizabeth was a Springsteen fan as well. Boldt knew the
Springsteen album, *Born to Run*. It was an old one and
Elizabeth had worn it out a few years back. Boldt suggested
they turn it down so the hidden microphone would not be
drowned out.

She said casually, ''Hey, it was the guys next door who
requested some tunes,'' and smiled at him. Boldt didn't
smile back. He was about to suggest she put a bra on, and
a shirt made of thicker fabric, and pants that didn't cling
to her quite that way, but realized he would be defeating
his own purpose. If Lange didn't go after her, he was out
of his mind. An ironic thought, it occurred to him.

Boldt looked around the apartment. He picked the doorway into her postage-stamp kitchen. From here, with the
door ajar, he could peer through the crack and see the front
door. He moved a chair into the kitchen then—if Lange
followed his pattern, he would use a knife from the victim's
kitchen—and sat down at his post.

Bobbie stood in the kitchen doorway for a few minutes,
passing the time with him. She was nervous, and he couldn't
blame her. The police-issue .38 was tucked between the
small of her back and her pants, the T-shirt hanging out

over it and concealing it. He still thought the music was too loud, and after prodding, she shut it off and they waited in silence. After a few minutes she left him and read a *Newsweek*, sitting on the edge of her bed.

The minutes seemed endless to Lou Boldt and he couldn't help but believe these minutes were more torturous for Justin Levitt, wherever he was. He knew he was only minutes away from seeing Milo Lange for the first time face-to-face. The thought made his heart race, his palms sweat, and he felt an unrelenting anger building up inside of him.

The click in his earphone brought him back. One of his detectives said, "We have a positive on the van. It just pulled up out front. Stations confirm."

Boldt checked his watch: four-fifteen.

Bobbie wasn't equipped with a radio. "Okay," he announced. "Here we go."

He heard the other stations verbally acknowledge having received the notice. There was an established order to the acknowledgments, to avoid jamming the radio channel. Boldt was last, and his confirmation was nonverbal. He clicked his SEND button on his walkie-talkie twice. The static popped in his ear.

"All in," said the same voice. "He's out of the van and moving toward the front door."

The buzzer rang. Bobbie depressed the CALL button and asked, "Who is it?"

A bland male voice, made small and thin by the speaker, said, "Market Video. Delivery."

She depressed a second button that unlocked the building's main door.

Boldt heard in his ear, "He's inside." He noticed his own hand was shaking.

He listened carefully as Lange's every move was detailed.

"Up the stairs . . ." said one.

"Coming down the hallway . . ." said another.

Station by station the reports came in. Bit by bit, Boldt felt his anxiety level rising.

Bobbie glanced over at him. Her forehead was shiny with perspiration, a vein there pulsed wildly.

"He's at the door. Right across from me . . ." came the announcement.

Then the knock on the door. "Just a minute," Bobbie said loudly. She wiggled her face, and locked a smile onto it like an actress preparing to take the stage. She straightened up, suspending the thin T-shirt from her pert breasts, and opened the door. "Hi!" she said ebulliently.

Boldt could see him through the crack. He was a pale man, with drawn features, narrow red lips, and thin hair. He was wearing a white Oxford shirt, blue jeans, and old black Converse sneakers. He had long arms, a narrow waist, and a chicken neck. He looked right through Bobbie Gaynes. *"Summer Knights?"* he asked.

She nodded. "That's right."

"Pickup's tomorrow before three, or you'll have to return it yourself."

"Okay."

He handed it to her. Nothing unusual. Nothing weird.

"Thanks," she said.

He turned and left. She hesitated a moment, then closed the door, studied the brown video case in her hand, and looked back at Boldt's single eye peering through the crack at her.

49

BOLDT HELD UP his hand to keep her from speaking. When, a few minutes later, he was informed via radio that Lange's van was on its way again, he nodded at her.

"Well?" she asked.

"He'll be back," he told her.

She looked at him curiously.

"Ground crew reports he placed a piece of duct tape on the latch of the side-door fire exit before leaving."

She crossed her arms tightly, as if she was cold. The apartment was anything but cold. She had the heat cranked up. "Looks like I don't get any flowers," she tried to joke.

"I wouldn't count on it," Boldt said. "I have a feeling that side exit is just in case he can't trick you. He's determined to get to you. He's just leaving himself an option."

"Is it cold in here?"

Lou Boldt shook his head.

She cooked him fish sticks for dinner. Boldt drank a half pot of coffee all by himself. She played Steve Winwood and finished the *Newsweek* before attempting a paperback she apparently couldn't concentrate on. She turned on the television and watched a rerun of a "National Geographic

Explorer." White-water rafting in Indonesia. Red apes and rainforests. Boldt watched from the kitchen door until he felt himself nodding off, and then spent several minutes splashing cold water on his face in the kitchen sink. LaMoia had offered to spell him, but Boldt had declined. He had been waiting for months for this opportunity.

Boldt became restless and began to pace the apartment, parting the blinds and looking down on a rainswept street. He watched the rain stream past the streetlamps, the silver rainwater rush in black opal gutters toward thirsty drains that swallowed it up. He saw a couple watching television in their apartment across the way. Each time an umbrella passed below, he anticipated word on his walkie-talkie and turned up the volume, only to turn it back down as a voice described and dismissed the possible suspect. Cars sped past, people on their way home from dinner, people on their way home from a movie or a night out with friends, people totally unaware of Lou Boldt and the fact he was awaiting the Cross Killer. There were people out there, Boldt knew, who would gladly pay hundreds of dollars—thousands perhaps—to know about this police operation. Boldt wondered if this operation would be compromised as so many had been lately. Would they get this close to the killer only to lose their chance?

The roof of a van passed below, and Boldt heard her say, "What is it?"

The van vanished into the blanket of rain. "What do you mean?"

"You stopped breathing for a second there. What did you see?"

"Just a van. A roof."

"You're eating yourself up, Lou, and you shouldn't be peeking out the window."

He turned and glared at her.

"Hey, I'm only repeating orders, Sergeant." His orders. He left the window and returned to the kitchen.

"We can talk, you know," she told him, unseen.

"About what?" he asked sarcastically. "What the hell do you talk about in a situation like this?"

"You talk about fun things. You talk about pretty things. You talk about whatever you can that will take your mind off of it."

"Nothing will do that," he said, rounding the corner and noticing that she wasn't watching the television. She was lying back on her bed, head on a pillow, staring at the ceiling. "Sorry. Nerves."

"Me too," she said.

At nine forty-five the crackling static of the earphone popped and a voice said, "Car nineteen. We have visual contact with suspect. Headed your way, station nine. Over."

"Roger, nineteen," said the voice of Billy Beacham, who was coordinating surveillance from the back of a green van parked down the street. "Stand by, everyone. You got that, nine?"

"Beach . . . This is Chubby in mobile thirty-five. We've got a visual. Repeat, we've got a visual. Suspect heading east. Over."

"East. Roger, Chubby. Over," confirmed Beacham.

Boldt felt his scalp prickle as he began to perspire. It *was* hot in here, damn it. He tugged at his collar and wiggled the earphone. "They've picked him up," he called out. Bobbie's anxious face appeared around the corner.

"Billy, this is Don, station four. Suspect is stopped at a red light. We got a blue Chevy wagon in front of him, red Volvo behind. Anyone confirm that? Over."

"I'm with you, Don," answered Chubby. "We're a couple cars back of the Volvo. You have us?"

"Roger," replied Don. "I got you now, Chub. Good. Just wanted to make sure I had the right van. Okay, he's turning right. Confirm?"

"Roger. Wish this rain would let up. Billy, we're going to drive by and let Pete pick him up. That okay with you, Peter?"

"This is nineteen. Roger, thirty-five. I've got him."

"Affirmative," Billy Beacham interjected, okaying the trade.

"Mobile nineteen. Suspect turning left; I'm going to have to drive by. You want me to drive by, don't you, Billy?"

"Affirmative."

"We'll lose him," said a worried voice.

"Affirmative. Drive by affirmative."

"Bastard's checking for tails," said Chubby from car thirty-five.

"Drive by affirmative," Beacham repeated. "Confirm mobile nine."

"We let him go, Billy. Car nine confirms drive-by."

The line popped loudly then and Boldt twitched in his chair. Someone had set their squelch too hot and it screamed in everyone's ear. A variety of voices complained and Billy Beacham called for order. There was much cursing before Beacham's request of, "Protocol, gentlemen!" silenced the line. The entire operation was being tape-recorded, and Beacham clearly wanted this handled as cleanly as possible.

The rain began to pound strongly against the apartment window. Boldt had to turn up the volume.

"Okay, I got him, Billy. Station six. I got him, Billy. Over."

"Direction, station six?"

"Okay. This is six. Turning left again, heading back toward you. Moving real slowly. Anybody confirm that? Over."

"Confirm," said the distinct voice of Michael Dundy, one of the Southerners on the force. Dundy was stationed in a dance studio across the street and down one block. He was one of two detectives equipped with "night-scope" infrared binoculars, though the binoculars weren't much good in heavy rain.

Boldt gained control of his breathing to try and slow his heartbeat. He inhaled deeply and exhaled. "Closer," he told her.

Over the radio he heard, "Billy, this is Quinn, station five. He's parking it. Over."

"Roger, five. Parking the van. Back to you."

"Roger. This is five. Okay, he's coming out. Stuffing something under his coat. He's wearing a blue raincoat. Repeat: blue raincoat. Over."

"Affirmative, five. All stations. Suspect is wearing a blue raincoat. Direction, five?"

"Heading around the building. Toward the front, Billy. Over."

"Roger. All stations. This looks like it. Confirm four through one."

"Four confirm . . ."

"Three confirm . . ."

"Two confirm . . ."

Boldt depressed his CALL button twice.

"Roger. All stations confirmed." Beacham hesitated, his line was left open, blocking the ever-present static. "Let's keep it clean and simple, boys. Mobile nine and thirty-five, positions as planned. Confirm when you're in position please. Over."

Moments later the two cars confirmed.

Beacham said, "He's at the front door. Repeat. Suspect is at the front door. Over."

"We've got it from here, Billy," said the voice of Paul Rathe, who was stationed in one of the ground-floor apartments.

The buzzer rang loudly. Louder than before, it seemed to Boldt.

She faced him, a bewildered look on her face.

Boldt nodded and pulled the kitchen door closed even further. He told her, "He's going to try and overpower you, Bobbie. Make sure he gets his chance, but you get your hand between the ligature and your neck. You hear me? You *must* be ready with that move immediately."

She stood before him, unmoving. She hadn't answered the buzzer. "Damn it, Lou, we've been over this!"

"Answer it," he said, annoyed by the ringing buzzer. "Quick!"

She stepped toward the panel on the wall and depressed the button. "Who is it?" she asked.

"Barbara Gaynes?" said a completely different voice than they had heard earlier. A different person, thought Boldt.

"Speaking . . ."

"I got a flower delivery for a Barbara Gaynes, apartment 209. That you?"

"Are you sure?" she said, repeating what she had been told. "For me?"

"Listen, lady," returned the voice. "I deliver until ten o'clock. You want them delivered wilted in the morning, that's up to you. Just say the word. But say something. It's pouring cats and dogs out here."

Cocky, Boldt thought. Complete change of personality. He *knows* she'll bite.

"No, no," she said, "come on up," and depressed the button. She released the button and looked over at Boldt. She was pale white. Her hand was shaking and she held it with the other.

She's too green, he worried. She's too green for something this big. I should have thought of that. Come on, Boldt thought, don't fall apart on me. I handpicked you for this.

"He's headed upstairs," said Rathe in a faint whisper. The whispering over the line, clouded with static, sent chills through Boldt. *Speak normally,* he wanted to say.

Distant footsteps as Lange bounded up the staircase.

"Roger, I got him. This is station three, Billy," whispered the detective in the apartment across the hall. "Right. He's heading down the hall toward you, Lou. You got him, Jimbo?"

"Station two, Billy. I think so. Come on, fella. Yeah, blue raincoat. That's him. I got him. It *is* roses. Just pulled them out . . ."

A creak on the other side of the door.

"Zero hour, Lou. He's all yours. We're right behind you."

The knock.

Bobbie looked to the crack in the door where Boldt was watching her from. He nodded.

She looked to the door, back to Boldt.

He nodded again.

Come on! he thought. "Go!" he whispered, risking the entire operation.

She stepped toward the door—forced herself toward the door. She stopped and took a deep breath. Boldt wondered what she felt like at that moment. He knew what *he* felt like and he couldn't imagine how she felt.

They needed to catch him in the act of attempting to get something around her neck. Assault. Attempted murder. They needed something more than him handing her a bouquet of silk flowers. Beyond that, they had him.

She opened the door. The flowers were thrust out at her immediately. She reached out to take them. "Wait a sec —!" she started to say, as if pretending to recognize him from his earlier delivery. But Milo Lange was exceptionally fast. Wiry. He sprayed something into her face, yanked her outstretched arm, spun her around, and pushed her through the door, the flowers falling onto the floor. He kicked the door shut behind him.

Boldt saw her face collapse and her body sag. He had hit her with some kind of powerful tranquilizer that had an instant effect. Pull out the ligature, Boldt commanded. Put the ligature around her neck. Standing there, gun in hand, Boldt began to take a step forward, but checked himself. They had him on breaking and entering now. Was it enough? He hesitated a moment longer. How many times had he pictured the killer's ritual? How many times had he wished he could have been there to stop it? And now, here he stood waiting for it to happen.

Lange yanked the roll of duct tape from his back pocket,

released her, letting her fall ungainly to the floor, and tore a strip of tape from the roll.

Enough!

Boldt pushed through the door, gun aimed at Milo Lange's head. "Police. Don't touch her, Lange!" he shouted loudly enough to be heard through the wall, much less over the radio transmitter. Lange snapped his head up, incredulous. The door kicked open behind him and the sound of two shotguns being cocked echoed through the room.

"Police!" the detectives shouted.

"Give me the excuse, Lange," Boldt said, waving the gun, wondering who was controlling his mouth and his thoughts. He had never experienced this degree of hatred. He was completely unprepared for it. He *wanted* to kill the man. Eager to kill.

"Jesus loves us all," said Milo Lange. He smiled and dropped the tape.

50

"ARE YOU SURE you feel up to this?" Daphne wondered. "You look awfully tired." Her brown eyes were red and glassy, her hair pulled back.

"I'm exhausted. But yes, I'm ready. I've made a list of things we discussed."

"You don't need any coaching from me. You're one of the best criminal interviewers this force has. What the rest of us spend years trying to learn, you seem to know by instinct. How about the public defender?"

"The PD's in there now. I'm told Lange won't discuss Justin. I don't buy that."

"His rules, Lou. You know that. He doesn't have to talk to us at all."

"Then why has he agreed to?"

"Control is a big factor here, Lou. By killing someone, he controls them. By agreeing to talk, he controls us."

"What crap! Should we refuse to talk until he tells us where to find Justin?"

"My professional opinion? No. He needs to talk to us. He may change his mind in there and tell you what you want to know. Work *with* him. You've read his statement. Use it. Thank him for it. You've done this kind of thing more times than any of us. You don't need me to tell you what to do."

Shoswitz rounded the corner at that moment, and Boldt cut her off. "How's Bobbie?" Boldt asked.

Shoswitz nodded. "She'll be fine. An animal tranquilizer is all. He stole it from the vet's. Suspended it in alcohol—damn near impossible to detect, I'm told. But she'll be all right."

"Here we go," Boldt said as he paused at the door.

Daphne offered a smile of confidence. Shoswitz nodded.

Lange's dark eyes tracked Boldt as the detective sat down and faced him. Boldt turned on a tape recorder and dictated the specifics of time, place, and persons present.

He knew the most important thing was to establish an immediate rapport with the criminal—to convince the man of his sincerity. He had done similar interviews dozens of times. Yet none was similar, he reminded himself. Right now, at this particular moment, this interview seemed the most difficult thing he had ever faced.

He said, "You offered to speak with me. Why?"

"I thought you would have questions." The man's voice was in a high register. He spoke softly and airily. "I thought you would want to know some things."

"Yes," Boldt admitted. "I do. I'm very familiar with what you've done. I've worked on this since April. You managed to elude us for quite some time." He swallowed and forced out, "You were very careful. Very thorough."

"I was. God helped me to do it." Proud. Defiant.

"I want you to know how much we—I—appreciate your agreeing to talk to us." He glanced over at the PD. "This can be very beneficial to us both. I think we can both get a lot out of this."

"Credit where credit is due, eh? Yes, credit where credit is due. I want to help, if I can." Lange paused, studying Boldt carefully.

The defender, a young man in a new blazer, interjected, "We would like my client's cooperation mentioned at the omnibus hearing, and would expect the courts to show some leniency regarding same."

Milo Lange said, "I want to teach you the difference between God's work and the work of his imitators."

"That would be good for me," Boldt acknowledged. "I'd certainly appreciate that. I'd also like to talk about the boy."

Lange shot the PD an angry look. Back to Boldt. "The boy?" he wondered.

"Justin Levitt."

"The boy? I don't know anything about any *boy*," he said.

"The young man."

"Oh, the young *man*." Lange rolled his eyes and for a moment only the whites of his eyes showed, and Boldt felt his stomach turn.

The PD jumped in. "My client will not field questions at this time concerning Justin Levitt."

"A boy's life is at stake here!"

"A boy?" asked Milo Lange, rolling his eyes the same way. "Bad boy," he said in the voice of a woman. "*Bad* boy." He shoved his hand into his crotch and squirmed.

"Off-limits, Lou. Completely off-limits," the PD demanded. "Or this ends right here."

"Your statement—your confession, Mr. Lange—raises several questions. I will address them in order, according to the statement. First, you stated you were instructed to 'free' these women—"

"The Lord is my shepherd," said Milo Lange. Another voice entirely from the ones he had used at Bobbie Gaynes's apartment.

". . . and that the instructions came in the form of voices—"

"His voice. There is only one voice. I said nothing about voic*es*. One voice. The voice of My Lord."

"Are you a member of the church? A member of a local parish?"

His thin, colorless lips formed a vague smile.

"Do you belong to a local parish, Mr. Lange?"

"I belong to God. I do the work of My Lord."

"You 'free' women?"

Another one of those nods. "Yes. That's correct."

"Women who were members of Market Video, the place of your employment, as is stated here."

"Filthy women. I do His work. I free them of the Devil."

"There's no mention here of placing the women under surveillance, Mr. Lange. Watching them. Did you watch these women before 'freeing' them?"

"I was to wait until they were alone. I had to be certain they were alone. He watched over me. He helped me to do it correctly. His work, you know? I do His work."

"So you watched them?"

"Yes, I watched."

"And you determined they were home alone? How did you do this?"

He smiled more fully. "He helped me."

"I need your help, Mr. Lange. I thought you would be willing to help. How did you do this?"

"Easy," he said. "If she comes alone and no one visits her, then she is still alone."

"So you did watch them?"

He nodded.

"And you knew they were alone."

He nodded again. "Credit where credit is due. It is His work. He told me when they were alone. He is never wrong." Again his pale lips curled.

"Did you do this on nights you were working?"

He shrugged. "I did this when He asked me to."

"But some of those nights you were working, weren't you? Could you clear that up for me?"

"Not many deliveries after eight. You see? It used to be some evenings I would sit and wait for hours. Nothing to do. He helped me to fill my time. I do His work." Lange asked for a cigarette. The PD looked for Boldt's permission and the detective nodded. The PD stuck a cigarette between Lange's lips and lit the cigarette for him. At the instant the match lit, Boldt recalled picking up the curled black paper match in the carport behind Croy's. Lange raised his cuffed hands to his face and pulled the cigarette out.

It made Boldt think of something. He asked, "Do you smoke grass, Milo?"

Lange shook his head.

"Any kind of recreational drugs?"

Again, Lange shook his head. "Just say no," he quoted with his strange smile.

Boldt realized they could confirm this a number of ways, but he believed him. It meant the profile had been flawed here as well. He said, "Did He ask you to take the boy?" Boldt tried once more.

"No way, Lou," interjected the PD. "You don't have to answer that, Milo," he told the man. Lange nodded. "I'll pull him out of here, Lou. I'm warning you."

"You want a dead kid on your conscience?" Boldt hissed at the man.

A buzzer on the wall rang and Shoswitz's voice came through the speaker. "Lou, can we talk a minute, please?"

Boldt didn't turn around. He raised his hand to ward off the lieutenant. They didn't need to talk. He and Lange needed to talk. Boldt took a deep breath. He was close enough to this man to kill him with his bare hands. And he felt tempted.

Boldt nodded again. "Where did you come from, Milo?"

"I'm the son of a *whore*," he screamed, his face distorted with rage. He had shifted personalities and Boldt had been unprepared for it. Lange's eyes grew fiery and intense. He glanced at his attorney. "I told you I would not discuss my family! Don't you people listen?" At Boldt he screamed, "I will *not* discuss my family."

"That's fine with me, Milo. Whatever you want. You're the teacher here. I'm just here to learn." Boldt bit back his anger. If he brought up Justin again, Shoswitz would pull him from the interview and assign it to someone else. After all this, Boldt had no desire to sit on the other side of a two-way mirror and watch someone else handle his case. He settled himself down and decided to get what he could.

"I work morning, noon, and night," Milo Lange said to the table. "I'm tired."

Boldt spoke extremely softly, trying to mirror Lange's tone of voice and even his body language—two important factors in maintaining rapport. "I worked morning, noon, and night on this case," he said, deliberately using the killer's words. "I'm tired too," he added, waiting.

"I know you did. But *he* confused you," Lange said.

"He?"

"The other one. He confused you, I think."

"Other one?"

"I *told* you!" he shouted. "I didn't free them all. I read in the newspapers . . ." His voice trailed off and he grew distant.

Boldt hesitated only briefly, deciding not to pursue "freeing them" yet. "Did you read the newspapers, Mr. Lange?"

"Call me Milo," he said perfectly normally. "Yes, the newspapers. Every day. Morning, noon, and night. I followed it all in the newspapers. What good are lessons if they teach no one? Every day," he repeated. "Did you know I've read the Bible sixty-three times?" He grinned, showing his horrible teeth.

"I read the newspaper every day also," he added.

Lange nodded. "We're a lot alike, you and I."

Boldt nodded back at the man. His stomach winced. "Why did you free them, Milo? Can you tell me that?"

"Certainly I can tell you. I ought to know, right?" He twisted his hands together thoughtfully. "They were dirty," he said in a whisper. "Filthy women. Unholy. I had to teach them. It was God's will."

"God's will for them to die?"

"For them to be punished. Yes."

"Was there one thing that told you these *particular* women had to be punished?"

"The videos. That *filth*. That showed me who I was after.

I knew which women were impure of spirit and heart. If I was told to deliver that video to a woman, I knew. I punished them. I did it for all of us. I punished them for such thoughts. I freed them of the Devil.''

"You raped them," Boldt blurted out, wishing he had not.

"I *punished* them. Of course I punished them. I didn't *rape* them. I fucked them. I screwed them. They wanted to be fucked, didn't they? Why else did they rent that movie? Answer me that! Yes, they wanted to be fucked. They wanted it bad. Just like the girls in *Summer Knights* wanted it bad. Just like that. Isn't it so? Isn't it so? I'm sure they did. I'm *certain* of it. Ha! Girls with filthy minds. They wanted to be fucked, so I fucked them. *He* wanted them killed, so I killed them. I do God's work. I thought that would make sense to you.''

"It does, Milo," Boldt said, fighting the stinging in his eyes. "So it wasn't to please yourself . . . the . . . fucking, I mean.''

"Me? Please me? You don't understand at all, do you? You think I fucked them to please me? They're filthy whores, all of them. Dirty-minded filthy whores. What pleasure could I derive from such a person? To please me? Of course not! *To teach them a lesson about the penalty for wanting something we shouldn't want!*'' he explained. Again he shoved his hands between his legs and rubbed himself.

"Earlier, you mentioned not killing them all. How many women did you kill, Mr. Lange?"

"Kill?"

"Free."

"Eight."

"Eight women. Is that correct?"

He nodded.

"For the sake of our records I would appreciate a verbal reply.''

"Eight. That is correct.''

"Do you remember their names?"

"The names of angels? Who forgets the names of angels?"

"If I may interrupt?" Boldt looked quickly over at the PD, who told his client, "You don't have to answer any questions you don't want to, Milo."

"You want their names? Of course I know their names."

"Yes. I'd like their names."

Lou Boldt felt himself sweating heavily. His throat was constricted, like he'd had a heavy workout.

"The Angel of Mercy. The Angel of Fate. The Angel of Forgiveness—"

"Their Christian names, please," Boldt interrupted.

"Those *are* their Christian names now."

"Before, then."

"Before what?"

"Before you freed them."

"Yes. I freed them. I do His work. I told you that. Did you know I've read the Bible sixty-three times?"

Boldt took a drink of water. "In your report you said eight. You said the papers had lied. Why did you say that?"

"The papers lie. Names like Saviria, Jordan, Kniffen, DeHavelin. These are not His work."

Boldt realized the man did know the names. "But Holmgren, Reddick?" He led him on.

Lange grinned.

"Were Holmgren and Reddick His work, Mr. Lange?"

"Call me Milo."

Come on! Boldt agonized at the man's avoidance. "His work, Milo?"

"Yes. Venessa Holmgren, Jan Reddick, Doris Heuston, Tanya Shufflebeam, Robin Bailey, Cheryl Croy, Diane Fabiano. All His work."

"And Nancy Levitt?"

Lange looked at the PD. He seemed to be asking "Who?"

The PD said, "He won't discuss the boy, Lou."

"I'm not discussing the boy. I'm discussing the boy's mother."

Lange said uneasily, "The little boy's mother is a whore. His father is a drunk. I saved the little boy."

Silence.

"Did you *free* the little boy, Milo?" Boldt asked anxiously.

"Boy?" Lange asked oddly. He repeated the word several times. Then he said, "I freed the whores. *Someone* had to free them, Lou. It's all right if I call you Lou, isn't it?"

Lou Boldt looked down at the photo I.D. clipped to his sports coat. He saw his name printed there, but it seemed the I.D. belonged to someone else. He nodded slowly. "Whatever you want, Milo. Whatever you want."

"I want to help you, Lou," Lange said. "I'm here to help you. God wants to help you." The man reached across with his bound hands and touched Boldt's hand. The small chain made a scratching sound on the tabletop. Boldt didn't dare jerk his hand away. He withdrew it slowly. He looked blankly at the mirror in the wall, knowing Daphne and Shoswitz were on the other side. Then he glanced back at Milo Lange and looked him directly in the eye.

"I'll need details," he said in a voice he didn't recognize.

51

"THAT WAS ROUGH," she said.

"Where's Shoswitz?"

"He's running down a bunch of the leads you picked up." She had let her hair down and combed it out. She ran her fingers into her hair, stretching the skin on her face. "His attention to detail suggests a true fantasy. The postcrime phase was interesting—from my point of view, Lou," she added, seeing his response. We don't think alike, you and I, Boldt thought. There are times your comments leave me cold. "It didn't occur to me that he might kill these women and then go back to work as if nothing had ever happened. One minute he was killing them, the next, delivering videos. Not the most comforting thought."

Boldt said, "It's hard for me to conceive of a man getting no sleep at all for days at a time. And he claims to have been doing that for what, three months? I don't know . . ."

"It helps explain the voices. It's fairly common, actually; this chronic insomnia is one of the early indications of psychosis. It will go on for days—sometimes weeks—at a time."

Boldt pinched the bridge of his nose and closed his eyes. "Insomnia's not my problem at the moment. I'm a walking zombie."

"You did a good job extracting his fantasy world. That will be extremely helpful to me."

Too cold. Too clinical. He missed the warmth of Elizabeth. "When's your interview?" he asked.

"Tomorrow, if the PD will agree. Mine will be short. The Prosecutor's office will call in an 'expert' to write the trial summary."

"I thought you were our expert . . ."

"They like to bring in outsiders. It gives a much cleaner look to things. They'll probably use Dr. Farris. He's the best there is."

"This seems so cut-and-dried to you. I have trouble with that," he admitted.

"To me, the Milo Langes will always have a piece of Mary Alice in them. His behavior is a result of something, Lou. I suppose to me it *is* cut-and-dried. There's a cause and effect at work here that as a policeman assigned to find him, you may not see—or care to acknowledge. He's not a monster. Not an animal. Not like your copycat is."

"Why did Lange help us?" Boldt asked, too tired to challenge her.

"It gives him a sense of superiority. By reconstructing the killings in such detail, it gives him a sense of cleverness and control. He wants desperately to control us now, to be the one dictating how the remainder of the investigation goes. His fantasy, which he believes involved God and the idea that he was purifying society, replaced reality for him. Reality has become the fantasy now; fantasy the reality. He's scared of reality." She paused. "We checked his record, you know. He *was* previously committed. Upon release from the institution he was prescribed a drug that costs about ten dollars a day. That's three hundred dollars a month for a man fresh out of an institution! When do you think his last prescription was filled?"

"Sometime in April?"

She nodded, lips pursed. "Right before the killings started."

"Damn." He shook his head. "I know you want me to feel compassion for this man." And you, he thought. He placed a hand on her shoulder. Where had that feeling of intimacy gone? "But right now I can't."

"At least you're honest, Lou. I can't fault you for being honest."

But I'm not being honest with you, he thought.

52

HE STARTED FOR HOME, but at the last minute stayed on Aurora for another two exits and then turned off. Shortly thereafter he was idling outside the entrance to his driveway. Her driveway now. Elizabeth.

He sat in the car and looked at the house and he could picture her in bed. It was just past two in the morning. He didn't imagine another man in his bed, he felt no great pangs of jealousy; he pictured himself in the bed, curled up with her, none of the last several months having ever happened. He missed her. He tried to rub the fatigue from his eyes, but it wouldn't leave. He tried to erase the last several months, but they wouldn't leave either. In his extreme state of exhaustion he bordered on the verge of tears.

He pictured himself with Daphne, embracing, making love, and he tried to convince himself it hadn't happened. Then he tried to convince himself it was all right that it had. But it wasn't all right anymore.

He was in a fine mess, he decided. He had scrambled up his priorities a long time ago, and was paying dearly for those decisions now. He recalled the doctor's waiting room. He recalled Elizabeth's begging to keep the child. He spoke quietly to himself, though he wasn't saying anything intelligible, nothing anyone sitting there might have understood. Faint apologies for things done and things said. Another failed effort at changing the past. Correcting the past. He could see the child out there playing on the lawn now, despite the darkness, despite the cold. She had wanted the child. He had not.

"We're a lot alike, you and I." He heard the eerie voice of Milo Lange, and wondered if that was what had triggered this.

A child kicking a ball. A boy or girl? He would never know. A child gleefully experiencing life and passing on the wonder of it all to her/his parents. He bit down on his knuckle, making it white, and fought back his tears. He blinked and the child was gone. There was no child playing in the yard. Only grass out there, grass that needed cutting. Empty, dark, and quiet.

I'm tired, he thought. That's all it is. I'm tired.

"Lou?" He heard the dreamlike tone of Elizabeth's gentle voice and the light tapping on the window and wondered where he was. The sun was up and he was lying against the door, mouth open, tongue dry. He opened his eyes a bit further and realized he was still in her driveway. He shook his head to wake himself, and when he looked over his shoulder he was face-to-face with his wife, a sheet of safety glass between them. She smiled at him genuinely. "How 'bout a cup of coffee?" came her muffled voice.

He shook his head. His refusal annoyed her and she took a step back, crossing her arms. She scrunched her eyes.

Not knowing why, he waved her away, like a teacher erasing the blackboard. *This never happened,* his effort seemed to say. He started the car.

"Lou," she pleaded, her voice even more faint. "Please."

He began to roll down the window, stopped, and shook his head, leaving the glass between them. He backed out of the drive. She followed the car on foot to the end of the short stretch of blacktop and, he saw as he glanced into the rearview mirror, stood in the road watching him drive away.

As he drove along, his imagination conjured up images

of Justin Levitt. It was at this peculiar moment in time that Boldt realized just how much this young man meant to him, recognized the fact that the emotional intensity he had felt before their separation was now being focused on the boy.

He faced the abortion now for the first time in eleven years. The act he had demanded of his wife back when she was still in school and he was a young patrolman unable to make ends meet. He faced her resentment now, and though he had told himself a hundred times that he *knew* what she went through, only now did he fully realize that he had not known. He had never even tried to understand. She had begged him—*begged* him—to let her keep the child, and he had steadfastly refused. Pigheaded. He could still smell the antiseptic odor of the doctor's waiting room. He could still feel his hands sweating as he pretended to read ancient magazines. His mind filled with images of what must have been taking place in the room just beyond those doors. He saw the nurse come into the waiting room and assure him everything had gone fine. *Fine?* he wondered now. His wife would lie down for an hour or so, he was told. She would be ready to go home shortly.

So what gave him the right? He had killed a human being of his own flesh and blood on that day. Elizabeth was not responsible; the doctor was not responsible. Only him. Only *he* had demanded they stop the life. Was it any wonder that Elizabeth had refused to have another child? Was it any wonder that she had buried herself in her work, had become a different person? Was it any wonder that she still kindled a sense of resentment?

"Am I glad to see you," Shoswitz said as Boldt entered the office area. The lieutenant looked surprisingly rested. "You look like shit," he said, appraising Boldt.

"I feel like shit," Boldt agreed. "Slept in my car."

"Different strokes . . ." Shoswitz said.

"We've got to find Justin."

"Agreed."

"How do you want to go about it? How many men can I have?"

Shoswitz shook his head.

"Phil!"

"Relax. What do you need?"

"We focus on any and all marinas, engine-repair shops, anything like that, in the immediate vicinity of Lange's residence. That mud we keep finding at all the sites is our key, Phil. It's still a dead-end lead. He's tracked it to a number of sites, into his apartment, but we haven't found the source. The mud is all we've got right now."

"So, we check the Yellow Pages for likely places?"

"That's what I would do. Yes. I'd check the Yellow Pages and pull out a map and start pinpointing locations near his place. Work out in a circle from there. If he has another place he uses as a hideout, how far could it be from his room? I doubt very far. Not with him."

"It could be near the video shop, or near the vet's, right?"

"True. That's a possibility too. I doubt the video shop. It's too centrally located, but the vet's worth a try as well. You don't mind working on this?"

"Listen, I'll talk to the captain when he gets in. He wants the kid as badly as the rest of us. If he can get the chief to okay it, we'll pull some overtime funds and get as many guys on this as possible. Right?"

"I'm going to start at his room and work my way out from there."

"It's pouring out there," Shoswitz reminded.

Boldt shrugged. "What's new?"

The rain was falling consistently, though not pouring, as Shoswitz had suggested. It was a typical Seattle rain. Boldt parked outside of Lange's rooming house and rang the door-bell until he awakened the super.

"Did you guys arrest that boy?" the super wondered. He had pulled on his clothes quickly and the man still looked half asleep. "Is that how come your people came back and gave my place that kind of going-over?"

"I need access to Lange's room. And I'd like a look from your rooftop, if you can arrange it."

The man nodded. "Shit, fella, it's your guys' tape that's across his door, not mine. And I already showed them the whole building—basement right to the top. They put that dust everywhere. Nasty shit, that dust is. But suit yourself."

The super unlocked Lange's room, and the door that accessed a small stairway that climbed to a small attic.

Boldt opened the door to Lange's room, breaking the bright orange sticker-seal marked SPD—POLICE LINE—DO NOT CROSS. The room was much as it had been the previous day, only now I.D. had returned and given it another thorough inspection. There was fingerprint dust everywhere. The room seemed painted with it. Boldt approached the window and looked out: a couple of low houses to his left, a taller brick building to his right. He could see the dark water of the canal over the roof of a distant building. But everywhere he looked he saw grass—thick, green grass. Not the kind of area one picked up gobs of mud on their shoes.

He stared out the window and thought of the boy. Was the boy alive? Did they have a chance of finding him? *We make what we want,* he heard Daphne tell him. *We create the way it is.* "I want to find him," Lou Boldt said aloud into the empty room, his voice sounding strange to him.

He climbed the narrow staircase and was reminded of his climb at the Fabianos'. But there were no dead women at the top of these stairs, only a cluttered, box-filled attic with an occasional blemish of fingerprint dust spread across a hard surface. Boldt rummaged through the room mindlessly, unsure of what he was looking for; when he didn't find it, he walked over to the wooden ladder that was built against the far wall and ascended to the hatch that led out onto the roof. He pulled himself up and through with some difficulty, his fatigue slowing him down, the short climb draining him. The rain fell more heavily now, and he tugged up his collar and checked the hatch before lowering it, ensuring he could get back down. The roof was thickly painted black tar and was graded slightly and rimmed with drains that were working feverishly to remove the rainwater. Boldt stepped into a puddle and soaked his right foot. He cursed and jumped from the puddle, but the damage was done. His shoe slurped and squeaked as he walked toward the edge. To the north were more buildings. Endless two-story buildings. A sea of rooftops and chimneys. Rain ran down behind his ears and down his neck. He tried to adjust his sports coat but it didn't help any. There was no way he was going to stay dry. To the west were more buildings, and to the east the same. He felt frustrated as he turned to the south and looked out toward the canal. Lange had walked around down there somewhere —had picked up mud repeatedly on his sneakers and had tracked the mud into several of his kill sites. Did the mud have something to do with his ritual? Did he have a hideout to go with his explosive personality, or was this rooming house all that remained? I can find him if I want to, Boldt thought. And I want to.

He studied the area before him carefully, rain soaking through to his shoulders. His pants were wet from his knees down. He began to shake from the cold. His eyes searched the various groups of houses, one by one. And then he lowered his eyes—he looked straight down into the small backyard behind this building, and he saw it. It wasn't mud—it was a chain-link fence with what appeared to be a tiny path cut into the weeds along its edge.

Boldt ran to the hatch, splashing through the same puddle and soaking his left foot as well. He lowered himself through, pulling the door closed over him, and slid down the ladder so quickly, he picked up splinters in the process. The attic smelled strange after the fresh rain, like mildew and dust. He bounded down the stairs and nearly knocked over the super, who was standing there, apparently wondering about all the noise. Boldt ran past with no attention to the man, and hurried down the creaking flight of stairs. A moment later he was back in the rain and that damp, almost electric, odor.

When he reached the edge of the chain-link fence he stopped cold. No mud here. The thin path was cut through spent weeds. He proceeded slowly, eyes trained on the ground. Despite the lack of mud, he liked what he saw—the path had not been used often. Without his bird's-eye view he might never have spotted it. It was narrow and it followed the fence as the fence turned left. Boldt glanced ahead briefly. The fence ran behind a small house, which Boldt now passed. At the end of the fence the path stopped. So did Boldt. The rain was intense now and Boldt felt discouragement pull at him. The water ran off the knuckles of his tightly clenched fists and cascaded to the weeds.

Boldt was no tracker. He knew nothing about tracking. But he walked on and quickly found himself facing a discolored picket fence. He was walking in an area where the backyards of opposing houses met, and he wondered if someone would call the cops on him. Would Lange have risked being seen? he wondered. He looked around. No yard lights on the back of either house, and to his left a row of shrubs a few feet inside the fence. He looked toward both houses, and then quickly vaulted the fence, dropping in between the row of shrubs and the fence. The jump hurt his knee. He remained bent over and something inside him told him that this was right—this was how Milo Lange had done it to avoid being seen. Then he realized it wasn't something inside him—it was something *outside* of him. The smell of gasoline. He looked down. He was into an area of mud, and on the surface was the rainbow haze of gasoline. He planted his hand firmly into the mud, covering it. It dripped from his fingers like gruel. He crawled forward to the base of the shrubs, to where the stream of colors was more intense—the source on the other side of the hedge. He lowered his head and butted his way through the thicket.

His coat sleeve, worn at the elbow, caught and tore. He pushed harder and broke into the cluttered backyard. His eyes settled on a fifty-five-gallon drum ahead of him. It was old and rusted, but the wooden length of board bolted near its rim told its purpose—it was filled to overflowing with gas-stained rainwater, a vat to test an outboard motor. The weathered length of board mounted to it showed several sets of circular impressions where the engine clamps had been screwed down tight. The drum, slightly tilted, was spilling its poison out onto the mud and into the narrow gap between fence and shrubs. Boldt broke back through the hedge, tearing his jacket again. A group of sloppy shoe prints in the mud. He moved along the property line, following the hedge until it stopped.

He snapped his head to the left. An overgrown lot with a partially burned, boarded-up house still standing. Behind it, closest to Boldt, stood a ramshackle garage—a shack of weathered wood. He ran through the tall, wet weeds to the door of the shack and stopped, winded.

Holding the front door shut was a recently added padlock. No more than a few months old, Boldt thought.

Lou Boldt had never considered himself a cop capable of an investigative ''sixth sense'' as some cops were purported to have. And yet he experienced just such a sensation now, standing in the pouring rain, soaking wet, cold, facing this door.

He believed the boy was inside. He *knew* it.

But was he alive?

He would reflect later that he was overcome with emotion at the time. And he knew emotion had no place in good police work. But good police work was not Lou Boldt's priority at that moment. Justin Levitt was his priority. The boy. The child. And that's why he kicked in the door without waiting for a search warrant.

The clasps tore from the decayed wood and the door blew

open from his efforts. It was dark inside and the roof was leaking, contained in several locations by rusted coffee cans.

Boldt felt the blood drumming at his temples, and the all-too-familiar knot in his chest. This was *his* domain. And if the other room had been the home of Jesus, this was the home of the Devil. Fast-food litter crowded the floor and the tops of crates Lange had rigged as a table. There was no bed, only a ratty, stained mattress in the corner. At the foot of the bed were several pieces of bloodstained clothing in clumps. The sight of the pieces of clothing returned the vivid photographic images of the various victims' faces fresh to Boldt's mind. Women screaming out to him with paralyzed eyes, stockings and handkerchiefs binding their necks. He felt short of breath. Nauseated. The stench was overpowering. The missing pieces of clothing! he thought. On the table, next to a Burger King bag, was a bloodstained serrated kitchen knife. Another lay in the dust on the floor. Boldt stepped forward and tugged open the black wool blanket that hung as a wall.

Pushed into the dark corner, his ankles and wrists wired together, Boldt saw the dull white eyes of Justin Levitt staring back at him.

The boy was alive!

53

BOLDT RODE in the ambulance with the boy. He experienced the pain of the victim: Justin Levitt was without family now, alone and left with only horrified memories of confinement at the hands of the man who had killed his parents. The boy had begun to cry as Boldt had unwired him, and the detective took this as a good sign. Justin had thrown his arms tightly around Lou Boldt's neck and had not let go. Initially, the paramedics had attempted to pry him away from Boldt, but the sergeant quickly convinced them that he should go along. Now the two of them were riding in the back of the ambulance, Justin strapped into a stretcher, uncomfortable with the restraint required by law, and Boldt at his side, one hand holding the boy's, the other stroking the boy's forehead. The boy sobered periodically, and except for his smell and the dirt smudges on his face, appeared all right—at least physically.

Once at the emergency room, he was taken away by a nurse, refusing to leave Boldt at first, then acquiescing after an encouraging word by the detective. Boldt summoned Daphne by phone. Less than twenty minutes later the two of them sat speechless in orange vinyl chairs, awaiting some word on the boy.

Time dragged on. In an awkward moment of consoling, Daphne reached over and took Boldt's hand. She had soft hands, but they were cold with fear for the boy. Boldt returned her hands to her lap—and with that came a message. Daphne's expression turned grave, and then she smiled somewhat pitifully and said, "It's all right, Lou. I understand." The two of them sat silently for another twenty minutes until finally an extremely young doctor arrived to consult them. Daphne introduced herself professionally and the two bantered in psychiatric jargon until Boldt stopped them. "Speak English, would you please?"

The doctor said they would keep him a day or two for observation, that the boy seemed to be handling the events remarkably well. He had not suffered physically at all. By all accounts, Justin Levitt was coming along fine. He had not witnessed the actual killing of his parents, had not seen the bodies. He had been too frightened to open his eyes after the struggle in his bedroom with Lange, and had been led from the house with his eyes shut. He knew his parents were dead—had been murdered—and seemed to be taking it as well as possible. "As well as any of us would," was how the doctor put it.

The boy was dressed in hospital pajamas. He said, "Hi."

"Hi," Boldt returned.

"I hear you got him."

"Yes."

"Thanks."

Boldt felt a frog in his throat. He could not recall having ever been thanked for solving a murder case. It seemed odd to him, now that he thought about it. He had been congratulated plenty of times, but never thanked. Suddenly the hospital room, the familiar smell, triggered that same image of his waiting for his wife to come through those doors after the abortion. He wondered if he would ever be free of the guilt. Is guilt something that chains itself to you and never lets go? he thought.

"My uncle's coming," the boy announced.

"That's fine," Boldt said, experiencing a degree of jealousy. Yes, he thought, jealousy.

"I suppose he'll take me back to Idaho."

Boldt nodded.

"He killed my parents," the boy told Boldt matter-of-factly. "Do you suppose my parents are in heaven?"

Boldt lowered the stainless-steel bar and sat down on the bed. "What do you think?"

"I think they are."

"So do I."

"I think they're probably happy that he didn't kill me, too."

Boldt nodded. His eyes were stinging. He didn't want to cry in front of the boy. Especially not the boy. He tried to get a word out, but it caught in his throat and he felt his fatigue and his emotions get the better of him. He looked down into the calm and gentle eyes and felt his throat swell with sorrow.

"It's all right," the boy said sympathetically, in an understanding tone only a child can convey. "It's not your fault, Mr. Boldt. You're the one who got him."

Big Lou Boldt rocked forward, pressing his heavy head against Justin Levitt's shoulder. The boy sat up to meet him, and hugged him strongly, his IV following his movements. Boldt shook violently as he felt himself in the young boy's arms. God, it felt incredible.

"I'm scared," Justin Levitt blurted out behind his own tears. "I'm scared of being alone."

Boldt placed his large hand on the back of the young man's head, and threaded his fingers into his hair. He pressed their cheeks together—the boy's, soft and warm; his own, rough and in need of a shave. He closed his eyes and for a moment could believe that this was his boy, his son, that he was a father, and he understood that there was nothing as important as this to him, nothing as moving or as meaningful. He smiled broadly through his tears, and the boy must have felt him smile for the boy began to chuckle and soon Boldt was chuckling too. And then, still clasped in each other's arms, the two began to laugh, neither fully knowing why—and they leaned back, away from each other, meeting eyes and throwing their arms around each other again and playfully squeezing the laughter away until it was gone altogether.

When Boldt left an hour later, Justin Levitt was fast asleep.

54

THIRTY MINUTES LATER Boldt found himself right back at his desk. He was attracted to it like bugs to floodlights.

The detailed interview with Lange had convinced him a copycat had indeed been responsible for four of the kills, Saviria, Jordan, DeHavelin, and Kniffen, and Boldt feared that with Lange arrested and charged, they might lose the copycat completely. If the copycat was indeed a cop, then he knew their energies would focus on him next.

He only stayed at his desk a few minutes. The parking tickets he had discovered in Judith Fuller's car continued to nag at him. He pocketed them and went down to dispatch, where a number of radio-telephone operators sat in front of panels that looked like something from NASA launch center. A variety of detailed maps of the city hung on the walls. Boldt searched the addresses on the tickets and, cross-referencing them with the maps, pinpointed the exact locations where Fuller had been ticketed. One was on Pill Hill near the school. The other two were on North Seventy-seventh Street and North Seventy-eighth. Pill Hill was filled with medical clinics, hospitals, libraries, and the college. He cross-referenced these locations against the approximate locations for the two dry-cleaning establishments. He saw no correlation. He returned to his desk and phoned Judith Fuller's Los Angeles bank.

The manager of Wells Fargo in Simi Valley was extremely pleasant. He agreed to share account information with Boldt, as long as that information was kept confidential, and out of the press.

Recent deposits into Judith Fuller's checking account included a fifty-dollar check from Irene Longet, Lincoln, Nebraska; a three hundred-dollar check drawn from the UCLA extension-course account; and six, all paid in large amounts, from *The Los Angeles Times*.

Boldt phoned the *Times* twice and spoke with seven different people before finally connecting with an editor named Tom Moriarty.

"Sure, I know Judy, Detective. She's one of my strongest stringers."

"A reporter?"

"Of course a reporter. She's an investigative journalist. Free-lance."

"Free-lance?"

"She comes in with an idea. If I buy the idea, I cover her expenses and pay for a first draft. Not like the stringer where I typically make the assignments. Judy's an independent. Very independent."

"Have you heard from her lately?"

"As a matter of fact, I haven't. I usually get a call every couple of weeks screaming at me for more up-front money. Haven't heard from her in nearly a month. I figured she was into the piece and getting ready to deliver. What's this about, anyway?"

"Can you tell me what she's been working on?"

"You say you're with the Seattle Police Department?"

"That's right."

"Extension?"

Boldt gave it to him.

"I'll call you right back, Sergeant. Sit tight."

Boldt hung up. He didn't like to be told to sit tight. It was a curious expression.

The phone rang. He picked it up. Moriarty said, "We get a lot of competition in this business. Your competition will try about anything to find out what your hot features are. Sorry for the delay, but I had to confirm that there was a Lou Boldt on the Seattle police, and that you were he. Now I'm convinced. You wanted to know what Judy is working on. I would appreciate it if you don't go broadcasting this. I have several hundred into expenses on this. It's more than worth it as long as we maintain our jump. We lose our jump and we've just pissed away several hundred and Judy's fee."

"I understand."

"Let me pull her file so I can give you any details you need. Hold the phone." Boldt could hear Moriarty rummage through his files. Then the man's voice said, "The idea she proposed involved a string of serial killings." Boldt listened more carefully. Moriarty paused while he evidently read from the file. "I don't mean a string, like a string. I mean one string in one city, another string in another city. Judy maintains she's found a connection between the different killings."

"Let me guess," Boldt said. "Denver and Tucson?"

"Right on the money, Sergeant. Are you familiar with those cases?"

"No, I'm not. Can you help me out?"

"Just that a number of women were murdered in each city last year."

"And the killer got away?"

"No, actually. A man was arrested and convicted in each case. However, in both cases—I've got the clippings right here—each murderer claimed he had not killed all the women blamed on him. That's what caught Judy's attention in the first place. She has this theory that there was, in fact, another killer working these same areas. As soon as the *real* murderer was arrested, this other guy would move on to another city where a serial killing was baffling police."

"Seattle . . ." Boldt said.

"On the money. She went from Denver straight to Seattle. I okayed that. She sent me clippings to support it. She checked papers around the time the Denver police caught the guy—the real killer—and found all sorts of headlines about your Cross Killer up there. That was the middle of May. I hear you guys got the guy, by the way. Congratulations."

Boldt thanked him. "Do you have her notes? Anything that might help me with this?"

"No. Nothing. Why not talk to Judy? I can give you her number if you haven't got it."

"I've got it," Boldt said.

"What's this about? You want me to call Judy?"

"I can't explain right now, Mr. Moriarty."

"Would my readers have any interest in it?"

"I'm afraid they might."

"What's that supposed to mean?"

Boldt regretted the comment. "No notes. No more details?"

"Listen, all Judy gives me is Xerox copies of ten thousand receipts. I send her checks. She sends me receipts. She's a damned good writer, Sergeant. If you see her, tell her I'm waiting on that article."

"One other thing, Mr. Moriarty?"

"Sure."

"Was Judith a windsurfer?"

"Wouldn't know anything about that."

"Any way to find out?"

"You could ask her, right? That seems like the most direct approach," he said somewhat condescendingly.

"Thanks for your help." Boldt hung up.

"I want to brainstorm this copycat thing with somebody."

"Jesus, Lou. I gotta ton of paperwork to catch up on," Shoswitz complained. "*Your* paperwork."

"Please?"

"Grab a seat," Shoswitz said.

Boldt sat down. He explained his conversation with Moriarty.

When Boldt finished, Shoswitz asked, "You suppose she was investigating the man who belongs to those Rockports?"

"Has to be, doesn't it?"

"Makes sense. So what do you suggest?"

"The first thing I would do is have records use the computers to search the entire force for anyone living on Boren, North Seventy-seventh, or Seventy-eighth. Those are where Fuller picked up those parking tickets. She could have been on a stakeout of her own."

"One of our men."

"Exactly."

Shoswitz, uncomfortable with the thought, reeled irritably. "Let's think backward—review the play-by-play, will you?"

"She's investigating the possibility of a copycat. Incidently, I've got a call in to Tucson and Denver. Good luck on a Saturday. Anyway, let's say Fuller makes some connection to someone. She has a lead, but nothing concrete."

"I'd like that lead," Shoswitz said.

"It was probably in her top drawer. Long gone now, I'm afraid." Boldt picked up where he had left off. "So she thinks she knows who the guy is. Maybe she put him under surveillance. Maybe she follows him."

"And it leads her to a place on Vashon," Shoswitz said.

"We had better include Vashon and Maury Island in our computer search, Phil. That could very well be it."

"I interrupted."

"I was just going to say that maybe it leads her to Vashon—or Maury. So why would she rent a windsurfer?"

"Maybe this guy's a windsurfer and she thinks it's her chance to create an 'accidental' meeting between them. She gets a chance to interview this guy."

"I like that," Boldt said. "That works for me." He thought a moment. "Something else that might play," he tried.

"Shoot."

"What if," Boldt said, eyes shut, thinking, "she's followed this guy to his place on Vashon once. She wants a look inside—"

Shoswitz interrupted, "But it's a remote location and she doesn't want to just drive up and say, 'Hi, I'm here to see if you're the copycat killer I think you are.' "

"And it's a place on the shore . . ."

"So she rents a windsurfer."

". . . and she intentionally screws something up on the board. She sails into his place from the waterside. She can head straight to the cabin, home, whatever. She has a perfect excuse for being there. She can even break in, once she finds no one home, with the excuse that she needed a phone and didn't think anyone would mind."

"Only she's caught, and the excuse doesn't work," Shoswitz added.

"But she's found something—"

"The dry-cleaning receipts."

"The dry cleaning itself. Clothes. Evidence. The souvenirs the copycat took to match the souvenirs Lange took."

"He kept them?"

"If Daphne's right, a psychopath would be *proud* of the crime." Boldt went on, "So he uses a fake name, always chooses a different dry-cleaning establishment, and has the item of clothing cleaned."

"Fuller finds the clothes in a closet and pulls the receipts."

"He catches her and tries to kill her," Boldt said.

"But she gets away somehow."

"Or he lets her get away. He toys with her."

"And she makes it to the water."

"But her trachea is hemorrhaging; she's drowning in her own blood, and she goes down."

"And now he's fucked," Shoswitz said. "The one that got away. So how does he know who she is?"

"Exactly! She's down and gone, and he's left holding a busted windsurfer." Boldt thought a moment.

Shoswitz theorized, "He gets rid of the windsurfer. First things first. Buries it, burns it."

"Burns it. This guy likes to burn evidence."

"But who is she? How's he figure out who she is?"

"She's windsurfing out on Vashon. Now for all we know, it didn't go down like this and maybe he gets into his torture routine and learns whatever it is he needs to know. But if he didn't . . ." He hesitated. "If he didn't, then he looks over the windsurfer real well. It's a rental, so it has some kind of identification. That store may mark hundred-dollar wetsuits with nail polish, but not a thousand-dollar board. So maybe he sees it was rented over in the city. . . .

"Wait a second. Even easier than that. She's going to have launched at one of the beaches or public landings, in any case. She'll park her car in one of the parking lots and put in from there. He's got to figure she drove to wherever she launched. She's not his next-door neighbor, for Christ's sake; not if she's caught snooping around his stuff. So he starts close and works his way out—same way we look for something. How many public accesses can there be on the east side of Vashon and Maury? A handful at best. Wouldn't take long for him to check them all, if it came to that. He goes that night and looks for an abandoned car. And she probably would have chosen a place close by. Why make it tough on herself? And there's a Mercury with California plates and a rented roof-rack sitting all alone when everybody else is gone."

"And guess where she's left her keys," added Shoswitz.

"We didn't find them on her. So either he got them off her before she went in, or they were in the car or hidden somewhere on it."

"He gets himself inside that car," said Shoswitz, "and he may as well be inside her brain. A piece of junk mail with her address. The key to her apartment. Her purse? It's all there. Shit.''

"Piece of cake.''

"I don't suppose we'll ever know for certain. Right? I mean even if we catch him, we may never know for sure.''

"She was one brave lady, if that's the way it went down.''

"Amen. Brave, or stupid, or both.''

"I prefer brave," Boldt said.

"And rightly so.''

"So how the hell do we find this bastard?''

"Did he pick his victims at random? Follow them. Kill them? Is he a traffic cop that takes their names off of their driver's licenses? One of my detectives wandering around out there?''

"Something we worked on before," Boldt recalled, "when we were talking about how he went about matching Norvak to Fuller. We thought he might have gone to the windsurfing areas and looked around for someone who looked like Fuller. Another thought . . .''

"Go ahead.''

"Norvak belonged to The Body Shop. We know that. And everyone at the club knew that Norvak was a heavy-duty windsurfer.''

"The club's where he found Norvak? I'd buy that.''

Boldt stepped out of the office and hollered, "LaMoia!'' He tried again, and the exhausted detective came at a run. They spoke in whispers, and a few minutes later, alone again with Shoswitz, Boldt had a ream of photocopies stacked on his lap.

He leafed through it.

"What have you got?" Shoswitz asked.

"Checking accounts and statements for Saviria, Jordan, Kniffen, and DeHavelin. John's making some calls.''

Shoswitz went back to his paperwork. Boldt reviewed the material. When LaMoia returned, both men looked up.

"They weren't all the same, but you were right, Sarge.''

"Let's have it," Boldt said, putting down the stack.

"Saviria belonged to Nutri-fit. She had been a member for years. Jordan belonged to the Sixth Street Gym. De-Havelin, Norvak, and Kniffen all belonged to The Body Shop. Most of Lange's victims didn't belong to health clubs, so we never saw a pattern. And these broads belonged to different clubs at that."

"Health clubs?" Shoswitz asked. "He spotted them at health clubs," he stated. "At The Body Shop?"

Boldt snapped his finger. It was right there dancing at the edges of his mind—the connection. He couldn't pull it to the surface. A man's voice, right there. It shot across his mind but he couldn't hold it there. A man's voice saying something. But who? Who had said it? Where? A man's voice . . .

"Lou?"

"The club . . ."

Shoswitz let him think.

"Something about the club." A long silence. "Group rates!" Boldt barked out. "Mike Sharff. Group rates."

"What?"

"The Body Shop sent out flyers a few months back. Don't you remember? They were offering group rates—five people or more. I ran into Mike Sharff at the club the night I was there. You know, Dixie's assistant. Short, stocky guy. He told me about the group rates. Said a number of our people worked out there too. If the copycat discovered Norvak and DeHavelin at the health club, and he's a member of this department, then he's more than likely in our group plan out there. We check their group-rate records and cross-reference them with the addresses where Fuller got her tickets."

"Or on Vashon."

"Or both."

"What is it, Lou? You look horrible."

Boldt didn't say a word. But in his mind was the all-too-clear image of Daphne coming through the door to The Body Shop. And right behind her was John Kramer.

55

A STUDY of the computer printout from The Body Shop revealed that twenty-two employees of the police department belonged to the group program. Of these twenty-two, seventeen were women, leaving five men whom Boldt and Shoswitz considered as possibilities for the copycat. Two of the five were patrolmen, and had no way of knowing the details of the Cross Killer investigation. Two others were in Narco, and were unlikely to have had access to the information, though they couldn't be ruled out completely. At the top of the list was John Kramer.

"I simply refuse to believe it," Shoswitz said. "Not John."

Boldt was staring at his copy of the printout. He had circled Kramer's name several times. There he lay, trapped by the ever-tightening orbits of ink. He looked out through Shoswitz's door. The back of Kramer's red head was visible thirty feet away. He was talking intensely to LaMoia. "Do we question him?"

"Shit." The lieutenant looked across at Boldt. "No way, Lou. You didn't hear this from me, but he's not smart enough to put this thing together."

"And he doesn't live anywhere near where Fuller was ticketed—if that relates to this. One way to find out."

"How's that?"

"Let's check with Jimmie down in the caves. If they haven't checked Kramer's print yet, we should do so now."

"Right." Shoswitz lifted the phone.

"Hold it! Forget it. Can't be Kramer. The guy we're after is new in town—Fuller followed him here."

Shoswitz closed his eyes, "Hallelujah," he gasped. He set the phone back down.

Boldt leaned forward. "It's not one of us, Phil. A cop couldn't switch a dental record." He hesitated and then said, "I know who it is."

56

THE THREE MEN, Boldt, Shoswitz, and Kramer, were behind the locked door of interrogation room A. Shoswitz had key-locked the small room that allowed viewing through the two-way mirror, as well as listening in. He meant to keep this private.

"So?" the lieutenant asked.

"It's James Royce," Boldt told them, "Dixie's autopsy assistant. It's my fault," he continued. "I had plenty of chances to see the connection. Mike Sharff, the other assistant, was at the club the first time I went. He told me about the group accounts—that a number of people from his office had joined. I knew Norvak was a member of The Body Shop—I should have thought it was connected. Being in the ME's department, Royce could alter evidence, plant evidence, cover his tracks however he saw fit. That's why the dental records matched Norvak's. That's what made me realize it. The autopsy assistant cleans the bodies and does the initial tests. Royce simply substituted a different X-ray of Fuller's mouth into Norvak's dental files and then let Dixie confirm. Dixie admits it wouldn't be hard to do."

He continued, "One of Fuller's parking tickets was issued on North Seventy-seventh Street. Royce lives in the same block of North Seventy-seventh. She had him under surveillance. It fits."

"You talked to Dixon about this?" Kramer asked incredulously.

Boldt nodded. "Dixie's had a terrible time with turnover in his department. Royce has been with him since mid-May—only days after the press picked up on the similarities between the Holmgren kill and the Reddick kill. We need a thumbprint in order to verify," Boldt pointed out. "I told Royce Bobbie was heading up the Jane Doe investigation. Two days later he asked her out on a date, no doubt worried about the apparent loose ends he'd left behind. He was trying to keep tabs on the investigation. It seems so obvious in hindsight. I didn't pick up on it at the time."

"We'll need that thumbprint," Shoswitz agreed. "The print will tie him to both Norvak's house and Fuller's car."

Kramer complained, "But we don't even have enough to get a warrant to get us into his place—as if that would help us any with a guy this careful. The prints may place him at Norvak's, maybe in both those cars, but where's the foul play? I'll tell you where—the foul play is in our heads."

It was a rare moment of truth for Judge Kramer's son, and Boldt acknowledged it. "Fair enough. So we need more than circumstantial evidence."

"And we'll never get it, right?" Shoswitz said, disappointed. "A guy like this."

"He's thorough, if that's what you mean," Boldt added.

"That's what *I* mean," Kramer said. "He's thought everything through. Covered himself well."

Boldt reminded them of Denver and Tucson. "He's had practice." Recalling his talk with Daphne he said, "His game is perfection. Perfect duplication."

"What we need is a confession," Kramer said.

"Good luck," snapped Shoswitz.

"There you go," suggested Boldt.

Both men looked at him curiously.

"He's a copycat. Literally. His game is perfect duplication. He sees how the bodies come in, he makes sure his victims are identical. That's the thrill for him."

"So?" Kramer wondered.

"With both Norvak and Fuller he had no one to copy. He made simple mistakes. Fingerprints, burning the clothing; he didn't understand the tidal currents."

"What are you driving at?" Shoswitz wondered.

"If we talk to Daphne, if we get briefed on his kind of personality, maybe I could go in on a wire and trip him up. Maybe we could get that confession after all. It's worked on schizoids before, using the third person and getting the suspect into a 'what if' situation. They can be made to stumble. It's a possibility."

"Those were trained professionals, guys from Behavioral Science, not city cops," Kramer reminded. "Besides, since when do we use wires? Narco doesn't even use them anymore."

"Daphne could do it," Shoswitz stated enthusiastically, ignoring Kramer. "I like it. Let's run it by her."

Boldt objected. "No way. She's not a cop. She's had no cop training. She's a psychologist. One of *us* should do it, and I've dealt with Royce. If I approach Royce—say about the tape on the mouth, something like that—he won't suspect it in the least. It should be me."

Kramer gave Boldt an angry look. "Is that the real reason?" he asked. "Or do you just want the limelight again. Your big chance to erase the Jergensen thing, is that it?"

"John!" Shoswitz reprimanded.

Boldt was tempted to slug the man. He was sick of Kramer's griping, of his jealousy and his ineffectiveness. He felt the warmth flood his face and he clamped his jaw down hard to keep himself from saying anything stupid.

"*She*'s the professional," Shoswitz reminded. "Let's run it by Daphne and see what she thinks. That's what she's here for, right: thinking?"

Lou Boldt wanted to object but knew it would fall on deaf ears. He knew what her answer would be, before asking. The thought of it turned his gut.

57

SHE SAT DEMURELY behind her desk, confident and excited. Her chestnut hair was styled in loose curls today. Her eyes sparkled. Shoswitz and Boldt sat facing her. She wore a tailored, navy-blue blazer, and a white, pleated blouse, sparkling gold earrings swinging from her lobes like fragile icicles. "It's a wonderful idea," she said, looking at Boldt and thanking him with her eyes, thinking, no doubt, this suggestion stemmed from their earlier talk where she had expressed an interest in getting to a psychopath prior to arrest. She was positively radiant.

Boldt felt the hair on the nape of his neck stand on end. This was wrong and he knew it, but he was helpless to do anything about it.

She asked, "How certain are you?"

"We only have circumstantial evidence," Boldt told her, disappointed.

Shoswitz interjected, "Nothing strong enough to put him away. He's been very careful. We may be able to link him to several crime scenes, certainly to The Body Shop, but that doesn't prove he murdered anyone—and for someone in the Medical Examiner's office, it isn't unusual to be around a crime scene. The defense would have a heyday with that, I'm afraid."

Boldt explained, "He more than likely chose his victims

from health clubs. Following the discovery of another Cross Killer victim, Royce would set up his next kill.

"We assume he spotted someone suitable at the health club," he added. "There's any number of ways it could go down from here: he could introduce himself using an alias; he could get himself invited over when he's out in the parking lot; but that's not how I see it. Too much could go wrong. His name could get mentioned; he could be seen leaving with her. I tend to think it was something *much* more subtle. Macho. He gives her the eye a few times from across the workout room. This is a good-looking guy, let's not forget. He eye-flirts with a few of the women and one of them bites. He keeps working on her until he knows he's hooked her—all without speaking a word. He intentionally avoids meeting her—they *never* meet. But he has her in his sights. He puts her under surveillance. And one night he walks up to her door and knocks. She answers the door. It's *him*. To her, it's *him*. He cracks a smile. 'Hi,' he says. She returns the smile and opens the door.

"No telling from here," he added. "Each time it's probably a little bit different. Sometimes he may step right in and kill them. Or maybe he goes out back for a little barbecue, like he apparently did with Norvak."

"Jesus, Lou. Where the *fuck* did you get that?"

Daphne nodded vigorously. "That fits, as far as I'm concerned: charm them to death. I like it."

"Like it?" Shoswitz said.

"He's a public employee. We've got a card on him. I.D. is comparing his prints against the partials. We won't move until we have print confirmation," Shoswitz added. "They're only partials, Daphne. That's our problem."

"I think I can help," she said, sitting back in her chair, hooking her fingers into her curls and combing them through. "It's a good idea, Lou. If I can get him talking he may give us what we want. It should simply be a matter of challenging him in the right way, putting his ego on the defensive."

"It's dangerous," Boldt contended. "It could go bad."

"We'll be right there," Shoswitz reminded. "We'll do it during business hours so the ME's is busy and there are plenty of people around. We'll put Lou in conference with Doc Dixon so he'll be close at hand. We'll have additional backup outside."

"I'm game. You don't have to sell me," she asserted.

"Any problems?" Shoswitz asked.

Boldt was about to speak up, but he caught the look in Daphne's eyes and fell silent.

I.D. matched Royce's thumbprint, linking him circumstantially to both Norvak and Fuller.

Daphne shut her office door and locked it. Lou Boldt recalled the last time she had done that. It seemed a long time ago now. She turned around and asked him to unbutton her blouse.

"One of the women from Special Assaults should be doing this," he said uncomfortably, placing the RF transmitter down, fingers working the buttons on her back.

"Nonsense. You're perfectly capable," she told him. She pulled off the blouse and turned to face him. Her breasts were cupped in a delicate, sheer bra, her dark nipples held in the very center of airy lace flowers. "Fix me up," she said.

"Daffy," he began in a dramatic voice that she quickly understood.

"Don't. Please, don't. I'm very much aware of what follows next, Lou. My God, do I know what follows next. 'It was just one of those moments. One of those wonderful moments.' I know *all about* wonderful moments. Believe me. I've heard this kind of thing before. Let's leave it at that."

"It *was* wonderful, Daffy. I mean truly wonderful. But—"

"Lou! Enough. It was one night. One moment. It was

a good time. I'm grown-up. I can handle it. Married men. Jeez.'' He looked up from his taping the small wire to her skin. He ran it up along her rib cage to just beneath her armpit and then followed the seam on the underside of the bra. She reached up to help him clip the microphone to the fabric, for it required pulling the bra away from her breast, and Lou Boldt was clearly uneasy with the task. He let her do it, standing back. "You're a married man . . . the kind who is *always* a married man. Once and for all, forever. I knew that as well. Believe me. People are my business, right? I'm the pro, right? Listen, it was good for me. Really good. Wonderful, in fact. I hope it was all right for you.'' He glanced up at her and he wanted to take her into his arms. But he resisted. He sensed she would have welcomed it. She finished clipping the miniature microphone to the center of her bra and he spun her around to run the wire along the top seam of her skirt and tape the tiny transmitter into the small of her back. While she was faced away from him she continued, "I've had my eye on you for a long time. And I got my chance, and I know you well enough to know it was a first and last chance. I know people, right? You bet I do. And you know something? I don't regret a single second. Not a single second.''

He handed her the blouse from behind and she fished her arms inside and pulled it around herself and he began buttoning it. "Listen, Lou, what I'm trying to say is that if it doesn't work out with Elizabeth—and for your sake I hope it does—then there's an understudy waiting in the wings.''

He hadn't finished buttoning her, but he took her in his arms from behind and hugged her tightly to him. She squirmed in his grasp and managed to turn to face him and pressed herself against him strongly. Held him tightly. She kissed his neck and along his cheek. "She's a lucky woman,'' she said.

She leaned away from him, suddenly a different person.

"Ready? Ready to go, Lou? I'm all set, aren't I? Sure I am."

He stared into her eyes.

"I have to finish buttoning you up."

"Yes." She smiled. "Do that." She turned around and straightened her spine. "Please finish it."

58

AS THEY CAME OUT of Daphne's office, Lou Boldt had her by the elbow. They took two steps and were face-to-face with Elizabeth. She wore a black dress, dark stockings, and white pearl earrings and necklace. She looked tired and sad. Her face was expressionless.

Lou Boldt didn't see the face that Daphne made—a face she tried to keep from showing—but he recognized the sudden flicker in his wife's eyes and he knew something had passed between the women.

"Can we talk?" Elizabeth said.

Daphne walked briskly past Boldt's wife with her impeccable posture and finely tuned gait. Boldt stopped, facing Elizabeth. He glanced at his watch and then held up a finger. He rounded the corner and stepped into Kramer's stall. The man was on the phone. He blushed and slammed the receiver down quickly.

"What is it?" Kramer said nervously.

"I need a few minutes of personal time. I wondered if you could organize everyone. Round them up, get them ready? I'll only be a few minutes."

"Sure," Kramer said, rising, the redness in his face subsiding.

"No, not in there," Elizabeth said, nodding toward interrogation room A. "Someplace else."

Boldt led her down the gray-carpet hallway and pushed open the door to the fire stairs. The building was old— much older than the recently remodeled offices indicated— and this stairway showed the age. He held the door at the last moment to keep it from latching, and then turned to face her.

"I've been thinking a lot," he said.

"Me too." She hung her head. "I'm sorry, Lou. It won't happen again."

"Not about that," he told her.

She snapped her head up, expecting the worst. "If it's what I think it is, don't tell me now, okay? I don't think I could handle it now." She took a step toward the door, already resigned to what he had to say.

He reached out and took her arms in his strong hands and stopped her. "About how I deserve everything I got."

"We lost touch. Wrong word," she said quickly. "Lost . . . We lost each other, I think. We had some wonderful times, Lou. The best. I'm willing to do whatever it takes to get those times back. Anything. Honest."

He swallowed deeply. "I've made it hard on both of us. I see that now."

"We *both* have."

"It goes back a long, long way, Elizabeth. It goes back to when you were first in school, I think."

She knew exactly what he was referring to and she nodded faintly. "Yes. That's right. I think it does."

"Boldt!" Shoswitz's voice interrupted from somewhere on the other side of the door.

He lifted his hand and gently brushed her hair back from the side of her face. He exhaled heavily. "I've missed you, babe."

"I heard on the news you caught him," she said. "Congratulations."

"That's why you came."

She nodded. "Yes. I thought we might get some time together. . . . I mean . . . if you wanted to."

"I do," he told her. "But it's not over just yet. I wish it was. A man—someone in our own ranks—has been misleading us for months. Without his interference we might have caught the other much sooner."

"A copycat," she said.

"We're pretty sure."

"Then you were right all along. You mentioned that to me back in June."

"A hunch was all. Back then it was only a hunch." Only an instinct, he thought, wondering why he failed to trust his instincts.

"You're a good cop, Lou Boldt."

Shoswitz called his name again. Boldt leaned forward and kissed her cheek.

"I won't wash for a week," she said in a whisper. He suddenly realized she was wearing little or no makeup.

He touched a finger to her lips. "It took a lot of nerve to come down here. Thanks."

"Come home tonight. Please come home tonight."

"I don't know."

"Dinner? How about a home-cooked meal?"

"Maybe dinner."

She kissed him briefly on the lips. He enjoyed it. She turned and opened the door.

Shoswitz stopped Boldt at his car, handing him a small radio and earphone. "You should be able to hear everything said on this, Lou. You'll be the closest to the scene. If it looks like it's going bad . . . use your best judgment. We'll have plenty of backup in the parking lot. We'll be listening and taping from outside—waiting for word from you. No heroics, Lou."

"Lieutenant, shouldn't we reconsider this whole thing? Let's think it through."

"You said yourself that the copycat could leave town anytime now. We may not get this kind of chance at him, and we both agreed that some kind of confession is about the only thing that will hang him. He's been pulling our chains for months, Lou. Don't you want this guy?"

The question was rhetorical. Boldt didn't dignify it with a response. He said instead, "What the hell's got Kramer in such a snit?"

"He always gets nervous in this kind of thing. You know Kramer. He always wants to be the big man. You're the big man on this, Lou. It bends him all sideways. He'll be fine."

"Keep him in his car."

"Will do."

A few minutes later Boldt was sitting with Doc Dixon, neither saying a word. Doc Dixon worked on his fingernails with the blade of a jeweler's screwdriver. Finally his telephone's intercom buzzed. Dixon answered it, nodded several times, and said, "Send her in."

It had been agreed that Daphne would go through all the proper procedures, in case Royce was keeping a careful eye out. She went into the office and both men stood.

"All set," she said strongly. She looked Boldt in the eye and quickly looked away. Elizabeth's arrival at headquarters had tempered her mood.

Boldt said, "In real life it would take you a few minutes to explain your case to Doc Dixon and then to get his permission to talk to Royce. Better stay in here for a few more minutes." The three waited in awkward silence. Daphne watched the second hand on the large wall clock.

"Okay," she finally said. "Where do I find him?"

Dixon gave her directions and she stepped toward the door.

"Hold it," Boldt said.

She stopped.

He switched on the receiver and stuck the earplug in his ear. "Say something," he said.

"What more is there to say?" she asked somewhat angrily now.

He looked into her eyes. "Okay. It works," he announced.

"Does it?" she wondered, forcing a bewildered grin, and she left the office.

Her arrival broke the ice. As the door shut Doc Dixon said, "Right here all along. The thing about it is, there was no way for me to know. I never would have suspected Royce. Royce of all people. Your theory's good, Lou, but I still think you've got the wrong guy, despite that print."

Boldt held up a finger. "Here we go."

He listened.

59

DAPHNE WAS OBVIOUSLY STANDING quite close to Royce, for the sound was exceptional. Boldt felt he was in the room with her, and he could almost picture every expression on her face, her change in posture, her rigid spine that indicated extreme concentration.

"How can I help you?" Royce asked.

"We've arrested and charged the Cross Killer—"

"Yes, I heard. What a relief."

". . . and I was told by Doctor Dixon that you performed the initial examination of many of the victims prior to autopsy." She let the statement hang. Royce was obviously considering how to respond.

"Part of my job is prepping the bodies for Doc Dixon, yes."

"As staff psychologist I'm trying to determine the why's and why-not's of some of our suspect's actions. Motivation can go a long way toward explaining deeds."

"I'm sure that's true. How can I help you? First, would you care for a cup of coffee or decaf?"

"Me? How kind. No thank you. But if you would like—"

"No, that's all right. Continue."

"To be quite honest, Mr. Royce—"

"James, please."

". . . and I assume I can take you into our confidence." She paused and Boldt could picture the handsome man nodding. "We—Homicide actually—suspect the involvement of a second killer. A copycat killer."

Royce hesitated and then said very convincingly, "My God."

"You haven't heard anything about it?"

"No. Nothing." He paused. "They're going to wheel a child's body in here in about two minutes. Why don't we move into here?" Boldt heard a door open. Daphne agreed, and when she spoke next her voice was filled with static. Boldt wondered how the reception was out in the van.

"He's moved her, Dixie. Moved her into another room. Said something about a child," Boldt said anxiously.

"That's right. A road kill. He's probably moved her into the smoking room." Dixon cleaned his nails casually.

Boldt heard her say, "I like this room better, even if the view is of the parking lot."

Boldt grinned. She was thinking like a cop. She had made sure that those listening in understood Royce had a view of the parking lot.

Royce asked, "So how exactly can I help you?"

"Like I said, it's important for us to understand the psychology of our suspect so that we build as strong a case as possible."

"Naturally."

"There are certain aspects to the conditions of the victims that tend to indicate a split personality. That is, a man somewhat in control of himself, sometimes, and psychotic other times. That, in part, supports the copycat idea and well, quite frankly, that makes it an entirely different case for us."

"I'm sure it does."

"The other interesting point is that our suspect is more than willing to discuss several of his victims, but claims no responsibility for four of the women, Saviria, Jordan, Shufflebeam, and DeHavelin, thus further supporting our theory of a copycat. Doctor Dixon is scheduled to do some last-minute examinations for us—''

"Concerning?"

"Well, it's interesting . . . James. One thing I wanted to ask you about''—Boldt could hear the tension rise in her voice, and he wondered if Royce had noticed it as well—"was the tape on the mouth. In cleaning the bodies up, did you notice any residue about the lips? We have reason to believe the copycat taped the victims' mouths shut, whereas Lange did not. That could help me assemble a profile. We think he may have tortured them quite severely before killing them. The suspect we have in custody was less brutal. As it turns out, he raped them.''

"Raped them! That's *impossible*,'' Royce shouted emphatically.

She paused. Boldt could hear her breathing. He thought if he could turn the machine up higher he might hear her heart pounding. He could picture right where that microphone was. . . .

Daphne said, "Doctor Dixon confirmed it. What threw us off was that he used condoms. There was no semen. He considered the women dirty and raped them with condoms. Most unusual. I'm sure no one will hold it against you that you missed that.''

It was her first direct challenge. Boldt felt a spike of heat run up his spine. *"Easy,"* he said under his breath. Doc Dixon looked at him oddly.

"Missed it?'' Royce said in a strange tone.

"He punished them,'' she said dryly. "He tied them to the bed, facedown—that's another place the copycat made a mistake—and then raped them while he forced them to watch porno movies. He worked in a video store, James. That's how he chose his subjects. You see, the only link to the four other women is membership at different health clubs. The copycat picked his victims at health clubs.''

"I could have cleaned the tape residue off by accident.

That's possible,'' he said. ''Just what exactly is Doctor Dixon checking for?''

''Doctor Dixon?'' she asked as if she had forgotten. ''Oh, he can run some more thorough tests to check for evidence of rape. We're certain he won't find any sign of rape on DeHavelin. The copycat killer did a poor job with De-Havelin.''

''Poor?''

''Yes. I mean the thing is, this guy thought he could do a perfect job. Can you imagine that?''

''But *I* saw all the victims. As far as I could tell they had all been killed by the same person. Now, granted I'm no Doctor Dixon—''

''Don't go underestimating yourself. Doctor Dixon speaks very highly of you. Still this copycat did a less-than-perfect job.''

''It looked perfect to me,'' he said.

''Oh, he did well on the Cross Killings, all right. Pretty well, except that he missed the rape evidence. Of course you missed it, too.'' She paused, leaving a heavy space. ''So did Doctor Dixon. It was on the other that the killer did such a poor job. A horrible job, really.''

''The other?''

''Jane Doe.''

''Jane Doe?''

''Judith Fuller,'' she said bluntly and paused. Boldt could picture her staring into Royce's eyes. Try and resist that stare, Boldt thought. He was proud of her. She was doing well.

''Fuller?'' he questioned.

''We know who Jane Doe is. Her name is Judith Fuller. We thought it was Betsy Norvak at first. Norvak belonged to your health club. Did you know that?''

There was a long hesitation, and Boldt feared she was trying for too much, too quickly. He mentally urged her to back off and take it more slowly. But he could tell by her tone of voice she was enjoying this. She was beginning to bat him around, like a proud cat with a dulled, senseless mouse. She would draw him into her confidence and then hit him with a complete surprise. Only Royce wasn't senseless.

"Betsy? Yes. I knew *of* Betsy."

"What amazing coincidence life deals out, isn't it true? To think she belonged to the same club you did. You might have been able to save her life."

"Was there something else, Miss Matthews?"

"Aren't you interested? I'm sorry. How rude of me. I just assumed you would be interested. You of all people."

"Why do you say that?"

"Well, since you were the first one to handle the victims. You and Doctor Dixon were the first ones to deal with the victims."

"That's true."

"The thing about Jane Doe is . . . the way I see it, as a professional, is that here we have a man who can duplicate the Cross Killings almost to the letter, if you discount the raping and a few other minor things, but when it comes to Jane Doe—to Fuller—he has nothing to copy from and, left to his own devices, he makes a mess of the job. Secondrate stuff, actually." She waited for him to say something, and when he didn't she immediately continued.

Boldt fidgeted nervously in his chair. Dixon asked what was going on and Boldt used hand signals to quiet him. The static was making it difficult to hear.

Daphne said, "Did you know that Judith Fuller was a reporter?"

"Me? How would I know that? I didn't know Fuller."

She spoke quickly like a gossipy female. "Oh, right. Well, she was a free-lance reporter on assignment for *The Los Angeles Times*. She had pieced together a fascinating story about a copycat killer in Tucson and Denver and had followed him here. Here to Seattle. The Cross Killings, you know. That's what attracted her."

"You said second-rate. What did you mean by that?"

"This guy has no creativity, James. None whatsoever. He's really not very bright. He made a lot of mistakes."

"Explain that," he said harshly.

"The thing about it is: he did such a *good* job copying the Cross Killings. You said so yourself. Didn't you think he did a good job?"

"Perfect," Royce said softly and in a voice that frightened Boldt.

"No, not perfect. But good," she corrected. "He taped the mouths of his victims because he wanted to torture them, James."

"Just what exactly did you want to ask me, Miss Matthews? I had better get back to work."

"Daphne," she said.

"Anything else?"

"How would you describe the condition of the victims? Did you notice anything different at all about them? I need to try and understand the copycat."

"The same. They were all identical."

"We've already determined they were not identical, Jimmy."

"Don't call me that!"

"You don't like the name *Jimmy*? It's a nice name."

Boldt heard the chair slide back. "If that's all . . ."

"Did your mother call you Jimmy?"

"What?!"

"Did she?"

"What do *you* know about my mother? What the hell's going on here anyway?"

"You know where the killer made the mistake with Jane Doe? Aren't you interested in that, James?"

"What do you want with me?"

Boldt was standing. The static was worse and he was losing the conversation, and it made him nervous. She was pushing too hard. She was trying too hard, and Boldt felt her control of the conversation slipping.

"What is it?" Dixon asked as Boldt stood. Boldt turned up the volume and pressed the earpiece hard into his ear.

Daphne shouted, "I need your help! Why do you think I'm here? You think I *like* this place? You were the *first* to see the bodies. Little things can tell us so much. I need your *help*, James, if we're ever going to catch this copycat. And we *must* catch him. We have to stop him, you and I, don't we, James?"

"Yes," Royce said, suddenly more calm. "Yes, it would be good to stop him."

"And you'll help me stop him, won't you?"

"I . . . I'd like to."

"You can help us identify any inconsistencies in the kills. We know four of the kills were done by another man. And though he may think he did a perfect job, we know he didn't."

"They *were* perfect," Royce insisted, again softly. "They looked absolutely *perfect* to me. I'll tell you that."

"No, not perfect. The copycat let DeHavelin get away because he tried to torture her a bit too slowly. And he left his prints at Betsy Norvak's house. And he didn't burn Norvak's clothes thoroughly enough. And he didn't know enough about Puget Sound. James, by just discussing the condition of the bodies—going over the details—you can help me to determine what the suspect might have been thinking when he killed them. You see, in order to prosecute we have to determine which women our suspect *did* kill and what mental condition he was in when he committed the murders. That's very important. I'm sure you can understand that."

"Who's that?" His voice sounded panicked but muted.

"Looks like the press," she said. "The parking lot is *filled* with them," she overemphasized, trying to alert Boldt. "Must be something going on upstairs."

"Why are the cops moving them out?" he wondered, his voice suddenly more clear, and Boldt realized he had been

looking out the window and was now once again facing
Daphne. "Oh Christ," he said. "You? You're a cop. Right?"

"James," she called out.

Boldt heard the struggle, her blouse rip, and the microphone go dead. Doctor Dixon had heard the cars. He opened
the curtains and Boldt saw dozens of reporters through the
high window. Someone had leaked news of this to the press.
He rushed through the door, heading quickly to the prep
room.

He burst through the door. A girl, no older than five, lay
dead on the table, a green cloth covering her to her chin.
She stared at the ceiling. Boldt froze at the sight, unable to
pull his eyes away. Then he jumped toward the far door,
withdrew his gun, and yanked the door open.

The room was empty, the radio transmitter and a piece
of Daphne's blouse scattered on the floor.

He ran into the next room, where a secretary stared at
him with an ashen face. Unable to speak, this woman pointed
toward an open door down a back hallway. At the far end
of the long hall, Boldt saw a door open briefly. Two silhouetted figures. Then the door closed, returning the hallway to darkness.

60

HE WAS FACED with choosing one of two options: he could use the small walkie-talkie clipped to his belt to inform Shoswitz that Daphne had been taken hostage (Shoswitz would then be obliged to pass the information on to Special Weapons and Tactics); or, he could go after them alone. In this brief moment of indecision he determined that the outside crew's reception of Daphne's transmitter must have been so intermittent that they had yet to discover she had been taken hostage. If they had suspected any trouble they would have already contacted Boldt by walkie-talkie, which meant they didn't know—a situation that couldn't, and wouldn't last long. He had to act quickly.

Duty demanded he inform his lieutenant of the situation; but his head—and his heart—dictated he ignore duty. He distrusted the SWAT team's ability to handle a crisis situation, despite their training. Boldt wasn't about to risk adding Daphne to their list of failures.

As he entered the basement corridor, he understood full well that he was violating procedure by not calling in, that he would ultimately be held responsible for his decision and, no doubt, for the outcome of the hostage situation.

Weapon drawn, Boldt ran down the long corridor past cardboard boxes and storage rooms.

He yanked open the door at the end of the hallway and

moved through swiftly, eyes darting about frantically, alert
for the slightest movement. This door accessed a fire stairway leading up to the ground floor of the medical center.

A man came hurrying down the stairs, eyes wide. He
avoided Boldt and continued his descent without a word.
Boldt rounded the landing, crouched, gun trained toward
the next level, and then stood and ran as fast as his bad
knee would carry him.

At this next level, which was actually the ground floor
of the medical center, he paused, out of breath. Had Royce
continued to climb the stairs, or had he entered the hospital
at this level? His answer came when two people casually
rounded the flight of stairs above him, no alarm showing
on their faces. Boldt shoved his weapon back into its holster,
tugged on the stiff door, and hurried into the hospital.

He spotted them immediately: Royce was holding her
tightly, walking her at a fast pace. Her blouse was torn open
and hanging from her. People were gawking in fear and
hurrying past.

The detective flattened himself into a doorway to keep
from being seen. The hallway was crowded, the people in
confusion. Royce continued to glance back over his shoulder as he forced Daphne along. In an effort to disguise
himself, Boldt pulled off his sport jacket and folded it up,
holding it pressed into his waist to cover his holstered weapon.
Face to the floor, he stepped out into the corridor, where
others had stopped to watch Royce. Shoulders slumped and
sagging, Boldt moved down the hall. He kept his eyes
trained on the scuffed toes of his shoes—shoes he had
meant to have shined for the past several weeks. He looked
up only twice.

The first time, Royce was looking away from Boldt,
steering Daphne clear of an orderly, shouting loudly, demanding the black man allow them past.

The second time, they were gone.

Lou Boldt knew there was precious little keeping Royce
from injuring or even killing Daphne. Hopefully he per-

ceived her as protection from the police, a deterrent. If this perception failed, there was no telling what he might do. The SWAT solution might have been confrontation. But for the moment Boldt decided against any such confrontation. Royce had too many options in this environment, too many potential hostages.

When Boldt reached the next four-way intersection, he saw them down the hall to the right, moving quickly. A stack of plastic directory arrows were screwed to the wall; the one marked EMERGENCY pointed toward Royce and Daphne. Boldt tucked his head down low again and continued on. This hallway was much less trafficked, and after only a few seconds Boldt realized he was essentially alone with them. If there was to be a confrontation, perhaps now *was* the best time.

He looked up: Royce was dragging her along at a run, his neck straining to keep an eye on Boldt. He had spotted him.

Boldt broke into a limping run.

"Stay back," Royce thundered, but Boldt continued to hurry. They were almost to the doors. . . .

Royce spun Daphne around, the scalpel appearing from nowhere, held it to her throat, the shiny metal glinting in the bright overhead light. The man pushed blindly back through two swinging doors. As the doors closed behind them, Daphne looked briefly into Boldt's eyes.

To his surprise, she showed little sign of fear. Instead, he saw in her face a devastating disappointment.

"Back!" he heard Royce shout.

Boldt pushed through the doors and found himself in the emergency room's reception area. Royce held Daphne at one of the doors to the outside, everyone in the room staring at him. A few turned their heads toward Boldt as he came through the doors, gun drawn.

Seeing him, Daphne made her move. She twisted and kicked backward, simultaneously driving her elbow into Royce's abdomen. It was a well-executed move, and had

Royce not been so physically fit it might have worked well. But as it was, it did nothing to free her. Royce choked her down in a headlock, his forearm across her windpipe, and stepped back, pulling her with him. The automatic doors swished open. He dragged her outside, the scalpel dancing dangerously close to her neck.

Boldt froze as Royce lifted the scalpel to her face, a move that subdued her quickly. He yanked open the passenger door to one of three waiting ambulances. Boldt watched silently through the marred glass as several EMTs moved away from the vehicle at Royce's insistence. He shoved Daphne into the brightly painted van and thrust her across to the driver's seat, pulling the door shut behind him, sticking the blade under her jaw.

The van's engine started up. Its tailpipe coughed out a single gray gasp. It sped away. Although the two entrances to the Medical Examiner's department were well guarded by unmarked patrols, no provision had been made for Royce escaping through the seldom-used basement corridor and up into the connecting medical center. As a result, there was no patrol car to stop the ambulance or give chase. The emergency room was located on the complete opposite end of the huge block-long facility. The ambulance turned right out the drive and was gone, Daphne at the wheel.

The last thing Boldt saw was Royce's smooth, slick face, distorted and pressed up flat against the glass of the side window.

The man was grinning proudly.

61

BOLDT WAS NOT PREPARED to turn Daphne's life over to a departmental effort. Boldt wanted to pursue the ambulance, but he had no desire to bring the entire force into it, especially the SWAT team. He hurried around the west side of the massive medical center. His car was parked across the street, on the other side of the small parking lot outside the Medical Examiner's department. His only hope of not being seen would be to stay close to the building, edging his way toward the parking lot, then lower his head and cut a straight line for his car. He moved carefully along a row of thick shrubs, realizing that with every passing second he was losing the ambulance.

Voices directly ahead of him, on the other side of a large cedar tree. Boldt heard the words, "Thanks, John," from a voice he recognized only too well. Marty Hanfield, a local crime reporter. He rounded the tree and there stood Hanfield, shaking hands with John Kramer. Kramer saw Boldt, knew he was caught, and immediately panicked, shouting, "He's been blackmailing me, Lou."

"What?" Hanfield said. "That's an outright lie!"

"You bastard," Boldt hissed, thinking of the Levitts, Jergensen, and now Daffy.

He recalled Kramer blushing while speaking on the telephone earlier, and suddenly Boldt knew how the press had been tipped off. This realization was followed by a succession of others. Who tried harder to shift blame than the person responsible for the act in the first place? Who on the force had *a thing* about media and press coverage? Who had tried to make Daphne the scapegoat for the Jergensen affair? Who saw control of the media as power, and power as the key to advancement on the force?

It had been Sergeant John Kramer who had leaked the BSU profile to the press several months earlier. That leak had cost Jergensen his life, and the force a huge embarrassment. Kramer had also alerted the press to Justin Levitt's involvement. He had gotten the Levitts killed, the boy kidnapped, and now Daphne. . . .

Boldt approached Kramer and stopped face-to-face with the man, ignoring Hanfield, who stood by. He reeled back his clenched fist and struck hard, putting his full body weight behind the punch and swinging through as if striking for the back of the man's head. The blow lifted Kramer off his feet and deposited him on his butt, jaw dislodged, mouth bleeding badly. He kicked him in the ribs, and turned to face the reporter, who shied away. Boldt backed him into the tree and hit him repeatedly in the gut until the man slumped to the ground. He turned and ran to his car. He heard Shoswitz shout his name but ignored it.

He jumped into his car, turned the key, and put it in gear, honking people out of his way as he cleared the area. In his rearview mirror he saw Shoswitz waving at a run. A crowd had gathered around Kramer and the reporter on the far side of the building. Lou Boldt reached under the dash and switched off his police radio. He unclipped the walkie-talkie from his belt and turned this off as well.

He didn't use his light or siren; he couldn't risk giving himself away. He was two blocks down Broadway, stopped behind traffic at a red light. Royce would certainly not head to his apartment on North Seventy-seventh. Then where? The light turned green but Lou Boldt didn't notice until someone honked from behind. The sounding of the car horn was nearly perfectly timed with the loud, haunting echo of a ship's horn reverberating through the city streets. He drove ahead slowly, his attention drawn to his throbbing hand and swelling fingers.

He sifted through the details of the investigation. Where would James Royce take his hostage? Or would he kill her as he had killed Judith Fuller? With the hollow sound of the ship's horn still ringing in his head, it occurred to Lou Boldt where James Royce—the copycat—would take her. He turned right—out of traffic—and sped downtown.

Three blocks from the Vashon Ferry pier, Boldt came across the abandoned ambulance. It was parked in front of a photo store. He double-parked and checked inside the vehicle. Empty.

Boldt left his car double-parked, blocking the rear of the ambulance, and hurried toward the pier. If Royce had any sense at all, he would take her high atop the ferry and would use this vantage point to examine the huge parking lot, eyes alert for any sign of the police.

For this reason Boldt stopped at a streetside vendor and paid five dollars for an umbrella. Its canopy was black nylon, its fragile frame hollow-stemmed aluminum. A slight breeze would spring it. He opened the umbrella and pulled it down low over his head, assuring that no one—even at street level—could identify him. He paid for his ticket and boarded the ferry, which was scheduled to leave in less than ten minutes. Oil-stained water slapped at the pilings. The wet air smelled of gasoline and salt. He climbed the narrow steel stairway to the main deck. He scanned the occupied seats of the expansive inside cabin, the many rows of brightly colored formed-fiberglass chairs and tables, looking for Royce and Daphne—or worse, Royce alone. Not spotting them, he walked out onto the deck that encircled the ship. Here he was able to open his umbrella again. He hid beneath its shelter and walked the perimeter slowly, a curious tourist perhaps, seemingly undisturbed by the harsh, inclement weather. In fact, he was worried the stiff wind would destroy his cover. Rain drummed against the tight fabric. He rounded the bow, one of only a handful of people brave enough—foolish enough—to remain outside.

The last of the automobiles was just boarding. The vessel would depart at any moment. Only a scant few minutes remained before there would be no turning back and he would be unable to disembark—trapped on a ferry to Vashon Island while Royce remained somewhere back in the city. He had been so certain—it seemed to make so much sense that Royce would flee to Vashon, where he had a boat, no doubt, a cabin perhaps. To the same place where Judith Fuller had found him, and was killed for it. But suddenly his certainty waned and he thought himself an idiot for thinking he could second-guess an insane killer. How good had be been at second-guessing the behavior of Milo Lange?

Then he spotted her.

He saw only her legs, but it was enough. The sharply defined calves disappeared up the stairway to his left, which led to the uppermost deck. Only a glimpse. Just a glimpse, but enough to know. He *knew* those legs. He pulled himself under the overhang, where anyone up top would not be able to see him. Heart pounding as quickly and as loudly as the rain on the deck. Mind whirring like the ship's engines. Did he dare follow them to the uppermost level? Could he hope to hide from them? He thought not. With only a few people outside, he would be spotted immediately. And yet, he had not actually *seen* her. Only a pair of legs. It was hardly enough to base decisions on, even though in his heart he *knew* it was her.

What to do?

Rain hammered more strongly onto the deck for a few short seconds, and then let up just as quickly. A drizzle now. In the distance the cloud cover broke and a beam of bright sunshine poured though, illuminating a passing freighter

in the shipping lanes. Boldt found himself hoping it woul
continue to rain. He needed an excuse to remain hidde
beneath the umbrella.

The retreating rain left him little choice. He had to get
look at the woman now; he needed the protection of th
umbrella while he still had it. He took two steps and foun
himself ascending the steel stairs toward the upper deck
peering out from below the umbrella's edge.

As he reached the middle of the stairs he saw the wom
an's shoes. Daphne's shoes? he wondered. Why couldn'
he remember? Then her calves. Her knees. The hem c
her skirt. Daphne's skirt? He doubted himself—he couldn'
remember what she had been wearing. Another step up
Her waist. A hand—a male hand gripping her waist firmly
and he thought it must be them! Dare he take another ste
higher? His feet moved independently of his thoughts. U
he went. Daphne? For the life of him he couldn't remembe
what she had been wearing. The woman's arms were crosse
tightly against the cold wind. Then he saw the gold rin
on her hand and his heart sank. He raised the umbrell
quickly to see her face.

It wasn't Daphne.

The woman was older; her husband, trying in vain t
keep a comforting arm around her, was both pointing towar
the shaft of sunlight and awkwardly holding a bright re
umbrella.

Angered, Lou Boldt looked away, stepping back, glanc
ing down toward the lower level. There, his eyes met thos
of Daphne Matthews, in the firm grasp of James Royce
who was himself looking down at the loading area. She wa
wearing his coat, her hair matted from the rain, clinging t
her face like seaweed to a rock. Her dark brown eyes reg
istered a faint flicker of hope and she passed beneath hin
smoothly, never breaking stride, not uttering a single gas|
of realization. Royce walked her along, firmly in control
remaining just under the overhang and out of the light driz
zle. Lou Boldt angled the umbrella to block himself fron

view, descended the stairs, and walked in the opposite direction.

The ferry's deafening horn sounded, resonating over the swelling water, rumbling up behind him through the narrow city streets. Boldt jumped with the blast and lost his balance momentarily; the ship was moving.

The ferry pulled away from the pier.

A handful of people waved toward shore.

62

THE OVAL CABIN AREA that formed the center hub of the ship was mostly glass to afford passengers a view. With his back to Royce and Daphne, Boldt headed toward the bow where a number of benches, bolted to the deck, sat beneath an overhang for sightseeing during nicer weather. A young couple in bright rain gear were huddled together here, kissing and talking softly, the only two people in this area. The sight of their innocent enjoyment of each other so contrasted with what he was feeling that he caught himself staring in disbelief.

Lou Boldt turned and tried to spot Royce and Daphne by looking through the cabin area and out through the windows at the stern, but he had lost them. He edged his way to the starboard side of the ship but stopped before rounding the corner, afraid he might end up face-to-face with them. He peered around this corner. The side benches were all empty. He waited impatiently for several minutes, wondering where they had gone. He thought his presence might provide Daphne with a degree of hope, no matter how faint, knowing that in hostage situations hope was essential.

He wasn't sure where to go with this. Should he confront Royce here on the ferry where the man was essentially trapped? Would such a confrontation work, or would it only end up with Daphne dead and another passenger taken hostage? Boldt refused to put Daphne in any more danger than she already was. He was overwhelmed with emotion as he thought of their passing a moment earlier—she had handled it so well, so professionally. She was trained to deal with unstable people while at the same time keeping a level head. Boldt, on the other hand, found himself nervous, agitated, and impatient. He wanted the situation over with. Now. He wanted Daphne safe and he wanted Royce locked up. Or dead.

He peered around the corner again expecting to see them. But they weren't there. He reversed directions and returned from where he had come, moving around the far side of the ship carefully, curiosity driving him on. He passed the very spot where they had seen each other and he continued on, umbrella pulled low, venturing an occasional glimpse ahead of him. The problem was that he had windows to his left. If they had entered the cafeteria area, they might be looking out in his direction. For this reason, he tilted the umbrella more toward the glass, exposing him to the front, a compromise he felt necessary. He walked slowly, not wanting to appear restless.

As he rounded the stern, he spotted them. They were sitting on a bench, outside, but blocked by a glass-and-steel panel that served as a windbreak. It was too late to suddenly turn around without attracting attention. Boldt, umbrella cocked to block his face from their view, walked to the far stern railing and looked down into the white frothy wake above which several sea gulls flew playfully. He could feel her eyes boring into him. He could not turn around to look, and it occurred to him that Royce could be approaching with the scalpel drawn, and that the last thing he might see of this world would be these carefree gulls riding the wind, and the churning waters of the ship's wake.

He was helpless to do anything, stranded here against the rail. He reached inside his coat, touching his weapon. Did he dare approach them now, abruptly withdraw his gun and kill Royce before the man had a chance to react? Would it work?

He edged along the stern rail, keeping the umbrella between himself and the couple, unable to see them, moving slowly but steadily around the ship's perimeter until he had cleared the stern. He risked one quick look through the corner of the cabin and saw the backs of their heads.

So close, he thought. So very close.

He had not formulated any particular plan. He dreamed up any number of ideas as he rode out the remainder of the ferry ride, but time seemed to work against most of them. If he phoned Shoswitz from Vashon and called in backup, it would take at least an hour to organize, and by that time he believed Daphne would be dead. Royce would have no more use for Daphne soon; she would be an unnecessary burden.

This was unproven territory for Boldt. He was used to examining a situation from the role of the victim—a dead victim. Now he was forced to join the living and consider this from the killer's perspective, something he found difficult, if not impossible, to do. Was there anything predictable about an insane killer?

Yes, he suddenly realized, elated at his deduction. Royce was a copycat, meaning the man felt safest in duplication. If he possessed any cognizant reasoning powers—which he must—then he understood he was best at *reproducing* events, not creating them. If one accepted this as fact, then there was little question what the man was up to: he was going to duplicate Fuller's murder, a murder he had already committed. He was not only headed to Vashon in an effort to elude the police, but also because he felt a certain comfort in duplicating his earlier method of killing. He didn't have to think, he merely had to reproduce the event.

This made him predictable. It meant he was headed to a specific location on the island and had a specific plan he was following. He had done this before.

Boldt recalled the tests they had run on the working model of Puget Sound and could visualize in his mind the approximate location of where Fuller's body had entered the tidal estuary. He remembered watching the tiny ball of wax being drawn along by the undercurrents.

The loud horn sounded and Boldt spun around to see the shore of Vashon quickly approaching. Time seemed to suddenly speed up. Royce brought Daphne to her feet. Boldt prepared to hide himself under his umbrella again, but a sudden gust of wind kicked up and the umbrella inverted, now a long and tattered mess of aluminum and nylon.

Through the corner of the cabin Boldt could see the two approaching him. He glanced over his shoulder: the nearest exit of any sort was at midships, what seemed like miles away. He dropped the umbrella, turned, and began the interminable walk toward the center stairs. Behind him the umbrella's skin flapped against the steel deck like the wing of a wounded bird. Bitter wind gnawed his face and tears formed in his eyes.

Nothing is ever simple, he reminded himself.

The ship was at least a half mile offshore, still a good ten minutes or more from docking. But, because of the horn, passengers were already collecting their things and moving toward the stairways that fed the bottom level. At this particular moment it left them the only three people remaining on the starboard deck. Rain began falling again, adding stinging needles to the wind.

How much further could that stairway possibly be? he wondered. It felt to him as if he had already walked far enough to reach the shore—a shore that seemed so close. Pane after pane he passed the cabin windows, catching glimpses of people inside. He knew that not far behind, the two of them continued their approach. He wondered what Daphne was thinking as she watched him walk away from her. I haven't deserted you, he told her silently, but he began to wonder if it was true or not. Since their one evening together he had begun deserting her, at least emotionally.

He had erected a wall between them, carefully avoiding her. He had begun to piece back together his feelings for Elizabeth, to convince himself it could work again, *would* work again.

The door. Finally! He leaned his weight against the tightly springed door and pushed his way through. He would not abandon Daphne any longer. He would act. He leaned back against the wall slightly behind the door, the rainwater running down his unshaven face like sweat pouring out in a tropical heat. His eyes remained fixed on the door's safety glass as his hand automatically gripped the butt of his gun and withdrew it from the holster.

Boldt spun, yanked open the door, and trained the gun on Royce. But Royce had the blade held to her throat and was awkwardly backing her up toward the rail. Boldt approached through the falling rain, water streaming from the V of his chin, gun held in both hands, arms outstretched. "Let her go, Royce. We can work this thing out."

"Listen to him," Daphne pleaded, stretching her head back to try and make eye contact with her captor, exposing even more of her long, vulnerable neck.

"You knew!" Royce said angrily to her, pushing the blade more firmly against her throat, maintaining his eye contact with Boldt. "You knew he had followed us." His face tightened manically and he shook her from side to side and shouted, "I should kill you!"

Boldt heard the door open behind him. One of the crew tried to restrain a small group of curious onlookers. Boldt felt out of his element here. He wasn't sure what to say, fully aware that the wrong thing would have disastrous results. "Release her, Royce. James. We can handle this. Just you and I. Is hurting her going to help your situation any? You going to hurt all of us?" he wondered, waving toward the unseen crowd behind him.

"Don't kill her," he heard someone yell from the crowd, followed quickly by the crewman's voice as he told everyone to move back through the door.

"Get back!" Royce yelled. "I want a car. I want a car
and some time. A head start. You leave me alone or I'll
kill her. *Worse* than the others." He drew the blade effortlessly across her neck and Boldt saw the line of blood
that resulted. Daphne cringed, but surprisingly maintained
her composure. It was a tiny cut—a warning—but the sight
of blood triggered images in Boldt's mind of all the earlier
victims, and he felt his finger tighten on the trigger. He
thought it might be possible to shoot Royce cleanly from
here, to put a single bullet into the man's head and kill him
before he had the chance to do Daphne any more harm.
Then again, the shot could cause the man's muscles to
contract, and Daphne's throat would be severed.

As if he heard Boldt thinking, Royce hid his head behind
Daphne's, his wild eyes peering over her hair. "Well? Deal,
Boldt? You've always struck me as a reasonable man. A
car. I want a car and a head start."

Boldt lowered his gun, still holding on to it, hoping to
relax the situation. He shook his head. "That's unacceptable, Royce—James—and you know it. I'm not going to
let you leave."

Royce glanced quickly behind him, down toward the
churning water.

Daphne told the man, "This isn't what you want, James.
Think about it."

"I'm willing to negotiate," Boldt added, "but Daphne
stays with me. You can have the car. We'll give you all
the time you want, but Daphne stays behind."

"Oh sure! Jesus Christ. You must be insane." His face
changed, now demonic with the realization that Boldt thought
him insane. "You don't have a clue, do you? You think I'm
like *him*? You think I'm like your killer?" Daphne tried to
shake her head, but Royce wouldn't have any of it. He
pressed the blade more strongly against her throat and drew
more blood. "You want to stand here and watch me kill this
bitch, it's up to you. Get me the car, Boldt. Now! Or say
good-bye." He lifted his elbow and the blade cut her skin.

Boldt watched as Daphne's eyes tightened with the pain.
He took a step back. He couldn't push any further. It was
time to give in. He stopped. Or was it? Wouldn't Royce
kill her eventually anyway? If Boldt let him take her, was
there any chance of seeing Daphne alive again? He took
another step back. There's always a chance.

As Boldt moved away, Daphne shouted gutturally, in a
voice that didn't belong to her, "No! No you don't, Lou.
You're not leaving me with *him*. Not with him. God, no.
Please. He's an *animal!*" she screamed, saying the one word
that came the hardest for her.

"You're a reasonable man," Boldt offered. "No bargain
is ever entirely one-sided. You have to trade this for that.
Right?"

"Put down the gun!" Royce demanded.

"Shoot him!" Daphne screamed into the harsh wind.
Blood had smeared her neck. Royce, seeing the effect she
was having on Boldt, cut her badly and she screamed and
fought wildly to get loose.

Boldt tracked Royce's movements with his gun. He nearly
had a clear shot. . . . He stepped closer.

Still struggling with her, Royce yelled, "Back. No closer.
Get back," but he was clearly losing control of her. She
didn't seem to feel the blade at her neck any longer. She
didn't seem to feel anything. She kicked and writhed and
fought against his strength despite the damage from the
knife.

Boldt brought his left hand up to steady the gun, Royce
looking back and forth between Daphne and Boldt. Royce
saw his situation deteriorating. Again, he glanced over the
rail.

Boldt took another step forward. He was close now. Very
close. All he had to do was aim and pull the trigger. A head
shot. But what if he missed. What if he hit Daffy?

Daphne whipped her head back and forth, her dark hair
flying, and some of her blood splattered across Boldt's face.
She was cut horribly, still fighting with all her strength.

Boldt squeezed the trigger. . . .

Royce drew the blade across her throat and threw her forward.

The gun discharged.

Royce went up and over the railing.

Boldt dropped the gun and caught her in his arms as she fell. "Oh God, no," he said, hand trembling in uncertainty, afraid to even touch her.

Out of the corner of his eye he saw the crewman pick up his handgun and step to the rail. He made no attempt to stop the man. Out of the corner of his eye he saw the man throw a life ring overboard.

"I'm a doctor," a distinguished-looking man in a blue Goretex jacket said, helping Boldt to lay Daphne down.

Boldt nodded, unable to get out a word, unable to take his eyes off of Daffy. He finally reached down and touched her matted hair lightly, brushing it out of her eyes. She blinked, squinting, rainwater pelting her. Her mouth moved, but no sound came out. She was losing a great deal of blood and from the awful sound, Boldt thought her windpipe must be severed. He watched her lips as they moved for the last time before her eyes shut and she passed into unconsciousness. He couldn't be sure, but he thought she said, "Thank you."

63

THE DOUBLE DOORS swung open, the silence of the offices suddenly shattered by reporters shouting loudly in the background, the lot of them restrained by a number of patrolmen.

"We're putting you under protection, like it or not," Shoswitz reiterated, leading the way for the disheveled Boldt and the member of the ship's crew, both wrapped in gray wool blankets bearing the ferry line's logo. "It's down to the minors for you, Lou."

"Water's too cold, Lieutenant. He couldn't possibly survive," Boldt objected. They were merely continuing an argument that had begun in the car. "Besides, I'm positive I hit him."

"Not according to your friend here. Right?" Shoswitz reminded.

Boldt complained, "He never even saw him."

"I saw him on the surface, just once," the young man corrected proudly. "He must have seen the life preserver."

Shoswitz interrupted, looking over his shoulder at Boldt disapprovingly, "What the hell was *he* doing with *your* gun?" He opened the door to interrogation room B and ushered the two inside. It was smaller than A, darker, and smelled worse, if that was possible.

"I was tending to Daphne—to Matthews, Lieutenant."

"Goddamned lucky thing a doctor was aboard or she'd be dead," Shoswitz said. "And no thanks to you, I might add. This thing was badly mishandled, Lou. You made bad calls right from the start, and there's going to be hell to pay. And it's yours alone, friend. I'm washing my hands of it. You hear me? All fucking alone. You want the list?" he asked, not waiting for an answer. He emphasized his points by counting his fingers as he spoke. "You didn't use your walkie-talkie to alert us in the very first place; you ignored or switched off your car's radio; you went after them *without* backup, *without* notice of any sort; you struck a fellow officer, who, incidently, has already filed a complaint against you; your gun turned up in the possession of a civilian. . . . Need any more than that? Jesus Christ!" He leaned back and collected himself. "We'll get him," Shoswitz added as an afterthought. "Coast Guard's out in full force."

"I hit him, Lieutenant," Boldt said.

"Yeah? Then I want the body. When I have a body I'll be happy. Until then, I take your shield and your gun and we put a couple guys on you."

"You take my shield because I hit Kramer?" Boldt objected. "That's absurd."

"Because you violated procedure. There will be an inquiry."

"And Kramer?"

Shoswitz nodded. "He came clean. It was him all along. He's a mess. A basketcase. The state'll press criminal charges. They've been waiting for an open-and-shut case like this. He'll do time."

"A long time, I hope."

"You're not careful, you'll be there with him," Shoswitz warned.

"Phil?"

"Don't start with me. Listen, our resident shrink is hooked up to a dozen tubes in the hospital, okay? No thanks to you. So you got my opinion to live with, like it or not, until we get another pro in here to evaluate this thing for us, and I say if this guy is still alive, then he has one of two possibilities: blow town right away, or kill your ass and then blow town.'' He paused, face scarlet from his shouting. ''If *I* were him,'' he added, ''I'd blow you away first.'' He raised his eyebrows. ''I probably ought to do it for him. Save the taxpayers the cost of a disciplinary review.''

''Lieutenant . . .''

''I'm not listening, Boldt. I don't hear. I'm not going to have you pretend everything's hunky-dory only to have you end up with a blade in your back. *If* you missed, and *if* by some flaw in the good Lord's better judgment this guy survived that water temperature and actually swam to shore, there remains the *possibility* he'll gun for you. And *if* that's the case, then maybe, just maybe we get another chance at this dingdong and do what should have been done in the first place. We *catch* him! And you talk about SWAT messing things up.'' He raised his hand as Boldt was about to interrupt. ''I know. I know. You think that if he lived through it, then he's left town by now. Same as Denver and Tucson. You've already told me that a dozen times. Fine for you to say, but you don't know any goddamned more than I do—and *don't* claim that you do. If I were him, I'd kill you. In his mind you're the one who screwed everything up. You're the one he has to thank. And right now, that's all you've got to think about. I got your shield and your gun. You got a little instant holiday coming while this whole thing is under review. What we're trying to do here—for your information—is prevent any surprises. I want you thinking like this guy is coming after you. That way it doesn't get any messier than it already is. You follow that?''

''Then how about my gun back?'' Boldt asked.

''You know the program, Boldt. You want a piece, go buy one like any other civilian. Register it, but keep it under your pillow. I catch you concealing a weapon on your person, and you'll have hell to pay. *No* exceptions to any of the rules. No favorites. The press is going to ride this tighter than a gnat's ass, and so's the captain, and so's half the goddamn city. Strictly aboveboard, all the way. You got that, Lou? Strictly aboveboard.''

"So what am I supposed to do, sit around and wait for this weirdo to come after me? I'm your bait, is that it? Dangle me out there and hope he comes after me. Is that what this is all about?''

"I thought you said you got him," Shoswitz said, scratching his scalp and unleashing his dandruff. "What's the big worry?''

64

BUT LOU BOLDT did worry. The possibility that Royce was still alive clung to him like two strong hands around his throat. He did not eat well; he slept hardly at all. And when he did sleep he had horrible nightmares about a final, bloody confrontation with Royce.

Seven days after his suspension he found himself stepping into the bright hallway of the hospital's intensive-care ward, so utterly exhausted and drained of energy that for a moment he believed himself in the middle of one of his dreams. In his mind, the ghostly faces gawking at him were, of course, not real, did not belong to real, living people, and so he could gawk back at them without concern. Which is exactly what he did.

The people walking the hallways of intensive care—people Lou Boldt believed imaginary—steered clear.

Daphne was lying in bed, various-sized tubes running into her limbs, mouth, and nostrils. A battery of electronic machines ticked, beeped, blinked, and pulsed, surrounding her: a gaggle of robotic nursemaids. The tracheotomy tube was still in place. Her eyes tracked Boldt as he entered the room, pulled up a chair, and sat down. He couldn't find a way to position the chair so they could see one another. Obviously frustrated, he eventually abandoned the idea of sitting and stood alongside of her. He reached down and took her hand in his. Her skin was ivory-gray, and her usually full-bodied hair now scraggly and in need of a shampoo.

"They tell me you're going to be able to speak. Good news," he said, squeezing her hand. "And for once I get to talk to you without suffering all your grief." He pointed to his own throat to indicate hers. "For once you can't talk back."

But she could talk back. Not in words but with her eyes. He thought she had the most expressive eyes he had ever known, for they spoke to him despite her silence. They had smiled when he had entered and now they teased him disapprovingly.

"Yes, sir," he said, obviously nervous.

She looked him over.

"I know. I know," he said. "Not looking too good at the moment." He forced a smile. "Don't you worry about me. Don't you concern yourself with me. Not for a second. Not for one instant." He looked around the room and then back to her. "It's *him*. You know how that goes. I'll get over it. . . . I ah . . . They searched both his places, you know, the one over on North Seventy-seventh, and they also found his place out on the island. A rental. He rented a place on Vashon, and they raided it, and they came up with some interesting stuff. They found the dry cleaning for one thing. The victims' stuff—two of the dry-cleaning stubs missing. That's what Fuller found evidently. They also found membership cards for all four health clubs.

"Don't be worried. If he's here . . . if he's here in town, we'll catch him. And if he's not, then he's not our worry anymore. FBI has all the stuff on him. There's a three-state manhunt underway and Canadian authorities are on the alert; Coast Guard is still at it. If he's around . . . if he lived, we'll catch him."

She squeezed his hand twice weakly.

"Me? You know how I am. Not a hell of a lot of sleep. That's all. That's the only reason I look like this. Honest.

I'm gonna be fine. I look a lot worse than I feel. This is my 'Miami Vice' look, right?'' he said, stroking his chin. "I'm gonna do a TV ad for razors." He winked at her. "Nah. This is my jazz look. I'm playing again. Did I tell you? Yeah. I'm going to be playing a couple times a week. The old stuff for now. You know, getting my chops back. Bear—my friend Bear—he wants me back full-time.

"Hey. Listen, it's great to hear your throat is going to be all right. That is *great* news. That's the best news I could have heard."

With each line he spoke her eyes seemed to change shapes and color under equally expressive brows. It didn't even occur to him that he was the only one talking. It seemed to him they had a two-way conversation going. If he had thought about it he might have become self-conscious and clammed up. But he didn't think about it. He looked into those eyes, was drawn into those eyes and rambled on, unaware of the singular sound of his own voice.

"Maybe you won't be singing any opera, but who cares? Never could stand opera. Hey, maybe you'll end up with one of those deep, husky, sexy voices, like you smoked a carton a day for most of your life. I love that kind of voice in a woman—rough and breathy and kind of from way down in here," he said, patting his gut. "Ooo!" He wiggled his eyebrows and got her to smile. "Yeah . . . You're gonna be fine, Daffy." He squeezed her hand. "I knew you were a fighter. I told Shoswitz you were a fighter." She closed her eyes slowly and he asked if she wanted him to leave, and her eyes told him no, and so he stayed. He looked around the room for another minute. There was nothing to look at except a few plants and some wilting white roses he had sent her a week ago. "You need some new flowers," he told her, his voice suddenly more quiet and more like Lou Boldt. "That was kind of weird out there. On the ferry, I mean. Wasn't it? I was scared to death."

Her eyes said, "Me too."

Boldt disagreed. "No, you weren't scared. You were the

brave one. You were the one who kept it together. You were amazing," he said, squeezing her hand. "Really amazing out there." He hesitated before saying, "The thing of it is . . . he wasn't the crazed animal I wanted him to be. He was like a kid, you know? Like a little kid. I actually felt sorry for him. I learned something out there . . . about myself, I mean. I can't put it into words so great, but I finally got the message. You finally got through, Doc. Thick head," he said, tapping his skull.

With great effort she lifted her hand and caught hold of his ear and twisted a lock of hair in her finger and then dragged her fingertips gently along his rough chin.

A teardrop had stained her pillowcase and he knew somehow that this was a tear of love, not of grief or pain, and he smiled broadly at her. He beamed at her. He saw the trace of a smile at the edges of her lips and he felt a sinking, heavy feeling. Like slipping on ice—that absolute knowledge of where you are headed. "You're very special to me," he conceded. "Very special." He placed her hand down gently and hurried from the room.

65

BOBBIE GAYNES entered The Big Joke and joined Chuck Abrams and Doc Dixon at a table that bordered the modest dance floor. She ordered a drink from the college coed cocktail waitress and waved over at Lou Boldt, whose head nodded from the other side of the baby grand. From behind the piano, with a bright light aimed in his eyes, Boldt could not make out her face, only the candles on each table, glowing yellow, and the faceless people seated behind them. The crowd noise competed with his music—not exactly a listening club. The music business hadn't changed much in the last fifteen years.

He hadn't noticed the helium balloons Bobbie had carried in with her. When he was between songs, she went across the empty dance floor with them and tied them to the prop that held the piano's top open. She leaned over and kissed Boldt on the cheek. "Happy birthday, Lou. I've missed you."

He played two bars of the melody to "Happy Birthday" and winked at her. She rejoined the others. He had two more songs remaining in his set. Elizabeth arrived, looking radiant, carrying a present, and he realized it was a conspiracy. His hopes of letting his fortieth slip by unnoticed were dashed. He played "All the Things You Are" and "Somewhere Over the Rainbow," both for Elizabeth. He felt a lump in his throat when she looked over and smiled at him during the second chorus of "Rainbow." Had these last few weeks ever happened? It's all what you create, he thought.

The crowd was modest but supportive. As Boldt crossed the dance floor to the table where his friends sat, the club's stereo came on playing Stevie Wonder.

"It's not until tomorrow," he complained, noticing that Abrams and Dixon both had presents for him too.

"You're not playing tomorrow," Dixon said.

He shook hands with both men and, sitting down next to Elizabeth, kissed her on the cheek.

"Look at the lovebirds," said Abrams.

Boldt squeezed her hand below the table where no one could see. She squeezed it back.

"Long time," he said to Bobbie.

She nodded.

"How do you feel?"

"Nothing physical." She shrugged. "Still a little shaky, I guess."

"Who wouldn't be?" Elizabeth gasped.

"Agreed," echoed Doc Dixon. "You'll get over it," he said paternally.

She grinned and then sobered. "It isn't the aftershock of the attack. It isn't that. It isn't Lange at all." She looked at them all, one by one. "It's James . . . James Royce. I went out with him. *Twice*. And he was absolutely normal. Polite, charming, attractive, intelligent. To think what he did . . ." Her eyes glassed over. "See? It still gets me."

Dixon stroked her back. "It gets us all, Bobbie. I worked with him for months." He shook his head.

"It could have been me," Bobbie said. "I could have been next. I probably owe you my life, Lou."

"Nonsense. He wouldn't have tried something like that. He was merely keeping tabs. And he had the added benefit of being with a pretty woman."

"Thanks," she said.

"So?" Doc Dixon said enthusiastically. "How's it feel to be forty?"

"You tell me," Boldt said.

"Me forty?" Dixon asked.

They laughed.

"No different," Boldt said. He glanced at his wife's profile. "Actually, quite different. It feels right for the first time in a long time."

"I'll drink to that," Abrams said.

They all toasted. Boldt's milk hadn't arrived, so he pretended to be holding a glass.

No one could think what to say for a few minutes after that. Abrams sat staring and smiling at Elizabeth and Boldt. He finally asked Boldt, "Where does your review stand?"

"No idea. I hear they're going to drag it out a few more weeks at least. Hanfield is filing criminal charges. Evidently I may have to go through that first."

"Jerk," Dixon said. "It used to be—in this free society of ours—that a man could get in a real good fistfight without being sued."

"That's progress," Boldt joked.

"We can handle it," Elizabeth said strongly.

"Do you miss it?" Bobbie asked him.

"What's that?" Boldt wondered.

"Do you miss work?"

"I have work," he said, looking Elizabeth in the eye and smiling, "despite a poor left hand."

"The department, stupid," she told him. Dixon grinned.

"The stupid department?" Boldt asked.

They all laughed.

"Sure I do," he admitted. "I miss the long days, the bad coffee, the arguing. The phone calls at night, the cold food and sinks that won't let the hot water stay on. I'm miserable, can't you tell?"

"You're a wiseass," Bobbie said.

"You got that right," Elizabeth echoed.

"Hey, no picking on the birthday boy," Boldt complained.

"I thought it wasn't until tomorrow," Abrams teased.

"And speaking of tomorrow," Dixon added. "That word comes up an awful lot when I bring up the idea of recording your albums."

"It certainly does," Abrams concurred.

Elizabeth intervened. "Tomorrow for lunch. Both of you. You too, Bobbie, if you can handle three *old men* gabbing like *old maids* about who played with whom when, where, and for how long. These three and jazz albums are like little boys with baseball cards."

"No thanks," Bobbie said.

"You're on," Abrams said, joined by a nod from Dixon. "If he cops out, we're counting on you, Liz."

"Deal," she said.

Boldt said to Elizabeth, "You were supposed to bargain them down."

"I'm an arbitrator, not an agent," she explained.

"Did you hear about Kramer?" Bobbie asked.

"I've been wondering," Boldt admitted.

"They're going to nail him," Abrams interrupted. "And he deserves no less, as far as I'm concerned."

"Civil court," Bobbie explained.

"He's off the force?" Boldt asked.

"Done and gone," said Dixon. "There's even talk of a manslaughter charge for the Jergensen thing. It's too bad, in a way, that it had to be John, but it's about time they did something to show they mean business about stopping leaks. This stuff has been out of hand for years now."

Elizabeth said, "Well, if Lou's not going to ask, I am, because I'm just as curious as he is, if not more so. What about Lange? Are the papers right?"

"About plea bargaining?" Dixon asked rhetorically. "No. I don't think so. What I've heard is that it's a standard insanity plea. Standard defense."

"So the confession holds?" Boldt asked.

"Absolutely," Bobbie answered. "Confession held up in the prelim, as did the transcription of your interview."

"We haven't had a single piece of evidence thrown out," Abrams said proudly. "He'll end up in a hospital somewhere, hopefully for the rest of his life."

"It was good police work," Bobbie added.

"The best," replied Elizabeth.

"Teamwork," Boldt corrected.

Abrams sang a piece of a beer commercial sarcastically. They all laughed and raised glasses. Boldt hollered over for his milk. The woman behind the bar let out a loud moo.

"You're not supposed to discuss the case with me, am I right?" Boldt asked all three friends.

"Bullshit to that," Dixon announced. He looked at Abrams and then at Gaynes. Neither protested. "Whatever your little heart desires," he told Boldt.

"Big heart," Elizabeth corrected.

They squeezed hands again, unseen.

"Why did Lange stop killing after Jergensen?" Boldt asked. "That's the only piece I don't have. Was he institutionalized? Did we miss that somehow?"

Dixon shrugged. "Out of my league."

Abrams said, "I can answer that one."

"Please do," Boldt said.

"The video wasn't rented by a woman. It was that simple. We've been over the lists a dozen times, LaMoia and I. *Summer Knights* wasn't rented with a woman's name on a delivery manifest until Croy and her boyfriend."

Boldt nodded. He didn't want to sound cocky by telling them that that was how he had figured it. "Thanks," he said.

Bobbie said angrily, "I can't see how they end up treating your case like a standard suspension. If you ask me, the whole thing is ridiculous. You caught two murderers, and they do this to you."

"Not me. Not alone," Boldt said modestly. "They gotta

do what they gotta do; same as they've always done, and always will. I'd be less than honest if I told you I was sorry about any of it. Besides, the time off is good for me. We're lucky in that the loss of income doesn't hurt us too badly.'' He looked at Elizabeth. He wondered why that had been so hard to say.

"But you're coming back?" Bobbie asked anxiously. She looked: "How am I ever going to get a promotion to Homicide if you don't come back?"

Abrams explained, "The rumor going around the office is that you're not coming back."

Boldt looked at his wife. "I wonder how a rumor like that might have gotten started."

Elizabeth grinned. "I wonder."

"It's only a rumor, isn't it, Lou?" Dixon asked his friend. In his voice was deep concern.

Before Boldt answered, Abrams's pager sounded. Within seconds Dixon's did the same.

"You're both on call tonight?" Boldt asked them.

Both men threw the switches on the pagers, silencing them. A few heads in the crowd had turned toward them. 'Needed an excuse to cut out on the shitty music,'' Abrams said. They laughed.

"I'll call it in," Dixon offered. He got up and left the table.

"You'll miss all the fun," Boldt told him, indicating the fairly sparse and quiet crowd.

Boldt's milk arrived. He drank half of it.

Dixon went back to the table and remained standing, all humor gone from his face.

"Dixie?" Boldt asked.

"A body, Lou. Male. It's the right size," he said, glancing at Bobbie. "Came ashore at Alki."

Abrams stood. "I've got my stuff in my car."

"Me too. The joys of being on call," Doc Dixon said by way of apology to Elizabeth. To Boldt he said, "You want to come along on this one, Lou?"

"No," Boldt said.

Dixon nodded. "Sure?"

"Sure."

"Okay." He hesitated. "I'd tell you that I'll try to be back for the last set, but you know how this business goes."

"No problem," Boldt said.

The two men headed for the door.

"Go with them, Lou," Elizabeth said.

Boldt shook his head, looking at his wife intently.

Dixon heard her comment. He seemed to have been waiting for it. He stopped and called out, "I can give you a ride over."

Elizabeth's look nudged him.

"You sure?" Boldt asked her.

"Positive. Bobbie and I will do a striptease until you get back."

Bobbie raised her arms and shook her breasts. Elizabeth laughed.

"Go," she told him again.

Boldt said, "I'll drive my own car, Dixie. You go on. I won't be staying."

The "strip" at Alki—less than a mile from where the body of Judith Fuller had been found—was void of the cars and vans that crowded its parking lots during the summer months. Tonight a miserable wet wind blew off the sound, cutting through to his bones. Boldt crossed his arms tightly, attempting to shield himself from the wind, but it didn't do much good. He shivered as he stepped up onto the seawall, and he wondered if this was because of the wind, or because of the sight before him.

There below him, a Parks Department four-wheel drive was parked on the beach, engine running, its headlights glaring out across the various cops milling about. The men and women formed an impenetrable circle through which Boldt could not see. He descended a short flight of wooden steps down to the beach, suddenly lost in the intense dark-

ss between the seawall and the four-wheel drive. He crossed
is distance slowly, very much aware of his solitude, eyes
xed on the backs of his colleagues.

No one noticed him as he approached. It wasn't until he
illed on a shoulder in front of him that he heard his name
entioned. And then the sound of it rippled softly through
ie crowd as it was repeated. He pushed his way through
id stopped.

The crabs and sea life had pecked holes in the man's
irearms. His fingers were reduced to bone, reminding Boldt
f a similar corpse several weeks before. There was a gap-
ig, bloodless bullet wound in the man's chest. The gray
ice, scarred and cut from two weeks in the currents of
uget Sound, stared lifelessly toward the lights of the four-
heel drive. Lou Boldt took one step closer and looked
own at the man. No eyes. It seemed to suit him. Boldt
irned and walked away.

"Good to see you, Lou," someone called from behind.
Boldt walked on.

"It's him. Right?" Shoswitz shouted, catching up at a
in. "Lou?"

Boldt stopped and turned around. The headlights blinded
im. He raised his hand to block the light, casting a shadow
cross his face.

"Glad to hear you're back with Liz. Right?" Shoswitz
id uncomfortably. Rubbing his elbow nervously.

Boldt nodded. He didn't feel comfortable here. Not yet,
iyway.

"How's things?" the lieutenant asked, the whites of his
es darting about. "What's going on?"

"It's him," Lou Boldt said, turning away. Disappearing
ito the darkness.

SHATTERED

. . . by a mindless act of violence that changed his life forever
James Dewitt decided to become a cop.

SHACKLED

. . . by a web of red tape and corruption, Dewitt now fights
desperately to solve a string of murders cleverly
staged to look like suicides.

SUBMERGED

. . . in the deranged world of the psychopathic mind, Dewitt
struggles to outwit the killer—before it's too late . . .

Pr⚫bable CAUSE

RIDLEY PEARSON

"FASCINATING . . . BREATHLESS!"
—*Chicago Tribune*

**AVAILABLE WHEREVER BOOKS ARE SOLD
FROM ST. MARTIN'S PAPERBACKS**